HAUNTED BY DARKNESS

HAUNTED BY DARKNESS

BL CLARK

SAPPHIRE BOOKS

SALINAS, CALIFORNIA

Sapphire Books LLC
Salinas, CA 93912
www.sapphirebooks.com

Printed in the United States of America
First Edition – February 2016

This and other Sapphire Books titles can be found at
www.sapphirebooks.com

Dedication

This book is for my Mom & Dad. Thank you for your love and support. I love you, both!

Acknowledgment

Chris and Schileen/Sapphire Books - Thank you for all your help and support. Thank you for taking a chance on me again. I am so very grateful for you both, and Sapphire Books.

Kaycee Hawn - Thank you for helping me to make this a better and stronger book.

Sapphire Family - You ladies are amazing! Thank you for your advice, help, and support!

Teri Thomas - Hmmm, thank you still doesn't really fit, but we're going to try and work with it again. You are a smart ass, pain in the ass, you like to be an ass…where was I going with this? Oh right, all these qualities and many more make you one of my closest and most cherished friends. Your support, encouragement, and well, pushing have helped to create another book. Thank you! So, are you ready to start this process all over again? LOL

Christian Slipper - Hi! Now, not only do you know a published author, you are in a published book. Pretty cool, huh? Thank you, for being one of my best friends and for sharing in that dream of becoming writers that we joked about years ago.

Tara Wentz - Thank you! You have been so supportive and helpful. I am a better person with you as my friend.

Ryan Clark - As a friend, you're pretty cool. As a cousin, you're even cooler. The fact that I can call you both is priceless. Thanks for always being there whenever and for whatever.

Lexi Meyer - Thank you for the support, pre-editing, and for tolerating my insanity.

Kathy Meyer - Thank you for the years of love and support!

Tony Clark - Meow!! You were the best, most opinionated and special cat. I miss you buddy!

Chapter One

I sat with my back to the wall of the old treehouse. The wood outside was weathered, but on the inside, the treated wood still looked like it was new. There were three windows and a doorway that exposed the interior to the elements, but you wouldn't know it. My best friend, Grace Barnes, and I helped to build the treehouse in the far corner of her parent's oversized backyard when we were six-years-old. Well, when I say helped to build, I mean more along the lines of we helped carry the trim pieces of wood while her father and older brother built the treehouse. Now, at seventeen-years-old and five feet eight inches tall, I had to admit that I was getting a little big to be coming up here, but after the week I had, honestly, I needed to feel the safety and solitude that this treehouse provided. Over the years, this treehouse had become my go-to spot, my sanctuary.

"Kris? Are you up there?" I heard Grace call from the bottom of the ladder.

"Yeah, I'm up here," I said, leaning out of the window and looking down at her.

"Is there still room for both of us up there?"

"No, you have to stay down there and yell up," I teased as I saw her flip me the bird and start climbing the ladder.

We sat together quietly for a long time in the treehouse before she interrupted the silence.

"How are you doing? I mean, with all that bullshit that went on at school today?" Grace asked, her blue eyes piercing right through my defenses. She was never one to beat around the bush. I loved that quality about her.

"Oh, you mean after that snobby bitch Jenna Patterson decided to tell the entire packed cafeteria that I was a lesbian, or do you mean when Trisha broke up with me rather than risk being outed or supporting me?" I said, a bit snarkier than intended. "Oh, I am doing just ducky good."

"Yeah, you definitely sound like you are doing ducky good," Grace said, raising an eyebrow at me.

"Sorry." I cast my eyes to the floor of the treehouse while my fingers continued playing with a loose string on my tattered jeans. "I'm hurt and upset. I'm not sure if I'll be luckier if my parents do or don't kill me for skipping the last three classes of the day."

Grace put her hand on my sternum and pushed me back against the treehouse wall. "Don't you dare talk like that. I will kick your ass here and now." The venom in her words was very evident. Her face was as bright red as her vibrant red hair. I could feel her directing the brunt of that anger at me. "Do I make myself clear?" I nodded. I knew better than to speak when she was that pissed off. I had made that mistake in the past; never again!

What you need to understand is that my parents weren't the nicest people, to me, that is. They were abusive, verbally and physically. Grace and her older brother, Tyler, were the only ones that knew about this. I made them swear not to tell their parents or anyone else.

"Speaking of skipping classes, how are you going

to intercept the automated call that the school makes?"

"I'll just have to be by the phone when it rings at six tonight to answer it. How'd the rest of the day go?"

Grace's bright blue eyes lost some of their brightness as they started to shift to looking around the room, everywhere but where I was. I knew Grace. I knew that it meant she was trying to avoid telling me something that was going to piss me off. I knew I wasn't wrong.

"What don't you want to tell me?"

"It's nothing."

"Dammit, Grace! Tell me."

"Fine, after you bolted, Trisha told everyone that you and I were dating and sleeping together," Grace said, tentatively. Trisha was the blonde hair, blue-eyed goddess that I have been dating and sleeping with for the past year.

"She *what*? I'm sorry, I must of have heard you wrong…" I managed to choke out as Grace gave me a single nod. "That bitch wouldn't stand by our relationship, and then she had the audacity to toss you under the bus with me?"

"It isn't a big deal, Kris. She felt cornered. Someone had mentioned that you two were seen together often, and she needed to deflect the attention."

"That's bullshit, and you know it. Maybe I should walk up to Trisha and plant a big kiss on her lips. Or hand her some of the pictures she and I took during that weekend we spent together sans clothing."

"Don't you dare do either. Wait, when did you spend the weekend with Trisha? Never mind. I don't mind people thinking that we're involved. I could do worse." Grace smirked, which she knew would melt my defenses. I didn't know why, but that smirk and glint in her eyes had worked on me since we were little kids. "It did get me asked out by three different people: two girls and a guy."

"Okay, wait, they asked you out *after* they heard that we were a couple?"

"Yeah, they thought that you being outed like that would cause me to break up with you." Grace laughed and then started to fan herself and speak in a southern tone. "Your auburn hair, your piercingly unnaturally green eyes, mmmm, and those long fingers, how could I possibly want anyone else? You have so ruined me for others."

We broke out into a fit of laughter. Grace liked to make me feel better, and she had a flare for the overly dramatic. Over the years, she had a lot of practice cheering me up, but this was different. This wasn't about my parents; this was about my friends, or at least people I thought were my friends.

We sat there for a long time, talking and laughing before I had to get going. If I wasn't home by a specific time, my father made sure to let me know how unhappy he was with me. He wasn't picky about what method he used to show me; his fists, his belt, the cigarette he was smoking, or anything he had handy. Mom, she loved to throw stuff, but never her liquor. That would be alcohol abuse, and she was not an abuser, of alcohol at least.

Walking up to the modest two-story pale blue house, I felt my stomach tightening. From the outside, it looked like your typical suburban family home. The front had a perfectly manicured lawn, flowers blooming in the flowerbed along the front of the house. White trim framed the door and windows. Nobody would ever fully understand the terror and disgust this place brought for me. When I got inside, I quickly put my books in my room at the top of the stairs and went into the kitchen to start on my chores. Walking into the unusually small eat-in kitchen, I saw the pile of dirty dishes left for me on the table. My parents must have had company over earlier. I hoped it was earlier and not that they were still there. I made quick work of clearing the table and washing the dishes. We had a dishwasher, but that took extra energy and made noise, neither of which my father would tolerate. I looked around the kitchen to make sure that I had cleaned it all up before I went into the living room.

The living room was my father's trophy room. By that, I mean he used the room to show off and impress people. There was a large flat screen television, complete with wireless surround sound. A large plush brown sectional, with a leather ottoman that had storage built into it, both complimented the warm mahogany colored walls. If it weren't for the memories of the beatings I had taken in this room, it would be very warm. As I walked into the living room, the phone rang, and I saw the handset in my father's hand.

"Shit," I thought. *"Could this day get any worse?"*

My father was a tall man. He stood about six-foot-four, muscular build. I had his auburn hair. It was about the only thing I really got from him, thankfully. My father glared at me and set the phone down as I came through the archway. I couldn't tell from the expression on his face if it had been the school or someone else. I'm also not sure which I was hoping for either.

"That was the school saying that you missed one or more classes today. Why?" he asked, his tone stern and demeaning.

"I had to do something for my computer teacher. She gave me a pass. I'll take it to the office first thing in the morning," I lied. Thankfully, I knew that my computer teacher would give me a pass for anything if I ask her. She adored me.

"Well, you had better," he said, turning back to the television. "What kind of teacher makes a student tardy or miss another class, anyway?"

He was grumbling that last part so I knew that it was rhetorical, and he wasn't expecting an answer.

❧ ❧ ❧ ❧

It was three months later when Grace found me curled up in a ball in the treehouse. I was grateful that it was dark out, because it hindered her view of me. That morning, I had been told to hurry home from school, but I got out of class late and therefore was late getting home from school. My father decided that he needed to punish me for my "repeated" tardiness. For some reason, he was particularly brutal that night. He must have had a bad day at work. The bits that I remember are several punches to my midsection and kidneys. I remember one catching me really off-guard, falling, and hitting my head on the end table. The rest of the abuse is a blur after that. For all the beatings I received over the years, I was grateful that I was never abused sexually. I am not saying that it wasn't a threat, but their threat was to farm me out to others. I am below my father's standards, and I'm sure you understand that my family has no clue that I'm a lesbian. After being beaten, I knew that I risked a lot sneaking out, but I couldn't stay there. It was more out of fear than disgust that I left this time. I was certain he would kill me if he were given the opportunity to hit me again.

"Kris?" Grace asked, tentatively entering the treehouse.

"Hey," I whispered. I turned my head slightly so that I could see her features in the moonlight. I knew she didn't mean to show it, but I could see the fear in her eyes. "I'm okay."

"Bullshit! How bad is it? Really?"

As I tried to sit up, the pain in my ribs was too severe, and I gasped for a breath. Grace hurried across the tiny room and carefully helped me sit up. The moment she had me sitting, she was able to get a good look at me, thanks to the moonlight. I heard her gasp.

"What the hell did that bastard do to you? Kris, you need to go to the hospital." Her hand was shaking as she brought it up and ran her fingers lightly over my swollen eye. She had always been so gentle. This time was no different; as she touched my eye, I could barely feel it.

"And tell them what? That my father beat the shit out me for being five minutes late getting home from school? Do you remember who my father is?"

"How can I forget who your father is? Kris, just because he is an executive assistant to the biggest business owner in our stupid state doesn't give him the right to hurt you."

"No, but it gives him added credibility. I'm just a stupid kid. He reminds me of that almost every time he 'disciplines' me."

"You aren't stupid," said Grace. I couldn't see her eyes, but I could hear the tears in her voice. I was trying like hell to ignore them, but I'm not that cold. Cautiously, I reached out for her and pulled her in close, stifling my own cries of pain.

"I'll be okay. I'm just going to sleep here tonight," I whispered into her hair.

"The hell you are," Grace said, pulling away quickly, causing me to wince in pain. Her movement was too much for my current injuries. "I'll be damned if I am going to leave you in this condition, here, alone. You are coming home with me."

"Grace, I don't want your family to see me like this. There would be a lot of explaining that neither of us wants to deal with. Plus, I got up here on adrenaline; I don't know that I can get down the ladder right now."

"Then I'm staying with you. Let me go to the house and get some blankets, pillows, and some food. Do you need anything else? Is there anything that needs bandaging? Ice? Splints?"

"I just need a blanket…thanks." I didn't have the energy to argue with her, plus I knew it wouldn't make a difference if I even tried. When Grace set her mind to something, it was rare that you could change it. She had been that way since we were five.

Grace hurried down the ladder to get stuff. While she was gone, I took the opportunity to poke and prod a bit to try to assess the damage my father has done. From what I could tell, nothing was broken. Not that I was a doctor, but he had broken a lot of my bones over the years, and I knew how it felt. I was going to have some good bruising on my ribs from where his fists made contact. I also would probably have a black eye from when I fell and hit my head on the end table, but at least that was the extent of the 'visible' damage. There was also possibly a cut or two on my back from the bowl he threw against the wall that shattered above me. I hoped there wasn't anything for Grace to see. She was already livid and scared; I didn't need her knowing the true extent of my injuries. I tried pulling gently on the hem of my shirt and I felt a tug midway up my back. Now I knew that I had at least one cut there that has dried and now stuck to my shirt. I was hoping that it wasn't big or too apparent. Why I couldn't have worn a black shirt that day? At least that way I would have been certain that Grace wouldn't see the blood. Grace had seen enough of my blood over the years.

I don't know how long it was before I heard Grace trudging up the ladder with a camping lantern to light the room. It was once she was up in the treehouse that I could hear she wasn't alone. I jumped and winced when I heard the sound of someone else climbing up the ladder. I don't think that Grace saw it.

"Please, don't be mad," whispered Grace, just before I saw her brother's red hair pop up and then the rest of his head into the doorway.

"Hey, Squish," Tyler said, as he came in carrying two sleeping bags and a backpack full of supplies.

Because I was hurting so much, that was the only reason that I let Tyler get away with calling me Squish. He gave the nickname to me when I was seven. Grace and I had been helping her dad with some home repairs, and he left Grace and me to mix the mud in the bucket, and it made this cute squishing noise when you moved your hand a certain way. Well, we sat there making that noise for a good ten minutes before we saw her father and brother watching us. Since then they've called me 'Squish.'

"Don't be mad at Grace. There is no way I was going to let her carry this stuff up here by herself." I knew it is safer that he did. Grace wasn't a big person. She was this little petite leprechaun. She hated it when I called her that, but it was what she reminded me of.

She's short, she had the red hair…she owned it. "It was me or Dad. I figured you would feel more comfortable with me."

"Thanks for helping her," I said, trying not to take too deep of a breath. When I jumped, I knocked the air out of myself with the pain that radiated through my midsection.

"How bad is it this time?" Tyler asked. I swear the Barnes family has this patented look that penetrates all of the walls and defenses I put up.

"Better than some, worse than others," I vaguely replied. I refused to meet either of their gazes.

"Gracie, don't let her go to bed without checking to make sure she isn't hiding any other injuries. Squish, you know that you just have to say the word and you can come to our house and live…you don't need to live like this. We can protect you. Mom and Dad can protect you."

"Thanks, Tyler, but this is how it has to be for a few more months. I won't put anyone else in harm's way. I wouldn't be able to live with myself if any of you got hurt."

"Kris, think about it, please?" I didn't know why, but the sincerity in his voice shocked me. Yes, I was friends with him. He was Grace's older brother, and he kept my secret. Why? I could only guess it is for Grace, but I truly didn't know, and I was smart enough not to ask.

After Tyler left, Grace checked my ribs and the various other places my father had hit me. I did my best not to let her see the back of my shirt, but Grace wasn't stupid either.

"Now, I want to see your back since you have been going out of your way to hide it from me," she said, affixing me again with that damn Barnes look. I really needed to learn to resist that look.

"I'm fine," I protested.

"Turn or I will turn you, and we both know that I am not going to be nice about it. We also both know how much that is going to hurt."

I turned and heard her groan a bit. I wasn't sure if the groan was because she saw I was hurt or if it was worse than I thought. I could feel Grace cautiously start to lift my shirt. I felt her stop when it reached the dried blood on my shirt. I felt something wet on the back of my shirt and realized she was pouring water from one of the bottles she brought to try not to hurt me when she removed my shirt.

"I should be taking you to the hospital," Grace said, bluntly. I could hear the anger raging beneath the surface within her. "You are already bruising back here."

"I know it looks bad, but really, I'll be okay." I turned my head and offered her a calming smile.

"I'm...*ugh*...dammit," she snapped in frustration.

Turning, I took her face in my hands and wiped away the tears that were streaming down her face.

"I am strong. I have you. I just need to get through the next few months and then I'm outta here. You are my best friend, and I love you for taking care of me and for caring enough to get mad. But, for me, don't give them the satisfaction of wasting your energy."

"How can you say that? I can't just sit by and watch my best friend get beat up for no reason by the people that are supposed to be protecting her. I need you around for a long time, Kris. Don't you get that?"

"A few more months, please, for me?" I asked, looking her in the eyes, hoping she could see my sincerity and give me this.

"Fine, now turn around. I figured you were hurt worse than you let on so I brought some other stuff and this is going to sting as I clean out the wounds."

I turned around and gritted my teeth. She wasn't kidding, and holy fuck did it hurt. If I didn't truly know Grace as well as I did, I would have sworn that she was pouring acid into the wounds just for her own amusement. After bandaging up the handful of cuts that I had on my back, Grace helped me get my shirt back on. We sat in silence for a long time. I had no clue what to say that would make this better. I was listening to the sounds of spring when my stomach decided it had had enough and let out a loud rumble.

"Wow, you haven't made that much noise in years." Grace laughed. I watched as she started digging around in her backpack and pulled out a couple of sandwiches.

"Thanks," I said, taking one, unwrapping it, and taking a bite. "Mmmm, I love your mom's cooking." My parents didn't regularly cook, so what we ate was whatever I made, and I wasn't a great cook.

"Yeah, I know you do. I snagged a few sandwiches from the refrigerator. It is nice that Mom preps all the sandwiches for our lunches ahead of time."

"Do you think she'll notice? I don't want to get you in trouble."

"Already covered. Tyler said he was hungry and snagged a few as a snack. Mom just rolled her eyes at him and reminded him soon he was going to stop growing up and start growing out."

We sat laughing, talking about college, and eating the snacks Grace had brought. A little while later, Grace helped me find a comfortable position, and it wasn't long before I was drifting off to sleep.

❧ ❧ ❧ ❧

I heard the birds chirping, and I could feel the sunlight on my face as it shined in from one of the windows. I opened one eye and found Grace was watching me sleep. "Creeper!"

"Shut up," she said, playfully.

"Why are you watching me sleep?"

"Well, it started as me watching you sleep since I couldn't. Then, you stopped breathing so that kept me awake. You actually stopped breathing twice last night. I was afraid you were going to die."

"I did not, did I?" I asked, realizing that there was a new fear that I had never heard in her voice before. "You're serious, aren't you? You've been up all night?"

"Yeah, I'm serious. You scared the shit out of me. I almost went to get Tyler and Dad to take you to the hospital, but I was afraid to leave you alone. Fucking battery on my cell died so I couldn't call them."

When I tried to sit up, I realized a whole new level of pain. The adrenaline that kept most of the pain at bay the previous night was gone. Today, there was a new level of hell for me. I was trying to play it off as if it didn't hurt, but there was no way I could hide this level of pain. At least, not from Grace; she knew me too well.

"Are you sure nothing is broken?" Grace asked.

"I don't feel anything broken," I said, running my hands over my ribs again. My shirt must have come up some because I heard a muffled scream from Grace. I looked down and yep, it was up a little and there were some very dark purple bruises.

"You need to get that looked at," Grace said, pointing to my rib cage, her hand shaking again like it had the night before.

"I'm fine," I insisted. I knew that she wasn't going to let this go, and I wasn't in the mood to argue with her and deal with the pain. No, I couldn't argue with her because it was taking everything I had not to cry or let her know how much pain I was truly in. I knew Grace; her knowing how much pain I was truly in would destroy her.

"Kris, what if you are bleeding internally? You can die from that, you know."

"I do know, and I know that I'll be okay. Please, trust me on this," I said as I pulled Grace into my arms. I hated seeing her upset, but the thought of explaining the injuries to a doctor is more than I could handle. I was not sure how I was going to get through the day at school, let alone anything else.

"Fine, but I'm watching you all day," Grace said, pulling back and glaring at me.

"I would expect nothing less."

We managed to get me down the ladder. It wasn't a fun trip, I will say that. We were walking to school, when I felt Grace tense up just before I heard my name being called. It was Trisha. She was one of the last people that I had wanted to see. My feelings were still hurt from the way she ended things. I had managed to avoid her almost entirely since that day. I was a pro now after three months.

"Kris, wait," Trisha was calling from behind us.

Grace grabbed my hand and started gently to encourage me forward.

"Kris, please!" I heard her running up to us. "Wait."

I stopped walking so that I could get this over with. Because I was so effective at avoiding her, I hadn't even talked to Trisha since we broke up, and today wasn't the day I honestly wanted to start. Grace let out a frustrated sigh and stood next to me.

"What?" I asked, exasperated as I turned toward her.

"What the hell happened to your eye? Baby, are you okay?" Trisha asked as her hand tentatively reached toward my face.

In my frustration, I had completely forgotten about my eye and the bruise on my face.

"Nuh uh, you don't get to touch, worry, or care about her after the shit you pulled," Grace said, stepping between us and slapping Trisha's hand away.

"Who the hell do you think you are?" snapped Trisha, stepping toward Grace. Both of them were puffing out their chests, trying to intimidate the other. Grace was shorter than Trisha, but not by a whole lot. Frame and build wise, Trisha had broader shoulders so she dwarfed Grace's mostly athletic build. In a fight, I wasn't sure who would be stronger. I knew they both fought dirty from playfully wrestling with them in the past. Well, with Trisha, it wasn't just playful wrestling.

I saw this situation getting out of hand very quickly. "As cute as it is to have you both fighting over me, Grace is right." I pulled Grace back and stepped between them sideways so that they would each have to back up a bit more. "You broke up with me, and you have ignored me for the past three months. That negates your right to pretend to care about me. I won't mention how I feel about what you did to Grace."

"I haven't ignored you, baby. I haven't seen you. Plus, I got spooked. I still love you…I never stopped.

I miss you."

"Like you know what love is," Grace was mumbling under her breath as I glared at her.

"Just forget about me, Trish. Move on with your life."

"It isn't that easy, Kris. Come on, please," she begged. "I'm sorry for how I reacted when you were outed, and for what I did to Grace. I still love and care about you. I still want to be with you."

"I can't be with someone who is ashamed to be with me and to admit to being with me. I'm sorry." As I turned to walk away, Trisha wrapped her arms around me tightly from behind. She pressed her body tightly to mine. I was starting to see stars from the pain when Grace quickly stepped in and got Trisha to let go. I staggered over to a nearby wall and tried to catch my breath. Blacking out here would not be good. Neither would throwing up, but I think I could handle explaining that rather than explaining blacking out.

"Just go," Grace said coldly as she glared at Trisha.

Trisha could see that she had hurt me with what she had done both physically and emotionally. Her look of confusion almost made me cave in, but she backed down. Trisha stood watching Grace and I for a long minute and then, slowly turning, she walked away. Once she was gone, I slid down the wall and carefully brought my knees to my chest. I was sitting there trying to use mind-over-matter and telling myself that my ribs didn't hurt. My body called me a liar and shot more pain to prove it. After I composed myself and got the pain under control, Grace and I headed to school. The day was a standard day, except I ran into Trisha more than usual. She was going out of her way to see me, but Grace was always there as well. Grace meant it when she said that she was going to be watching me.

Over the next few weeks, while I was healing, Trisha slowly started to put distance between us and for that, I was grateful. I had also made it a point to keep Grace as far away from my parents as I could. I wasn't afraid of what she would say; I knew she would do nothing to hurt me or get me hurt. It was more that I didn't want *her* to get hurt.

≈ ≈ ≈ ≈

As the school year ended, my parents were oddly enough becoming more and more detached from me. I wasn't complaining; I think over the last three months my father only hit me twice. Going from several beatings to two was an eerie change. I kept waiting for him to snap, but he hadn't. As our graduation neared, I was starting to get my stuff packed up and I was more than ready to leave. The morning after graduation, Grace and I were out of there.

"You know the only reason you are being allowed to go anywhere for college is because it makes me look good," my father said to me as I was clearing the table after my graduation dinner.

"Yes, sir," I said, avoiding eye contact.

"Are you sassing me?" He raised his arm, poised to swing and hit me.

"No, sir. I would not do that. I know that my scholarships and ability to go to school are the direct results of the way you have raised me."

"Damn straight, Skippy," my mother drunkenly interjected, causing my father to roll his eyes as he lowered his arm.

After finishing my chores, I went up to my room to make sure I had everything packed. It was a little after midnight when I grabbed what I had packed and climbed out my bedroom window. I shimmied down the nearby tree and made a break for the treehouse in Grace's backyard. I had planned to hide out there until morning, and then I would go and get Grace, and we'd put our plans into place.

Now, as I sat there in the treehouse, I felt safe, safer than I had in a long time. I was going to miss this place. I didn't know if I would ever be back. There were a lot of memories from up there that I was taking with me.

Chapter Two

It had been six months since Grace and I left town. Grace had, of course, stayed in touch with her family. Her brother, Tyler, told her that my father was telling people that we had planned for me to leave right after school so that I could start college early with some summer classes. As it was, my family had no idea where I was. I'd turned eighteen a few days before graduating so legally my parents didn't have a say in my life. Hell, I didn't even go to the college that they thought I was going to. I didn't go as far as changing my name, although it did cross my mind.

"Hey, slacker," Grace said as she entered my dorm room. It wasn't a big room, but they never were. The painted cinderblock walls did nothing to block out the sounds of the others in the hall or next door. Two twin beds flush against the walls, two desks separating the beds, two things posing as dressers at the end of the beds. It was a sad sight, to be honest, unless linear was your thing, then it might be kind of cool.

"What's up?" I asked, watching as Grace flopped down on the bed next to me.

"I'm bored. The girls here are boring."

"I haven't had that same experience," I said, offering Grace a sly smile. "I've found several that are quite outgoing and fun."

"Yeah, but that is because you are just sleeping with them."

"Trust me when I say that there is little to no sleep going on."

"Gross! I don't want to know about your sex life…especially when it is better than mine." Grace pouted, causing me to laugh.

"So, what are your plans for tonight?"

"Well, it's Friday night, and I have my fake ID. I'm thinking bar hopping," Grace said with a smile. "You know some drinking, some dancing…"

"Some getting laid?" I asked, raising an eyebrow to her.

"I'm not sure that is in the cards for me. I'm not looking for a one-night stand."

"Well, there are some girls out there looking for a relationship. I'm sure we can find you one of them," I said, and I totally meant it. It wasn't what I was looking for, but if it was what she wanted, I was willing to support her.

Grace and I had gone to a couple of bars near campus and had a few drinks. She danced with a couple of girls, but she didn't find anyone wanting more than a hook-up. I, however, was having a great time. There were a couple of steamy trips to the bathroom with girls whose names I didn't even get. Then there were the few whose name and number I did get, oh, and the two that I was taking back to the dorms with me. I knew Grace wasn't amused that our night out was ending early with me picking up a couple of girls, but we were in college, and who was I to deny beautiful women their experimental fun?

I know what you are thinking, and no, my roommate Kendra didn't mind me parading women through our room because she was never there. Kendra had the room for appearances and for her parents, but in reality, she was living with her boyfriend on another floor.

It had been several days and I hadn't heard from Grace, which was unusual, seeing as we usually talked daily. I'd stopped by Grace's room several times, but her roommate said she wasn't around. I wasn't sure if she was covering for Grace or not. I had even resorted to trying to call Grace on her cell phone at various hours of the day and night, but she still hadn't picked up. I finally realized that she was truly pissed at me and she was avoiding me. Yeah, I know, I'm a regular Sherlock Holmes. Now, I just needed to figure out where she was and how to get her to talk to me. The problem with several of the classrooms on campus was that they had multiple entrances and exits. I knew that after at least three of her classes Grace saw me waiting and went out the other door.

I decided to give Grace some space and wait for her to come to me. The days passed and turned into weeks, weeks into months. It had really been months since I last talked to Grace and I knew she was going to be heading home for Spring break. Her family was very close. I had two days left to find her and get her to talk to me and allow me to make this right. I missed my best friend. I finally broke down and enlisted the help of one of the girls that I knew had several classes with Grace. Sarah sent me a text telling me that Grace hadn't been in three out of the four classes they had together. I could feel the panic starting to rise inside me. It wasn't until I received the next message from Sarah that I realized that I was going to have a chance. Sarah messaged and said that Grace was in class and that she would try to figure out a way to get Grace to go out the main door. As I stood outside the small lecture hall, I made sure that nobody inside could see me until class was over.

"Grace, wait," I said, putting a hand on her shoulder as she hurried past.

"I have to get going, Kris," she said, annoyed. "I'm sure you have someone better to spend your time with."

With that, Grace pulled away, leaving me standing there with my mouth opening and closing like a fish. I knew I had to go after her, but I couldn't make my feet move. It wasn't until I was standing alone in the hallway that I was able to move again. The silence of the hall was deafening.

"Shit," I thought to myself. *"Now what?"*

I looked at my watch and saw that, if I hurried, I could still corner Grace in her room. I knew this was a desperation move, but it was my last hope. If she really was heading home, she was going to be leaving the following day right after classes. I quickly left the building and ran to position myself outside her dorm room.

"Hey Kris, Grace isn't here yet," said Grace's roommate as she exited their room.

"I know, but I still can't get her to talk to me. So I'm hoping if I wait here she'll give me a chance, or I can make her listen to me."

"She's really pissed at you. Why don't you wait inside? That way you can corner her without an audience. Maybe she will talk to you then."

"Thanks," I said, as she let me in the room. Their room setup was different from mine. They had chosen to set the beds up as bunk beds. Grace's was on the bottom. Heights weren't her thing. They had the desks facing out the windows. I don't think I would get anything done with my desk looking out the window. I looked at Grace's bed and saw that she had all of her stuff packed up and ready to go. It looked as if she were leaving today. My heart started to race at the thought that I could have missed her. I sat down in the desk chair nearest Grace's bed and waited. Thankfully, I didn't have to wait too long before I heard Grace on the phone as she unlocked the door and entered.

"No, Tyler. I am not bringing Kris back with me. We haven't spoken in months," she was saying as she entered. I watched her enter the room and close the door and then she turned and saw me sitting in her chair. "I'll call you back, it appears someone broke into my room and is still in my chair. No, I'm okay, I just need to deal with this situation, and then tomorrow I'll be heading home. I love you, too."

"I didn't break in," I stated in my defense. "Your roommate took pity on me and let me in."

"I'll have to have a chat with her when I get back from break." This was the coldest Grace had ever been with me, and it was creepy and scary. "What do you want, Kris? I've left you to 'enjoy' your college experience."

"I didn't want you to leave me to my own devices. I wanted you to share in those experiences."

"Sorry, ménage à trois with you is not something I'm interested in."

"That isn't what I meant, and you damn well know it," I snapped. "What the hell has gotten into you? I thought you were my best friend. The one person who would always be there for me."

"I'm not going to watch you self-destruct. If you want to do that, you do it alone."

"How am I self-destructing?" I could feel myself

getting defensive.

"Besides me, is there any female in this building that you haven't slept with?" Grace asked. I could see both anger and concern in her eyes. I wasn't sure which feeling was going to win, though.

"Yes, there are," I said, knowing that there were many, but there were also a great many that I had slept with. "So, you have ignored me for months because I was having fun?"

"No, I have been ignoring you because you are being reckless and dangerous. I'm not going to watch as you blow your scholarship and future away."

"I've got a perfect GPA. I'm not throwing anything away."

"Are you going to keep sleeping with any woman that you can coax into your bed?" Grace asked.

"I'm just playing the field…" I started to say before she interrupted me.

"Great, that is the only answer that I need. Now get the hell out of my room. When you decide to get your head out of your ass, let me know," Grace said, ushering me to the door.

"Have a great vacation," I whispered as I rushed out of the room so that she couldn't see my tears. I was grateful that my room wasn't far from hers. I wasn't fond of crying, and I was even less fond of having other people see me crying.

That was the last conversation that Grace and I had for almost a year. I went out of my way so as not to even see her because it hurt too much. I know I did it to myself, but that didn't make it hurt any less.

After Grace and I stopped talking, I continued to play the field and enjoy my freedom. I'm not saying that jilted lovers didn't burn me once or twice, but their partner made the choice to sleep with me. I recall one night in particular that I was out at a club, and I was dancing with one girl. We were getting friendly, touching, bumping, and grinding, maybe a kiss here and there, and then her girlfriend showed up. She was taller than me and definitely a bit intimidating. Because of my upbringing, I didn't like violence, and when the girl went to hit me, I just let her. I know how it feels to take a punch from someone. I won't be the one to inflict that on another person. Although, that was the night that things started to change for me. I had been through enough drama and realized I didn't want it anymore.

It was several months after the club incident; I was walking along the dimly lit sidewalk, bundled in my hoodie, headed for my dorm. It was rather brisk because it was still early spring. As I neared the library, I could see the silhouette of what looked like a woman leaving. She was carrying a bag that appeared full of what I assumed were books. As I got closer, I saw her stumble and drop her bag, causing books to go flying down the stairs and all around. I hurried over to make sure that she was okay and to help her pick up the books.

"Thanks," said a timid, yet familiar voice.

"No problem. I'm glad I was nearby," I said while stacking the books that were nearest me as neatly as I could.

I pushed the hood off my head and turned to face the person I was helping for the first time. That was when my eyes met a familiar bright blue pair. There, kneeling next to me was Grace Barnes. I didn't know what to say or do. She hated me the last time we spoke. I couldn't be here; I needed to hurry so that I could get away from her. I could hear her breathing pattern change. I wasn't sure if it was out of hatred, disgust, or what. I wasn't certain I wanted to stick around to find out, either.

"How are you doing?" she asked, softly. So soft I almost didn't hear her.

"I'm okay. How have you been?" I replied, handing her the books I had collected while still avoiding making eye contact with her. It was hard because it was one thing that we both believed in doing.

"I'm okay."

"How is your family?" I asked, mentally kicking myself for still caring so much and for asking. I had been fooling myself for the past year. I told myself that Grace and her family didn't matter, but they did. They always would.

"They're good. They miss you."

"I, um, miss them, too. I should, um, I should get going," I said, standing and awkwardly turning to get away from her.

"Kris, wait," Grace said, reaching out and grabbing my arm to stop me from running away. I stood there as still as a statue before I felt Grace turn me to face her. I still wouldn't meet her eyes. "Look at me, please."

Looking up at her for the first time in almost a year, our eyes met, and I could see worry in her eyes, worry for me. She still cared. I won't lie when I say that this confused me. Why would she still care about me? It didn't make sense to me.

"Hi," I said dumbly, before offering her a slight yet forced smile. "You, um, didn't get hurt when you stumbled, did you?"

"Hi. No, I didn't. I'm okay," she said, returning the smile, only her smile was genuine. It lit up her eyes. "I've missed you."

"I've missed you, too," I said, looking away from her eyes. "I'm sorry for how I acted. I was out of control, and I've gotten it out of my system. I don't go out like that anymore."

"I'm glad."

"I just...I don't know why I felt it important to tell you that. I guess part of me just doesn't want you to totally hate me and regret our time growing up together."

"I don't regret it, and I don't hate you."

"I should let you get back to your night. I'll, um, see you around," I said, taking a few steps backward.

"Kris, wait. Please."

I was ready to bolt, but something in her voice made me stop.

"Why do you think that I hate you? Or that I would regret our childhood?" she asked.

"Think about how things were left between us. Think about how awkward this feels." I was motioning between us. "Why would you want to acknowledge someone like me? I'm nothing."

"Yeah, things ended badly, and I agree, this is beyond awkward, but you and I have been through so much." I watched her step into my personal space. "I could never hate you. I would always acknowledge you, because I know you are an amazing person. But, I know you want to go so I won't keep you."

"Grace," I started while reaching out my hand and caressing her cheek for a moment before letting my hand drop to her shoulder. "I hope at some point we can make amends."

I didn't give her a chance to respond. I kissed her forehead and then I put my hoodie up, turned, and walked away. I didn't walk at my normal pace, no. I needed to get away from her. I practically ran away. Yes, I'm a coward. I admit that freely.

❧ ❧ ❧ ❧

Three weeks had passed before I saw Grace again. I was walking through the courtyard at school, and she was sitting at one of the benches. It was a sunny but cool day. Spring is always unpredictable.

"Kris, wait," Grace called after me. I turned, and she was standing two feet away. "Can we go someplace and talk? Maybe, for a coffee or somewhere that is more private and warmer?"

"Why?" I asked.

"I miss you, and I'm worried about you," she admitted. She made eye contact with me. This was her way of letting me see that it was the truth. I could always see it in her eyes when she lied.

"I have a single room. We can go back there to talk," I offered. "Unless you'd like someplace public so you aren't alone with me…"

"Kris, relax. Let's go back to your room and talk. I'd like that."

"Okay. I'm not far from here." After picking up a couple of her books, we walked in silence to my dorm. Once inside my room, I set Grace's books on my desk, and she followed suit. The single room was a little smaller than the double room I had the year before. The nice part was that there was just the one bed, a single desk, an actual dresser for my clothes. I also had a bulletin board with built-in whiteboard. My schedule was written on the board along with when my tests were.

"You have a nice room," Grace said, looking around and smiling. "I'm jealous."

"Why?" I asked as she sat down on the edge of my bed, and I sat down in the desk chair.

"I've got the roommate from hell this year," Grace said, laughing. "She's not in the slightest bit clean. And I mean that in more than the putting stuff away sense. Smelly clothes, body odor, food that I'm certain is growing antibiotics or fungus of some sort strewn all around the room."

"Nasty," I said, laughing. It felt weird to laugh with Grace. "Why didn't you request a change?"

"I don't know. I guess I never thought about it. I just try to spend as little time as I can there. That's why I was at the library so late that night. How did you get your own room?"

"Um…er," I stammered. Now came the hard part, what I should just tell her. Would the truth hurt her? Would she still hate me? Would she hate me more? I knew that I couldn't lie to Grace; plus, she deserved to know the truth. "Because I stay here over the summer, I am here when the room assignments first come out. I found out that I was in the same building as you and on the same floor, two rooms down actually. It hurt too much to be that close to you and know that I couldn't just pop over to talk to you or see you. So, I went to my advisor and requested a change. I told her that it was personal, but I couldn't be there. She did some hunting and checking and this was all they had available at the time."

"You moved because of me? Seriously?"

"Yeah," I said, sheepishly looking down at the ground.

"Tell me the truth. Have you been avoiding me for almost a year now? Since that night?"

"Yep."

"Why?"

"You hate or hated me. I could see the disgust in your eyes that day before you left for spring break. It has haunted me nightly, whenever I closed my eyes. I couldn't keep seeing you and not want to talk to you. You are...were my best friend, the only person who ever stuck up for me and chose to be there with me. When you walked away, I was...empty, I guess is the best way to describe it. I had nothing inside me worthwhile. Every time I saw you, it hurt and I felt the loneliness of my life become overwhelming. I tried to fill it with meaningless people, but that didn't work either. No, I don't mean with sex. I actually tried to make friends, but they weren't you, nobody could ever be you. So, now I just keep to myself. I go to class, study, and then come home. The isolation of it reminds me of home, except without the beatings. There is some comfort in that."

"I never hated you, Kris. I just couldn't stand by and watch you destroy yourself. You were being reckless. I had never seen that from you and it scared me. After I left, I spent that spring break worrying about you. When I got back, I had a hard time finding you. I wondered why I stopped seeing you around. I'd catch a glimpse of you every now and then, but it was only that, a glimpse. I guess because you were avoiding me, that would explain it."

"I just couldn't handle the pain and seeing you. I knew it was my fault, but that didn't make it hurt any less. I finally resolved that you and your family were better off forgetting about me. I looked in to changing schools, but my scholarship wouldn't allow it."

"I'm glad you didn't. Mom, Dad, and Tyler ask about you every time I talk to them."

"What'd you tell them?" I said, fearing the answer. The Barnes family has always made me feel like I was a part of their family and that I belonged with them.

"I told them that we were both busy with classes and homework and we had drifted apart, but I saw you around campus every now and then. I don't think they bought it, but they never pressed for more details."

"Thanks for not telling them what a jackass I became."

"I didn't think you were a jackass, and I still don't. Besides, I would never tell them anything like that anyway. That is disrespectful to you. You are now and will always be my best friend, Kris. I love you, and I really don't like not having you around. Not having you a part of my life, it feels wrong."

"I love you, too. I have missed you, a lot," I said, getting up and pulling Grace up and hugging her tight.

We spent the rest of that day and night together in my room hanging out. We ordered a pizza and talked about everything that had gone on over the past year. I told her about the women, the club fight, everything. She told me about how she had shut herself off to some people, but how she had also made some friends out of everything that had happened. I was happy for her, and I honestly felt a large amount of jealousy rear up inside me. I was used to being Grace's closest friend; now, I didn't know if that was even possible again. I was certain one of the new friends had replaced me there. We talked until early in the morning, and Grace ended up spending the rest of the morning sleeping in my room. We skipped classes that day and spent the time hanging out together. It was the first time in a year that I had felt whole, and like I wasn't alone in the world.

Chapter Three

Kris, you should come home with me this weekend," Grace said. The weather had finally starting to warm up so we were eating lunch in the courtyard.

"Grace, have you forgotten that my parents, the people I am hiding from, live like two blocks from your parents?"

"Actually, they don't. You really don't know anything that has gone on back home, do you?"

"Why would I?" I asked, dumbfounded. "I don't want to know about the people that abused me as a kid."

"Well, there was this huge scandal, and your dad lost his job. The CEO was stealing from state contracts, and your dad was implicated in it. They both got in a lot of trouble. After that, your dad couldn't get work so your parents had to sell their house and move. The last we heard was that they went to live with his parents."

"Wow, I want to feel bad for my grandparents, but they allowed my parents to treat me like scum, so I guess it is karma."

"So, will you come home with me?" Grace was looking at me with puppy dog eyes. She wasn't playing fair and she knew that.

I didn't have any excuse not to go home with her. I agreed, and we made the plans. Grace decided not to tell her parents I was coming with. I wasn't sure that was a good idea, but I'd go along with it.

It was a short flight back home; Grace and I were taking turns and sharing the window seat. I think the man in the aisle seat was a bit annoyed with us, but we were having fun so I didn't care. I started to get a pit in my stomach as we were walking into the airport terminal. It had been a year and a half since I had seen Grace's family, let alone been 'home'. That pit was also bringing with it a flood of 'what if's.' What if they didn't believe Grace's story that we'd drifted apart? What if they didn't want me around? What if they didn't want Grace to hang out with me anymore?

"Hey," Grace said, placing a hand on my arm.

"Huh?" I said. Her soft touch startled me. I had been lost in my own world.

"Where'd you go?"

"I just got lost in my head," I said, avoiding eye contact.

"Kris? Talk to me." Grace pulled me aside and the concerned look on her pale face was making me feel even worse. "Are you okay with being here? Is it me? Did I do something? Or not do something?"

"I'm just nervous about seeing your family. I started playing the 'what-if' game in my head."

"Well, stop it," Grace said, smiling. "My family loves you, and they've missed you."

I felt Grace wrap her arms around my neck and hug me, and I felt myself relaxing into her embrace. Once I was calmer, we made our way toward the exit to meet up with her family.

"*Grace,*" we heard called repeatedly.

I realized that this place was very crowded. Everywhere I looked, there were people and luggage. Then I finally found the source of the voice. It belonged to Tyler. He had seen Grace and I could see him running toward us. When he saw me, he bypassed his sister and picked me up in a bear hug.

"Oh, I missed you," he said, swinging me around.

"I missed you too," I said, once I was back on the ground.

"What am I?" scoffed Grace.

"I see you all the time. I haven't seen Squish in forever," replied Tyler, sticking his tongue out at his sister. She returned the gesture.

As the three of us walked to Tyler's Jeep Wrangler, I found myself sandwiched between the two redheads. This was the closest I had been to any of the Barnes family since Grace and I had our blowout. It felt amazing!

"Why didn't you tell me she was coming with you?" Tyler asked, glaring at Grace, who was seated in the passenger seat.

"If I would have told you, it wouldn't have been a surprise. Duh, dumbass."

"Shut up or I will pull over, and you can walk home."

I loved listening to the two of them go at one another. When I was younger, it made me miss having a sibling. As I grew older, I was glad I didn't. I didn't want anyone else to be treated like I was.

As we pulled into the driveway, I could see Grace's parents coming out of the house. I watched them making their way to Grace. Just as they were about to hug her, I got out of the back of the Jeep. My movement caused them to look in my direction and they bypassed Grace and hugged me. That was what I loved about them. They always had a way of making me feel as if I were a part of their family. Although, I didn't have the same red hair as they all did.

"Oh, Kris," cried Grace's mom, Erin.

"It is nice that you finally decided to come home for a visit. I thought we were going to have to come down to the school and kidnap you," said her father, Sean.

"I'm sorry," I said, sheepishly.

"Um, hello? Your daughter is here as well," Grace said, but her tone told us she was joking.

"Yeah, yeah, we see you all the time," said her mother as we all headed inside.

Grace took my bag and put it in her bedroom while her parents were grilling me on school. After finishing filling them in on the 'parent rated' version of my college life, Grace and I went downstairs to the basement to play pool. I had always loved how they had turned their basement into a sort of family game room. The walls were painted with chalkboard paint. They had an area for playing video games with a large flat screen TV. There was the pool table, complete with a small bar table and stools. They had a section for playing darts. When they first set that area up, they just had the dartboard attached to the wall, but after Grace and I stuck several darts into the wall, Sean put up a corkboard and then the dartboard. Now if you miss and hit the wall, you have issues or your name is Grace Barnes.

"I told you they missed you," Grace said with a smug look on her face.

"I know you did—"

"But you were still skeptical."

I smiled at her and shrugged my shoulders. I wish I could tell Grace how much I loved being here and being a part of her family. I never once felt this way in my house. We had dinner and played cards. I had picked up a few tricks at school in my 'player' days. I won most of the hands that I played. It had been an emotional day so I excused myself and went to lay down in Grace's room early.

❧❧❧❧

I was leaning up against the window frame when Grace finally came into her room. I felt her wrap her arms around my waist and lean her chin on my shoulder. We had always had a touchy closeness in our friendship. Trisha always resented how close Grace and I were.

"I thought you would be asleep by now," she said.

"I tried."

"Wanna talk about it?"

"There isn't a lot to talk about. I just forgot how good it felt to be a part of a family. Like I matter or belong someplace."

"Kris," Grace said, turning me to face her. "You do matter. You matter a lot to me. As for being someplace you belong, you will always have a place with me, and I am pretty certain my parents and Tyler will agree."

"Thanks for not completely giving up on me," I whispered, and she hugged me closer.

"We'll get through this. And, I never gave up on you or hated you. Now, let's get some sleep."

The two of us were sharing her queen-sized bed. I don't know why it felt different that night, but I couldn't relax with Grace next to me. Maybe it was being back in this town. Maybe it was because she and I had spent so much time apart. It just felt off. I was restless.

☙ ☙ ❧ ❧

The air was crisp as I walked down the street of our little patch of hell, er, little town. I was checking out how much things had changed since I was last here. Everything seemed older, smaller, and dirtier. As I was walking, I bumped into a storefront bench, and it crumbled before me. I hadn't bumped it hard. I had really just grazed it.

There was a ground-shaking thunderclap that startled me. I glanced up at the sky and saw the dark menacing clouds roll in. Something in the look of the clouds told me to get my ass moving and get out of there. As I hurried away, a bolt of lightning struck where I had just been standing.

"Wow, that was close," I said to myself as I raced down the street.

I rounded the corner hurriedly and came face to face with my father. His eyes glowed red with fury and hatred.

"What are you doing here?"

"I'm just v-visiting," I stuttered. My heart was pounding in my chest. I felt the fear welling up inside of me.

"Not anymore," he said, grabbing me by the hair and dragging me into a black utility van that was next to us.

Once in the van, I felt my hands being taped behind my back as I squirmed and tried to scream. Then a piece of tape put over my mouth made the probability of my screams being heard almost nothing. I couldn't make out the face of the person with the tape. I could tell it was a man, but who, I wasn't sure. My mother and father had no siblings. I fought to see who it was, but then came a searing pain on the back of my head and then it went dark.

As I awoke, I could hear the sound of water splashing. It sounded like I was on a boat, but I neither lived nor went to school near water. My life was in dry dock. I tried to open my eyes, but I couldn't see anything. My head was throbbing, and my mouth tasted like metal. I knew the taste well. It was blood.

"What are we going to do with her?" said one of the male voices.

"We're going to dump her overboard and watch her sink, you jackass," said my father. His voice I could never forget.

"Weigh her down, you fools," said my mother, another voice I could never forget.

I felt something heavy being tied to me, and then it was wet. All sounds were muted, and I couldn't breathe. I felt myself thrashing.

"Kris? Hey, wake up," I heard Grace's voice saying repeatedly.

"Beep...beep..."

"Kris? Hey, wake up," I heard Grace saying. Her voice seemed to be coming from everywhere.

As I was gasping for air, I opened my eyes. I started pulling away from her until I felt myself pressing against the wall. Frantically, I looked around to figure out where I was. What was going on?

"Kris, look at me. Come on, it's me. It's Grace."

"Is everything okay?" said Tyler, opening Grace's door. Her parents followed him in.

"It's fine. She just had a nightmare. I need you all to get out of my room so that I can calm her down,"

Grace said. I could hear the annoyance in her voice.

I watched them turn and leave without question. It was as if I was watching a movie and not reality. I watched Grace slowly extend her arm and brush her fingertips on my cheek. I felt a wave of uncertainty wash over me. It threatened to drag me under again. I could see her lips moving, but the sounds were as if I were underwater. I felt Grace take my hand. I allowed her to pull me back down onto the bed.

"Grace?" I whispered, feeling her arms tighten around me. I've had nightmares since I was a kid. Nothing like this, but Grace had seen or heard me wake from them before.

"You're safe," she said, kissing the top of my head.

I draped my arm across her body and pulled her closer. I was shaking so bad I was certain I was going to vibrate us out of the bed. We were closer than we'd ever been, but I needed to feel her there. I needed to know that I was in the real world and not a dream.

Beep…beep…beep…

"Grace, do you hear a beeping noise?" I asked, my voice low and full of fear.

"Look at me." Grace tilted my head up so that we were looking at one another. I could see the worry in her eyes. Worry really doesn't look good in bright blue. "You're here, with me. I'm not going to let anything happen to you. You're safe."

I couldn't stop myself at that moment. I'm not sure I would have if I could. I leaned up and kissed her. It was hesitant at first, but then the need to feel something, the need to be consumed, took over. The kisses became deeper and hungrier. We definitely crossed that friendship barrier. When we finally broke apart, I found myself lying on top of Grace. Our bodies were pressed tight together. I could feel skin on skin where our t-shirts had risen up. We were both panting, reeling from what had just happened.

"Are you back with me now?" Her voice was soft and comforting; she didn't seem the least bit upset.

I nodded and dropped my head onto her shoulder. I felt Grace wrapping her arms protectively around me, holding me close. I don't know how long she let me lay there, but she never once tried to push me away. I rolled off her and onto my side. She rolled with me, keeping her arms around me. We drifted to sleep and I felt at peace for the first time in almost two years.

⁂

I could feel the warmth of the sun on my face. Morning was here. My whole body ached. That wasn't uncommon after having one of those nightmares. My muscles frequently locked in the tensed state. I could feel Grace pressed up against my back. She was still holding me and keeping me safe. How had I survived without her for the past year?

"Morning," Grace said, softly.

"Morning," I said, turning in her arms to face her.

"How are you feeling?"

"I hurt like hell, and I'm embarrassed…"

"You have nothing to be embarrassed about. You had a nightmare. It wasn't the first, and as much as I hate to say it, it won't be your last."

"Yeah, that isn't that part that I'm most embarrassed about. I'm sorry if I crossed the line—"

"Stop right there; you did nothing wrong."

"I just needed to feel something real. To feel like I was real again."

"I understand, I think that I partly needed it as much as you did. I was afraid I was losing you. How long have you been having the nightmares like that?"

"I've always had them. I mean since we were kids. You have to remember me waking up during our sleepovers." Grace nodded. "They got worse after everything went down between us at school last year."

"Are they always that powerful?"

"That was actually a rather tame one. There have been more times than I care to admit that I have been so paralyzed with fear that I couldn't leave my dorm room."

"How did you get past them?" Grace asked. Her eyes were fixated on me.

"Time. I would sit in a corner of my room until the fear passed," I said, averting my eyes. The sheet between us was very interesting all of a sudden.

"How long did or does that take?" asked Grace. Hearing the tension in her voice made me uneasy. I didn't like upsetting her.

"It varies."

"Dammit, Kris! I'm serious, stop being evasive with me." Her tone made me look up at her.

"Okay. But it does vary. It can take a couple of hours to a couple of days." I hung my head because I knew the look she was going to give me. I didn't want or need to be pitied. "The hard part is when they pass. I have to figure out how long I have been out of it. I don't usually remember the terrors. That is the only good thing to come of these."

"Kris, look at me." Grace waited in silence until I complied. "You are never alone. You could have, and can, call me for whatever you need. You don't have to do this by yourself. I'm glad I was here last night for you."

"But the kiss…"

"Oh that. I don't regret that either. I now know the rumors I heard about you in high school were true. You aren't a half bad kisser." Grace giggled as I blushed.

"What rumors?"

"Oh, nobody knew who started them…well, you and I know it had to be Trisha, but yeah, it was rumored that you were quite good at kissing."

"Ugh," I groaned, burying my head in the pillow.

"Although, the next time you want to kiss me, a little warning, please. I had morning breath and couldn't let loose," teased Grace. "I prefer a minty fresh mouth."

"Very funny," I said, sticking my tongue out at her.

"Don't tease me." Grace was having way too much fun at my expense.

❧❧❧❧

By the time we headed down to breakfast, the entire Barnes family was already up. When we walked into the kitchen, I could feel all eyes on me.

"How are you doing, dear?" asked Erin.

"I'm okay," I said, feeling a bit uncomfortable.

"Kris, what happened last night?"

"It was a nightmare, is all, Dad," Grace said, before looking at me.

"I'm sorry—" I started, staring at my feet.

"Honey, we don't care about anything other

than that you are all right and safe," Erin said, before hugging me.

"She's right," said Sean. "Like it or not, you are a part of this family and we care about you. I will never forgive myself for not doing something sooner to get you safely out of that house." I could hear the venom in his tone. "I wish my kids would have told me something sooner than last night. I am so sorry for whatever you had to endure."

"Sorry Squish," mumbled Tyler. I could see the guilt on his face for telling his parents even a little bit of the secret that he and Grace had kept for years.

"It wasn't your responsibility," I said, offering both Sean and Tyler a reassuring smile.

"You are like a daughter to us," he started.

My mind quickly flashed back to kissing Grace a few hours prior, and I started to blush. I don't know that Sean would feel the same way about me if he knew that Grace and I had a rather intense make-out session earlier. I glanced at her and saw a smirk on her face. She was loving this, loving seeing me squirm.

Breakfast passed quickly, and I was quiet throughout the meal. I was still dealing with the emotions of the dream. Grace told everyone we were going out for a bit. We walked a little but ended up in the treehouse, as usual.

"You enjoyed watching me squirm way too much," I said, once we were in the treehouse.

"I wouldn't say that it was too much enjoyment, but I did enjoy it."

"How loud was I last night? How embarrassed should I really be?"

"You were almost completely silent. That was what freaked me out more than anything. It was me trying to wake you up that alerted them to there being a problem."

"God, I should have stayed at school," I said, burying my head in my hands. "This was a very bad idea."

"I don't agree. Kris, you aren't alone. I'm here, Tyler, my parents…we're all here for you. Here to support and help. Do you want to talk about the dream?"

"It's one that I have frequently." I told Grace the details that I remembered from the dream. It felt good to confide in someone, but I didn't want to burden her.

Grace sat silent for a few minutes. I'm guessing she was processing what I had told her. Then she lunged at me and wrapped her arms around me. I could feel her crying on my shoulder. Her wet tears were dripping from her cheek onto my shirt, causing the wet material to cling to my skin. I did the only thing I could do; I held her like she had held me earlier.

"Sorry," Grace said, sheepishly. Once she was able to compose herself, she pulled back and took my hand in hers. "You know that I'm never going to let that dream come true."

"I don't know that either of us really has a say in that dream coming true or not."

"I don't care. You are my best friend, and I'm not going to let it happen."

The remainder of the weekend passed without incident. I had forgotten how much fun it was to hang out with Grace's family. While waiting for our plane to be called, Grace's parents made me promise to come back with her more often.

Over the next few weeks, Grace and I had a running breakfast 'date' at eight in the morning. I know that this was her way of making sure that I was okay, without blatantly saying it. I had one nightmare during that time, but it was the tamest one I've had in years. The more time I spent with Grace, the more things started to feel like they did when we were growing up. I had my best friend back.

"Hey, slacker," Grace said, when I found her sitting outside my dorm room door one afternoon.

"You are calling me a slacker, and yet you are the one sitting outside *my* door doing nothing."

"I'm not doing nothing," she said, showing me the game she was playing on her phone.

"Free Fall? Really? Get up and get inside. I don't want people knowing that we're friends. It'll ruin my crusty bitch reputation." I extended my hand and helped Grace stand up before gently pushing her into my room. "Plus, that game is embarrassing."

"You could be so lucky to be associated with me," Grace said, sitting down on my bed. "What are you doing tonight?"

"I have no plans. Why?"

"Good. I need a movie marathon with junk food."

"Who broke up with you?" I asked, giggling. When we were younger, every time someone dumped her, we did this. Even when we were eight, Disney movies and popcorn with M&M's mixed in were the key to soothing a broken heart.

"Nobody, I just have had a harsh week. We don't have to."

"I'm teasing you. I'd love to do the movie and junk food. Do you want to do it here or go over and hang with smelly?"

"Here, please."

I had finally met Grace's roommate. She had understated the stench. Okay, maybe if she hadn't understated the smell and had she told me the truth, I would never have set foot in her room. The scent in her room reminded me of the scent of a wet dog mixed with spoiled milk. It wasn't pleasant. Since that fateful night, we've made sure that we either go out or hang at my place.

"So, do you want to go get the food? I'll go get us some movies?" I suggested.

"Okay. Just don't get anything gory."

"I'll get some frou-frou movies." Grace stuck her tongue out at me, and we both laughed.

We agreed to meet back at the room in an hour. I went and got three movies that I knew were Grace's favorites. I wasn't sure what had happened in her week, but I wanted to be there for her the way she had been for me. I stopped and got her some flowers. Yes, I know, but they make her smile and that was so very important.

"I hope you are ready for pizza, chips, chocolate, and caffeine," Grace said, entering the room.

Hurrying over, I took the pizza and one of the bags from her. We spread of food out on my desk. I set up the first movie and we got comfortable on my bed.

"All right, you want to tell me what happened?" I asked.

"There are just some people in a couple of my classes that are making it a bit difficult."

"Tell me who, and I'll make sure they stop," I said. My defenses were up instantly. I was a bit on the over-protective side when it came to Grace.

"No, you will not go all butch and 'talk' to them.

Just, let's have a fun night. Please?"

I relented for the time being, but I swore to myself that I would find out whom it was making her life difficult, and I would make their life difficult.

We ate, watched movies, laughed, and she cried. It was a great night. We fell asleep on my bed. When I woke the following morning, I was drawn to watching Grace sleep. She looked so peaceful and relaxed. I wasn't trying to be creepy, or creepier than I already was. It was just, ever since we kissed at her parents' house, I'd felt a little different toward her. I think I was developing a crush on my best friend. My true fear was that she would find out and then she would pull away.

"Hi," I said as I saw Grace's eyes opening.

"Hey." Grace gave me a tired smile. "Have you been up long?"

"Nah, just a few minutes."

We stared at one another for another minute, and then Grace did something that I totally hadn't expected. Grace leaned up and pressed our lips together. I let out a moan of enjoyment when I felt her lips on mine. I brought a hand up, ran it along her jaw, and then threaded it in her hair. I deepened the kiss and heard Grace moan when our tongues touched. When we finally pulled apart, we were both breathing hard.

"I've wanted to do that since that day at my parents'," said Grace. I wasn't sure if she was blushing or just flush from the kiss.

"I have too," I admitted.

"Then why didn't you?"

"I was afraid of losing you again. You have no clue how bad it was for me without you."

"I have a pretty good idea," Grace said, moving

her body closer to mine. "I was miserable without you."

I pulled her into my arms and kissed her again, this time without restraint. I had kissed a fair number of women. Not a single one felt as amazing as it felt to kiss Grace. We got lost in the kisses, and when her stomach finally protested and voiced its need for food, we'd been kissing for over two hours.

"Wow," I said, barely above a whisper.

"Yeah, you won't get an argument from me," said Grace as she started to giggle.

"Care to share the joke?"

"Sorry. It's just, who would have thought that you and I would have ever ended up kissing?"

"Almost everyone that I have actually dated," I said.

"Huh?"

Grace and I sat up and faced one another. "Trisha and I fought often about how close you and I were. She accused me often of cheating on her with you. Others have said that we were too close. Hell, one of the girls that I dated while we were here at college but not speaking said that she would never consider getting serious with me because of you. And she had never met you."

"Wow, I had no idea. How come you never told me this before?"

"It was never relevant. If I would have told you about what Trisha said when we were in high school, what would you have done?" I asked.

"I would have backed away and given you both more space."

"And that is why I didn't say anything. I didn't want anything between us to change. If they couldn't accept that you were a large portion of my life, they didn't need to be there."

A tear rolled down her cheek. I wiped it away and gave her a light chaste kiss. We got cleaned up and headed out to get something to eat. As we walked, I wrapped an arm around Grace's waist to hold her close.

Chapter Four

Grace and I spent the next three weeks growing closer, romantically. I was taking things with her slow. Sex changes things. Sex, too early, destroys relationships. I wasn't going to risk doing that with Grace. We went out for dinner and movies. We held hands. We cuddled; there was a lot of kissing, and some incidental minor groping.

"Hey, babe," I said as Grace entered my room after classes one day.

"Hey," she said, sadly.

"What's wrong?" I asked her, closing my books and setting them on the floor next to the bed where I was sitting.

Grace came and sat down on the edge of the bed.

"Can we talk about something?"

"Of course, sweetie. What's up?"

"Remember when I told you there were some girls making my life difficult?" she started, and I nodded. "Well, are you still willing to help?"

"Always. Nobody messes with my girlfriend. Just give me their names."

"The main one is Alyssa Ames. I don't know what to do about her. In Psych, we are seated alphabetically so she sits right next to me."

"What's she doing?"

"It's like we're back in high school. She knocks stuff off my desk, calls me names, and today she announced to everyone that I was gay. One of her friends mentioned I had a girlfriend. She laughed and said that my girlfriend must have been blind or desperate to choose me."

"Trust me when I say your girlfriend is neither blind nor desperate." I pulled her onto my lap and held her body close to mine.

Grace started to squirm until she was sitting on my lap with her legs wrapped around me.

"Show me," she whispered, before kissing me hard.

"Well, so much for taking it slow," I thought to myself as I adjusted us so that I was lying on top of her.

"Are you sure?" I asked. I needed to make sure she was ready for this step, and it wasn't just because of that bitch, Alyssa.

"Oh yes, I am very sure," Grace said, her hands slipping under my t-shirt.

I groaned and kissed her passionately. Slowly, we stripped one another's clothes away and made love for hours. They say that the first time with someone can be awkward. For me, with Grace, it was perfect.

"Mmmm, you are amazing," I said, nibbling on her neck.

"Oh, god. That feels so good."

We eventually got up and went to get dinner. While we were out, Grace pointed out Alyssa. I would describe her as a prissy brunette who appeared to have been popular in high school, and she felt that entitled her to something special in her college years. As I veered toward Alyssa, Grace stopped me. She said that she didn't want to spoil our newfound closeness with the memory of me beating the shit out of Alyssa, even if she did deserve it. I respected that, but it didn't quell the annoyance I felt for this woman.

❧❧❧❧

Two days later, as I was heading to class, I saw Alyssa standing alone. I knew that this was a perfect time to walk over and exchange some words with her.

"Hey, good looking," she said to me.

"I'm sorry?" I asked, shocked at her boldness. I also didn't get hit on often, so I'm wasn't used to it.

"Well, you are beautiful. What do you say that you and I go find some place to get better acquainted?" said Alyssa, suggestively.

"I don't know that my girlfriend would approve of that." I could feel the anger inside me rising.

"What she doesn't know won't hurt us." Alyssa moved closer. There was barely any space between us. "I promise it will be a night you won't forget."

"Well, I'm very happy with my girlfriend."

"Does this girlfriend of yours have a name? This is a pretty small campus. I probably know her."

"Grace Barnes," I said. I couldn't help but laugh as Alyssa placed the name and took a step back away from me. I stepped forward into her personal space. "Leave her the fuck alone, or you and I will be up close and personal, and not in the way you are hoping for."

Stepping back again, Alyssa fixed her gaze on me. She was shocked, and I was happy to see that. "Her? You are turning me down for her? Seriously?"

"I wouldn't do you with a hazmat suit and a twenty-foot pole. Now, do we understand one another?"

"Yeah, you want to play hard to get. I like a challenge."

She gave me a wink, and then I felt her hand on

my ass as she gave it a good squeeze before walking away with a smug look on her face. I felt like I needed to go shower again. I could see Grace standing outside my class as I neared it. I was trying to smile, but I know it didn't meet my eyes.

"What's wrong?" she asked, pulling me aside.

"It's not important," I said, leaning over and kissing her.

"Something upset you. That to me is very important."

"I ran into Alyssa on the way over here, is all."

"With her that is never 'all.' What else happened?"

I knew I wasn't going to get lucky enough for her to drop this. "She hit on me. When I told her that I was very happy with my girlfriend, she hit on me again then asked who my girlfriend was."

"And?" asked Grace. Whenever she got angry, her face would turn as red as her hair. We were well on our way there now.

"I told her that my girlfriend was the incredibly sexy Grace Barnes," I said, pulling Grace's body flush against mine. "Once I saw she had placed the name, I told her to leave you the fuck alone, or she and I would have some physical contact, and not the kind she was hoping for." I gave Grace a chaste kiss.

"So far I'm not seeing why you had that disgusted look on your face."

"She then said that I was playing hard to get and she liked a challenge…and then she squeezed my ass. And we aren't talking a light squeeze." I wrapped my arms around Grace and gave her butt a similar squeeze.

"I'm sorry, she did what? She touched you? She has a death wish," Grace said. The ire in her voice was the same one that she had taken with my parents on several occasions. "Bitch thinks she can touch my girl…"

"Hey," I said, interrupting her thought process. I cupped her face in my hands and kissed her. It wasn't a gentle kiss, but one that had purpose. "Why don't we skip class and go back to my room? You can touch me and help me forget that I had skanky hands on me."

"Mmmm, I like how you think, Ms. Holt," Grace said. She took my hand and led me away from my class and back outside.

On the way back to my room, we saw Alyssa talking with a couple of her snobby friends. Grace made sure she had Alyssa's attention before pulling me into a steamy kiss. I must say, I do enjoy Grace's jealous side. We heard Alyssa let out a low growl. That confirmed for us that she saw the show. Grace waved to her, grabbed my hand, and we raced to my room. We barely made it in the door before we were pulling each other's clothes off.

"You are so hot when you are jealous," I said, kissing Grace as we fell into bed.

"You are so fucking hot at any point," she said, grinding into me.

We took one another hard and fast. When we were done, we lay there basking in the afterglow and the comfort that comes from being with someone you knew you could love, trust, and know that they loved and trusted you as well.

"I have to go home this weekend. Do you want to go with me?" asked Grace.

"I can't. I have a paper due on Monday, and two tests that I have to study for. I am going to miss you though."

"Poop." Grace pouted.

"And you kiss me with that dirty mouth?" I teased.

"Oh, that isn't all I do with it." Grace started to kiss her way down my body. We spent the rest of the day lost in one another.

Friday morning, I took Grace to the airport. It was hard to say good-bye, but since we started dating, my attention to my schoolwork had faded. I needed to get caught up, and if possible, get ahead.

❧❧❧❧

I studied until noon and then went out and got lunch. When I got back to the room, I saw that Grace texted me and told me she was home and that she missed me. I couldn't help but smile. I was never this happy with any of the other girls I dated. I looked forward to seeing and hearing from Grace. Once I got situated in the room, I decided to take a nap. I really enjoy not having to go to class on Fridays.

As I was walking through campus, all I could think about was Grace: how beautiful she was, how funny it was that until that nightmare I had never thought of her and I romantically. I was smiling, the birds were singing, sun shining bright. I could even smell the fresh cut grass. Rain had always been my favorite sound and scent. My second favorite thing used to be fresh cut grass, but that moved to third. Now, my second favorite smell was Grace. Yes, I knew that I was falling in love with her, and it was scaring me.

I stretched out on the grass in the quad, watching the squirrels playing over by a nearby tree. They were just babies. Then I saw him, lurking, staring, and menacingly smiling. I tried to get up, but I couldn't move. I looked down my body and saw ropes tying me to the ground. I started to struggle, but it was useless. I couldn't get up. The ropes were biting into my skin, cutting me.

"Hello, daughter," said my father, looking down on me. "Did you really think you could get away from me?"

"You aren't here. This isn't real," I said, my voice cracking.

"Tell me if this feels real." I saw him pull his leg back, and then I felt a searing pain in my ribcage as he kicked me. I cried out in pain. "You wouldn't have felt that in a dream, would you?"

"Just let me up, please," I begged. My breathing was labored from having the air kicked out of me and from fear.

"Oh, I will."

I felt another blow to my ribs. As the pain radiated through my body, I felt the air rush out of my lungs for the second time. I tried to move, and again I felt the ropes biting into my skin.

"Stop struggling," said a male voice. It wasn't my father. It was the voice from the other dreams. I wish I knew who the mystery man was. His face was always just a blur.

I felt myself being lifted up. The ropes were now wrapped around my body instead of trapping me to the ground. I felt the mystery man punch me in the other side of my ribs. I doubled over and felt a blow to my jaw, snapping my head to the side. Then I was hit with the metallic taste. Oh how I loathed the taste of blood.

"You are coming home with us. You are going to take care of your mother and me."

"You don't need me. You just want a slave," I said, without thinking.

"Oh, you aren't going to tell us what we need. You

are going to do as we say or that pretty little girl you have been dating and her family are going to pay. They may pay with blood, they may pay with beatings, or maybe we'll show her what a real man is like."

"Don't you dare touch them," I spat, blood flying from my mouth. "I'll kill you if you touch Grace. I will fucking kill you."

"Then maybe you should show some respect and do as you are told. Your mother and father have spent a lot of time, energy, and money trying to locate you."

"Who are you?"

"You'll figure it out," said the mystery man.

I tried to see him, but the sunlight was so bright. I couldn't shade my eyes with my hands being tied to the rest of my body.

"You have grown quite tempting," he said as he ran his calloused hand down my neck and grabbed my breast.

"Don't touch her," my father said, pulling the man's hand off me. "You can have her when we're done with her. Until then, if I catch you touching her again, I'll kill you."

"Fuck you," said the man as he walked away and everything around me went black.

When I opened my eyes, I could smell blood. I looked down and saw a pool of it at my feet. I tried to locate the source, but I could only move so much. Then I heard a scream; it was Trisha. She staggered into the room, bloodied.

"Kris, help me," said Trisha. She fell to her knees, and it was then that I saw the wounds on her back. I was standing in her blood. I knew it. I thought I was going to get sick.

I began to shake. "Trish, no! Why her?" I screamed,

but there was no answer. I tried to get to her, but I couldn't move.

I heard a whooshing noise just before I felt pain in my arm. I heard the crack. I knew it was broken. This wasn't the first time it had been broken. I heard another whoosh and something hit that same arm.

"Beep...beep..."

I jolted awake. I couldn't see where I was. Was I still in that room? Oh god, was Trisha's body still at my feet? I couldn't open my eyes and look. I felt my way to my safety corner and slid to the floor.

"Beep...beep..."

"What is that noise?" I mumbled, before blacking out again.

⚜ ⚜ ⚜ ⚜

I heard a knocking sound. Oh god, they are coming for me again. I felt bile fill my mouth and fear fill the rest of me. Why didn't they just kill me? I tried to curl up even more. I just wanted to make myself invisible or so small that nobody could or would see me.

"Kris?" said a soft female voice. "Baby?"

"No, you are a dream," I said. "You are trying to trick me. I won't let you hurt her. You killed Trisha. I won't let you hurt Grace. Just kill me and get it over with."

"No, baby. It's really me. Come back to me."

"Stop," I said, pressing myself harder against the wall.

"Baby, open your eyes and look at me," Grace said, lifting my head up so that we were now eye-to-eye. Her beautiful blue eyes were looking into my green eyes with a mix of fear and concern.

"Grace? Run. You shouldn't be here. They'll get you. I can't have them get you. I have to go with them so they don't hurt you and your family. Please forgive me."

I felt myself being pulled forward. It wasn't like it had been. It was gentle.

"Kris, honey. Please," I heard Grace say. I could tell she was crying.

"G-Grace? Is that really you?"

"Yeah, it's me. You're safe. We're in your dorm room. Come back to me."

I was looking around and I could see that she was right, that I was really in my dorm room. Grace watched as I was looking at my arms, my body. There were some bruises, but nothing like I knew there should be from the abuse that I had endured. I could feel the tears welling up and then spilling out.

"I'm going to be sick," I said. Grace grabbed the nearby trashcan, and I threw up in it. I threw up mostly blood and bile.

Grace left the room for a minute, returned with a wet washcloth, and dabbed at my forehead.

"You're safe now," she said, pulling me close to her, allowing me to feel her body against mine, allowing me to know what was real and what was part of the dream.

"W-what day is it?"

"Sunday," she whispered. She was crying again.

"Oh, god. Why me?" *Why couldn't this torment go away?*

Grace held and rocked me for a long time before helping me get up and into the shower to get cleaned up and wash the horror off. After I was clean, she helped me get dressed into a t-shirt and pair of boxers.

"Kris, touch me. Feel reality."

Grace knew that I needed to feel to know I was okay. She brought the palm of my hand up to feel her breast. I felt the nipple harden under my touch. I groaned at how good it felt. We made love, and Grace gave herself over to me to allow me the chance to root myself back in reality.

I loved feeling Grace next to me. I had always calmed in her presence, but this was entirely different and more intense.

"What is the last thing you remember doing?" Grace asked, running her hand along the space between my breasts and inner thighs.

"I remember taking you to the airport, I remember getting something to eat, studying, and then laying down to take a nap."

"Baby? You've been like that since Friday?" Grace started to cry again. "I shouldn't have left you."

"Hey, no. You saved me. That is the important part. You had to go home. The nightmares, they would have come if you were here or not."

"I could have gotten you out of it sooner, though."

We kissed and laid there holding one another, processing what had happened.

Chapter Five

So, tell me how your trip home was," I said as we sat in the cafeteria Tuesday night. This was the first chance Grace and I had to talk about her weekend. We had been lost in each other on Sunday, and then Monday was a very full day for me. I didn't get back to the room until late.

"It was good," Grace said, though her voice was sullen.

"Baby," I started, taking her hand. "You need to let this go. You saved me from the nightmare. You had no way of knowing what was going on. Had you not come into my room, who knows, I could still be there. Please, stop dwelling on this."

"I should have known there was a problem when you didn't answer my messages."

"Grace, baby, I told you I was studying. You know I turn my phone off when I study. You had no way of knowing."

Reaching over and cupping her face in one hand, I could feel her lean into my touch. She smiled a soft smile that melted my heart. We finished eating, and as we were walking out the door, we came face to face with Alyssa.

"Well, hey there, cutie," Alyssa said, her eyes roving the length of my body.

"Back off," I heard Grace growl. The tone in her voice was enough to make Alyssa look at her. I hadn't ever heard it from her, either. Apparently, Grace still had a jealous and possessive streak. I hoped she realized that I was hers.

"What? Are you scared of a little competition? Afraid that I might show her what it is like to be with a real woman?" Alyssa taunted Grace, looking at her smugly.

I knew if I let this keep going, it wasn't going to end well. I wrapped my arms tightly around Grace. Her body was rigged, but I could feel her start to relax. I did it partially to hold her and keep her from doing something stupid, but I also felt the need to make a point to Alyssa.

"She doesn't have to be scared of competition. You aren't even worthy of being in her league. And for the record, trust me when I say that she is a real woman. I have spent hours and hours exploring her body." I nipped at Grace's neck a couple of times. "Now, if you'll excuse us, I feel the need for some more exploring of both taste and touch."

Yeah, I'm mean and it may be a bit childish, but Alyssa deserved it.

"I, er," stammered Alyssa.

"That is what I thought," I said, moving my hand along Grace's hipbone.

"Yes, please," Grace whispered.

We left Alyssa with her mouth hanging open.

"You are a huge tease," Grace said as we were walking back to my dorm room.

"Who said I was teasing?" I leered at Grace and heard her audibly gulp. She grabbed my hand, and we picked up the pace to my room.

As soon as we entered my room, I found myself pressed against the door. Grace's hands worked their way under my shirt while her lips latched onto my neck.

"Oh, god, Grace," I moaned.

It didn't take her long to divest my shirt and bra. Grace brought her hands up and started to tease my breasts. I pulled her lips to mine and kissed her passionately. She removed the remainder of my clothes while keeping me pressed against the door.

"You are so hot," Grace said, taking my left nipple into her mouth and teasing it with her tongue.

"Yes," I whispered, sharply. I felt her shift from one breast to the other.

With her help, we quickly removed her clothes. Grace pressed her body against mine. The heat emanating from her body was like being on fire. The cold wood of the door on my back was the only thing keeping me from overheating. Our breathing was becoming ragged. I quickly spun us around and pressed her back against the door.

"Fuck," Grace moaned. The only time Grace used the F-word with me was when she was really turned on or when she was really mad at me.

We made our way to my bed, and I slowed things down. We made love more passionately than we ever had before.

"I love you," I said, looking into Grace's eyes, before leaning over and kissing her, trying to show her how deep my love was for her was.

"I love you, too."

This was the first time that either of us have said 'I love you' without it being because of our friendship.

"You never did tell me how things went when you were home," I said, running my hand over her naked body. I just couldn't seem to stop touching her. We were covered partially with the sheet, but any part of her exposed was fair game to touch.

"I did. I said it was good."

"And that is you avoiding something. Normally when I ask you to tell me all about your trip home, you tell me every detail, even what you had to eat. Now, you won't? Talk to me, please."

Grace let out a long breath. "I told them about us…"

"And they don't approve," I said, stopping my hand on her stomach.

"They just need some time." I started to pull my hand away, and Grace grabbed my hand. "Baby, please. My family doesn't decide whom I am going to love. I am here with you, because that is where I want to be."

"I won't make you choose between me and your family. You know that."

"I know that and nobody is asking me to choose. It was just a surprise to them. I mean we've been best friends since we were five. I don't think that anyone ever pictured us dating. Did you ever picture us dating? I know I didn't." I shook my head.

"There's more, isn't there?"

"No," Grace said. She was a terrible liar.

"Grace?" She wouldn't make eye contact with me, so I had to play dirty. I rolled on top of her, pinning her still naked body beneath my naked body. I watched her eyes close and then flutter open again. She let out this moan of pleasure that almost made me forget why I was doing this. Almost.

"That…isn't fair," she said, her hands caressing

my sides.

"I know, but it is effective. Now talk to me." I felt her hips start to move, and I gave her a stern look, causing her to relent and let out a sigh of frustration.

"Tyler has a new girlfriend."

"And you don't like her? Why is this an issue? Details." I ground my hips into hers. I know it wasn't nice, but she wasn't talking to me. And technically, she started it.

"Oh, god. You had better put out after this," she said, smiling. I kissed the tip of her nose and nodded. "Fine, Tyler is dating that bitch, Jenna Patterson. You remember, the chick that outed you in school senior year."

"Ew! I thought your brother had taste."

"He did, but I don't know what happened to it."

"Well, hopefully she has matured."

"She hasn't. She was rather crude when I spoke with her. My parents weren't happy with what she had to say, but Tyler said he'd talk to her."

"Was that before or after you told them about us?"

"Before," she groaned.

"I love you. Thank you for telling me."

"Like you left me a choice. You play dirty, Ms. Holt."

"You loved every minute of it," I said, before I leaned down and kissed her soundly. "Now, let me reward you for being open and honest with me."

"It's about time," Grace said, flipping us over so she was on top and taking control.

❧ ❧ ❧ ❧

Over the next two months, Grace moved into my dorm room with me. The room definitely wasn't made for two people to be living in, but we were making it work. I can honestly say that I had never been happier. I know, with how my childhood was, it wouldn't take much, but this was so amazing. School was going great, I had the woman I loved living with me. I then realized that school would be ending soon. Grace would be going home for the summer. I would be alone, again. That single thought felt like a punch to the gut. How was I going to survive the summer without Grace? Life had just gone from amazing to sucky in three seconds flat.

"Hey, baby!"

"Hey," I said, trying to hide the tears. I knew a few had slipped out and left streaks down my face.

"What's wrong?" asked Grace as she dropped her bag on the floor and raced over to my side.

"Nothing. How was your day?"

"Kris, come on. What's got you so upset?"

I let out a large sigh. "I was laying here reveling in how good my life has become, and how much I love you. Then it hit me…the semester is going to be ending soon, and you are going to be going back home, and I'll be here, alone again. Last year it wasn't a big deal. I didn't have you, but now…"

"Baby," Grace said, cupping my face. "You aren't going to be alone. You can either come home with me, or we can both stay here. I don't like the idea of sleeping alone any more than you do."

"Your parents don't approve of us, and I don't think that it would be a good idea for me to go back there, let alone the idea of us sharing a bed in their house."

"Well, then we will stay here."

"Grace, I can't let you blow off your family for me. I know how much your time together means to all of you. I always envied it." I tried to look away, but she still had my face cupped in her hands. Grace kissed me softly.

"Well, I am not going to be able to spend all my summers with them. I will, at some point, have a job."

"Yes, but that isn't now. Now is when you are to spend time with your family. Cherish the closeness."

"I love you, Kris. I want and need to be where you are. If you don't want to come home with me, then we will stay here."

"I love you, too." I kissed her softly. My emotions were still raw, but I felt better knowing that she wanted to stay here with me.

"Come on, I am in the mood for an ice cream cone."

We headed out in search of her ice cream cone. We found the one spot on campus that carried her favorite flavor, chocolate marshmallow. I was certain we'd never find it. While we were out, Grace asked if I would be there with her when she called her parents to tell them that she was staying here over the summer. I reluctantly agreed. When we got back to the room, we curled up together on the bed with Grace wrapped safely in my arms. Once situated, she gave me a weak smile before calling her parents and putting the phone on speaker.

"Grace, Sweetie!" said Sean, her father.

"Hi, Daddy!"

"How is my little girl doing?"

"I'm not that little, Dad. Plus, being your little girl implies innocence—"

"Stop. You are about to venture into an area where this father doesn't want to know. To me, you are still my innocent six-year-old daughter."

"Who are you talking too?" asked Erin in the background.

"Grace. She is trying to get the inheritance by giving me a heart attack."

"Gracie, we talked about this. No giving your father a heart attack until *after* I make the life insurance payment."

"Sorry, Mom. I saw a really cute pair of shoes."

I loved the playful banter between her family. It made me wonder what my life would have been like if I would have had parents like hers. Parents that actually cared if I was alive or dead.

"So, what's new?" Grace asked, nervously.

"Tyler and Jenna were over last night for dinner," said Erin.

I felt Grace tense when her mother said this. I kissed the side of her head, hoping to remind her that it didn't matter; we had each other.

"That's nice." Grace wasn't convincing at all. We all knew that was her humoring her mother.

"So, when do you need us to come and help you move out of the dorms?"

"Um, that is part of the reason for my call. You see, I'm going to stay here for the summer."

"This is because of Kris, isn't it?" I tensed at her father's tone.

"Yep," Grace responded tersely. "It is."

"Grace, you know that your mother and I adore Kris. She has and will always be a part of our family."

"Yeah, Dad, but she can't be a part of it as my girlfriend. That's where you were going with this, right?"

I held Grace closer. It took everything I had not to pipe in and let them know that I was there and that I wasn't forcing her to stay here. Grace turned and gave me a chaste kiss.

"That isn't what your father means. You know what her family life was like—"

"Yeah, I know what she went through day after day. I know how bad it got. You guys don't even know the tip of the iceberg about what her life was like. I love her, and she loves me. You claim that she is a part of our family, but you treat her marginally better than her parents did."

"Grace Marie Barnes! That was uncalled for," snapped Erin.

"Baby, don't," I whispered into her ear. I didn't want her starting a fight with her parents because of me. I'm not worth that.

"Yeah, it was called for. You claim that you love her, that she is part of our family. And yet you have done nothing but try to talk me out of my relationship with her. You have implied that she will turn out like her parents. She is nothing like them. You wouldn't have a problem if we were still just friends."

"You deserve better, honey," said Sean. The disapproval in his tone was very apparent

"No, Daddy. I deserve her. She treats me with respect. We are equals in our relationship. She has told me numerous times that she will never ask me to choose between my family and her. You and Mom are asking me to choose though. Kris tried to talk me out of staying here. She knows how much family time means to us."

"Well, she didn't do a good job, now did she," said Erin, sarcastically.

"Actually, until you said she wasn't good enough, I was going to come home for a visit. Now, I don't think I am. I'm going to do what Kris is doing and take a couple of classes to get ahead." Grace turned and smiled at me. I mouthed 'I love you' to her. My stomach was in a knot.

"Where are you going to live? How are you going to pay for things? Your father and I aren't just going to toss money at you."

"I haven't asked either of you for a dime since I started here. Why would I do that now? No, I have money saved, plus I can pick up a job or do some tutoring. As for where I will live, I'm going to live with Kris in the dorms."

"Are you sure that living together is such a good idea?"

"Oh crap, please don't say it. Please don't..." I thought, sensing where this was going.

"Yeah, Mom, I do. We've been living together for the past two months."

I cringed when I heard her say this. I knew that she was saying it out of spite to wound them. Yes, it bothered me to hurt people who had always been so caring for me, but I kept quiet. I buried my face in her hair and enjoyed the coconut scent of her conditioner.

"Does the school know this? What does her roommate think?"

"The school does know, and she has a single room, so there is no roommate to worry about. I love you both for caring, but you are out of line and completely wrong about Kris. I love her, and I'm going to build a future her."

"Well, have a great summer. You are always welcome home if you want to come see us."

"I'll talk to you another time."

Grace hung up the phone and turned in my arms. I could see the tear trails across her face.

"You don't want to burn your family ties because of me. I'm not worth that," I said, unable to meet her eyes.

"Don't you ever fucking say that to me again. You are more than worth it. I love you and by saying that you belittle my love for you. Do you want to do that? Do you think that little of our love?"

"No, baby. I love you so much. I just don't want to come between you and your family."

"You aren't. They are."

We were silently lost in our thoughts for a long time. Then Grace sat up abruptly.

"Let's get out of here. I want to stop dwelling and start living."

We headed out hand in hand to go find something fun to do.

❧❧❧❧

The remainder of the school year passed in a blur. Grace and I made plans to take a couple of classes. Since we were taking classes, we were allowed to keep my dorm room, only it was now registered to us both. Life was good. That is when you know you need to be cautious, when things seem too good to be true.

After the school year ended, the campus was deserted for a few days before the summer session started. Grace and I spent the time just enjoying our new relationship. We went out on a couple of movie dates, and we would walk around campus, holding hands. There were a few romantic picnic lunches. It was nice just to spend time together without any worries or stress. Yes, we have been friends forever, but this was different. I finally understood what people meant when they said their relationship was better because they were with their best friend.

Grace and I had chosen to take a class together over the summer. When we arrived for our Photography/Photoshop class that first Monday morning, we saw that Alyssa and one of her friends were also in the class. Grace let out a low groan.

"You know that I love you, so don't let her bother you," I said, putting a hand on the small of her back. I nudged her shirt up a little so that she could feel my hand on her back, skin to skin.

"That is easy for you to say. She isn't checking out your girlfriend. You'd feel differently if she were."

"You're right, she isn't. And why she isn't, that is beyond me. My girlfriend is smoking hot."

Grace turned, raised an eyebrow, and then rolled her eyes before we took a seat in the back of the room.

"You are cheesy, you know that?"

"Yeah, but you love it about me," I said. I kissed the back of her hand, and when I looked up, I saw Alyssa watching us. I ignored her. I wasn't going to play her games. Nor was I going to let her ruin my time with Grace.

The teacher let us pick our partners for the session. Of course, Grace and I were partners. It was close because he was randomly pulling names out of a hat and my name was chosen first. The second name chosen was Alyssa's.

"Professor?" said Alyssa. "Don't you think it would be better if we picked someone that we didn't know to work with?"

"Well, you are welcome to choose whomever you want. I am not going to make um, Kris and Grace unpair because that would be unfair. Unless, you two ladies would like to?"

"No, sir," Grace said, smirking in Alyssa's direction.

Alyssa let out a low growl and chose her friend that was sitting next to her. After everyone had been partnered up, the professor handed out the cameras. The camera was far from new. I looked at the model, Ricoh KR-5 Super II. It was heavy, well, heavier than the point-and-shoot that Grace had when we were growing up. This one even took 35mm film. I started to wonder how old these cameras had to be when Grace poked me in the side and motioned for me to listen to the teacher. He told us that our first assignment was to go out and find beauty in nature. A couple of guys started to giggle as if they were twelve years old. The professor rolled his eyes and told them that it meant plants, animals, and not people. He stated that we had a week to take pictures. When the week was up, he would show us how to develop the film. We thought that was going to be it for class, but then he said that the fun part was over and it was lecture time. I let out a groan; I hated lectures. Grace, of course, loved them and was all ready to take notes. She had her notebook out and opened to a clean page. She had the date and class name at the top of the page. I giggled when I saw that.

"This is going to be a great class," said Grace as we were exiting the room.

"You like it because you got to take notes," I teased.

"Shush you! I noticed that you didn't take a single

note."

"Nah, I sit next to this hot, smart chick. I'm just going to cheat off of her."

"What if she won't show you her paper or give you her notes?"

I smiled mischievously and licked my lips. "Oh, I think I know of a way or two to make her see things my way."

"Hmmm, I like how you think."

We were laughing together in the hallway when Alyssa and her friend came up to us. I wrapped an arm around Grace's waist and held her close. I'm not certain if I did it to reassure Grace or to try to get it through to Alyssa that I was only interested in Grace and that she had no chance whatsoever with me.

"Well, if it isn't beauty and the beast," said Alyssa, glaring at Grace.

"Oh, trust me; beauty is a beast when she wants to be. Like last night in bed," retorted Grace. I was so proud. I saw a smile start to form on Alyssa's friend's face.

"That's a pretty immature comeback," Alyssa said.

"Maybe, but that doesn't make it any less true. And weren't you the one starting it by calling us names?"

"I was just stating the facts."

"As was I."

"Okay, that's enough." Grace and Alyssa had started to move closer together. I stepped between them to keep this civil. "I get that you don't respect Grace, but I love her. Do you really think you'd win points with me by being insulting and being mean to the woman I love? Are you that dense? And Grace, sweetie, as cute as it was watching you and Trisha or now, you and Alyssa, fight over me, baby, I'm all yours." I was hoping that this would bring some peace.

"Who's Trisha?" asked the other woman standing with us. "Alyssa, you didn't say that there was another person. You just said one. I don't understand."

"Trisha was my high school girlfriend," I clarified for the lost and confused woman.

"Now, if you'll excuse us, we have some photos to take," Grace said, taking my hand in hers.

We walked away with Alyssa glaring at us, and the woman standing next to her looking more lost and confused. She was the type of person that you wondered how she managed to tie her own shoes in the morning. Then, I looked at her feet and giggled. She was wearing flip-flops. No laces to tie.

After leaving there, we went for a walk in a local botanical garden. We found several plants that were both unique and breathtaking. I hadn't realized that nature could be so creative.

It wasn't until class the following week that this class really caught my attention. We were learning how to develop the prints. The professor took each pair into one of the dark rooms and taught us how to develop our film. Now, yes, being alone in the dark with Grace was definitely appealing, but I also loved the process for making the prints. Using the different washes: the Developer, Stop Bath, Fixer, and Hypo Clear. Then there was the projector and its various knobs and features. He taught us about making the contact sheets from the negatives, setting up the prints, creating the prints. I was in my element. This was incredibly cool.

"You're loving this, aren't you?" Grace said after the teacher left us alone to experiment.

"Hell yes," I said as I started to play with the pictures we created.

I heard the professor tell us that class was over, and that we would continue to work in the dark rooms in our next class.

"Grace, will you help me find some books on this stuff?"

"Of course, sweetie."

Grace and I headed off to the library to look for books. I needed to know more. Four books later, we returned to our room, and I immediately sat down on the bed and opened one up.

"I have to go out for a little bit. Do you need anything?" Grace asked.

I glanced up and shook my head. I had my books; I was content. She leaned over and kissed me before she left the room, and I went back to my books.

⁂

There was a red glow in the otherwise dark room. I was developing some pictures that I had taken of Grace. Pictures that weren't for class or for anyone else to view.

"Grab her," I heard my father's voice say, and then I felt strong hands on my arms.

I felt the coolness from the chemicals spilling onto my body.

"Well, now aren't these some nice pictures," I heard the man holding me say.

"Don't you fucking touch them," I spat. I felt something hit me in the stomach that knocked the wind out of me. As I doubled over, I noticed it was my father's fist.

"Shut up. Another sound out of you, and I will not only let him have the pictures, I will personally go get

her for him."

I knew my father well enough to know that he wasn't one to joke about that sort of stuff. I closed my mouth and gritted my teeth, willing this to be over soon, and for Grace to be safe from these monsters always.

"That's better."

"I want a picture for my troubles," I heard the man say.

"No, now let's get out of here."

They dragged me out into the light. I had to close my eyes. I had been in the dark room for hours, and it hurt too much to be in the sunlight. I felt myself being shoved into a vehicle. I heard two doors close. We had to be in the black van again. Then I felt a jolt, and we were moving.

"You thought you could stay away from us, but you can never escape us," said my father.

"Why?" I asked.

"Shut up," said the mystery man, before he hit me in face, knocking me out.

When I came to, I could taste the blood in my mouth from being punched. I could feel my hands rubbing on a metal bar. My eyes were covered, and I couldn't hear anything around me. The room was cold, not freezing, but definitely not summer weather.

"Hello, daughter," said my mother. Her breath reeked of whiskey. I wanted to gag, but I had done that once as a kid, and I spent the next week sleeping next to the garbage cans. My parents made sure to put as much rotten food in them as they could find or create. It was her way of teaching me a lesson about what truly smelt bad.

I went to say something to her, but I felt something tighten around my throat. The blindfold was removed, and I found a rope tied around my hands and another around my throat. I was standing in what looked like an old warehouse. The walls were dirty with some black marks on them that resembled scorch marks. I could see rusted out shelves with specks of yellow paint. The floor was covered in debris, and I could smell old, wet cardboard boxes. It was not an appealing scent.

"This is just a pit stop. We won't be staying long. Nobody will miss you, though," my father said with a menacing tone. He was baiting me, and I knew it. I wanted to give in, but with this rope around my throat, I wasn't going to risk it. One good yank on the rope and I wouldn't be able to breath and could easily be strangled to death.

I heard someone come up behind me and then it all went dark. The blindfold was back. I felt my hands and throat being untied from the pole. I was being walked out of the building. The air smelled of smoke, like a bonfire. The smoke got thicker and thicker. I started to choke. I couldn't breathe.

"Beep... beep..."

"Kris? Wake up, baby," I heard Grace say.

I thrashed, trying to free myself from the hands holding and leading me toward the fire.

"Kris, you're safe. Wake up and open your eyes," I heard Grace say again.

I started to fight what was holding me back. I broke free and opened my eyes. There was Grace, my lover.

"Grace?" I said, my voice very raspy. My throat felt raw. The only time I really remember it feeling this raw was when I had strep as a kid.

"Yeah, baby. I'm right here," she said.

I could tell she wanted to hold me, but I was a

bit hesitant. I was still stuck between being awake and asleep. Grace just kept talking to me. She told me to focus on her voice. I did and finally I was ready for her to hold me. I moved slowly, my muscles still tense, my throat still tight. I relaxed into Grace's embrace.

"I love you. My savior," I rasped out.

"I love you, too."

I lay there in her arms for a long time. Once my muscles had relaxed, I was able to concentrate on putting the nightmare behind me.

"Are you okay?" Grace asked.

"Yeah, I am. Thank you."

"Do you want to talk about it?"

"It was just another nightmare. I was in the darkroom developing some very special pictures of you," I started, wiggling my eyebrows at Grace. She laughed and kissed the side of my head. "I didn't hear them enter." I finished telling her about the dream.

"I wish I could make these stop. I don't know what to do. I feel so helpless."

"You aren't. You bring me out of them. You make me feel safe so that I know it is okay to come out of the dream. Baby, nobody else has ever been able to help. The two nights I stayed with Trisha, I had nightmares, and she wasn't able to make me feel safe. You've always been able to help me."

"I didn't know that you had spent nights with Trisha. When was this? Why didn't you ever tell me about it before?"

"Baby, please don't be jealous. I love you; I am here with you."

I could tell that what she had just learned still bothered Grace. I sat up and cupped her face in my hands. I looked her in the eyes and then leaned in and kissed her softly.

"Only you," I said when we pulled apart.

I put my books away and pulled Grace to lay on the bed with me. I held her in my arms. I kissed her. This wasn't about sex, this was about connecting and reassuring. We spent the night like that. There were no more nightmares that night. There was just Grace and me.

Chapter Six

As the days and weeks passed, I noticed that Grace's mood seemed to dim. She wasn't the same. She smiled and laughed less. It wasn't right. Every time I asked her what was wrong, she would tell me that everything was fine. I knew Grace well enough to know that this was really because she was missing her family. She would never admit it to me, but I knew. The Barnes family was always very close. They loved doing things together.

I knew that I could be selfish and think of my own happiness and how good I felt being with Grace, but that wasn't what being a couple meant to me. There were still three weeks left of summer. Classes had just ended, and now I had to do something drastic that was going to hurt more than anything ever had. It was definitely going to hurt more than anything that my parents had ever done to me.

"Hi, babe," Grace said, entering the room with a smile on her face.

"Hi," I said. I tried to make it sound upbeat, but there was no way to make that happen.

"What's wrong?"

"I'm just having an off day." If she only knew the reason the day was so off.

"Wanna talk about it?" Grace turned the desk chair so that she was sitting across from me as I sat on the edge of the bed.

"There is nothing to talk about. It's just an off day. Do you want to go out tonight?"

"Like a date? Or just go out someplace?" she asked.

"A date," I said, smiling at her. We could have one last day and night together before I gave her a reason to leave and go see her family. God, I am a horrible, rotten person. "Get your gorgeous self all dressed up, and we'll go out for a special night."

"Okay, I need to shower," Grace said. She kissed me softly before grabbing her shower tote and heading off.

I felt sick to my stomach. How was I going to get through the night, let alone the next day? I loved Grace so much, and I just wanted her happy. I knew that she would never be truly happy unless her family is a part of her life, and that wouldn't happen as long as she was dating me. This fucking sucked! Okay, now I needed to get ready. I needed to make tonight memorable so that maybe she wouldn't completely hate me, or hate me forever.

I dressed in a fitted royal blue silk button up and a pair of fitted black leather pants. Grace came back into the room in just her towel. My mouth went dry. The fluid was pooling in other places. God, she looked so beautiful.

"Well, hello," she said lustfully as her eyes raked over my body.

"You in that towel, yummy," I said, swooping in and kissing her. As we kissed, I slipped my hand inside the towel and cupped one of her breasts. I heard her moan, which only served to heighten my arousal. I lowered myself as I removed the towel and butterfly kissed my way down to her breasts. I teased and sucked on her nipples; hearing her sounds of lust and pleasure drove me on.

"Oh, god, yes," Grace moaned. She threaded her fingers into my hair to hold me to her body. When she couldn't take it anymore, she pulled me up and our lips connected again.

I could feel Grace unbuttoning my shirt, and then my pants. By the time we made it onto the bed, we were both naked. Well, she already was, but we had managed to divest the rest of my clothes. I straddled her thigh and pressed my thigh into her heated center. She arched and started to rock her hips. I started to rock my hips with hers as my upper body hovered over her.

"I love you, so much," I said, leaning and briefly kissing her. "Never forget that."

"I love...you, too," she panted.

I kissed her and she climaxed. Hearing her call out my name was enough to help me climax as well. We lay there kissing and enjoying the closeness, until Grace started to giggle.

"Why are you giggling?" I asked her, running the tips of my fingers along the side of her face and along her jaw line.

"I thought we were going on a date and not just a booty call."

"I still want to take you on a date. I just couldn't resist you in that towel."

"Well, did you really think that I would be able to resist you in those leather pants?"

I kissed the tip of her nose. "I was hoping not. Now let's get dressed and go on our date. Do you want me to wear the leather pants or put on something else? Something less distracting?"

"Like you have to ask. I want to see that hot ass

in those leather pants," Grace said, squeezing my butt.

"You keep that up, and we aren't leaving this room," I teased. Grace winked at me, which made me giddy inside before I remembered what I was doing tomorrow, and then I felt like shit.

We got dressed, and we went out for a romantic dinner. Grace and I walked through a nearby park and up a small hill to look up at the stars. I wrapped my arms around my love and held her close.

"I want to die," I thought to myself. *"I know this is gonna hurt us both. I hope that someday she'll forgive me, or at least understand* why *I'm doing this."*

"What are you thinking about?" asked Grace as she turned in my arms.

"How beautiful you look in the moonlight." I kissed her. It was meant to be a light kiss, but she leaned in more, pressing her body to mine, pressing me back into the light pole I had been leaning against.

"I think we should head back to the room."

I could see the lust in her eyes. I know she had to be able to see it reflected back in mine. I pulled her in and kissed her again. We exchanged 'I love you's' and then, with her hand in mine, we started back.

As we neared an alley, we could hear two women screaming. One was clearly getting her ass kicked. I recognized both voices, but couldn't place either one.

"Stay here." I told Grace as I pulled her phone out of her pocket. "Just in case we need to have someone to call 911."

"The hell I'm letting you go in there alone," she said, following me.

"Baby, please. I'll die if you get hurt. You can follow, just don't get too close."

She nodded her agreement, and we went into the

alleyway. There, I saw Alyssa on the ground, bloody and whimpering. I saw the woman who had fought with me over a year ago standing above Alyssa, screaming at her. There were two others in the alley cowering in the corner. At a glance, I knew by the way that they were dressed that they were Alyssa's friends.

"Do you get your place, bitch?" yelled the woman standing over Alyssa. Alyssa couldn't respond, and the woman kicked her again.

"*Hey*!" I screamed, making my presence known.

"This doesn't concern you; turn around and walk away. Unless you want me to kick your ass again?" I don't know if it is a good or bad thing that she recognized me so quickly.

"If it means you will leave her alone, then let's go." I stepped closer to the woman and Alyssa.

"Kris," I heard Grace whisper. I could hear the fear in Grace's whisper. I wanted to reassure her that it was going to be okay, but how could I? This woman was hell bent on someone hurting. Now it was going to be me.

Alyssa and her friends were staring at me as the brutish woman stalked toward me.

"Time to pay," she said as she neared me. "You're a worthless piece of shit."

I let her hit me in the stomach once, twice, three times. She continued to scream insults at me, and then I felt something inside me snap. I lost my calm, and I ducked under her next swing that was aimed for my head, slammed my shoulder into her stomach, and pushed her toward the wall. I heard her head hit. It had happened to me several times before, and I knew the sound.

"Your ass is mine, bitch," she said, charging me.

We exchanged blows, and after a while, I heard Grace telling me to stop, but I couldn't. I stood my ground. It wasn't long after that the police showed up and placed me and the other woman in handcuffs. I saw an ambulance arrive and the medics attending to Alyssa. Grace was in tears. I could see the fear in her eyes as well.

When we reached the police station, I was booked and put in a cell. The woman I had been fighting with was booked and taken to another cell. I sat there 'alone' in a cell with seven other women. I thought about the events of the night. The day had started with promise and then gone mostly downhill. I started to drown in self-pity. I looked up and saw Grace walking toward the cell. I hurried to the empty side of the cell and met Grace's eyes.

"Are you okay?" she asked, reaching through the bars and running her hand along the side of my head.

"I've had worse." I offered her a weak smile.

"That's not funny."

Seeing the hurt and anger on her face made me flinch. "Sorry, bad taste. It hurts, but I'll be okay. Did you hear how Alyssa was?" I was shocked when I heard that question come out of my mouth. It wasn't as if Alyssa and I were even remotely close to being friends.

"Had you not stepped in, she would be a lot worse off. Her friends told the police the full story, and about how you stepping in had saved her. They explained that the other woman threw the first punches at you as well."

"That's good. I'm sorry our night got ruined." I reached my hand up and placed it on her hand that was wrapped around one of the bars.

"We'll have other nights. They said that, because

of what happened, you have to spend the night here. They haven't said if you are going to be charged with anything or not."

"You know I wouldn't have been able to look at myself in the mirror if I didn't step in. Even if it was for Alyssa."

"I know. I have to go. They weren't supposed to let me see you, but the officer doing the interviews took pity on me. I love you."

"I love you, too."

I watched her walk away. All I wanted was to be home in bed making love to her or holding her. Instead, I was locked in this cell overnight, my fate still pending.

❧❧❧❧

Morning came quicker than I thought it would. I had spent the night thinking, dwelling, preparing myself for what I was going to do. Preparing myself to break both Grace's and my own heart. Several women had already been escorted out of the cell. There were just three of us left.

"Kristine Holt?" said the female officer.

I stepped forward, and she motioned for me to put my hands through the slot in the door. She put the handcuffs on me and then opened the door. I was then escorted to a small courtroom. Seated inside were the officers from the previous night, Grace, and Alyssa.

I was led to the front of the room where I stood in front of the judge.

"Ms. Holt," started the judge.

"Yes, sir," I answered.

"I have read the police account, I have read the

witness accounts, and I have spoken with the woman who was being assaulted when you stepped in. In light of all of that information, there are not going to be charges filed against you. You are a very lucky woman. I don't want to see you back here. Is that understood?"

"Yes, sir. Thank you, sir."

The judge banged the gavel, and the cuffs were removed. The next thing I knew, Grace was in my arms, hugging me close.

"Are you okay?" Grace asked, still holding on to me as if I was going to float away.

"I'm fine, love. I just feel horrible about ruining our date." I pulled back and kissed her forehead before we made our way to the door. Once we were in the hall, Alyssa came up to us.

"Thank you. I don't know why you did what you did, but thank you," Alyssa said. I could tell from how she was breathing and how she was standing that she had a couple of broken ribs.

"I did it because it was the right thing to do. Nobody deserves to have that done to them."

"That sounds like it comes from experience," said Alyssa.

"It does," Grace said. I could tell by the guilty look on Grace's face that she hadn't meant for that to be out loud. I smiled at her, letting her know I wasn't upset.

"I'm glad you were there. I'm glad you weren't charged with anything, and I'm glad you weren't hurt too badly."

"That is a lot of glad." I laughed. "I hope your ribs heal quickly. I need to get going. I'm exhausted."

"Thank you, again," Alyssa said, before Grace and I walked off.

Grace asked how I knew about Alyssa's ribs. I told her that I could tell from her breathing pattern and the way she was cradling her ribs. We took a cab home. I was too exhausted to walk all that way. Once we were in our room, Grace helped me out of my clothes and into a t-shirt and boxers.

"Rest, baby. I know you are exhausted," Grace said, pulling me into her arms.

"I wanna talk," I said as my body betrayed me, and I yawned.

"Sleep first." Grace kissed the side of my head and held me close.

How could I break this woman's heart? I drifted into a dreamless sleep. When I woke, I was still in her arms. God, it felt amazing.

❧❧❧

"Afternoon," Grace said.

"Mmmm, it is? How long did I sleep?"

"About three hours. We'll go to bed early tonight."

I felt my stomach clench when she talked about later tonight. After all that I put her through last night, this morning, and even this afternoon, how was I going to find the words and the courage to do this? Yes, I could wait, but then I was just prolonging the inevitable.

"How are you feeling?"

"I'm a little sore," I said. I was trying to adjust when the full force of the pain hit me. I gasped and the room started to go black.

"Baby? What is it? What's going on?" I could hear the fear in Grace's voice.

"Maybe I'm a bit more than a little sore. I'm maybe

a lot sore."

Grace leaned over and kissed me to distract me from the pain. It worked, but it also got me very worked up. I wanted to make love to her, no, I needed to make love to her. I couldn't do that to her. I couldn't make love to her and then break her heart. That would be cruel to do to myself. It would be unspeakable and unforgivable to do to her.

"Let me help," Grace said. She adjusted so that she was able to massage my legs.

"Mmmm, that feels good," I said as she moved up my legs. I reached down and eased one of her hands under my boxers.

"Are you sure? I don't want to hurt you."

"I need you," I said.

Grace eased my boxers off. She then helped me remove my shirt. She allowed her hands to rub along my body, feeling me, tracing every inch of my body. I felt her lips on my body; every place they touched felt like it was on fire. I pulled Grace's shirt off, pulled her up to my lips, and kissed her hard. That is when everything caught up with us. The emotions we were feeling were amplified. We made love with intense passion. I knew we would both feel it in the morning.

"I love you," Grace said, trying to catch her breath.

"I love you, too," I said.

We drifted off to sleep, holding one another. Morning would come, and so would the heartbreak.

❧ ❧ ❧ ❧

The sunlight streaming in through the window woke me up. I went to move to close the curtain, but

Grace had a firm hold on me.

"Not so fast, you need to pay to be released," she mumbled.

I turned in her arms and kissed her gently.

"How was that?" I asked.

"Good enough to let you up for a couple of minutes."

"I just need to close the curtain more. It's blinding me."

"Well, we can't have that."

I closed the curtains and curled up back in bed. We slept for another hour, and then we got up to get dressed. I stalled enough so that Grace went to shower alone. I couldn't handle the idea of showering with her and then doing what I had to do. By the time we were both showered and dressed, it was lunchtime.

"Do you want to go get something to eat and talk or do you want to talk first?" Grace asked.

"Um, maybe we could get something and come back here? I really don't feel like being in the public eye right now."

Grace agreed that it was a good idea. I was still sore from the beating I took, plus running into people and explaining my split lip and black eye wasn't anything either of us wanted to deal with. We got our food, and we came back to the room.

"So, what did you want to talk about?" Grace asked.

I sighed deeply. "I really don't know where to start."

"This sounds serious."

I nodded, before looking down at the chips on my plate. "It is. I think we should separate."

"W-what do you mean by separate?" Grace

choked on the air exiting her lungs.

"I need some time alone."

"What does it mean that you 'need some time alone'?"

"I need to work on some things."

"I love you, Kris, you are my world," Grace said, a quiver in her voice that caused my heart to break even more.

"I know that, but, Grace, I completely lost it the other night. I could have killed that girl. You could have been hurt. I could never live with myself if you got hurt, especially because of or by me."

"And you think hearing you say that you want to break up with me doesn't hurt? Yeah, I know what the hell you're saying. I'm not a fucking idiot. Separating is breaking the fuck up."

"Grace, I never said you were—"

"No, you just used me like I was one." Grace had tears streaming down her face. She jumped up and was now up pacing the room in front of where I was sitting.

"Baby," I started. This was so much harder than I had imagined it would be. "I didn't use you."

"Bullshit. So what was last night? You just had to get a last fuck in?"

That last statement hurt worse than anything that had ever been done to me. "This doesn't mean that I don't love you. And no, dammit, I have never 'fucked' you. I resent you even saying that." I was now standing as well.

"Oh, you resent that being said. Well, then I must be in the wrong." The angry sarcasm in her voice was something I had never heard before. "I don't care if you resent a fucking thing."

"Grace, you aren't happy. You haven't been happy

for weeks." I tried reasoning with her. I know it was mostly to curb my own guilt.

"Oh, so this is my fault? That's right. The great and powerful Kristine Holt can do no wrong."

"I can and do plenty wrong. I'm not saying that you being unhappy is why. I am the one that needs some space. The other night was an eye opener for me. It proved to some extent that your parents are right. I am a danger. I love you so much that I don't want to risk you being hurt by me or anyone else, especially because of me."

Tears were now pouring down both of our faces. I had never seen Grace this upset before. I just wanted to take her in my arms and tell her that I was sorry, that the idea of living without her was killing me too.

"Well, I'm glad that we are in a dictator relationship. That you feel I am too inept to be involved in the decision-making, and when it affects both of us. Fuck you, Kris."

"I'm sorry."

"No, you don't get to say that you are sorry. You shouldn't even be allowed to cry. After all that we have been through over the past few months, you are just willing to give up and not even try to work on things. You are a weak coward. I alienated myself from my family for you. Have a great life, Kris. Stay the hell away from me. I'll have Tyler come get my stuff. I never want to see you again."

With that, Grace grabbed a few things and left. I had never felt so empty and alone. The woman I was madly in love with had just walked out of the door and my life, for good. I sat down on the bed and hugged her pillow. It smelled like her. I missed her already. I wanted to die. How was I going to live without her?

Chapter Seven

It had been a week since Grace left. I'd barely left my room since that fateful day, the day that I broke up with Grace. I could still feel the open wound where I ripped my own heart out. It was for the best. It was what needed to be done. No matter how many times I told myself that, I kept calling myself a liar. I hurt her. No redemption can come from that. I knew that I would forever be broken inside. I would have a scar, an easily opened, self-inflicted wound.

I was driving myself crazy sitting in this room, thinking about her, about our last night together. I decided that self-torture was the way to go today. I decided to go and retrace our steps from the night of our date. As I walked passed the restaurant where we ate, I could smell the garlic, and it reminded me of the pasta she had and her fear that it would keep me from kissing her. As I walked through the park and up the hill to where we looked at the stars, I could still feel her body pressed against me as we kissed. It hurt; it was still too raw. I needed to get out of there. The bonus was that on the few trips out that I had made, I hadn't seen Grace around, so I could only assume she went home to be with her family.

As I wandered aimlessly around campus, I heard my name called. I saw Alyssa coming toward me and internally groaned. I was truly not in the mood to be hit on or to deal with any of the drama that she was going to bring with her.

"Kris, are you okay?" asked Alyssa. I could hear the genuine concern in her voice.

"Nope," I said. I wasn't able to meet her eyes. Hell, my eyes had barely left the ground since Grace left.

"Where's Grace?"

"I...um...we broke up," I managed to get out before I felt my gag reflex kick in.

"I'm sorry. You two seemed so happy together. Was it because of the night that you helped me? Not that it is my business."

"We were happy. It was my fault. I'm the one that ended it," I blurted out. I don't know why I blurted it out, but it just came out.

"I would ask how you are doing after the alley thing, but I get the impression that is the least of your concerns."

"Eh, that was nothing. I've had worse. How are you doing after everything that happened, Alyssa?"

"Please, call me Aly. Alyssa is too formal for my liking. My ribs still hurt a lot, and I'm afraid to go out after dark, but otherwise I'm okay."

"Your ribs will hurt for a while. The fun part is after they heal and the weather changes. That is when you realize how much of a pain broken bones are."

"You sound like you've had some experience in this."

"I have."

"Do you want to get some coffee?"

"Alyssa, really, you don't need to be nice to me."

"You stepped into a fight that you didn't need to. You could have just walked away."

"No, I couldn't have. That isn't the type of person I am."

"I know I was a bitch to you, but please, you look like you can use someone to talk to instead of the walls of your room."

"Fine," I relented with a sigh. Alyssa wasn't wrong. I did need someone to talk to. I just wasn't entirely sure that she was the one that I should be talking to.

Alyssa and I walked to a nearby coffee place. We ordered our drinks and then found a table out of the way. After sitting for several minutes, I decided to break the silence.

"You don't have to tell me, but why was that chick attacking you?"

"One of the girls with me was her ex. She started being rude to her, so I stepped in. I had no idea that was what was going to happen."

"She seemed a bit unstable. I've had my own run in with her."

"So, is that what she meant when she said something about kicking your ass?"

"Yeah, I sort of slept with her then girlfriend," I said, offering a sad smile. I couldn't sit still, so I motioned for us to leave. We walked out of the coffee shop, and we headed toward the dorms. "It was my freshman year. Long before Grace and I ever got together."

"When did you and Grace meet?"

"We met when we were five. I was new to the neighborhood. We've...er...we'd been best friends ever since. I had a rough childhood, and she was always there for me."

"Hey, Kris!" I heard my name shouted by a male voice. I looked up to see Tyler stalking toward us. "What the fuck is your issue?" He was standing in front of me, standing within my personal space. "After everything we've been through together, how could you do that to her?" He pushed me back a couple of steps. "How could you hurt Grace like that?" He pushed me a second time, knocking me back a couple of more steps.

"It isn't what you think, Tyler." I put my hands up to stop him from coming near me again.

"Did you or did you not break my sister's heart?" I nodded. "Was it for her?" Tyler asked, motioning toward Alyssa.

"No, I didn't break up with Grace for her. Can we not do this here?" I could feel the eyes of people nearby watching us.

"Fine, where should we do this?"

"Let's go to the dorms."

"I'll see you around, Kris. Thanks again for saving my ass," Alyssa said, before ducking out.

Tyler and I walked to the dorm room I had shared with Grace for the past several months. I had already packed up most of Grace's things. I had left some stuff until the very end. They were things that allowed me to hold on to her. Tyler sat down in my desk chair, and I sat down on my bed.

"So, talk," demanded Tyler, coldly. The color of his blue eyes was now more of an ice blue rather than the bright blue that he usually shared with Grace.

"I didn't want to hurt Grace—"

"Well, you succeeded at that one. You beyond hurt her, you devastated her."

"Did Grace tell you the full story of what happened the last few days prior to the breakup?"

"Enough of it for me to piece things together. She wasn't really in the talking mood or state of mind."

"Then you know that I spent a night in jail."

"Yeah, I know. Grace kept that little bit of news

from our parents. Not that you deserve that kindness."

"You're right. I don't deserve that kindness. Tyler, I lost control that night. The girl I was walking with today when you found me? She was the one getting her ass kicked. The person I got into a fight with was insulting me, and she started to sound like my father and my mother. I snapped. Every time I hit her, all I could see were my parents. I wasn't thinking about Grace, Aly, or anyone else. *That* was a problem. That night as I sat in that bleak cell, I took a long hard look at life. Grace hasn't been happy being apart from you guys and your Barnes family connection. She's been missing you guys and even though I told her to go visit several times, she wouldn't because of that one weekend months ago when she went to see you and I had a stupid nightmare. She blames herself that I spent Friday thru Sunday in that corner," I said, pointing to the corner of the room that was my safe place. "Between her being unhappy and my losing control, I love her too much to risk her safety. What if all those years of my parents beating me did make me that type of person? What if your parents are right and I am a danger? I'd rather die than ever raise a hand to Grace."

"So, you did all this for my sister? I'm supposed to believe that?"

"I would like you to believe it because it's the truth. Today was one of the few times that I've left the room since Grace walked out the door. I love her, Tyler. I don't know how I'm going to live without her, but I have to. I won't risk her getting hurt. She deserves a life without the chaos or the risk that I bring to the table."

"Kris, you aren't your parents. You get that, right?" asked Tyler, sitting forward in the chair.

"I may not be, but I won't risk Grace. Your parents were right. I was going to hurt her. I just did it on my own terms."

"Your own terms? Dude, you slept with her the night before you broke up. She said you had wanted to talk, but she made you wait."

"I didn't sleep with her. We made love; there is a difference. I know she is your little sister, and you probably don't want to hear that, but it is a fact. None of what I have done was with malice intent. God, Tyler, I love you sister more than my own life. I'd give my life for hers without a second thought. I broke up with her to protect her and so that she would stop alienating you and your parents. It wasn't because I wanted someone else, or I didn't care enough about her. If anything, I care too much." I was pacing the room like a caged animal at this point.

"Kris, you should have talked to her. You should have told her this—"

"She wouldn't have listened. Tyler, I was here when she talked to your parents. I heard every word they said about me. Every painful word about how I was like my parents and that she deserved better."

Tyler got up and wrapped his arms around me. I'm not sure if it was because I was pacing or what, but having him hold me and let me cry helped me not to feel so alone.

"My parents are wrong about you. They would've seen it."

"There is nothing we can do about it. It is over and done with. Grace told me to stay away from her and that she never wanted to see me again."

"I'll talk to her. This isn't beyond hope, yet."

"Please, don't. Let her heal and find happiness. I

can't risk me hurting her anymore," I pleaded. "She's been through enough over the years."

"You don't have to lose her," said Tyler, sitting back down at my desk.

"I already have. It will never be the same between us. Not romantically, not our friendship. She is better off this way."

"You are a special one, Squish. Gracie was lucky to have you in her life. You will be there again, I promise. And I will always be here for you."

"So, you'll keep this between us?" I asked, looking him in the eyes.

"Not that I want to, but I will," said Tyler. "On one condition."

"I'm scared, but shoot."

"You at least stay in touch with me. If you don't agree to it, I'm telling Grace everything."

"Deal. Thanks, Tyler. What are you going to tell everyone about how this went?"

"I'm going to tell them I ripped you a new one, and that you're miserable. They don't need to know anything more. And it is true…"

"Thanks. Please, look after Grace."

"Always. I know in time she is going to forgive you, and you'll be friends again."

"I hope so."

I helped Tyler load Grace's stuff into his car. There were only four boxes. Once he was gone, I went back to the room and daydreamed about what life could have been like for Grace and me.

❧ ❧ ❧

It'd been six months since my breakup with

Grace. I hadn't seen her around campus, but Tyler and I had stayed in touch as I promised, and he assured me that she was indeed still going to school here. I kept to myself. I think you could have called me a borderline hermit. Aly and I exchange pleasantries and hung out once and a while. She wasn't that bad, well, once she stopped being a snobby bitch, that is.

I received a call from the photography professor who taught the class that Grace and I had taken over the summer. He had asked me to stop by his office. I couldn't think of any reason why. I was headed to meet him when I ran into Aly, who was heading the same direction.

"Hi," she said.

"Hey. Where are you headed?" I asked.

"Photography room, the professor said he wanted to see me. You?"

"Same. Did he tell you why?"

"Nope, just that he wanted me to stop by."

As we neared the room, I saw her. There was Grace walking toward the room. She had her hair pulled back and she was wearing a pair of baggy jeans and an oversized school sweatshirt. I stopped in my tracks. I couldn't breathe. She was still the most beautiful woman I had ever seen.

"What's wrong?" asked Aly.

"Grace," I whispered. I had broken down one night and, in a drunken stupor, told Aly about some of my past and why I broke up with Grace.

"What do you want to do? Do you want to skip the meeting? I'll go in and can tell you about it later."

"No, um, you can go in. I'll be in. I just need a minute."

"Are you sure?" I nodded. "Okay."

Aly went inside, and I took several long, deep breaths before I made myself walk into the room. I could feel both Grace and Aly watching me. I glanced up and saw Grace quickly avert her eyes, and Aly gave me a reassuring smile.

"Good afternoon, everyone," said Professor Lenz. "I appreciate you coming in. I was so impressed with your work over the summer that I want to use some of your photos in a book that I'm putting together. I need your permission to use the photos and for you to sign these release forms."

He handed out the release forms for us to sign. We all signed them, and he thanked us for our time. Then he asked Grace and me to stick around. I saw Aly looking at me with sympathy. She knew how hard this was on me.

"You two had such a great dynamic together that I was wondering if you would be willing to help me with another project I'm working on."

"What's the project?" asked Grace. She didn't even glance in my direction.

"I'm doing a section on campus life and was hoping that the two of you would be willing to take some pictures around campus. Pictures of statues, buildings, and even the occasional student."

I let Grace take the lead this one. If she said okay, I'd work with her. If she said no, I'd either go it alone or bow out as well.

"I don't have a problem with that," said Grace, turning to glance at me.

"Sure, no problem," I said.

"Great. I have a camera for both of you, and if you want to work together to get the shots, that is fine with me as well." The teacher handed us each a camera.

These were much newer and nicer than the ones that we were using over the summer.

"When do you need the pictures by?" I asked.

"Would two weeks give you enough time?"

"Yeah, Kris and I can have your pictures ready by then."

"Great!"

The professor turned and left the room, leaving Grace and I standing there, alone, together.

"I don't think I can work with you, but if you want to take a certain area of campus, I can take the other," Grace said, her voice shaking.

I swallowed hard. "Anything that is easier for you."

"Oh no, you don't get to pretend to be nice, to care, or anything. You don't get that, Kris. Now, I ask again, where would you like to work?"

"Let's call this center point. I'll take everything east including the library, and you can have everything west of here. That way you don't have to see me."

"Fine," Grace said in a clipped tone.

We exited the building, and Grace hurried away without even so much as a backward glance. I started to walk away and found that my resolve was fading and my legs were turning to rubber. As I made my way to a nearby bench, I heard Aly coming up. She put a supportive arm around me and helped me to the bench so that I could sit before I fell.

"So, how'd it go?" asked Aly. I was certain she only asked to fill the awkward silence.

"Well, she definitely still hates me. The daggers that shot out of her eyes after everyone left were enough to confirm that." Aly put her arm around me and held me. I leaned my head on her shoulder.

"What'd the professor want?"

"Oh, he asked Grace and me to take some shots around campus. He thought that the pictures we took over the summer were really good."

"Ouch."

"Yeah, she said that she can't work together with me. So, I'm taking east of here, and she's going to take the west."

"You know it is going to take her some time. You still aren't even close to being over her either."

"I know." Aly was right. I wasn't even close to being over Grace. I was still deeply in love with her. I felt Aly lean her head on mine.

"Do you want some company while you are taking pictures?"

"Thanks for the offer, but I think I need some time alone right now."

"Call me if you need anything," Aly said, getting up and squeezing my shoulder in support.

"Will do. Thanks."

I watched her leave and sat there trying to control my emotions before heading back to my lonely dorm room. I took me a couple of days to get full control of my emotions again. I had no idea what seeing Grace was going to do to me. It wasn't pretty, but once I got myself under control, I decided to start with taking pictures. Being the glutton for punishment that I am, I decided to start at the hilltop where Grace and I had our last date. I always felt closer to her up there. I knew that wouldn't help me get over her, but dammit, I loved that woman and I was certain that I always would.

"So, are you dating Alyssa now?" I heard Grace say as I was about to take my first picture.

"No, Aly and I are just friends." I turned and saw

tears in Grace's eyes. I just wanted to wrap her in my arms and tell her I was sorry and that I loved her still.

"That's convenient."

"Grace, I swear to you that there is not anything now nor in the past going on with Aly and me. I also can tell you that there will be nothing in the future with her either. She's not someone that I'm interested in that way."

"Why not? She's pretty."

"She's not you," I thought. "I have enough issues. I don't want to burden anyone else with them. I did that to you and your family for too long." I tried like hell to keep the tears from falling, but down they went. You would think after crying for six months, I wouldn't have any tears left, but I did.

"You look like hell."

"Thank you," I said, softly. She wasn't wrong. I had lost a lot of weight, and I didn't really have any to spare at the time. I have always had a thin, athletic build, so my losing weight was very apparent. I didn't really care what I looked like, so my hair was usually messy, and my clothes had more of the grunge look, if you closed one eye and partially covered the other.

"Kris, I didn't mean it as harsh as it came out," Grace said, backpedaling. "I meant that you aren't taking care of yourself."

"I get by."

"Getting by isn't going to cut it in life, Kris. Why aren't you taking care of yourself?"

"Why does it matter, Grace?" I said, bitterly and somewhat defeated. "I don't have any reason to care if I am alive or dead, if I look good or not. Nobody gives a shit."

"Well, isn't that a special pity party you have

going," Grace said, sarcastically. "You were the one that ended it with me."

"Yes, and I don't feel that I need to explain my reasoning to you, but I did it for a damn good reason."

"No, you did it for a selfish reason. Tyler told me last week why you broke up with me."

"What? What did Tyler tell you?" I asked, trying to play it cool, but my insides were doing raging flip flops. How could Tyler betray me like that?

"He told me that you did it so that I would go see my family and so that you wouldn't end up physically hurting me one day."

"Dammit, he fucking promised," I mumbled angrily.

"Yeah, well, there may have been some extenuating circumstances…" Grace said, averting her eyes.

"What'd you do?"

"It was nothing major." Grace still wouldn't meet my eyes.

"Grace Marie Barnes, either you tell me, or I am going to make Tyler tell me. He owes me that much considering he swore he would never tell you."

"Fine, whatever," Grace said in a huff. "I was home visiting, and we went out with a group of people. Trisha was there, and she and I got to talking, and drinking, and more drinking. I sort of ended up with alcohol poisoning and spent a day in the hospital."

"That's not cool, Grace. Why did you drink that much? What the hell was wrong with Trisha that she allowed you to drink that much?"

"I drank that much because I hurt like hell still. Oh, and just so you know, Trisha is still hoping you'll come back to her. You are a very hard woman to get over, Kristine Holt."

"It was the safest thing to do, Grace. And for the record, you aren't that easy to get over either."

"It was selfish, not safe. You didn't give me a choice. That is inexcusable."

"If I had come to you with my fears, what would you have said?"

"I would have said that it was my choice."

"Exactly."

It was then that I realized that Grace had been moving closer and closer to me. She now had my back against the lamppost, and she was definitely in my personal space. I could smell her perfume, the scent of her conditioner. My eyes closed on their own while I was enjoying the familiar scents. I felt Grace press her body to mine as she had done so many months ago. I let out an audible moan, and then I felt her lips on mine. I wrapped my arms around her and pulled her as close as I could. We kissed for a long moment before she pulled away.

"You still make my stomach flutter whenever I think about kissing you. But, kissing you does so many other things to my body," Grace said as she stepped just out of my reach.

"I...wow..." I said. Words were lost; my brain was not functioning. I believe that everything had migrated elsewhere. "Woman, you are playing with fire here."

"Yeah, you are still pretty hot. Now, let's go back to your room and finish this discussion properly."

Grace took my hand, and we hurried our way back to my room. I was still in shock that Grace was talking to me, let alone that kiss. I repeatedly told myself that we needed to talk before we did anything else. How was I going to resist her? That I didn't know.

God, I wanted this woman.

As soon as the door closed to my room, I found Grace's lips attached to my neck. She knew the right spot to drive me crazy.

"Oh, baby," I moaned, my body was on fire. "We need…to talk first."

Grace pulled back from my neck and looked me in the eyes. "Is that really what you want to do?"

"Hell no, but I think we need to," I struggled to get out. The lust in her eyes was driving me crazy.

"Okay, you are right, but we need to talk fast." Grace licked her lips, and I almost lost my resolve right then.

"What changed between the classroom where you said you couldn't work with me, and the hill?"

"Alyssa."

"Aly? Why?"

"I was jealous. I watched you cuddle up to her, then as the two of you talked, and then I followed you. I heard you crying from outside your door. Today when I saw you were going to the last place we were before things went to hell, I knew I had to get you back."

"Why, were you jealous?"

"I thought you and Alyssa were dating…the thought of the two of you together just wasn't right." Grace had been pacing in front of the bed where I was sitting. She stopped directly in front of me and a predatory look crossed her face. "You are mine, you will always be mine."

I gulped and then stood up quickly, cupping her face in my hands and kissed her hard.

"All yours," I said into her lips. "I love you, Grace Barnes."

"Mmmm, I love you, Kristine Holt."

We continued kissing for several minutes before Grace pushed me backward onto the bed and covered my body with her own. The weight of her body on mine felt heavenly. She moved to straddle my hips while kissing me deeply. Her tongue brushed against mine, causing me to let out a loud moan. When neither of us could take the burn in our lungs, we parted, breathing heavily. Grace sat up and removed her shirt and bra. I found myself mesmerized by her body; she was so beautiful. I ran my hands up her thighs, across her stomach, to cup her pert breasts. God, I'd missed how perfectly they fit in my hands. Sitting up, I kissed the valley between her breasts while my hands caressed her breasts and my thumbs teased her hardening nipples. Grace leaned her head back as she arched into my touch.

"Oh, Kris," moaned Grace.

The look of raw passion on her face excited me more than I ever remember it doing before. I brought our lips together, and they started to move as if we had never been apart. We took turns sucking on each other's bottom lip.

"I've missed you," I said, pulling my shirt and bra off before pulling her body flush against mine, feeling our breasts brush together.

"I missed you too," said Grace as her hips started rocking into me. "Kris, make love to me."

"Oh, god yes."

I briefly flashed to the last time we were in bed together, how intense it was. Shaking my head, I brought myself back to the here and now. I positioned myself on top of Grace, our now naked bodies moving together as one. I traced around her nipples with my tongue, feeling them harden and then nibbling on them, causing Grace to arch her back, pressing her breasts into my mouth. We both moaned. I couldn't believe that I had let this woman go. As her hips rocked faster, I lowered my hand down her body.

"Please...Kris," panted Grace as I eased two fingers inside her. "Oh, god yes!"

"Baby, you feel so good," I said, watching her writhe in ecstasy below me. I wasn't paying attention to what her hands were doing until I suddenly felt two fingers enter me. "Oh, Grace!"

Our hands moved inside one another, our lips pressed together, and we both groaned loudly. I could feel Grace getting closer. I started to move faster. Grace mirrored my actions. We came together in a powerful orgasm. I collapsed next to Grace, panting and trying to catch my breath. It hadn't been too long, but damn I was out of shape.

"That...was...incredible," panted Grace.

"Uh huh," I replied. I didn't have the mental capabilities to find words. I loved this woman so much. I had almost blown my chances with her. I could never let that happen again.

Chapter Eight

A knock on the door woke me. Looking around the room, I couldn't help but smile at the clothes that had been flung everywhere in our need to get naked. Grace sighed in my arms. I kissed the side of her head before slipping out of bed and into my robe. I was surprised to see Aly standing at the door when I opened it.

"Hey," she said, smiling.

"Hi," I said, pulling my robe tighter, and then glancing back at my bed to make sure that Grace was fully covered or that Aly at least couldn't see anything.

"Judging from the hickey on your neck, I'm guessing you aren't alone."

I smiled and whispered, "Grace is here."

"All right, well then, call me—"

"Baby?" Grace said, wrapping her arms around me from behind. She used our closeness to hold the sheet she had wrapped around her body in place.

"It's okay, love," I said, kissing her cheek as she rested her head on my shoulder.

"I just wanted to make sure Kris was okay. I'll let you two get back to better and more important things."

Aly practically sprinted down the hall away from my door.

"She still has a crush on you," Grace said as we made our way back to bed.

"Well, I don't think it will be an issue anymore.

She seems to understand that you are my one and only love. Plus you weren't very subtle in staking your claim."

"Mine, Holt. You…are…mine," Grace stated with an incredibly sexy growl and punctuated her words with nips to my neck, darkening the hickey that she had given me at some point in the night.

Not much talking took place the remainder of the day. We were lost in one another, reconnecting, reaffirming, and reminding each other of our connection and our history together.

It wasn't until the following morning that we heard Grace's phone started to beep.

"Baby, who the hell is trying to get ahold of you at six in the morning?" I asked as she tiredly rolled out of bed and grabbed her phone out of her pants pocket. I couldn't complain too much; my eyes were enjoying the view of her beautiful and naked body.

"It's Tyler. He has had me check in daily since the drinking incident. I guess I was a bit distracted yesterday and missed my check in," said Grace, her eyes raking over my naked body.

"Well, tell him that you are okay and then get back over here. I'm not done snuggling with you yet."

"We have classes today," she reminded me.

"Ugh, but I don't want to get up. I want to stay in bed with you…" Whining wasn't one of my more attractive attributes, but Grace was used to it. I gave her my best pouty face.

"I want to stay in bed with you too," she said as she licked her lips. "But we have to be adults. Maybe, if you are a good girl, I'll spend the night again."

I perked up at this. "Tonight?"

"If you are good," Grace teased.

I got out of bed and wrapped my arms around Grace's naked body, grabbing her butt and using it as leverage to hold her as close to my body as I could. Hearing her whimper, I started to nibble and suck on the pulse point at the base of her neck.

"Oh, I am very, very good," I said, with a sultry growl.

"Oh, god, yes, you are," she said, breathlessly.

Her phone beeped again. Grudgingly, I let her go so that she could answer her brother.

"Shit, he wants me to call him." She looked between the phone and me. I could see the distress in her eyes.

"Do you want me to leave?"

"Hell no. You are going to help me calm his ass down. He has sent me forty-six text messages and called fifteen times."

I handed her a robe, and I put one on myself. I knew if we were naked, Tyler was going to learn more about his baby sister than he could ever want to know. Plus, it was awkward thinking about talking to him without clothes on.

Grace dialed Tyler's number and put him on speakerphone. I sat up against the wall and Grace sat between my legs. Feeling her leaning back into me was heaven. The past day and a half had been heaven.

"For fuck's sake, Grace. Where in the hell have you been? I was about to call the police. I've already called two hospitals."

"Relax, Tyler. I am fine."

"Have you been drinking? You know the doctor said that one more drink and you could have died."

This bit of news surprised me. Grace hadn't mentioned that it was that serious when she told me about her drinking binge. She looked back at me and gave me a wry smile. We were going to discuss this little fact, and she knew it.

"I haven't touched a drop of alcohol. I swear."

"Then where the hell have you been? And don't lie to me."

"I lied to you once right after I got back to school. I haven't lied to you since. Geez, you are worse than Mom, you know that?"

"Deal with it and quit stalling. Where the hell have you been?"

"I have been in bed—"

"Are you okay? Was it from the drinking? Do you need me to come and get you?"

"Relax. It was from having sex."

I stopped breathing. I couldn't believe that Grace had just said that to her brother. I think Tyler stopped breathing as well.

"Please tell me you are kidding."

"Nope, I am being honest."

"Do you, er, did you know this person before?"

"Yes, I knew *her* before. I've known her for a long time actually. I was in bed with Kris."

"Kris who?" asked Tyler, sounding very confused.

"Kris Holt. You know, love of my life, lust of my loins…"

"Stop talking about sex. It creeps me out to think that my little sister is having sex, let alone that she is having more sex than I am."

"Ew, I don't want to know about your sex life, or lack thereof," Grace teased. I pulled her closer to me. The feeling of her body pressed against mine was incredible.

"Very funny. Now seriously, who were you with?"

"Hi, Tyler," I chimed in.

"Squish? Really?"

"Yeah, and I'm mad as hell at you for telling her why I broke up with her. I will, however, forgive you because I have her back in my arms." I kissed the side of Grace's head.

"When? How? What?"

Grace saved her brother from his mental breakdown and told him the story on how we got back together. I reassured him that Aly and I were not, nor had we ever been a couple. I reminded him that he saw her when he came to get Grace's stuff.

"I'm happy for you both. You better not fuck up again, Squish. I won't be as nice and understanding next time."

"I promise you, I will not fuck up again. I love Grace too much to let anything come between us."

"We have to get going, Tyler. We both have classes today."

"Okay, Gracie. I love you both, and I'm happy you made it back together."

"Thanks, Tyler. We love you too. I'll check in soon, but we're still making up for six months apart, so it may not be daily."

"Ew, stop talking about your over-active sex life," Tyler squeaked.

"But it is fun to torture you. Oh, gotta go, Kris is waiting for me to shower with her. Bye."

Grace hung up the phone, and I ran my tongue up the sensitive part of her neck. "I think showering with you sounds like a lot of fun." I heard Grace whimper as I smiled into her neck. My hands worked their way into her robe and cupped her breasts as I continued to nip at her neck.

"You aren't making this easy," said Grace.

"I'm not trying to," I said, smugly.

We got up and showered together before deciding that we should get some breakfast. We hadn't eaten food in almost twenty-four hours.

❧❧❧❧

Grace and I were walking across the quad, holding hands, and I realized that this was the first time since our breakup that I had truly been happy. After we ate, I walked Grace to her class.

"I'll be back to get you after class," I said, before kissing her.

"You don't have to. I have been walking myself to and from classes for six months without an escort."

"Yes, but now you don't have to, unless you don't want me to." I realized that maybe this was too much for her. A frown crept onto my face as I started my internal panic at the thought that maybe I was rushing things.

"Calm down, Kris. I would love for you to walk me to my classes. I know that look on your face; stop over-thinking things."

"Sorry. I gotta get going, but I'll see you after class." I kissed her again and then headed off to my class.

I walked into class and saw Aly sitting inside already.

"Hey, hey, Aly-meister," I said as I sat down next to her. I couldn't help the enormous smile that was plastered on my face.

"You seem to be in a good mood. What's up?"

"One word. Grace." I felt the smile creep even bigger on my face.

"I'm going to need more than a single word, Kris. What about Grace?"

I explained to Aly about the events of the past two days. Well, not in too much detail. Unlike what Grace did to Tyler, I didn't think it's as much fun tormenting Aly with my sex life. Especially since less than a year ago, she was hitting on me. And if Grace was right, Aly still had the hots for me and that would just be rude.

"I'm happy for you, Kris. It's good to see you smiling again. You deserve to be happy."

"Thanks. You do too."

After class, I hurried to meet Grace. I got to her class just as she was coming out of the door. I walked her to and from every class that day. I hadn't known how close her classes had actually been to mine. By the time we finally made it back to my room, it was after dark.

"I hate long days," I said as we entered the room.

"Usually I do too, but today was surprisingly nice."

"Oh, and why is that?"

"Well, you see, the love of my life dropped me off and picked me up from each of my classes."

I couldn't help but give her a cheesy smile. Yes, we are back at the honeymoon stage. Or is it called the hornymoon phase? Anyways, we both had homework. After we finished, we decided to reconnect some more.

⁂

Grace hadn't told her parents that we were dating again. I didn't know if that was for my protection or hers, but as summer approached, I could see the unease starting in her again. No, I wasn't going to break up with her again, but I wasn't going to let her stay here either.

"Grace," I said, sitting down on the bed as she worked at the desk. "What's wrong?"

"What makes you think that something's wrong?"

"Well, you are very tense lately. You avoid direct eye contact with me unless we are making love. Is it because summer is coming?"

Grace let out a loud breath and then turned to face me. "I don't know what to do. My parents are pressuring me to come home—"

"And since they don't know about us…"

"Yeah, I'm torn. I don't know that I can handle that much time away from you." Grace took my hands in hers and kissed my knuckles.

"I don't like the idea of being away from you that long either. You could always come and visit for a long weekend or a week."

"I could do that, or we could just tell my parents, and you could come with me."

"That brings us to another subject."

"Now I'm scared. You just went from playful to serious."

I could see the tension in her eyes. I reached up and ran my fingers through her hair. "What would you think about getting a place, just us, after summer?"

"What about your scholarship? I mean, I'd love it, but you have your scholarship to think about."

"Yes, but that won't matter." I could see the concern growing inside her. I pulled Grace out of the desk chair and onto my lap. She adjusted and wrapped her legs around me. "I only have two classes left. Grace, I'll be graduating at the end of the summer session."

"How? Kris, that is like a year early. How'd you manage it?"

"I've been taking an extra class every semester, plus summer classes."

"Baby, that's fantastic. I'm so proud of you." Grace leaned forward and kissed me. I loved it when she kisses me.

"So, that means I can't go home with you," I said, tucking some hair behind her ear. "But I don't want that to stop you. And maybe on that long weekend visit, we can start looking for an apartment."

"Wait, if you graduate and we get an apartment, what are you going to do about rent?"

"I may already have a job lined up." I grinned.

"How long have you know about this? What else don't I know?" I could see the hurt look on her face.

"I didn't know until last week about graduating, and I found out about the job yesterday." I could see the wheels in her mind turning. "I love you."

"I love you, too."

"I didn't want to say anything until I knew for certain. I wasn't trying to keep anything from you. Talk to me, beautiful. Tell me what you are thinking?"

"I'm thinking that I'm going to miss you this summer. I still cannot believe that you are graduating before me, and the reality that our life together is truly about to begin."

"I thought we already had a life together?" I asked.

"We do, but I mean our adult life. This is a big step. You sure you want to put up with me?" she teased.

"Maybe." I kissed her. It was meant to be a chaste kiss, but it quickly started to escalate to more. "How much homework do you have left?"

"Kris, I swear," Grace started to say, but was quickly silenced as I attached my lips to her neck and my hand slid down her body and into her shorts. "Oh, god yes."

Touching Grace and feeling how turned on I made her was like nothing I'd ever imagined. We moved together as one, as though we were made for one another. Hearing her call out my name was intoxicating.

Loving and having Grace love me made me feel invincible. As we lay in bed together, enjoying the afterglow of our lovemaking, I could feel Grace running a single finger across my stomach. I felt content for the first time in a long time.

"Can I tell my parents and Tyler about you graduating?"

"Do you think they'll care? I mean, I know Tyler will, but you parents don't like me much."

"They are going to have to get over that. I love you, Kristine Holt, and I intend on spending a very long time showing you."

"I love the sound of that." I kissed her neck and then her lips. "I love you, too."

※ ※ ※ ※

There was just one week left before Grace was going to be leaving to spend the summer with her family. This was also the week of finals. Grace and I were both on edge and trying not to step on one another's toes.

"How many finals do you have today?" asked Grace as we were both attempting to study.

"Two. I have two tomorrow and one the following day and I'm done."

"I still can't believe that I never noticed that you were taking extra classes."

"Well, in your defense, we have had some rather large separations in our time here."

"And now, I'm abandoning you for three months," Grace said, tears filling her eyes.

"Baby," I said, wrapping her in my arms. "You aren't abandoning me. You are going to spend the summer with your family. You have already promised two trips back here to see me, for hot and sweaty lovemaking, oh yeah, and for looking for an apartment. Plus, you said you would be here for my graduation. I'm not saying that I'm not going to miss you like crazy, and I'm not saying that I'm not going to text, email, and video chat with you every chance we get. Trust me; you are going to be sick of hearing from me."

"I know. I just hate the idea of leaving you here, alone. What if you have another nightmare? You could be in that corner for days." Grace was starting to panic; it wasn't cute.

"Hey, for starters, if you don't hear from me often, are you really going to wait days to have someone check on me?" Grace shook her head. "Aly is going to be here, and if she doesn't see me for several days, she will check on me."

"Yeah, like I want her helping you back to reality," Grace mumbled, forgetting how close her mouth was to my ear.

"Excuse me?" I said, pulling away from her.

"I know she still has a crush on you. It makes me nervous leaving, knowing that she can be here for you."

"That sounds an awful lot like you don't trust me. Do you honestly think that I am interested in Aly? Do you think I would cheat on you? Do you think I would allow Aly to initiate anything between her and me?"

"That isn't what I was saying," Grace said, pulling out of my arms and walking to the other side of the room. "I do trust you, Kris."

"That almost sounded believable." After all that we had been through, how could she not trust me?

"Kris, let me explain. I know you love me. I know you would never cheat on me. Do I trust Aly not to try something? Not on your life. I see the way she looks at you. No, I don't trust her. I get scared because I know what happened between us after you had a nightmare."

"You think I'm going to fool around with Aly because I need to feel grounded? Really?" I was starting to get angry.

"Kris, when you first kissed me after that nightmare, was that planned? Had you hoped for an opportunity to kiss me?"

"No," I said. I had a feeling where she is going with this, and I didn't like that she didn't believe in me remaining faithful.

"Exactly. If you have a nightmare and need to feel grounded, Aly is the one that is going to be here, not me."

"Either you trust me or you don't. You need to decide that. I'm going for a walk." I stormed out of the room. I knew if I stayed there, one or both of us were going to say something that we both regretted.

Aly knew that I was head over heels in love with Grace. She had even commented that she hoped to find someone that she could have the same type of connection with. We had spent time together, Aly, Grace, and I. How stupid was I to think that it would calm my jealous girlfriend after seeing that I was only friends with Aly? What the hell did she want me to do, just ignore everyone so that she didn't worry? I did my playing around my freshman year. It almost cost me my friendship with Grace.

I walked around campus for an hour before it started to get dark. As I neared the room, I could hear Grace crying. It sounded like she was on the phone with someone as well. I didn't want to be nosy, but I decided to listen to the conversation. I wasn't proud of my decision to do that, but I needed to understand. I leaned my head up against the doorframe so that I could hear better.

"Why can't things for Kris and me just be easy?" cried Grace.

"Gracie, you need to trust her if you want your relationship to work," I heard Tyler say.

"I do trust her. I don't trust Aly."

"Why don't you trust her?"

"She's an opportunist. I've seen her take advantage of Kris' kindness, or guilt Kris into doing stuff she wants."

"And you think she can manipulate Kris into cheating on you? Grace, have you really looked at how devoted Kris is to you?"

"What do you mean?"

"Gracie, she loves you so much that last summer she was willing to risk spending her life being miserable in order to protect you from harm."

"That wasn't fair."

"I don't give a shit if it was fair. Grace, she loves you enough that she was willing to be miserable rather than risk you getting hurt. That takes a lot. You told me that your freshman year she avoided you so that neither of you hurt more. Do you think she had to do that?"

"No."

"Does she ever look at anyone else? Does she treat you differently when others are around? Does she make you feel safe and loved?"

"No, she never looks at anyone else. She always makes me feel like I'm the only woman in the world when we're together. That is in private or in public."

"Then get your head out of your ass. She loves you, and she isn't going to cheat on you. Aly doesn't stand a shot in hell with her."

"You're right. I do trust Kris. I'm just going to miss her. I wish she didn't have classes and could come home with me."

"I know you are going to miss her. I'm certain she'll miss you too," I heard Tyler say. I couldn't stay outside anymore. I opened the door.

"I'm going to miss you more than you will ever know," I said.

"Call me back later. You two need to talk," Tyler said, before hanging up.

"How much did you hear?" asked Grace.

"Enough. Baby, every single thing in this room reminds me of you. I sit and watch you studying at the desk, the bed, loving you, holding you, just being close to you, the pictures above the TV of us as kids, the pictures on top of the dresser from our photography class. I'm going to have to look at all this day after day and miss you."

"I'm sorry. I do trust you. I just get jealous and insecure."

"Well, stop it," I teased. I pulled her into my arms and kissed the side of her head. "I love you. You are my world."

Chapter Nine

We were walking back from having a nice romantic dinner. I had thought about spending the last afternoon and evening in our room, lost in one another, but taking Grace out seemed more romantic.

We were holding hands as we passed by the library. I couldn't help but smile. It wasn't so long ago that Grace was coming out of the library and stumbled. It was that incident that helped us get our friendship back and then for us to become a couple. Well, maybe it had been a couple of years, but in the grand scheme of our lifetime, it wasn't that long. "I can't believe that you're leaving tomorrow. I'm going to miss you." I wrapped my arm around her waist and kissed the side of her head.

"I'm going to miss you, too," said Grace.

"What do you want to do now?"

"I want to go back to our room, and I want you to hold me close and later show me how much you love me."

"I love the sound of that." And that is what we did. We spent our last hours before she left for vacation making memories to get us through our time apart. Any time with Grace was amazing, but that night was just about us; it was perfect.

The night had been perfect, but morning came all too soon. When I dropped Grace off at the airport,

I made her promise not to cry until I was out of sight. She made me promise the same thing. I never saw a tear from her, although I think that was because my eyes were full of my own tears.

Yes, I know it's grossly sappy, but we're talking about the love of my life. Grace called me as soon as the plane landed. We talked for a few minutes and then she said she would call me later. I'm ashamed to say that I pretty much sat on the bed waiting for it to be later for her to call.

"Hey, baby," I said, answering the phone. I could feel the smile creep onto my face at the sound of her voice.

"Hi. I miss you so much already," said Grace in her sultry, sexy voice.

"How's it going there?"

"Not bad. Tyler wants to know if he can come to your graduation."

"I'm okay with that. Are you still going to tell your parents?"

"Yeah, I'm going to tell them about us too."

"Grace, are you sure that is a good idea? I mean, they don't like me much, or at all."

"Kris, I love you. And I am not going to let my parents dictate my life. I want them to know that I love you. That you make me happier than I have ever known possible."

"I love you, too."

We talked for an hour before I heard her yawning. It took a bit, but I convinced Grace to go to bed. After we hung up, I couldn't stop thinking about her. My dreams that night were of a hot and steamy reunion with Grace.

Over the next few days, Grace and I talked on the

phone, sent text messages, and daydreamed about one another. It didn't help me miss her any less, but it at least made the distance tolerable.

"Knock, knock," said Aly as she poked her head in my room.

"Aly, hi. Come on in," I said, motioning to the desk chair.

"How are you holding up without Grace?"

"I miss her. It has only been a few days, and I'm going crazy."

"Wow," said Aly, laughing. "You know, you could always take these classes when the semester starts, and you can spend the summer with your girlfriend."

"I could, but I have my job lined up already. I want to start my life and future with Grace as soon as I can. I can't do that hanging around here."

"I get it. I was just trying to give you an out."

"I appreciate the offer. Wanna go get some pizza?"

"Sure."

Aly and I went to Scooter's, a local campus restaurant for pizza and a beer. During dinner, we started to talk some more about our past. She told me about her childhood. I told her more about growing up with Tyler and Grace. It was nice to just relax and talk with Aly. She was a good friend. I was glad that she was going to be around, but she did make me miss my lover more. As soon as I got back to my room, I received a message from Grace to call her as soon as I had a free moment. I smiled and called her.

"Hey, Kris," Grace said, sounding stressed.

"My love, what's up?"

"I told my parents about you graduating. They were happy for you."

"I'm surprised about that. I figured that they just

hated me."

"They don't hate you. I also told them about us. That we are dating again and that you want us to get an apartment together."

"How did that go over?" I asked hesitantly as I lay back on the bed.

"Not well at first. Tyler jumped in and helped them to understand why you did what you did last year. I told them how I got jealous seeing you and Aly together. Tyler had a good laugh at that one. Then we discussed how we got back together. Mom was the first to come around. She is willing to give you a shot. Dad is still on the fence. Tyler said it is because I'm his little girl. I think he's full of shit."

"So, if all is going well on that front, why are you sounding stressed?"

"I just miss you. Like, a lot."

"I miss you, too. It is just three more weeks, and you get to come and visit."

"I can't wait. How was your day?"

"I missed you, I went to class, I came home to study, I missed you some more, and now I'm talking to you. It may not be having you in my arms, but it is a nice second."

"How am I going to survive this summer?"

"The same way I do, holding on to the idea that when you get back here, we're going to get a place of our own and start our future together. And maybe a lot of dirty phone calls, sexting, and vivid dreams." I heard her giggle; that helped.

"Goof! I do like how that sounds."

"Good. I have to get some sleep, but I will dream some very nice and naughty things about you."

"I bet you will. Just make sure it is only about

me."

"There is no other my love! I will talk to you tomorrow."

"Okay, I'll see you in my dreams. I love you, Kris."

"I love you too, Grace."

❧ ❧ ❧ ❧

The next three weeks were hard. Missing Grace, the academic load of the accelerated courses I was taking, and then I had a couple of minor nightmares. They weren't bad ones, just ones that made me wake up in a cold sweat.

"Sports drinks…check. Snacks…check. Love of my life…missing, but arriving as soon as I head to the airport to get her." I glanced around the room one last time to make sure everything was set. I felt like a little kid waiting to go to an amusement park. Jittery, bouncing around the room, a complete freak. I knew that it was just because I couldn't wait to see Grace. I'd already checked three times to make sure that her flight was on time. I hailed a cab to the airport.

As I stood there looking around the terminal at all the people waiting, I couldn't help but bounce on the balls of my feet when I heard her flight called and that it was arriving on Gate Four. I hurried to that gate. I needed to be there when she came down the stairs. I was leaning against a column support when I saw her. I am glad that I had the column for support. Grace looked more beautiful that I had remembered. Her normally pale skin was bronzed from her time out in the sun. Her red hair was a lighter shade, bleached from the sun. When we were kids, her hair would turn blonde in the summertime. I saw that she had her carry-on bag over her shoulder.

Grace ran toward me, while I propelled myself toward her. We met and I picked her up as she wrapped her arms around me. Within seconds, her lips were on mine. I hadn't realized how much I had missed the silky feeling of her lips on mine, but damn she felt good. I heard someone whistle at us, but I didn't care; the only thing that mattered was the woman in my arms.

"I…missed…you," Grace said between kisses.

"I missed you, too. Do you have any other luggage?"

"Nope, but we need to get back to the dorms so I can properly show you how much I missed you."

"I love the sound of that," I said with a growl. We hurried out of the airport and back to campus. We entered our room, and as soon as we were inside, I used my body to press Grace back against the door. Our lips met in what could best be called a feral kiss. I didn't only want to consume every inch of this woman; my body ached and craved it.

"I…need, mmmm…you now," said Grace.

She didn't have to say more; that feeling was very mutual. I tossed Grace's bag off to the side and walked her backward to the bed. As we reached the bed, she turned us and pushed me onto the bed. I moved to the middle of the bed and watched Grace slowly crawling up from the foot of the bed. She looked at me as if I was her prey. I have never seen that look in her eyes, but damn it was sexy-hot.

Grace slowly made her way up the bed, and she covered my body with hers. It was the most incredible feeling. I moaned as she kissed me hard. I started to remove her clothes; she started clawing at mine. We both managed to get naked, and then it was as if our bodies were one. I could feel the warmth of her breath on my neck, her teeth scraping along my skin. God, this woman was turning me into putty. I could feel our hips starting to rock; I could feel her wetness coating my leg.

I threaded my fingers through her hair and pulled her up meet my lips. We both groaned as soon as our lips touched.

"Yes…Grace," I moaned as our hips started to move faster.

"Fuck, you feel…so good…below me," Grace panted.

"Don't stop…please…faster, baby."

We were now frantically grinding into one another. The room was filled with moans and grunts of pleasure. I could hear Grace's breathing becoming ragged, and I knew she was getting close. I pressed my thigh harder into her as she ground into me.

"Yes, Kris, yes, oh god yes."

Grace and I came together. She went to roll off me and I held her in place.

"Please don't move. I need to feel your weight on me. I need to know that this isn't just another hot and horny dream. I've had several of them over the past few weeks."

"If it is another hot and horny dream, then we're both having it."

I closed my eyes, reveling in that thought. I kissed her gently, savoring the taste of her lips.

"Hi," I said, smiling up at Grace.

"Mmmm, hi."

"How was your trip?"

"It took too long to get here."

"I agree; it took you too damn long to get here." I

rolled us over so I was on top. "Next round."

After several rounds of lovemaking and reconnecting, we fell asleep, both exhausted.

❧❧❧❧

"Tyler, wait for us," a seven-year-old Grace called after her older brother as we tried to catch up to him.

"Hurry up, you two," he called back.

Grace and I ran as fast as we could. When we finally caught up to him, we were standing in the woods near my house. There was a tree that we could see the full neighborhood from when we climbed it. Because of the age and size of the tree, our parents had told us that we were not allowed to climb the tree.

Grace went up first; she was the best climber of us all. I went next, and then Tyler came up after us. We were looking around the neighborhood when I saw my father looking at us.

"I-I gotta go," I said, trying to hurry down the tree.

"Kris, what's wrong?" asked Grace.

"My father saw us," I said.

Tyler and Grace had followed me down. I was shaking, and I knew they both saw it, but I could do nothing to hide it.

"Kristine Kay Holt, you get your ass home right now," yelled my father. "You two had better go home as well. You should feel lucky I don't tell your parents what I saw you doing."

I watched as Grace and Tyler hurried down the path that would take them to their house. My father grabbed my arm roughly and dragged me home.

"How many times have you been told that tree is off limits?"

"Several, sir," I replied to the ground. I was too scared to look up.

"Well, since telling you doesn't seem to get anything through your stupid thick skull, you leave me no choice but to use pain as a deterrent." I watched as my father removed his belt. He sat back down and wrapped the belt around his hand. I gulped and felt a tear roll down my face. "Oh, you are going to cry, but only babies start before their punishment."

My father motioned, and I leaned over his knee. I felt him raise his arm. I cringed and felt the belt hit. I tried not to, but it hurt so bad that I cried out. I knew by doing that it meant he was going to hit me more. He always did. He swung again and again. After five hits, he told me he was done with the punishment for the tree, now I had to face the punishment for crying out. There were two more swings of the belt.

"Now, go to your room. You will not get dinner tonight or breakfast tomorrow. Maybe that will help you remember what you are told."

"Yes, sir," I said.

Monday, as I was getting dressed for school, my mother commented on the bruise on my arm from where my father had grabbed me. She told me that I had better not let anyone know what happened. If I were asked, I got it from bumping into something. I nodded and headed off to school.

"Kris," Grace said, walking over to me. "How much trouble did you get in?"

"I got yelled at and had to spend the weekend in my room or doing my chores."

"Tyler and I are really sorry you got in trouble."

"It's okay."

In gym class that day, my sleeve came up, and

Grace saw the bruise. She knew what it was but asked anyway. I told her I got it from falling while jumping on the bed. She knew I was lying but didn't press it. She knew. She was the only one that knew.

"Kristine, you were late getting home. Why?" screamed my father.

"There was a lot of traffic," I said.

"Then you should have walked faster," he snapped.

"I was trying."

My father looked at me, his eyes turned red. "You sassing me?"

"No sir."

I saw his hand come up and there was only a moment before I felt his hand make contact with my cheek. The searing pain was almost too much for me to take.

"Beep…Beep…"

"Baby, wake up," Grace said, softly into my ear. "Kris, baby."

I started to stir, my dream fading to the back as I became more aware of what was going on. I could see the concerned look in Grace's eyes.

"Hi, angel," I said, placing a chaste kiss on her lips.

"Are you okay?"

"Bad dream."

"I would hope so. Otherwise you were on a ride that I wasn't on." Grace kissed the tip of my nose and then my forehead. "Do you want to talk about it?"

"It was stupid. I was dreaming about when we were seven and we climbed that huge tree."

"You mean the beating that you took because of me?"

"It wasn't because of you, my love. It was because

he was a vile man."

I knew that Grace had always felt guilty for that day. It had been her idea. I have spent years telling her that it wasn't her fault and that I had no ill feelings toward her, but she continued to beat herself up about it. I knew that this dream wasn't going to lessen her guilt either.

"I'm sorry I woke you."

"I'm glad I was here," she said, nuzzling her head into the crook of my neck.

We drifted back to sleep. When we awoke still wrapped together, I realized then how much I had missed waking up in her arms.

⁂

Grace and I had spent the first three days of her visit lost in each other. We did manage to go look at a few apartments, briefly. I liked one, but she wasn't sure about it. We had two days left before she went back to her parents, two very short days.

"I can't believe that you are going to be leaving in two days," I said. We were walking hand in hand to get some coffee.

"I don't want to go back. I'm having all kinds of fun here with you," Grace said, smiling.

"I know you are, and I love having you here." We stopped to get a cup of coffee. We found a table outside to sit at. It was a pub table so it was taller. Grace was standing between my legs instead of sitting. We were about the same height this way. I pulled Grace close and kissed her.

"Get a room," Aly said, walking toward us.

"Hi, Aly," said Grace, a bit tense.

"Hey, Aly. What brought you out of your cave? You know that this is daylight, and you might burst into flames."

"Very funny. Ass! I go out in the daylight. I just prefer nighttime."

In the two minutes Aly and I had been talking, Grace had managed to position herself as close to me as she could without blatantly climbing on my lap. I couldn't understand her jealousy, but I did love feeling her up close and personal.

"Are you taking summer classes?" asked Grace as she leaned into my touch.

"Two. I failed one last semester, so I'm retaking it over the summer with a different teacher. It makes a world of difference. How has your summer been?"

"It's fun being with my family, but I missed Kris."

"You two grew up together, right?"

"Yeah. Grace and her family allowed me to be part of their family when I was growing up."

"I don't know how you do it, Grace. I could never date my best friend from my childhood. She knows way too much."

"Kris does know an awful lot, but then, I know a lot about her as well. In all honesty, I hadn't thought about Kris and I dating until she kissed me."

"Well, it is great to see her smiling. I don't want to invade on your time together anymore. I'm glad you gave her a second chance. You two always look so happy together."

Aly waved as she walked away.

"That seemed to go okay," I said as Grace tried to pull away, but I just held her close.

"She seems a bit more relaxed. Her eyes weren't traveling all over your body."

"I'm certain that had nothing to do with the fact that you were covering most of my body." I poked Grace in the ribs, and she squirmed.

"I have to protect what is mine." The smirk that crossed her face sent shivers down my back and heated up other areas. "And later I intend on showing you how much I love that you are mine."

I let out a groan. Grace loved to tease me and see how flustered she could get me. We finished our coffee and then went to look at one last apartment while she was here. Once we were done walking through it, we went back to the room.

"So which one did you like the best?" I asked. We were laying snuggled together on my bed.

"I liked the one we saw today. It is close to campus, close to where you will be working, and the rent is not the cheapest of the ones we've looked at, but it is still reasonable."

"I agree. So, wanna sign a lease with me before you go back?"

"I don't know. Do I really want to be tied to something that is going to have your name on it? I'm going to have to think about that," teased Grace.

I started to tickle her and as she squirmed and rolled around on the bed, trying to get away from me. Grace ended up pinning me down.

"Of course I want to sign a lease with you before I head back to my parents'."

Grace leaned down and kissed me. The passion that I felt in the kiss was more than I have ever felt kissing her. We were moving into a new phase in our life together. We made an appointment to sign the lease the following day.

After signing the lease, Grace and I went and

started to look at furniture and other items we were going to need. We both knew we wouldn't be able to get them all at once, but Grace felt that as long as we had a list, we had a good start.

"Are you going to tell your parents about the lease?"

"Why wouldn't I?" asked Grace. "Kris, I told them that I love you. They know we were living together before and that we are now. Yes, they aren't happy about you breaking up with me, but seeing me happy outweighs that greatly. I promise. Plus, they don't decide my life and future. We do."

I loved this woman. With one short speech, she was able to calm my fears and make me feel more loved than I could have ever imagined. Yes, I know that was a seriously sappy statement, but that doesn't make it any less true.

That night was Grace's last night there until she came back for my graduation. It was bittersweet. I loved her being there. I missed her when she was gone. I knew she would be back in a few weeks, but those were going to be long weeks. Especially since I knew when she got back, we were going to move into our new place.

Chapter Ten

Will you please stop pacing?" pleaded Aly. "Grace will be here for the ceremony."

"What if she gets delayed? What if she changed her mind over the past few weeks about everything? What if she..." I panicked.

"What if she kicks your ass for being stupid?" asked Grace's voice from behind me.

I spun around and saw the most amazing sight. There was my beautiful girlfriend. She was wearing a very sexy emerald green dress. She could have been wearing a burlap sack and I would have thought she looked very sexy.

"Grace!" I rushed over, hugged, and kissed her. "You look so beautiful."

"Thank you. What's with the 'what if' game?"

"You know me...you know my mind."

"Yes, and they rarely play nice together," said Grace. "You look really hot in your cap and gown. Whatcha got on under there?" Grace pulled at the top of the gown to look down the front of it.

"Grace, be nice. She looks nervous enough," said Erin.

I hadn't heard her come in, but when I looked over, I saw Erin, Sean, and Tyler standing there, smiling.

"Hi," I said, sheepishly. I was still holding onto Grace. She always kept me grounded.

"I'm going to leave you to say your hellos. Grace,

I saved you a seat in the second row."

"Thanks," Grace said. She seemed friendlier to Aly. I was grateful for that.

Erin, Sean, and Tyler took turns hugging me.

"We're very proud of you, Kris," said Sean. "I always knew you could succeed beyond expectation."

"Thank you." I blushed at his compliment.

"Good job, Squish."

"We should get seated. Congratulations, Kris."

"I'll be right there," Grace said. We watched her family leave before she turned to me. "I love you. They meant what they said. They are here because they chose to be. There are a lot of things that were said back home, but the important part is that they support us."

"I'm glad. I missed you so much."

"I missed you too. I'm going to go sit down and tonight we party."

"Can I request a private party?" I asked, waggling my eyebrows at her.

"All night long, if you want," whispered Grace in my ear. The warmth of her breath on my ear sent my already hyperactive hormones into overdrive. I let out a small moan.

"I love you. Now go before I skip the ceremony and take you in the coach's office."

"I love you, too."

I watched Grace leave. Once she was gone, I found a water fountain and took several large drinks. Once my nerves were calmed, it was time to line up. We were lined up alphabetically. As our names were called, you could hear family and friends responding.

"Kristine Kay Holt," called the person reading the names. I walked up onto the stage, and I heard cheers of 'way to go, Kris,' and 'you rock, Squish' coming from Grace and her family. I blushed as I shook the Dean's hand.

After the graduation was over, we went to the hotel so that the Barnes family could get checked in. We then all changed our clothes and went out for dinner. The dinner conversation centered on the summer session and the graduation. I could tell that Sean and Erin wanted to discuss something, but were holding back. Erin must have read my face because she squeezed my hand and told me we'd talk tomorrow. I can't say that I was completely relieved, but I wasn't upset.

We said our goodnights to Grace's family and made our way to our dorm room. Once inside, Grace and I removed our clothes and spent the night making love. I think that was the only way I was truly going to relax with her parents and brother in town. When it was time to get up, we showered together and then headed to meet Grace's family for brunch at a restaurant near our new apartment. I had picked the keys up on the way to the graduation the day before.

"Wow, I'm impressed you made it on time," teased Tyler as we entered the restaurant.

"Tyler," Erin said, offering her son that patented mother eye.

"Yes ma'am."

At breakfast, the Barnes' told me about their time together. They talked about how they were remodeling the house. Grace talked about how nice it will be when they are done and she didn't have to sleep on the couch anymore.

After brunch, we walked over to the new apartment. Sean and Erin seemed pleased that the building was security locked. We had a corner unit, which we were told ran a bit bigger than the others. It wasn't anything spectacular, but for two people just starting out, it was perfect. Grace's parents took us shopping and helped us furnish the place. I felt guilty and grateful. I wish I could have put more money toward furniture. After we were done, Erin and Sean sent Tyler and Grace to retrieve some of our things from the dorm.

"Thank you both for the furniture and for being here. I want you to know how much it truly means to me," I said.

"Kris, we have spent a lot of time talking with Grace, and I believe we have an understanding on why you did what you did last summer," said Sean. "I just wish you wouldn't have had to hurt Grace."

"Sir, that was the last thing I wanted to do. I just couldn't get it through her head that she needed to go home. She was miserable and missing you all so much. I also couldn't risk me possibly hurting her. I didn't want to prove you both right."

"Now that you two have an apartment together, that can't ever happen again," Erin said. "We are entrusting you to take care of our daughter."

"With my life, I promise you both," I said, with the most conviction I think I have ever had.

"Good. Kris, can I ask you something personal?" asked Sean.

"Uh, sure."

"Why did you never come to us when you were growing up? We would have gotten you out of there."

"I've been waiting for years for you two to ask this question. I appreciate that you would have been willing to help, but my father, if you can really call him that, told me when I was six-years-old if I told anyone or tried to get away, he'd kill them and me. I wasn't willing to test that theory. He had several guns in the house, and he had ways of getting around the law. I was always grateful that you allowed me to feel as though I was part of your family, but I knew where I had to stay."

"I am so sorry you had to go through that. Grace wouldn't tell us anything other than you weren't as clumsy as you claimed to be. May we ask how often?"

"How often they hit me?" I asked. I saw them both nod. "Four or five times a week. It really depended on how drunk my mother got, or how bad of a day my father had. I will always carry the guilt that Grace and Tyler knew any of what happened. They didn't need that darkness in their childhood."

"I don't think that our children would agree with you. I think that Grace would say that she wanted to do more, and if keeping that secret was all she could do, then she was glad she could do it," Erin said.

"That sounds like something Grace would say." I couldn't help but smile at the thought of Grace and her amazing heart.

"Well, your parents are no longer in town or the area, so you are now required to come back more often. If you are going to be involved with Grace, it is a packaged deal," Sean said, smiling.

"Oh, nobody told me that," I teased. "I may have to rethink this now."

We were all laughing as Grace and Tyler came into the apartment. I jumped up off the floor and quickly took the box out of Grace's hands. She offered me a questioning look, and I gave her a wink and a smile, telling her that everything was okay.

We hung around for a bit longer while the bed was delivered. I was glad we had started with that. The store had a cancellation and was able to squeeze us in for same day delivery. We went out and picked up some food, pots, and pans. Grace and I wanted to spend the night there. We knew we were being silly, but it felt as if we needed to start our life together as soon as we could.

The next day, Grace's family had to head home. I was sorry to see them go. I knew that we were finally in a good place again. Things were falling into place. After seeing the Barnes clan off, Grace and I went and gathered the rest of our stuff from the dorm and finished moving into our apartment. The following day, the rest of the furniture we had gotten with her parents was delivered. Grace started classes the following week, and I started my new job. Adult life had begun.

❧ ❧ ❧ ❧

The school year had gone by quicker than we thought it would. Grace and I had settled into a good routine where we were able to support one another. It was an amazing year. I had received two promotions in that time. It wasn't something normal for my company, so I had a few people who didn't like me, but overall, it had been great. Now, we were three days away from Grace's graduation. She had two finals left. I volunteered to run out and get us dinner so we didn't have to cook. I knew that for us, splurging wasn't always a good idea, but dammit, Grace needed brain food. I was out getting us Chinese. Why? Well, it was Grace's favorite.

I walked into the house and heard the sound of something heavy hitting the ground followed by a loud groan. I quickly put the food down and made my way into the bedroom where Grace was sitting at the desk pretending to study.

"Is everything okay in here?" I asked.

"I'm going to fail the last of my finals," said Grace in defeat.

I knelt down in front of her, put my hands on her thighs, and moved them in slow long circles. "Why do you think you are going to fail?"

"I'm too stressed out to study and remember anything."

"What can I do to help?"

"Take the tests for me?"

"Love, if I took them for you, you'd be guaranteed to fail. I love you, but I am not the nerdy one in this household."

"Fine," Grace said with a heavy sigh. "What'd you bring for dinner?"

"Your favorite, Chinese."

"Yay!"

We ate dinner, and I held her on the couch while she studied. Grace seemed to relax while I was holding her. Well, it could have been me holding her, or the nibbling her neck that I kept finding myself doing.

"Kris, if you keep that up, I'm not going to be able to finish my studying," Grace warned as I nibbled on her earlobe, again.

"Sorry. I thought that if you got stuck, you could just think of me doing this, and it would help you remember."

"You did not. You just wanted me to think about you and get all turned on."

"Um no, not while you're in class. Hello, you are mine, mine, and only mine. I am not sharing your sexy goddess body with anyone." I pulled her body closer to me.

"Then behave and hold me. I just need another half hour, and you will be rewarded for good behavior."

"Interesting, rewarding good behavior with naughty behavior. Don't they cancel one another out?"

"Kris."

"Sorry," I said, grinning. I held her close and allowed her to finish her studying.

Once Grace finished her studying, she turned around and pressed me down onto my back. The look in her eyes told me that this was definitely going to be a way for us both to burn off some extra energy.

We made love on the couch before moving to the bedroom and making love again. I had set the alarm a little earlier than usual and snuck out of bed, to make Grace and me breakfast. I made it back into the room with the tray of food just as her alarm went off.

"Morning, gorgeous," I said, setting the tray on the floor and crawling back into bed next to Grace.

"Morning." Grace kissed me softly. "Where were you?"

"I was making my beautiful girlfriend a healthy breakfast to make her finals today a piece of cake."

I reached down, pulled the tray of food up, and set it on the bed. I saw Grace's eyes widen when she saw what I had made. I had some orange juice, coffee, chocolate malt-o-meal, and a white rose on the tray for her.

"You made all this for me?"

"Yes. I love you, baby. I want you to have the best start. I know that chocolate malt-o-meal is your favorite on test days. So, I went out and got some and your rose this morning."

"You are so sweet. I love you."

"I love you too. You eat while I finish getting ready."

Chapter Eleven

After Grace graduated, she got a job doing IT for a major company. The job involved some travel, which neither of us liked. We had been together for almost two years, but because of my nightmares, Grace didn't like to be away.

"Hey, Aly," I said, entering the coffee shop and sitting down at the table.

"Hey, Kris! Where is your other half?"

"Grace is out of town on business."

"How long will she be gone?"

"She's been gone for a week, and she isn't due back for another week." I pouted.

"Awww, you poor baby." Aly laughed.

"You wait. Some day, you are going to feel that way about someone."

"Don't you threaten me." Aly laughed. "I don't know that I will ever find that one special girl. Well, I had found the one, but Grace beat me to her."

"Yeah, yeah, you two are still fighting over me. It is such a curse to be as amazingly hot as me."

We both laughed. We talked for a couple of hours while we drank our coffee and their refills. After we finished, we decided to walk off some of our extra energy from the coffee. It was nice still having Aly in our life. She had become a trusted friend for both Grace and me. Yes, Grace had finally learned to trust Aly. Well, I guess trust is a relative term. Grace always said there were three facets to our relationship. There was that which affected her, that which affected me, and that which affected us as a couple. This mentality had saved us in several disagreements. But when it came to Aly, Grace said that as long as Aly knew her place was not with me other than as a friend, she would overlook her jealousy. Aly and I made jokes about her and Grace fighting over me, or Aly still pining for me, but we knew that my heart belonged to Grace and it would always belong to Grace.

The week dragged by, and then finally on Friday, it was time to pick Grace up at the airport. I drove over there and picked her up. When she finally entered the terminal, she looked tired, but she was still my ever-beautiful girlfriend.

"Hey, sweetie," I said, kissing her cheek and taking her bags from her.

"Hey," Grace said, tiredly.

"How come you are so tired?"

"The past two days have been long, and I have missed my own bed."

"Well, then let's get you home."

I drove us home in silence. There was more than just being tired going on with Grace, but I wasn't going to push it until she had rested. I didn't do a lot of business trips, but the ones I had done were exhausting. This one had been for two weeks, one of the longest that Grace had ever done.

Once we were home, I made us dinner while Grace unpacked and showered. After we ate, Grace said she was tired and went to bed. Although I couldn't prove it, I swear that she was still awake when I finally made my way into the bedroom. Something about her breathing pattern didn't sit right, but I let it go. She had told me that she was tired and I needed to trust that if there was a problem that she would talk to me when she was ready.

Saturday morning, Grace was still very quiet and reserved. It was unusual, and it scared me. She didn't seem happy to be home or to see me even.

"Grace? Did I do something wrong?" I finally asked.

"No, it was just a long trip."

"I get that, but you have been very distant. Even in your sleep, you pulled away from me."

"I just need some space, okay?" Grace had rarely snapped at me like that because of the environment that I was raised in. She knew it had a powerful effect on me. It took me aback.

"Fine, I'll give you your space." I grabbed my keys and headed out the door.

I went and walked around for several hours. I didn't have a destination or anything. I had left my phone at home, so I was completely off the grid. I started to wonder if Grace had tried to reach me, if she even cared that she couldn't reach me. I wasn't the most confident person, so what was going on here really threw me.

It was evening before I went home. When I got there, Grace was sitting in the living room with an almost empty bottle of wine.

"Where the hell have you been?" she asked. Her tone was tense, but she wasn't yelling at me.

"Giving you your space," I said without making eye contact. Because of my family history, drinking was not something I liked. Drinking for emotional reasons was worse than for social reasons.

"You didn't take your phone. I have been worried

about you."

"So worried that you polished off a bottle of wine?" It was a low blow, but somehow I didn't mind that at that moment. It seemed fitting.

"Yeah, I know your stance on emotional drinking, but there are other things going on here. I needed the fucking wine. I'm certain that Aly is ready to file a missing person report on you. She has been checking in with me almost every half hour since you left."

"Why is she calling you? How does she even know that I was gone?"

"Because I called her. After you left, I called to tell her that you were out and I had no idea where you had gone. I told her that you didn't take your phone which was really unlike you."

"I left to give you the fucking space you wanted. I wasn't concerned with my phone. I just knew *you* didn't want me here. I don't know what I have done, but just fucking tell me." I sat down in the chair near the sofa where Grace was seated. Our apartment living room wasn't large. We had enough room for a chair, sofa, loveseat, and coffee table between them all, but it worked for us.

"You didn't do anything, Kris. I did and the guilt of it is killing me."

"What do you mean *you* did?" I could see the stress and anxiety in Grace's face when I asked this. The inner turmoil that she was feeling played across her face.

"I love you so much. You are my world…"

"Just tell me, Grace." I didn't like how this was going.

"Kris, I slept with one of the interns that I was working with."

Hello, reality check. Did she just say that she slept with someone else? Did my ears hear her right? What the hell...

"Grace, repeat that very slowly..." I stood and started to back away from her.

"I am so sorry, baby," said Grace as she started to cry. "I didn't mean for it to happen. I mean, why would I? But you have to believe that I love you, Kris. It will never happen again."

"Grace, I said to repeat what you said very slowly." I could tell she was scared; the coldness in my voice always scared her. It was when I started to disconnect.

"I said that I slept with one of the interns." Grace's voice was barely audible, yet deafening.

"You slept with someone else. I'm going to assume that you aren't talking about sleeping in the same bed with a pillow barrier so you didn't touch."

"Yes," whispered Grace.

"So you fucked someone else?"

"Kris, I am so sorry. Please, give me a chance to make it up to you. It meant nothing. We were drunk and—"

"And drinking makes it all right? Do you remember my childhood? If drinking makes what you did all right, then every god damn thing my mother fucking did to me, every painful hit, every thrown glass, everything that fucking woman did was all right because she was drunk."

"Kris, that isn't what I meant." Grace was on her knees in front of me, sobbing. "I am so sorry, baby. I fucked up. I broke the trust we had. Please, give me a chance to make it up to you."

Watching Grace beg for forgiveness at my feet felt wrong. The thought that she had violated and betrayed my trust and love for her, not to mention our relationship, made me sick. Some people may be willing to forgive, or to work to get beyond something like this. After everything that I had been through, I didn't know if I was that type of person. I looked down at her sobbing and holding onto one of my legs like a two-year-old does with their parents.

"I need to leave. I can't be here now, I can't see you." I pulled my leg away from her. Grace flopped into a heap on the floor. Part of me wanted to scoop her up in my arms and hold her, but then the thought that she had let someone else hold her, kiss her, and touch her disgusted part of me. It was that thought that was driving me out of the house. I went into the bedroom, I grabbed a bag and packed some clothes in it, and I grabbed my phone and headed toward the front door.

"Kris, please, say something. Don't leave like this." Grace had managed to get up to her feet, but she was unsteady. "Please, don't leave me."

"Grace, right now I'm disgusted with you, the idea that your mouth was on another woman, that you let another woman touch you, feel you…I can't do this right now. *I* need some space and time to sort out what this means."

I turned and walked out the door. I heard her throw her body into the door as I leaned against the other side. I called Aly and told her that I needed a ride, that me driving was not a safe idea. She was there to pick me up in less than fifteen minutes. We rode back to her apartment in silence.

"Kris, what's going on?" Aly asked once we were inside.

I went through everything since I picked Grace up at the airport. To say that Aly was shocked would be an understatement. She was also furious with Grace. Aly let me cry on her shoulder for a long time. Well, until I was too exhausted to cry anymore. I went into her guest room and spent the next three days curled up in that bed. I got up to pee, that was it. I didn't eat, I didn't really sleep, I just lay there blankly staring at the wall.

❧❧❧❧

The sound of Grace and Aly arguing loudly awoke me. At first, I thought that I was dreaming.

"Grace, Kris is sleeping. She will talk to you when she is ready."

"I need to talk to her. I need to make this right," I heard Grace pleading. "Come on, Aly, just let me see her."

I knew Grace wasn't going to give up. I got out of bed and walked out to where the two women were talking. I found Aly standing with her arms crossed, blocking Grace from coming any further into the apartment.

"Kris, baby," Grace said, the moment she saw me.

"Grace, what are you doing here?" I was rubbing my eyes. They were sore and crusty from crying.

"I tried to get her to leave," Aly said.

"It's okay. I'll take it from here. Thanks."

Aly grabbed her phone and her keys and headed out the door. She had been on her way out when Grace arrived.

"Kris, please, can't we talk about this? I love you." Grace stepped toward me, and I took a step backward.

"Grace, how can you say that you love me? You slept with someone else." I sat down in the recliner that was closest to me.

"I did and I am so sorry. I know that doesn't make it right, but I'm not ready for us to be over. I love you. I need you." Grace was now kneeling before me.

"Grace, every time I close my eyes, I picture another woman kissing you, caressing you, loving you. It makes me sick to my stomach. I'm now left to wonder if she touched you the way I do. Did you like her touch more than mine? Did her mouth on your body make you feel more alive? Did you like how deep she was able to penetrate you? All of which disgust me."

"Kris, nobody could ever make me feel the way you make me feel. Please, don't let this be the end of us."

"I'm sorry, Grace. I need to figure out how to get over these thoughts in my head before I can say yes or no regarding our future."

I could feel the tears rolling down my face. I could see the hurt in Grace's eyes. I wanted to tell her that things were going to be okay, but honestly, I didn't know if I could honestly not think about it. My own self-doubt was enough to make me self-destruct. Her giving it this added fuel was almost more than I could take. I still loved Grace, I would always love her, but this was something huge. There wasn't an easy fix for this.

"Please, come home. Kris, we can't work on us when you are living here."

"I wouldn't call what I have been doing here living. I would call it barely being alive. I'm pretty certain that Aly came in with a stick to poke me a few times to make sure I was still alive." I wish that were just a joke and I was trying to ease the tension, but it wasn't. My breathing had always been shallow, but now it seemed like it was even worse. Aly said it was the hurt; she might be right.

"Please, come home. I'll sleep on the floor, on the couch, in the car if you want. I just can't handle being there without you."

I thought about her request for a minute, then told Grace that I needed another night away, but that I would come home the next night and we could work out who slept where. This seemed to pacify her. She hugged me and kissed the side of my head before she left. She looked back as she was closing the door and told me again that she loved me.

After Grace left, I messaged Aly that it was safe for her to come home. When she got there, I replayed the conversation that Grace and I had. Aly told me that I needed to do what my heart felt was best for me, but that giving Grace another chance wouldn't be a bad thing. She said that she could tell that Grace meant what she said when she said she regretted it and that she loved me. I knew that, but the thought that she had allowed someone else to do what was sacred to us and our relationship still disgusted me.

I didn't sleep that night. I just kept thinking about how I could get beyond this. I had resolved that if it was just one time as opposed to one night, I might be able to work past that. But if it was more than once and/or wasn't just one night, then I couldn't and Grace and I were through. That thought made me throw up in my mouth.

When I got home, Grace had made dinner for us, and she had moved bedding for herself to the couch.

"Grace, I have one question and I need you to answer it honestly."

"Of course." Grace turned from where she was

doing the dishes.

"Was this a one time or one night thing?"

The guilt that played across her face was all I needed for an answer. I raced for the bathroom and threw up. I thought that I had prepared myself for this, but honestly, how do you prepare?

"Kris," Grace said, standing at the doorway.

"Get away from me. You...you...oh god," I managed to say, before getting sick again.

Grace left. I could hear her crying in the other room. I couldn't move. How did this all go so wrong? How did she honestly expect me to forgive or forget this betrayal?

I messaged Aly and asked if I could stay with her for a while. She said of course. I told her I was going to stay here tonight and then I'd be by tomorrow.

❧❧❧❧

I was curled up in bed, my head throbbing from crying. My mind was reeling from all that had taken place this week. I was happy, I was hurt, I was cautious, I was devastated. I just wanted to be happy, to have a good life. Why was that so hard for me to obtain?

"Kris? Can I come in?" said the voice on the other side of the door.

"I'm not in the mood to talk."

"Please, I just have one thing to say and then I will leave you alone."

I got up, walked over, and opened the door. There, standing before me was Grace, the woman who had caused the emotional rollercoaster I had been on this week. I moved back to the bed as she entered the room.

"Kris, I know that what you have learned is painful.

I'm sorry you got hurt but did you really think that you could have a normal life? That you could truly be loved by someone?" Grace said. I saw she was holding something in her hand. I couldn't make out what it was until the probes shot out of it. Tyler had given her the stun gun as a joke when we started college. Oh god, those probes hurt. I tried to cry out, but I couldn't. "You are a fool if you believed that. I will admit that we had some good times, but that intern, she was so much better. Maybe it was the forbidden fruit appeal, or maybe she just had more skill."

"Grace, stop, please. You're hurting me."

"That is the plan. I am going to make you hurt, and then I am going to turn you over to your parents and let them finish you."

"Please, Grace," I pleaded.

"You see, I can't do that. I only have a few minutes before your parents arrive."

I saw a glint of light hit the knife that Grace now held. She moved toward me slowly, but with a purpose. I saw the knife go up high above me and then I felt it plunge deep into my chest.

"Your heart, you don't need it. I'm going to keep it as a souvenir. It is something to remind me of how stupid you were to believe in us and to believe that you could ever have a happy life."

The pain in my chest continued. I saw Grace holding my heart in her hands. How was this possible? I watched as Grace put my heart into a box. She looked at me and grinned. I heard a knock on the door and Grace left to answer it. While she was gone, I tried to move, but the stun gun effects still hadn't worn off. All I could do was lay there. The pain was growing more and more intense. I heard people entering the room and moved my eyes to see who it was. There Grace was, standing with my parents and her arms wrapped around another woman.

"Are you ready for a little trip?" my father asked.

"Get her out of here. I need to help my intern with some stuff," Grace said, licking the woman's neck as I saw her hand slip into the front of the woman's shirt.

"Grace, don't do this," I repeated over and over again.

"Kris, good-bye."

It went dark again. All I could smell was dirt and wetness around me. I could hear the sounds of someone working, but I couldn't make out what they were doing. I tried to open my eyes, but all I saw was darkness.

"Dig faster," I heard my father snap.

"Fuck you. If you want it done faster, you can get your ass down here and help," said another man.

"You talk to me like that again and you'll find yourself living in a grave just like her."

I heard a growl from the other man and he continued with his work. It wasn't long before I felt myself being tossed down into the grave. Then, I tasted the soil that was being pushed in and burying me.

"No, don't do this. Why? Why are you doing this?" I screamed.

"Beep...Beep..."

"Kris, open your eyes," I heard someone say. "Come on. You're okay. It is safe to open your eyes."

"Beep...Beep..."

I felt comforted by the voice. I tried to open my eyes. At first, it was just a flutter, then a little more. It looked like Aly was the one talking to me. Why was Aly asking me to wake up? My eyes fluttered open again and this time they focused on Aly's face. She looked scared. I looked around and saw I was in a corner of the bedroom holding my chest where I remembered Grace had plunged the knife in and pulled out my heart.

"Hey there, are you awake?"

"Yeah," I said. My voice was very hoarse. I tried to swallow, but I didn't have enough wetness in my mouth to do anything. I saw a hand give Aly a glass of water. Aly helped me to get a drink. "Thanks."

"Are you okay? Physically?" Aly asked.

"I don't know. I'm in a lot of pain. My chest really hurts."

"Well, I don't doubt that. When I got here, Grace said you were trying to stab yourself in the heart with your brush."

"Huh?"

"You looked like you were trying to stab yourself," Grace said, quietly. I groaned. I still have the vivid memories of the dream. "When I couldn't get you to respond to me and stop crying out, I called Aly."

"I think I'm going to get sick," I said. I was still unable to move from my spot. Grace handed Aly the puke bucket we kept, for this reason. Aly got it situated so I could hold it myself and then she backed off.

"I love you, my friend, but I am *not* going to let you puke on me. We aren't that close," Aly said. She was trying to alleviate the tension in the room. Little did she know that there was no way she was going to be able to do that.

I threw up several times before it became just dry heaves. Grace brought Aly two damp washcloths, one to wipe my face and mouth with, and the other to put on the back of my neck. I felt the shakes starting to take over. Grace moved over and even though I protested, she and Aly picked me up and moved me to the bed. Once I was in the bed, they tried to cover me in blankets but my memory of being buried alive overtook my logic, and I started to panic.

"Kris? What's going on?" Grace asked. "What was the dream about?"

I could see the fear in her and Aly's eyes. "You shot me with a stun gun and then cut my heart out with a knife. Then you turned me over to my parents, who were burying me alive."

Grace was more than devastated hearing my words. I could tell that she was barely hanging on and this made her slip even closer to the edge. I wanted to feel bad, but I couldn't. Grace bolted from the room in tears. Aly wrapped an arm around my shaking body.

"Oh, buddy. You definitely won't cut yourself a break, will you?"

"It wasn't one time, Aly. She fucked that intern multiple times that night," I whispered, before the tears started to flow.

"That explains the dream, and you wanting to move in with me. You know you are welcome to stay as long as you want or just to become my roommate. We'll get through this."

I moved in with Aly the next day. I left Grace enough money for the remainder of our lease and for utilities. I changed my phone number. I made Aly get rid of anything that had Grace's picture on it. Yes, this seemed like an extreme overreaction, but I didn't know how else to deal with this at the time. I didn't want to be reminded of Grace Barnes and the level of betrayal that I felt.

Chapter Twelve

I had been living with Aly for four months when one night her phone rang and she went outside to take the call. When she came back inside, the pallor of her skin was unnerving.

"Aly? Is everything okay?"

"I, um, I need to go out for a while."

"What's going on? Talk to me."

"I, I can't just yet. I need to go. I won't be gone long."

Aly grabbed her keys and hurried out the door. I was left standing there staring at a closed door.

"What the hell just happened?" I thought to myself.

This was something that I had never seen from Aly. She wasn't the most open person about things, but she had certainly never shut me out like this either. About four hours later, Aly came back to the apartment. She looked even more ragged than she had before she left.

"Is everything okay?" I asked, hesitantly.

"No, but I can't talk about it now. I'm sorry. I'm supposed to get a call tomorrow morning. Then maybe, I just..."

"That's fine. I'm here for you whenever you are ready to talk or for whatever you need."

"I appreciate that, I do. I think I'm just going to go to my room."

Aly didn't wait for a response; she just turned and

walked into her room and closed the door. I had never seen her like this. Shortly after I moved in, her best friend from high school was in a climbing accident. Aly was upset, but nothing like this. I could only think that it had something to do with her parents or another family member that she was close to.

I gave her the space she requested. The next day, she took two calls outside. She still seemed to be harboring something big. I could see it weighing on her. Aly told me that she needed to talk to me about something serious. Ominous, I know. She scared the shit out of me with that, to be honest. How do you prepare yourself when someone says something like that?

"Have I done something wrong? Do you need me to find my own place?"

"No, you haven't done anything wrong and I'm not throwing you out or anything. I just have something to tell you and I don't know how you are going to react. I want you to remember that I am here for you."

We both sat down on the couch. "You're scaring me now. Aly, what's with the mystery?"

"Kris, Grace is in the hospital."

"I'm sorry to hear that." The coldness in my tone appeared to take Aly by surprise. "I don't know why this affects me. Grace is not a part of my life anymore. She made her choices."

"Kris, it's pretty serious. The doctors say that Grace could die. Put the pettiness aside. I know you still care about her. You don't love someone the way you two loved and just stop caring."

Okay, so she had my attention. "What do you mean Grace could die?" My voice cracked like a teenager in puberty.

"Grace has been drinking a lot over the past few months—"

"How do you know this? Who has been calling you? What the hell is going on?" I could feel my anxiety rising.

"Tyler found my number in Grace's phone yesterday and thought that maybe I could either get you to call him since you changed your number or at least let you know what is going on."

"What happened?" I asked, tears welling up in my eyes. Dammit, I didn't want to cry, I didn't want to waste more tears on Grace Barnes. I had cried often enough the first couple of months after I moved out.

"Grace was in a car accident. She was hurt pretty bad."

"How bad? Tell me the truth, Aly." My voice was stern. Yes, I was still very hurt by what Grace had done, but I didn't want her harmed. "What do you know?"

"Grace was at a party two days ago. She got in the car with someone to go home, well, they were both very intoxicated and the driver lost control of the car and ran them into a bunch of parked cars. It wouldn't have been so bad, but neither was wearing their seatbelt. The doctors said if she made it through the next forty-eight hours that she stood a good chance to live. The forty-eight hour time frame ends today."

"Is that why you didn't tell me last night?" My voice was increasing in volume. "Is this why you went out yesterday?"

"Yes. Tyler asked me to wait until they knew if she was going to be okay," said Aly, bowing her head.

"Why? Because if she were to die it would be easier to let me know? Where is she? Can I see her?"

"Yeah, I'll take you."

Aly and I headed to the hospital. When we arrived, the Barnes clan had overtaken a small section of the waiting room. Aly stayed next to me. I didn't honestly know what, if anything, Grace had told them.

"Kris," Erin said, moving out of her chair and enveloping me in a hug.

"Hi, Mrs. Barnes," I said, softly. I could feel her shaking as I hugged her. Grace's mom was one the strongest women I knew. Her being this scared, well, it scared the shit out of me.

"You haven't called me that since you were six. Please, don't start now. I won't accept or allow it. Am I understood?"

I could see the pain in her eyes. I had no interest in being the cause of more pain.

"I'm sorry," I said, hugging her close again.

"Grace told us what happened. How are you doing?"

"One day at a time." As we were talking, Sean came over and hugged me.

"You are still family, never forget that. You don't have to be dating our daughter to come to us if you need anything."

"Thank you. How is she?"

"She's asleep. Do you want to go in?"

"I, I don't know. I don't know if I can."

"May I go in with her?" Aly asked. I had almost forgotten that she was there.

"Sure," said Sean. The sadness in Grace's parents' eyes looked wrong.

Aly and I stood outside the door to Grace's room. I saw Grace through the window. There were a lot of bandages and tubes. I looked back at Aly. She gave me a supportive smile and put a hand on my shoulder. I took a deep breath and pushed open the door.

The sterile scent in the room was the first thing that I noticed. Next was the constant beeping of the machines. Grace was never one to be able to sleep with noise in the room. She wouldn't even let me listen to music with headphones on in bed. I looked over at Aly. I wasn't sure I could do this. Aly placed her hand on the small of my back. She moved us forward.

"Talk to her," Aly said softly.

"Hey, Grace." I sat down on the edge of the bed. I made sure not to touch any of the wires or tubes. I glanced over at Aly and she mouthed for me to talk to Grace. What the hell did she want me to say? "What the hell?" I laughed nervously. I had no clue if she could even hear me.

"Kris?" Grace said, opening her eyes slowly.

"Yeah, I'm here." I took her hand in mine. She was so cold. Grace hated to be cold.

"Why are you here?" Her voice was raspy; it barely sounded like Grace.

"Because you were stupid." It came out a bit blunter than I had planned.

"Don't hold anything back." She tried to give me a smile, but it never made it to her eyes.

"Grace, what the hell? If you wanted to get me back in your life, there are other ways."

"Well, you didn't leave me a whole lot of options. You changed your number, closed your email account, and removed any other way of contacting you."

"You knew I was staying with Aly." I glanced over in Aly's direction.

Grace turned her head slightly to see where I was looking. "Hi, Aly."

"Don't mind me. I'm just going to step out and

let you two talk. Please don't kill each other. It would look very bad."

Aly bolted out the door, leaving Grace and me alone.

"So, are you sleeping with her yet?" Grace asked, bluntly.

"Not that it is any of your business, but no, I'm not. She is my roommate and a friend. If this is what is going to happen, I'm just going to go. I didn't come here to fight with you."

"Why did you come, Kris?"

"I came because I heard you were hurt. We may not be a couple, we may not even be friends, but we have a history together and because of that history, I'm always going to care about you."

"Why bother?" Grace said, dismissively.

"You're right, Grace. Why should I care that the only person who ever gave a shit about me was almost killed?"

"I wasn't almost killed."

"Yeah, you were. You don't even know what happened, do you?" My heart was pounding in my chest. I was running out of ideas to get through to this woman. Grace was looking at me with a blank look. I told her what Aly had told me. I don't know if they wanted her to know about it, but she was acting stupid and needed a kick in the ass.

"How bad do I look?"

"You are going to be funny colored for a while."

"Great."

"Eh, just say you're an oompa-loompa." Grace gave me a playful scowl, or it would have been if she weren't so bandaged up.

"Even when you don't like me, you're an ass."

"It isn't a matter of liking or not liking you, Grace. It is about trust and respect. Relationships don't work without those. Well, they will, but it won't be a long or healthy relationship." I started to stand up and she stopped me.

"I'm sorry. I have wanted to apologize for a while now."

"I know you are sorry, but that doesn't make it hurt any less." I looked down at my hands. I couldn't bring myself to look at her.

"I miss you. There are days I wish I were dead. It would hurt less than not having you a part of my life," Grace admitted. I could feel her eyes fixated on me.

"Don't talk like that. We'll figure it out. Please, no more stupidity." I closed my eyes and pinched the bridge of my nose. I could feel a stress migraine starting.

"Tell me that you'll forgive me someday."

"I will forgive you. I can't forget it though."

"I just want you back in my life. I'm empty without you, Kris." I could hear the sincerity in her words.

"Get better, then we'll start working on our friendship. Now, I need to leave so you can get more sleep. I will come back in a few days, if that is okay?"

Grace nodded her agreement. I kissed her forehead and then quickly exited the room. I leaned up against the wall to center myself. I could feel the eyes from the waiting room watching me. After a few minutes, Aly was by my side.

"You okay?" she asked as she ran her hand up and down my upper arm.

"Not even in the slightest way possible am I okay. Can we get out of here?" I asked.

"Yep, whatever you want or need."

"Thanks." I waved to Grace's family and then Aly and I left.

"Where do you want to go?" asked Aly once we got in the car.

"Anywhere but here."

Aly drove us to a local nature preserve. It was the perfect choice. We walked along the trail for a long while in silence.

"What was it like, seeing her?" Aly asked.

"It hurt. It was a sadness hurt. My mind started to race between what happened between her and me. The pain of her admitting that she cheated, it was still pretty powerful. On top of it, seeing her injured was hard too. I still care about her, if that makes any sense."

"It does. You and Grace have been together as friends for a long time. You had an intense romantic relationship. Do you ever think you'll be friends again?"

"I told her we'd try to find a way to make it work. I don't know how to trust her again."

I stopped in front of a small rock bench that had been placed alongside the trail. I let out a sigh and plopped down. I felt Aly sit down next to me and wrap an arm around my shoulders. I rested my head on her shoulder. I was at a loss on how to deal with the myriad of emotions going on inside me.

"What's going on inside your head?"

"A lot, actually. On the plus side, my feelings for Grace have certainly started to change. On the downside, seeing her and knowing that I couldn't trust her hurt and made my mind go into overdrive. I'm questioning my whole friendship with her."

"Kris, you can't let one huge mistake negate your entire friendship."

"But," I started to say, pulling my head from Aly's

shoulder and looking at her. "But, what if that wasn't the only lie she has told me?"

"What if it is? Are you willing to risk it all on the possibility that she lied to you in the past, a past that cannot be changed?"

"I don't know..."

Aly and I sat there for a few more minutes. I was watching Aly while we sat there. She had been great through all of this. Then, I don't know what came over me, but I found myself straddling her thighs and sitting on her lap. I essentially pinned her to the back of the bench before leaning down and kissing her. It wasn't a tentative kiss; it was passion-filled. She was stunned at first, I could feel that, but then she started to respond. I felt her arms holding me close as our lips, our tongues, and even our bodies moved together as if we were one.

"Wow," I breathed once we pulled apart from the kiss.

"Yeah, definitely wow."

"Aly, I'm so—"

"I swear, Kris, if you apologize for kissing me, I will bury you somewhere in these woods where nobody will find you. You didn't force me, you surprised me, but you didn't force me to kiss you back, to hold your body against mine." Our bodies were still pressed together. It felt amazing. "I could have dumped your ass off my lap if it weren't what I wanted. I still might... dump you off," Aly said, smiling at me. "But, you need to make sure that I'm not a rebound or replacement. I won't be what helps you get over Grace."

"You aren't a rebound or replacement. Yes, I am still dealing with my feelings for Grace, but you are someone I have cared about for a while as well."

Aly pulled me close again, and we shared another

steamy hot kiss.

"Good, then you will understand and respect me telling you that I want you to wait a week at least before you try that again. I want you to make it right within yourself. Make sure you are ready to move forward. If you can't do that, then we may need to have another talk."

"I respect that. I guess I should probably get off your lap then." We both laughed because neither of us had given it a second thought that I was sitting on her lap still.

"Yeah, you probably should."

I got off Aly's lap and we continued our walk along the trail for a while longer before heading back to our apartment.

❧❧❧❧

Three days later, I found myself stepping off the elevator at the hospital, going to visit Grace. I had called and spoken to Tyler. He said that she was improving and that she would like it if I would visit. I wasn't sure that I could do this alone, but Aly had to work, and after kissing her the last time we were there, I wasn't sure it was the best idea to associate her with the emotions that came from seeing Grace.

"Hey, is now an okay time?" I asked, poking my head into Grace's room. I saw that Tyler was sitting there with her.

"Yeah, Tyler is boring, I need some fresh blood," quipped Grace.

"Well, lamb chops, you're up," said Tyler, grinning at me.

"I liked it better when you called me Squish."

"Yeah, well, today you're lamb chops. I'm older and wiser, so therefore, I am correct."

"In your dreams, snacky-crack." I loved it when Tyler and I were able to exchange wit. You see wit your way; I'll see it my way.

I watched as Tyler kissed his sister on the side of her head and said he would be back later. As he passed me, he squeezed my shoulder and offered me a warm smile.

"How are you feeling today?" I asked. A majority of the bandages had been removed and the bruises that were bright purple the last time I was here had started to yellow and fade.

"Sore. They took me off the big dog meds. I'm grateful because now I can stay awake for more than thirty minutes at a time, but I feel the pain and injuries more now."

"I can see where sleeping all the time could get annoying. If you nod off, I brought a Sharpie to draw on you with." I pulled the marker out of my pocket and showed it to Grace.

"You wouldn't dare."

"Grace, you have known me for twenty years. You know damn well I certainly will do it."

"But I'm injured and defenseless." Grace pouted.

"So?"

"You're supposed to be nice to me."

"I'll think about it." I smiled and put the marker back into my pocket. "Have they said when you get to go home yet?"

"They are thinking another two days. Do I still look like an oompa-loompa?"

"Yeah, but not because of the bruises. You're short." I loved teasing Grace. It felt a bit awkward, but it was still fun.

"You're an ass."

I turned my head and looked as best I could at my butt. "Yeah, it is kind of cute too. So, what else have you been up to? Well, before you got injured that is."

"Not a whole lot. I spend a lot of time either working or drinking. I guess that car accident is going to put a stop to that for a while."

I sat down on the edge of the bed in the same spot that I sat in the last time I was here. "Why do you drink?"

"It helps me forget that I lost you as my girlfriend, my lover, and my best friend. I know it was my fault, and the only person I can blame and make pay is myself."

"Well, you know that I won't be around if you are going to be doing that shit. One or two drinks every now and then, maybe, but from what I have heard about your current drinking habits, not a chance. I won't have anything to do with you."

"That's fine, I get it. What have you been up to? I've missed you."

"I've been putting in a lot of hours at work. That and reading have been the main things in my life. Aly tries to get me to go out, but I usually find a way to get out of it."

"Does this feel as awkward to you as it does to me?"

"Yeah. Listen, Grace, I want to work on us rebuilding a friendship. I miss it."

"I want that too." Grace took my hand in hers. She still felt cold, but it wasn't as bad as it was the other day when I was here. "I know that it will take time. I just hope that we can be close like we were before."

We talked for another thirty minutes before Tyler came back in. The three of us were joking and laughing when a woman in a black business suit came in. I saw both Grace and Tyler tense.

"Hi sweetie," said the newly arrived woman as she walked over and kissed Grace on the lips.

"Hi," Grace said, her eyes shifting from this new woman to Tyler, to me.

"Oh, I'm sorry. I didn't realize you had company. Hello, I'm Daeva Wagner, Grace's girlfriend," she said, extending her hand to me.

"Girlfriend? Seriously, Grace?" I felt as though I had been punched in the stomach.

"Maybe we should go outside and talk," Tyler said, reaching for my arm, but I pulled it away from him.

"Honey, who is this? Why does she seem surprised that you have a girlfriend? I appear to be missing something."

"H-how long have you two been together?" I asked in barely a whisper.

"Grace and I have been together for four blissful months, last Wednesday," Daeva stated proudly. "Why?"

"Kris, please, let me explain…" Grace said, wincing as she reached for my hand, and I quickly pulled it away from her reach.

"What is there to explain? I'm guessing this is the slut that you cheated on me with. Wow, you said that it meant nothing, you wanted us to still be together, yet here you are still fucking her."

"Kris, please," Tyler said, moving to stand between Daeva and I.

"Please what? Huh, Tyler? You all told me that

she was miserable without me in her life. Grace, you said that you wanted to work things out between us. The whole time you were both lying to me."

"Listen, bitch," Daeva started. "Grace wouldn't have cheated if you were keeping her happy. If you are going to keep upsetting her, I am going to see to it that you are banned from this hospital. I know people. Powerful people."

"Daeva, stop," Grace said. "Kris, I do want for us to make amends. I do want you back in my life."

"Why? So you can lie to me some more? If any of you can give me an honest answer, does Aly know about you and the wonder tramp over there?"

"Bitch, I am warning you." As Daeva threatened me, I saw the spittle flying out of her mouth toward me. It was gross.

"Kris, please calm down," said Tyler.

"Fuck you, Tyler. Is someone going to answer me? Does…Aly…know? Is she lying to me as well?"

"No," said Grace, shaking her head. "We didn't tell Aly. I was going to tell you, but then we started talking. I couldn't find the words. I have missed our talks."

"Well, get used to missing them again," I snapped back at her.

"Kris, please," Grace pleaded as tears rolled down her face. The machines were beeping and going crazy.

As I saw the fleet of nurses staring in our direction, waiting to see if she would calm down before they had to come to the room, I knew I had to get out of there. Daeva was standing on the far side of the bed, trying to keep Grace still. Grace was trying desperately to reach for me. Tyler was trying to keep me from putting Daeva in the hospital. She was mouthing off and really needed me to slap the taste out of her mouth.

"Let…me…go, Tyler." My voice was quiet and eerie. I knew that because it sent a shiver up my spine.

"Kris, please, let me talk with you," Tyler said as I tried to wiggle from his grasp. "Outside, please."

"Kris, don't leave like this."

"You fucking lied to me, again. And again it was for that troll. I thought I knew you, Grace. I guess I don't."

"Kris, you are just mad, once you cool down, call me and we can talk."

"Tyler, you and Grace stay the fuck away from me. And leave Aly alone as well. Don't drag her into your convoluted mess. Grace, I hope you and the slutty troll have a good life together."

"You fucking—" Daeva said, trying to lunge for me.

"Daeva," snapped Grace, reaching for Daeva's arm. "Shut the fuck up. Kris, please, let me call you when I get out so I can explain. Please. Don't let things end like this."

"How can I trust you or believe you? Why should I even try? Good-bye, Grace, for good."

I turned and walked out of the room. I could hear Grace and Tyler calling my name, but I didn't turn around. I was shaking as I got in my car. I sent Aly a text telling her that things went worse than I could have ever thought and that I was headed home. When she asked if I was okay to drive, I almost told her that it didn't matter. But, I knew that wasn't the right answer. I told her I would be careful and would meet her at home, but it would take me a little longer than usual.

Chapter Thirteen

When I finally arrived home, Aly was already there. I could see the look of concern on her face. As soon as I closed the door, the tears started to flow and instead of sliding down the door, I found myself wrapped in Aly's arms. She led me to the couch and held me while I cried.

"Shhh, you're safe here," Aly said several times, trying to calm me down.

I wanted to calm down. I was tired of giving Grace and her family my tears and energy. I felt Aly kiss the side of my head. I took comfort in her closeness and caring.

"When you are ready, we can talk about it." We sat there, Aly holding me for a long time until I felt that I was able to calm down enough.

"G-Grace is still seeing the intern. No, seeing is not the right way to describe her, the intern is her girlfriend."

"What? Sweetie, oh, I am so sorry. Did Grace tell you this?"

I shook my head against her chest. "Fucking slutty troll showed up."

"I'm sorry, what?"

I pulled my head away from her chest and repeated, "The fucking slutty troll showed up there."

"The chick showed up there?"

I sat back a bit; Aly was still holding onto me. I

told her what had happened at the hospital. About my talk with Grace, about Daeva showing up, about how I left things.

"Kris, I swear I had no idea. I wouldn't lie to you or cover for them." I could hear the fear in her voice that I wasn't going to believe her.

"I know. I have to say that I was relieved when they said you didn't know. I was afraid I was going to lose everyone in my world. I wasn't sure if I should believe them, but I trust you."

"Not only that, but I'm sorry, you are stuck with me for life."

"I'm okay with that." And I truly meant that. I was so grateful for the friendship that Aly and I had created.

Aly held me while I processed the events of the day. We had dinner together and after, we cleaned up. That meant throwing the pizza box away. I heard Aly let out a loud sigh of frustration.

"What's wrong?" I asked.

"Tyler has called me several times, and I have a voicemail that I am assuming is him."

"I told them not to contact you," I growled, loudly. Why couldn't they just listen for once? I supposed that since my feelings didn't matter to them, they had no reason listen to me.

"Hey, before you get too upset, let's just listen to the message and see what it says." Aly dialed into her voicemail and put it on speakerphone.

"Hi, Alyssa, I'm sure by now Kris has told you about what happened today. Please, can you at least let us know that she is okay? Grace is going nuts here. She has already pulled out several of her sutures. Also, can you also tell Kris that we didn't mean to lie to her?

Thanks." said Tyler.

"What the hell does 'we didn't mean to lie to her' actually mean? Was it an accident? Did they lose their brains? I don't get that."

Aly wrapped her arms around me from behind and rested her chin on my shoulder. "I don't know. I wish I had an answer for you, sweetie. Do you want me to let them know you are, in relative terms, okay? If you say no, I'm okay with that as well."

"I told them not to contact you. To leave you out of this. So no, don't bother to let them know. They don't deserve the right to know how I am or anything about me anymore."

"That is fine with me."

"You know that after today, I'm not going to be able to kiss you like I did the other day."

"I know, but you are also working through that and maybe soon you will be able to. I'm seriously not going anywhere, Kris."

We made our way to the living room and put in a movie. I was so emotionally spent that I fell asleep about twenty minutes in. I don't know when, but Aly covered me up and let me sleep there.

⁂

Over the next few weeks, the not-so-subtle flirting between Aly and I increased. We hadn't heard from or seen Grace or her family since Tyler's voicemail. I was very happy about that.

As I entered the kitchen, I heard Aly say good morning as she was leaning against the counter, waiting for the toaster.

"Good morning," I said cheerfully.

"You aren't a morning person. Why are you cheery? Is the world ending? I haven't done my laundry yet. I don't have clean undies. I don't want to die in dirty undies." Aly stuck her lower lip out and pouted.

I took two large steps toward her, putting me mere inches away from our bodies touching. I cupped her face in my hands and brought our lips together. The kiss started slowly, but rapidly heated up to hot and steamy. I found Aly's arms wrapped around my waist, pulling my body to hers.

When we finally broke apart, I kissed the tip of Aly's nose and said, "I was cheery because I knew that I was going to do that."

"Well, in that case, you are welcome to be cheery like that anytime."

"Good." I leaned in and slowly brought our lips together. We both let out a loud moan.

Aly and I spent the next few days taking every opportunity we could to kiss. We didn't move further than that. This felt right, for the time being. There was no need for us to rush into things.

One night, after dinner and after we had gotten into our jammies, we were making out on the couch when my hand inadvertently grazed her breast. I was bringing it up to cup her face and she moved just enough that it went right across her erect nipple. Alyssa groaned and arched into my hand. Hearing her groan sent a signal to my body that it was done with restraint. I needed more.

I watched as my hand cupped her breast, running my thumb over the erect nipple protruding through her T-shirt. I could feel the heat from her body, feel her arching into my hand. I was mesmerized at how perfect that nipple appeared. I continued to rub it and felt it get harder. I could hear Alyssa's breathing becoming more ragged.

"Baby, fuck, you are…driving me…insane," panted Aly.

I moaned at her words, lowered my head, and wrapped my lips around the shirt-covered nipple. I heard Aly whimper. I pulled back, cupped the other breast, and repeated my actions. I felt Aly's hips grind into mine. She had me so turned on; there was no turning back for me at this point.

"Take…my…shirt…off…touch me."

I was more than thrilled with this request. I quickly removed her shirt and let out a groan of intense desire at the gorgeous body splayed out before me. With every breath, I could see the rise and fall of her breasts and the perfect buds perched atop her soft, sensual breasts. I leaned forward and teased her nipples with my tongue. I felt her hand come up to the back of my head and pull me tighter against her breasts.

"God, Kris, you are, oh so good with your tongue."

"Your skin tastes so sweet."

"I want you," Aly said. I could see the desire burning in her eyes. "Now."

I stood up and helped her up. We walked back to my bedroom. I didn't want to have our first time together on the couch. I slowly finished undressing her. This meant removing her panties. She was stunning. Aly slowly undressed me, and we came together on the bed. Feeling her body under me was incredible.

"Oh, Kris." I heard her moan as I sucked on her neck. "Baby."

Our bodies moved together as we pleasured each other. Hearing Aly call out my name sent me over the edge. We lay together panting, trying to catch our breath.

"I think I like what you being cheery in the morning eventually leads to," said Aly, laughing.

I leaned over and kissed her. "It did seem to turn out well. Didn't it?"

"Let's just not wait as long the next time," Aly said, before pulling our lips together again.

We kissed and explored one another all night. After showering together and getting dressed, we made brunch and spent the remainder of the weekend cuddling, kissing, and having sex. When I think back to how it all began with Aly and I, it made me laugh. She was so cocky in college, but after that night in the alley, she changed; she let her guard down and let us see the real Alyssa. The real woman was an incredible person, and I was honored to have her in my life.

❧ ❧ ❧ ❧

My relationship with Aly had been growing deeper and more intense following that fateful morning. It had been several weeks, and that honeymoon period was still very much intact.

Aly and I were holding hands while walking along the outer fringes of the Farmer's Market early one Saturday morning. "I can't believe I let you talk me into coming out this early in the morning, on a Saturday, no less."

"Babe, it really isn't that early." Aly wrapped one arm around my waist and with the other, she took my hand and looked at the watch on my arm. "It says it is 8:30."

"Yeah, that is early, especially when you keep me up until the early hours of the morning." I nipped at her neck, causing her to giggle.

"Is that a complaint?"

"Dear god, no," I said, placing a chaste kiss on Aly's lips. "You can keep me awake doing amazingly naughty things to my body anytime."

"Mmmm, good," whispered Aly. We shared a toe-curling kiss. "Shit…"

Shocked by Aly's outburst, I turned and saw, coming right at us, two of the people I least wanted to see.

"Well, well, is this your new girlfriend? You may want to leave now. From what I understand, this one couldn't satisfy a gnat," Daeva sneered.

I heard Aly growl. It was not a friendly noise. Not like the one she makes when I…well. You can use your imagination.

"And you keep your distance from Grace, bitch," spat Daeva, glaring at me.

"Daeva, stop," Grace said through gritted teeth. "Now."

"Listen, you slutty troll, I don't want anything to do with her. Especially since she is willing to go slumming with the likes of you." I wasn't in the mood for her shit today. I was with Aly; I was happy.

"Compared to you, I am almost royalty. Do you realize the amount of physical and emotional pain you caused Grace that day? You owe her an apology."

"No, I don't. If I had wanted to apologize, I would have. She hurt herself that day. I didn't cause any of her hurt."

"No, you were the cause of her moving around and ripping out her stitches. Apologize to her, now." Daeva's voice had deepened and her tone was colder.

"Not you or anyone else is going to get me to

apologize for something that she brought on herself. Grace, control your pet," I said, before turning to Aly. "Sweetie, aren't there leash laws for pets in this state?"

Aly gave me a look that told me that she was done tolerating this situation and that she was rather pissed at me for engaging Daeva and antagonizing the situation. "Enough, Kris. Let's just leave."

"Your bitch hasn't apologized for hurting Grace. She isn't going anywhere until she does."

"You keep telling yourself that. I can't believe that you would be with someone like it," I said to Grace, motioning toward Daeva.

"Kris, Daeva, please, stop." Grace's tone was barely audible. She actually looked as though she were in truly in pain. I felt bad about that, but not bad enough to stop.

That seemed to be the last straw. Aly stepped between Daeva and me. "Babe, enough." I stopped at the look on Aly's face.

"Awww, you're not strong enough to fight your own battles. Your girlfriend needs to jump in." Daeva was taunting me. I was trying to remain restrained, but what I really wanted to do was rip her ugly head off.

"Daeva, one more insult toward Kris or Aly, and we're done. Am I clear?" Grace turned to face her girlfriend; her face was a very pissed off shade of red. I wasn't sure that I had ever seen that shade of pissed off from her either. Trust me, over the years I'd seen many different shades.

"Grace, baby, I am defending you. That whore owes you an apology."

"That is it! No more…we are through! Don't call me. Don't come near me. Nothing."

"Grace, you don't mean that. You are just putting

on a show for them. They aren't worth it, baby. You know how much you mean to me..."

Aly and I just stood there, silent. I personally was in shock. Here was Grace Barnes standing before me, and she was actually dumping this slutty troll because she was being a bitch to me. I think Aly was either waiting for me to spout off again, or she was waiting for Daeva to come after me. Either way, she wasn't going to allow either to happen. I knew better than to test her. The look on her face was downright scary.

"Daeva, I have told you since I lost her that I need Kris in my life for it to be complete. Yes, I fucked up majorly by having an affair with you. And trust me when I say that you are not even remotely close to being as skilled at kissing or in bed as that woman is," Grace said, motioning toward me. I blushed; I know it. "Kris, on her worst day, can bring you to climax by just kissing you. Let alone what she can do with her tongue."

"Amen to that," Aly interjected, causing us all to turn and look at her. "Shit, sorry, that was out loud, wasn't it?"

"Yeah, it truly was," Grace said, smirking as Aly turned a very dark shade of red. "But you are correct. Amen to Kris' talents."

"Grace, Snookie," Daeva pleaded. "Don't do this. I love you."

"Ew," I said involuntarily as I shuddered. I received glares from both Grace and Aly. I mouthed 'sorry' to them. I seriously hadn't meant for anything to come out like that.

"Daeva, I have told you that you are *never* to call me Snookie. I am not your fucking pet or stuffed animal. Now, we're done. Good-bye. Stay out of my life."

"How will you get home? Baby, let me drive you, and we can talk about this."

"I'll give you a ride, Grace." We all turned and looked at Aly. "I don't think you are in any condition to be dealing with much more. Kris and I are parked not far from here."

"Thanks," Grace said softly.

I wasn't sure how I felt about this, but the fact that she had just broken up with Daeva, maybe there was still hope for us as friends. After the hurt passed and trust was rebuilt, maybe we could salvage something. It was definitely going to take time.

Daeva stormed away, and Aly wrapped an arm around Grace's waist and helped her walk toward where we were parked. I noticed then how much physical pain Grace was truly in. I didn't notice it before because I had been too fixated on the slutty troll. Once we got in the car, my petty side took over, and I started to hum to myself, or I thought it was to myself. I was in the back seat so I didn't realize how loud I was actually humming.

"Kris, babe, what are you singing?" asked Aly. I saw her eyes glance at me in the rearview mirror.

"Um, nothing," I said. I couldn't tell them what the words were going through my head. They may both kill me.

"Come on, Kris. You always had some melody tweaked to your own amusement when we were kids. What is it this time?"

I looked at the two women and said, "And nobody is going to be pissed or hurt me?" They both nodded, so I sang my song for them.

"Ding dong the evil bitch is gone. Ding dong the

evil troll is gone. She was a plague. She destroyed a lot, but in the end, the evil spirit lost and I won. She can kiss my ass. I don't care. Ding dong the evil bitch is gone."

"That is horrible, Kris." Grace was smiling when she said it. She always loved my songs.

"Babe, why do you call her an evil spirit?" asked Aly. "You've said that before about her."

"I looked up her name…it means evil spirit."

Both Aly and Grace rolled their eyes at me, but I saw smirks touch the corners of their mouth. I sat back and hummed my song while we drove Grace home. Aly helped her inside, and then she and I went home.

❧❧❧❧

A couple of weeks after the Farmer's Market incident, I was flipping channels when Aly came in to the living room, flopped down on the couch next to me, and put her head in my lap. I instinctively started running my fingers through her hair. "Hey, gorgeous."

"Hi. It has been a couple of weeks, and I was wondering if you were ready to talk about what happened with Grace?" My hand stopped when Aly said this.

I don't know if I was in denial or if it was just wishful thinking, but I was really hoping not to have this conversation.

"Um, okay," I said. I started to play with her hair again. This time I think it was more of a nervous habit than an affectionate reason.

"How are you doing with it?"

"I don't know, I guess okay." I wasn't convinced with what I said, and Aly didn't look like she was convinced either.

"Kris, you don't have to be okay with it. You can be conflicted or pissed off."

"I don't know what I feel, honestly. The bottom line is that Grace and her family all lied to me, I know it was more than once, so I have to question a lot of what the Barnes' have said and done over the years. Plus, Grace cheated on me. That's a pretty huge betrayal. Trust has always been a hard thing for me. What they did hasn't made it any easier."

"I know, and that is why I wanted to talk about things. I know how your mind works overtime. And it usually isn't in your favor."

I smiled down at her. She wasn't wrong, but I was trying not to think about things.

"Aly, I don't know what to do. I mean, yeah, it was cool that Grace dumped Daeva. And yeah, it was cool as hell to see it happen, but what does she want or expect from me? How do I trust her again? I just don't know." I let out an exasperated sigh.

"We'll figure it out, babe. I ran into Grace today. She wants to sit down and talk with you. At least start opening the lines communication."

"Why?"

"Kris, you were her best friend for twenty years. She misses you in her life. I haven't known you nearly that long, and I know I'd be lost without you." Aly liked to flirt with me even though she had already won my heart. I have to admit, I enjoyed it as well. Aly sat up, took my face in her hands, and pulled me in for a gentle kiss.

"So, what do you think I should do?"

"Do you miss Grace?"

"That depends. I miss her until I remember what

she did, and then I don't. I go numb, actually."

"Do you think you can ever forgive her?"

"I don't know, I'd love to say yes, but I don't know. I don't know that I am that big of a person. What do you think I should do?" I looked to Aly on this one. I knew that I was too emotionally scarred to make a good decision. Plus, it was going to affect her as well.

Aly explained how she felt about Grace and me becoming friends again and that she thought that I should try to forgive Grace. Aly said that she hoped that Grace and I would be close friends again. I told her that I would try, but I wasn't making promises, and I knew that it was going to take a lot of work for both Grace and me to move forward.

The following week, Aly invited Grace over for dinner. I was still on the fence on if this was a good idea or not, but I was willing to try. Or, I promised Aly I would try. I heard the door buzzer go off and knew that it was now or never. I took a deep breath and headed into the living room.

"You ready, gorgeous?" Aly asked, before kissing me softly on the lips when I met her in the living room.

"As ready as I am going to be," I said.

There was a knock on the door. Aly kissed the side of my head and went to answer it. I could hear her and Grace exchanging pleasantries. Then there she was the ex-love of my life.

I waved as they came into the living room. "Hi."

"Hey." Grace smiled but avoided making eye contact with me. This was something she did to avoid facing whatever she wasn't comfortable with in a situation.

"Okay, now I am going to go and make dinner while you two start talking. And, I mean talking. None of this staring at one another or looking at the walls shit. Talk. I have a wooden spoon, and I am *not* afraid to use it."

Grace and I nodded and then watched Aly leave the room. Now, this felt awkward. Here I was, sitting with Grace and I was scared to talk with her.

"Would she really use the spoon?"

"Yeah, she isn't shy about that shit," I replied, laughing.

"Okay then…"

"How are you doing? Are you still in a lot of pain?" I asked to keep us from going back to the silence.

"I'm okay. I have good days and bad days with the pain. The doctor told me that I appear to be healing okay, but the plate they put in my arm and the screws in my knee and ankle, those will take some extra time. The good news is that there will be no real long lasting effects from the accident."

"That's good."

"Wanna feel the screws?"

"Hell no, that's gross."

"Come on." Grace lifted her pant leg a bit and I could see the marks on her ankle where they put the pins in. I did a full body shiver. "You are such a wuss."

"Bite me, Barnes."

"Hey, she will not bite you. Do you hear me?" Aly raised a wooden spoon and Grace and I started to laugh as Aly came over and kissed the top of my head before heading back into the kitchen.

"I'm sorry about Daeva," said Grace.

"Listen, Grace, I have given this a lot of thought. I don't think I will ever forget the pain that I felt the day you told me that you cheated on me, or the realization that…well, we all know. I also won't forget that you and your family lied to me. But, I am willing to work to move past some of the wonky feelings and see what we have after that."

"I want my best friend back, Kris. My life is lonely and incomplete without you in it. I know I have a long way to go to prove to you that I mean it when I say I'm sorry and none of it will ever happen again."

"What else did you lie to me about?" I asked, bluntly. "I don't just mean the Daeva shit. I mean over the years. I'm having a hard time wrapping my head around her being the breakpoint for you to start lying to me."

"I promise you I never lied about anything else. The only reason that I slept with and started dating Daeva was because, well, you know me when I drink. I turn into a ball of hormones with wandering hands."

"No wine for Grace," muttered Aly, playfully. "Set the table with a butcher knife by my side in case of wandering hands." Neither of us had heard Aly enter the room.

"Babe, didn't we agree that it was rude to maim our guests?"

"We did, but it is different if the hands are touching what is mine," Aly playfully whined and pouted as she sat down next to me.

I wrapped my arm around Aly's shoulder and kissed the side of her head. "I know it is, but we cannot maim Grace."

"Yet, you mean yet, right?"

"Yes, baby, I mean yet."

"As much as it hurts and it does hurt, you two are cute together. Although, I seem to recall, Kris, you saying in college that you would never date Aly," Grace pointed out.

"Shush you."

"No, sweetie, she's right. I remember…oh, what was it? Oh, right, 'I wouldn't do you with a hazmat suit and a twenty-foot pole,' if memory serves correctly me, that is."

I turned several shades of red. I knew that I did because I felt the flush of the color change. I didn't think that either of them would have remembered that. Or maybe I was just hoping that neither would remember that.

"Don't I smell dinner burning?" I asked, trying to get out of this before anyone recalled anything else that I said.

"No, but I am going to go finish making dinner."

Aly leaned over to kiss me, and I pulled back from her. "You want me to kiss you after you just embarrassed me?"

"Yes, now give me a kiss." I obeyed and kissed her softly. "And anyway, Grace started it."

I gave her another chaste kiss before she bounced off to the kitchen to finish dinner.

"How does life get so messed up?" Grace asked.

"I don't know, Grace. I really don't know."

The rest of the night went off without a hitch. There was no dwelling on the past; there were no more apologies. We just simply enjoyed one another's company. Grace didn't drink, so Aly didn't have to maim her. The night was left with Grace and me agreeing to process our feelings and call each other when we were done. I knew that I would take longer than Grace, but I also had Aly; she was something very positive that came out my broken heart.

As I worked to put things back together with the Barnes family, to rebuild the relationship that we once had, life moved forward. Aly and I found a small house to get together. It was a small three bedroom, two baths, ranch style house with a finished basement. It was on a quiet street not too far from our apartment. We had made a deal with the owners that it would be a longer than normal closing since they still hadn't found a new place. Grace gave me a lot of crap for the fact that I was becoming domesticated and buying a house and settling down. One day, Grace and I were walking around town looking for something for me to get Aly for our anniversary.

"I can't believe that you, Kristine Holt of all people, bought a house."

"Why not?"

"Okay, it isn't so much that you bought the house, it is that you bought the house *with* someone." Grace looked me in the eyes and laughed.

"Yeah, well, I love her, what more can I say?" I gave Grace a cheesy grin.

"Less, please say less, because, ew, I don't want to know the details of your love life."

"You're just jealous," I said, sticking my tongue out at her.

"Damn right. How is it fair that you have a better more stable love life than I do?"

"I'm damn cute, and according to you both, I'm awesome in bed."

"Yeah, yeah, rub it in."

We continued to look and then I found it, the one perfect gift for Aly for our anniversary. Grace was busy looking at other things so she didn't see what I bought. That truly was my plan. This was going to be a special anniversary. I was going to prove to Aly that the romance wasn't slipping and that we were still so perfect together.

⁂

Beep...beep...beep...the sound surrounded me. I could smell the faintest hint of perfume. I did not know that scent. I heard the sound of footsteps getting closer and closer. I felt something cold touch my arm. It was brief, but after it was pulled away, I could still feel the cold resonating through my arm. I tried to open my eyes, but they wouldn't open.

"Such a pity," said an unfamiliar voice.

I tried to open my mouth to speak, but no sound came out. The beeping continued. It was steady most of the time; there were occasional lags, or it would speed up.

I heard the sound of feet shuffling away again. I tried to move, but I couldn't. I started to struggle and the beeping got louder and faster. I relaxed, and it slowed down. Who was doing this? Why were they monitoring me? What was going on?

It was silent again. Silent except for the rhythmic beeping of the machine. After listening to it for so long, it had become hypnotic. I couldn't move, I couldn't speak, I couldn't see, but I could hear. Was I tied up? Or, more accurately was I tied down to the bed? Was there a gag over my mouth? I didn't feel one, but I could not speak. Was there a blindfold over my eyes? Was I blind? Why could I not see?

I heard the sound of a door opening and then softly closing. I heard footsteps again, coming toward me. There was the coldness on my arm again.

"At least you are holding your own," said a female voice. "Most people in your position just give up, quit fighting, and quit trying. Don't let them win."

What was she talking about? Who gives up? Why? Who was I stopping from winning? What the hell was going on? I wanted so badly to talk to her, to move so that she would tell me more. But I just laid there like a turd.

I heard the footsteps, the door, and then nothing again. I tried to force my limbs to move, but I knew they wouldn't. I tried to force myself to speak. I think I heard a grunt. That was something. Maybe I could get someone's attention when they came in next. I practiced until I was too tired to practice anymore. I must have drifted to sleep.

I woke feeling someone touching my neck this time. I let out a grunt. I felt the hand on my neck stop moving. I grunted again. I needed to know that they heard me. Please, say something.

"Keep it up, and I'll crush your air pipe," said the deep voice. I knew that voice. Sonofabitch, it was my father. "You grunt again, and I will kill you right here, right now."

I stayed quiet. I know he wouldn't think twice about doing it. I felt his hands wrap around my throat and then, there was no more air. I couldn't breathe.

"See how easy it would be? I could crush your windpipe, I could break your neck, and you are helpless to do anything."

"Kris, honey?" I heard Aly say as my eyes shot open.

I could see. I could breathe. Oh god, I was panting and light headed. Don't pass out, don't pass out. I pleaded with my body. My eyes met Aly's eyes.

"Aly?" I managed to croak out. My voice was very ragged. It hurt to speak.

"Yeah, babe. I'm right here. You're okay. You're safe."

I rolled on my side and cuddled into her embrace. I could feel my body shaking as she held me tighter. I don't know how long we stayed like that, but I was so grateful that Aly didn't try to make me move.

I felt her lips on my head. I felt the air from her nose on my ear, and I heard her whisper in my ear. "You are safe, my love. I will never let anything happen to you."

"Why does this keep happening?" I asked, softly. I could still feel the pressure of my father's hands on my neck, the ease at which he could kill me.

"I don't know, but we'll figure it out. Do you want to talk about it?"

I laughed and told her no, but I needed to or I was going to dwell on it. I told Aly about the nightmare, the helpless feeling that I had. How I hurt, but I didn't. I felt as though I were in limbo. I told her about what the woman said about my fighting and others giving up. Neither of us knew what to make of this. I told her what my father was doing. I showed her where he had placed his hands on my throat. I stopped when I saw the tears forming in her eyes. I hated that these nightmares didn't only hurt me, they hurt the woman I loved. Aly kissed the spots on my throat where the hands had been.

Later that day, I had just finished with the dishes when I overheard Aly on the phone. She was relaying what I had told her to someone. Why? Why would she do this?

"Aly?" I said, entering the room.

"Hi, sweetie. Would you be okay if Grace came over, and we all hung out for a bit?"

"Yeah, that's fine." I agreed, but I also resented that fact that she had told Grace about my dream. She had done this without my permission. We had agreed early on that anything that I dreamt was private, and she needed to check with me before telling anyone.

I puttered around the house until Grace arrived. Mysteriously, once Grace arrived, Aly had to leave for an errand.

"So, you get to babysit the freak, huh?" I asked, my tone more snide than joking.

"I am not babysitting, and you are not a freak. Stop talking like that," Grace snapped.

"Why? You don't think that I know that she told you about my nightmare?" I saw Grace's eyes widen when I said that. "Yeah, I overheard her. Is she afraid to be alone with me?"

"Kris, it is nothing like that. Yes, she did tell me about your dream, but she is concerned. Aly loves you, you know this."

"Then why did she arrange for me to have a babysitter? Is she afraid I'm going to do something stupid?"

"Should she be? Did you ever think that I might have asked for some time alone with you? Kris, I know you better than you know yourself."

"Did you ask to be alone with me?"

"Yes. Are you going to hurt yourself?"

"No, I'm not. I promised you years ago that I wouldn't."

"Good. Now tell me what you didn't tell Aly about the dream. I know that there is more to it than what you told Aly."

I told Grace every detail about my dream that I could remember. She seemed shocked at the level of detail that I had. After I told her, we talked about what we thought it meant. Mostly I told her that I was scared at how real it felt.

"Have you thought about going back to a therapist?"

I knew Grace was asking to be helpful, and I tried to tone down my anger when I answered her. "No, after those two broke my trust and tried to have me committed for that special study, I don't trust them."

"They aren't all like that, Kris."

"I am sure they aren't, but I'm not willing to take that chance."

"I respect that but promise me that you'll at least be as candid as possible with me. I know you hold shit back from Aly to protect her. Which you know you don't have to, right?" I nodded. "Good. She loves you a lot."

"And that is why I hold stuff back. I know how much she loves me and how much it hurts her to hear some of the details. I don't really like telling you everything either, but like you said, you know me better than I know myself."

"We'll figure it out and how to get them to stop. You won't be in this alone, ever."

"Thanks. I just hate feeling like a burden."

"Well, you aren't, so stop it and let those of us that care about you help."

Chapter Fourteen

Roses in the vase, check. Candles lit, check. Dinner cooking and not burning, check. I wanted this night to be perfect. I mean, honestly, how many three-year anniversaries do you get with the woman you love?

I had been planning this night for a month. I had finally decided that I was ready to ask Aly to marry me. That is right. I, Kristine Holt, was truly ready to settle down. No, I wasn't drunk, nor had I been hit on the head. I had finally accepted how much I love Aly. I hadn't thought after what happened with Grace that I would get to this spot, but I was happier than I had ever been in my life.

I looked at the clock and saw that I had just enough time to shower, get dressed, and put the rose petals on the bed. Aly was going to be so surprised with all that I have done. I wasn't the most romantic person. Oh hell, I sucked at romance, but I wanted tonight to be special. Something memorable for her and me to look back on.

After I showered and slipped into a silky little black dress I had picked up for tonight, I finished the rest of the prep work for the night, and then I sat on the couch and waited for Aly to get home. The living room had an overstuffed brown leather couch with built in recliners, with a matching loveseat and two leather chairs. The sofa faced a wood-burning fireplace with an aged wood mantle. I was especially proud of the mantelpiece as I had been the one to build, stain, and install it. I looked at the clock and started to hope and pray that Aly would be home soon. Thankfully, I didn't have to wait too long. If I had to wait much longer, I'm certain my overactive brain would have tried to talk me out of what I had planned. I heard Aly's car pull into the driveway just as my anxieties kicked in. What if she said that she didn't want to marry me? Dammit brain, shut the hell up.

"Hey, sexy," I said as I opened the door for her.

"Wow, you look incredible," Aly said, entering and kissing me softly. "Why is it so dark in here?"

"Well, it is our anniversary," I said, taking her hand and leading her into the living room. I picked up the single rose I had set on the coffee table. "I love you."

"I love you, too," she said as she sniffed the rose and gave me a coy smile. "What else do you have planned?"

"Well, you are just going to have to wait and see. Dinner should be ready soon. You have time to get out of your work stuff."

Aly went and changed into a blue dress that I had laid out on our bed. We sat on the couch and cuddled until the timer went off in the kitchen. I went and got dinner and brought the plates out before I led Aly to the table.

"Wow, more roses and candlelight. I'm not sure what to make of this."

"I know it isn't my usual, but, I am trying to work on the things that we talked about last week."

"Thank you for that," Aly said, before she kissed me...deeply.

"You keep kissing me like that, and we aren't going to get to eat."

"Oh, we'll eat," she said, wiggling her eyebrows and then laughing as she heard my audible gulp. She had no idea what she was doing to me.

We ate, we kissed, we shared wine, and enjoyed being close. After I cleaned up dinner, I found myself pulled into an embrace as I entered the living room. Aly had turned on some soft music and we danced, close. My arms wrapped around her neck as she wrapped her arms around my waist. As we danced, I softly whispered in Aly's ear that I had a gift for her.

"Baby, you didn't have to get me anything. What you have done here tonight is more than enough. I mean, this whole night has been dreamy."

"I am glad that you are enjoying the night, but this gift is something that is long overdue," I said. We sat down on the couch and I reached behind one of the pillows on the couch, pulled a thin rectangle box, and handed it to her. "Happy anniversary, my love."

Aly took the box and I held my breath as she turned it in her hands before she started to open it. I could see the apprehension in her eyes. I knew she couldn't have guessed what it was. I had been so resistant to the idea of making any big commitment since she first asked me on our one-year anniversary. It wasn't that I didn't love her and hadn't wanted to be close to her. It was that after everything that had gone on with Grace, her lying and cheating, I was hesitant. I felt that by remaining in the 'darting' status that I was keeping my own space and independence. Yes, we had bought a house together, but I still felt as though it wasn't that intense of a commitment. People sold houses every day.

"Kris, baby, you need to breathe," Aly said.

"Sorry," I said as I let the breath that I had been holding out.

I watched as she opened the lid to the box, her eyes gazing at the bracelet that was inside. I could tell she was confused as to what it was or what it meant.

"What?" she said in a confused tone.

"I love you, with all my heart and soul," I said. I pulled the bracelet out of the box and affixed it on her wrist. I could see the bewilderment in her eyes. I had just put a small diamond ID bracelet on her.

Aly continued to look at me and then she inspected the bracelet closer. Her eyes widened when she read the inscription.

"Are you serious? You want me to marry you? This isn't something you joke about, Kris."

"Yes, I am very serious. I want to make love to you in our bed as my wife, shower with my wife in our shower. I want to come home to you, my wife, nightly. Please, say yes."

"Yes, yes, I will marry you," she said, tears rolling down her face. She leaned over and kissed me soundly.

I reached into the box and below the velvet padding that the bracelet had sat on was a ring that I had hidden. I was going to keep it in my pocket, but then I found the dress and had to improvise. I slipped the ring on her finger and then kissed her hand.

"Take me to our bed and make love to me."

"My pleasure, my amazingly beautiful fiancée."

That night we made love for hours. When we finally drifted to sleep, I felt as though we were one.

"Aly, I can't believe that you tamed the one and only Kristine Holt," Grace said one night when we were out at the bar celebrating our engagement.

"You make it sound like I'm a wild animal," I said defensively as I felt Aly wrap her arms around me from behind and her chin rest on my shoulder.

"You have your moments," Aly growled, before she nipped at my neck, causing my eyes to flutter closed.

"Ew, hello, none of that."

"Why not?" I teased Grace as I leaned into Aly's embrace.

"Why not? Because, I'm single and not getting any. I don't want to see you two getting all hot and bothered."

"You can live vicariously through us," Aly said as she pulled me closer and, using a single finger, turned my head and teased my lips with her tongue before bringing our lips together.

"Ew, gross! I've had Kris. I already know how good she is…now you and I…" Grace joked, wiggling her eyebrows, calling Aly's bluff and making her blush.

"Sweetheart, you have to watch out, playing sexual chicken with her. She has very few fears and very little inhibitions," I said, before kissing Aly on the tip of her nose and then turning to Grace. "As for you, eyes and paws off my woman."

"Awww, you are so cute when you go all cave woman." Grace pinched my cheeks and laughed as I blushed.

We danced and they drank for a few more hours before saying our good-byes. Grace went her way, and Aly and I made our way home.

"You were really cute when you got all protective

of me," Aly said, running her finger up and down my arm as I tried to drive us home.

"Well, you just bring that side out of me," I said as we stopped at a stoplight. I leaned over and kissed her. The kiss left us both breathless and with a new urgency to get home.

❧ ❧ ❧ ❧

Life for us was great for the first six months of our engagement, and then I started to feel like the walls were closing in on me. Aly wanted to know where I was, what I was doing, when I was going to be home. She wanted me to account for every minute of the day. I felt smothered. Getting engaged was a huge step for me, but this control that she felt the need to have over my free time was getting a bit unnerving.

"When are you going to be home?" Aly asked as we were getting ready for work.

"It's going to be late. I have meetings all day, so I am going to have to stay to make up the work that I wasn't able to get done during the day."

"Do you want me to bring you some dinner while you work?"

"No, I will just grab something out of the Wheel-of-Death."

"That isn't healthy."

"I know, but for tonight it will be fine. I love you for wanting to bring me dinner, though."

"Well, if you change your mind, just let me know."

I smiled and kissed her before heading to work. I would never eat out of the Wheel-of-Death, but tonight was my night to myself. I wasn't really going to be making up what I couldn't get done during my meetings; I was going to relax and read. I know what you are thinking. Yes, relationships are built on trust and honesty, but dammit, she wasn't giving me any room to breathe. We had only been engaged for six months. Six short little months. One hundred and eighty days.

⁂⁂⁂⁂

I didn't stay late often, maybe once every week or two. I just needed some time to myself. Over the next couple of months, Aly was understanding, but then she started to get suspicious. I didn't blame her; hell, I was the one that was lying to her. That was when the fights started. We had some seriously intense ones. And then there was the night that it all came to a head.

"Well, it was nice of you to come home," Aly slurred as I entered the front door. She was sitting on the couch, a bottle of wine on the table in front of her.

"What do you mean by 'it was nice of you to come home?' I live here, with you. Where else would I be going?" I asked her as I entered the living room and sat down on the couch near her.

"I'm not sure, it isn't like I know where you really are when you are out late like this," she slurred and tried to move away from me.

"You're drunk," I stated.

"What the hell do you care? I'm drunk and you lie. Aren't we a good fucking pair?" she snapped and then downed the last half of the oversized wine glass she had been holding.

"Baby, I don't want to fight with you…"

"I asked you a question. Where have you been?"

"I was at work. I told you that."

I could see the doubt in her eyes. I could feel the room getting colder and colder.

"I was there, jackass, now, let's try this again. Where have you been?"

"You were where? I don't understand."

"I was at your work," she said as she poured the last of the bottle of wine into her glass.

"When were you at work?" I asked, completely baffled by what she was saying. I didn't know if she was dreaming this because of the wine, or what I should think. I had been at the office the whole night. I was down in the break room for most of it.

"I brought dinner for you. You always say that you are going to get something there. I was trying to be sweet and bring you dinner. The joke was on me."

"Alyssa," I started and got up off the couch and walked toward the fireplace at the end of the room.

"Kristine," she replied in the same tone, before downing the rest of the wine.

"I was still at work. I was in the break room for most of the night."

"Bullshit. Why must you lie to me? I am not as stupid as you give me credit for being. Are you that stupid?" she yelled, before hurling the oversized wine glass at the fireplace that I was standing next to. It shattered into a million pieces.

I felt several stings on my face and arms. It took several moments before I realized that the pain I was feeling were cuts from the shattered glass.

"Oh, god. Kris? Baby, I am so sorry…"

"Don't," I said, fighting to contain my shock and anger. I couldn't look in her direction. I wanted to, but I just couldn't.

After a minute of standing there gathering my

composure, I turned and walked passed the couch, avoiding her arm as she extended it, trying to reach me. I could hear her crying. Well, it was more of a drunken wail. I went to the master bath, closed, and locked the door behind me. At that moment, I didn't care about my wounds; I let gravity take over and my body slid down the door until I was sitting on the floor. That is when I started to cry. I didn't cry often, but when it happened, I was unable to control it. I have no clue how long I sat there crying. At some point, I heard Aly come into the bedroom and knock on the door. I didn't respond. She begged me to open the door, but I couldn't move. I was frozen there on the floor.

"Kris, please. I am so sorry. Let me help you get cleaned up," she cried through the door. "Please, open the door."

It was a long time before I responded. "Just leave me alone."

I heard her start to cry harder. I didn't know what else to do. I pulled my phone out of my pocket and sent a message to Grace, asking if I could stay at her house tonight. I needed to be out of this place. Grace replied immediately and said that she had been waiting for me to message her. I guess Aly had already messaged her. I love that my fiancée screwed up and then messaged my best friend. Now I needed to clean up a bit, pack, and then manage to get out of the house.

I washed the blood off my arms and face. I found a couple of small pieces of glass embedded in my arms, but nothing in my face, thankfully. I cautiously opened the door and looked around for Aly. I saw that she was passed out on the bed. I quickly went into the closet, packed a few things, and slipped out into the living room. I stopped and stared at the fireplace. I could see the mark on the wooden mantel where the glass had hit and shattered. Six-inches or so to the left and that would have been a dead-on shot to my face. I shook my head and then grabbed a piece of paper out of the desk near the fireplace and wrote Aly a note.

"*Aly,*

I have gone to stay at Grace's house for at least tonight. Please, give me some space to process what happened tonight. You know that I was abused as a child. You know how bad the nightmares have been over the years. This has brought up some very deep scars/memories/feelings. I will call you when I am able to talk and we'll see where things stand.

I love you.

Kris"

I placed the note on the table where I knew Aly would see it. I grabbed my stuff and walked out the door, locking it behind me.

Chapter Fifteen

When I pulled up outside of Grace's house, I took a deep breath. I looked toward the house, and she was already outside on the porch. I smiled to myself, knowing that I could always count on her. We had been through some good and bad times over the years, but no matter what had happened, we found a way to get one another through the bad times. This was one of those bad times.

"Hey," I said softly as I walked up to the porch, trying to hide my face. The long sleeves I had put on covered my arms.

"Hey," Grace said. The tone of her voice caused me to glance up, and when I did, I heard her gasp. "What the hell happened to your face? Are you okay? My…wha…get inside."

I followed Grace inside, set my stuff down in front of the couch, and then plopped down and went to bury my face in my hands when I hit one of the cuts and flinched. Grace sat down next to me and pulled me into her arms. That was all it took, and I lost my composure again and started to cry.

"What happened, Kris? Talk to me."

"I don't know what to say."

"Well, you need to come up with something…" Grace spat. I knew that tone. She was in her defensive mode. The last time I heard her like that, she almost beat someone up. I didn't need her doing that to Aly.

"Aly and I had a fight," I started.

"No shit. I gathered that part when she called me, drunk and crying, telling me that she had hurt you and that you had locked yourself in the bathroom."

"Well, if you knew that much, why'd you have to ask?" I snapped, looking up at Grace before relenting. "Sorry. She has been smothering me lately, and I have been taking time to myself, claiming to be working late. Tonight was one of those nights. I guess she brought me dinner, but when she didn't find me in my office, she assumed I was lying and wasn't at the office."

"Were you there?"

"Yeah, I was in the break room most of the night. A couple of nights per month, I stay late just to get some time to myself. I miss reading. She doesn't let me do that when we're home."

"So then what happened?"

"When I got home, she was drunk. She accused me of lying, and we went back and forth, then she threw one of those oversized wine glasses she likes so much at the fireplace that I happened to be standing next to. The glass shattered and well," I said, showing Grace my arms and the couple of marks on my face that my hair mostly covered.

"Geez, do you need to go to the ER or something?"

"No, they are all pretty superficial. I pulled some glass out of a couple of the cuts, but the others I didn't see anything."

"Kris, you cannot be so blasé about this. The glass could have seriously hurt you. It could have cut your artery, or gotten in your eye. I, ugh," Grace said in frustration. "I thought she was good for you. I never in my life thought she would hurt you."

"She didn't do it on purpose. And they aren't

that deep, so no arteries are in danger of being cut."

"I don't give a frilly fuck if she did it because purple elephants were holding auditions in her ass for a new musical. She had no right!"

I couldn't keep a straight face. I started to giggle, which pissed Grace off more.

"This isn't funny, Kris. You could have been seriously hurt."

"I know that, but seriously, you want me to keep a straight and serious face after you give me that image? Her ass isn't all that big either. It could be a tight fit." I continued to giggle until Grace joined in.

"That was good, wasn't it?"

"Very, and I love you for being my best friend and worrying. I am okay, physically. Mentally…"

"Oh, honey, you have never been mentally okay," she teased. "Come with me. I want to double check those wounds, and then we're going to get some sleep. You can share my bed, but don't try any funny stuff."

"You didn't mind the last time I did," I teased.

"Yeah, but that was years ago."

"Oh, but, Grace, I have learned some very new tricks," I taunted. It was fun trying to distract Grace and calm her anger.

"Ugh, dammit, this is serious. I am worried about you."

"I know you are, but really, I'm okay. Let's go play doctor so that we can get some sleep."

⚘ ⚘ ⚘ ⚘

"Mom, may I go outside and play with Grace?" I heard my timid voice say.

"No, you go back to your room and be quiet," she

snapped as she grabbed her tumbler full of ice and a bronze liquid with one hand and brought the cigarette in her other hand to her mouth.

I sniffled loudly, causing my mother to turn and look at me again.

"I said go back to your room. You can stop that sniffling shit. One more noise like that and I will give you a reason to sniffle."

"Yes, ma'am," I said as I turned and walked toward the doorway.

There was a loud crash on the wall next to me and then I felt the spray of liquid on my face. I looked up to see the wet mark on the wall and then I looked down to see the shattered tumbler and ice.

"You ever sass me again, and I'll break your arm," spat the woman as she lit another cigarette.

I nodded and hurried out of the room and back to my bedroom. I cowered in the corner, trying to make myself small enough to disappear.

"Girl, get out here," called my father hours later.

I slowly emerged from my room and walked out to where he was standing in the doorway of the kitchen.

"I hear you were sassing your mother. Didn't I tell you never to do that?"

"Yes, sir," came my scared little voice.

"You clean up that glass, and then you are going to be punished," said my father as he removed his belt from his pants.

As I cleaned up the glass, I cut my fingers several times. Thankfully, I had a black shirt on and could wipe the blood there and not get in trouble. Once the floor was clean, I hesitantly went into the living room to receive my punishment. My father picked up the belt and hit my backside six times. One time for each year of my short *little life. I knew that school for the next couple of days was going to be really hard. My father put the belt down and grabbed my arm tightly.*

"This is becoming a bad habit, and if it doesn't stop, we are going to have to look at new forms of punishment. Do I make myself clear?" he snapped.

"No more," I practically yelled as I sat up in bed, panting and feeling completely disorientated.

"It's okay, Kris," Grace said, sitting up next to me.

Grace and I sat there together for a very long few minutes. Me trying to catch my breath, and Grace waiting until the episode had passed so that she could comfort me. Once I felt calm enough, I nodded and Grace wrapped her arms around me and held me close.

"Which one was this?" she asked. "It isn't often you wake yourself up screaming."

"One of the oldies, but goodies. It was one from when I was six, and my mom threw her glass at me as I left the kitchen."

"Of course, Alyssa throwing her glass brought it up, I bet."

"I don't disagree, but she isn't like them."

"No, she isn't, but that doesn't excuse what she did."

As we sat there, I heard Grace's phone buzz. She reached for it and rolled her eyes. When I asked whom it was from, she told me that it was from Aly. I leaned over and started to read the conversation as it unfolded.

Aly: *"Grace, please tell me she is there with you... I'm worried."*

"I left her a note."

Grace: *"Yeah, she's here. She said she left you a*

note. How could you? You know what her childhood was like!"

Aly: *"I messed up. Tell Kris I'm sorry…I love her so much."*

Grace: *"Actions speak louder than words."*

Aly: *"You are one to talk. I get that you are pissed…Can you ask Kris to message me when she feels ready? Please."*

Grace: *"Fine. Not that you deserve for her to do that, though."*

"You were a bit hard on her, weren't you?" I asked Grace.

"No, I wasn't. She hurt you both physically and emotionally. She is the reason that you had to relive that horrible nightmare. I will not cut her some slack or be nice. You are my best friend and that means that I will always look out for you."

"Thanks, Grace," I said, before a large yawn overtook me.

"Do you think you can sleep again?"

"I have no idea, but I'll try."

We lay down and got comfortable. Grace placed one of her hands on my back to help ground me. I drifted off to sleep. When I woke a few hours later, I was pretty out of it, but within seconds, the memory of the previous night came racing back. I let out a loud groan before getting out of bed and following the scent of freshly brewed coffee.

"Good morning," Grace said as I entered the kitchen.

"Good morning." I grabbed a mug off the counter and went to pour myself a cup.

"How are you feeling?"

"Emotionally, not so great. Physically, stiff and

a bit sore."

"You know that you are welcome to stay here as long as you want."

"I know and I appreciate that," I said, putting a hand on my friend's shoulder. "I need to get home today."

"Can't you make her sweat it out another day? She needs to learn that what she did was wrong."

"She knows that."

"How do you know that she knows that?"

"She sent me plenty of text messages overnight. I told her that I wasn't going to work today, and that I would come home, and we could talk."

"Are you sure?"

"Yeah, I am. I also made sure that she knew that you were not happy with her, and that you wouldn't be happy with the idea of me going back there."

"Well, you got that right," Grace said as she took a bite of her breakfast.

"I love her, Grace. I need to try to make this work. I failed us. I don't think I get another chance if I blow this one."

"You didn't fail us. I did that. I am the jackass that cheated on you. I think the reason I am still single is my own punishment for that. Or, maybe it is because you are a very hard woman to get over."

"Shut up." I laughed and rolled my eyes at her.

We finished eating and I went and changed. I hugged Grace before heading back to my place. I have to admit that I wasn't really thrilled with the idea of going back there, but I had to be an adult and face the issues and not hide from them. I did enough hiding as a kid.

❧ ❧ ❧ ❧

When I got home, I saw that Aly's car wasn't there. I won't deny that I felt relieved that she wasn't there. I know that she was drunk and didn't mean to hurt me, but as the nightmare I had proved, I was damaged and still had a lot of things from my past to deal with. When I entered the house, I could smell the scent of coffee. I was grateful that it wasn't the smell of stale liquor. I had enough of that growing up. I saw a piece of paper on the table next to the one that I had left for Aly the night before.

"Kris,

I had to run out for a bit. I will be back by ten and then maybe we can talk about things.

Love always and forever,

Aly"

I looked at my watch and saw that I had about thirty minutes before she would be back. That, I thought, would give me time to go shower, get changed, and prepare myself for this. True as she said, at ten on the dot, I heard Aly's car pull into the garage. I was seated at the breakfast bar. I had tried to sit in the living room, but my mind just kept playing tricks on me.

"Hi," Aly said, sheepishly as she walked toward me.

"Hi," I said, unable to meet her gaze.

"Why are you sitting here?"

"My mind was messing with me in the living room," I said as she sat down on the stool next to me.

"I am really sorry about last night. I know that doesn't make up for my actions, but I still want you to know that I know that I was in the wrong. I thought a lot about last night, the things that you said. What did you mean that you were at work?"

"I was in the breakroom most of the night."

"Why?"

"I was starting to feel smothered. So, I thought that if I told you that I was working late, I could get some time to myself, and it wouldn't affect us. I was wrong on that. I'm sorry for not talking to you or telling you the truth."

"Smothered? How in the hell were you feeling smothered?" she said, angrily.

"We spend every minute outside of work together. When I do go out without you, you ask where I am going. Who is it with? When will I be home? Is it really important that I do whatever it is? I'm an adult. I need some space. I love you, but you know me."

"I thought I knew you. I'm not so sure anymore. What else have you lied to me about?"

"Nothing, and don't you pretend that you are squeaky clean and innocent here."

"I have already admitted that I messed up," Aly snapped.

"And now I have admitted to my mistakes. The question is, where do we go from here? What next?"

"I don't know. Why is the living room messing with you? What does that mean?"

"My mother threw a drink at me when I was six. Well, that wasn't the only time, but that was the one I dreamt about last night."

"Oh god," Aly gasped as she covered her mouth with her hand. "I caused that memory to come back, didn't I?"

"You didn't know it would happen. You were drunk and didn't mean to throw the glass. You said that in your messages."

"I bet your mom wasn't sober when she chucked the glasses at you either."

"No, she was rarely sober," I said, staring down at the counter. I had always been ashamed of my past, and this was just bringing it all back up.

Aly wrapped her arms around me and held me close. I don't know why she did it, but I was so grateful that she did. I hated remembering my past and my childhood. I wasn't fond of the dreams, but I could lie to myself and say that those were just that, dreams, things that never really happened. I suppose I could tell myself that I was remembering it wrong, but I had the scars, both emotional and physical, that proved otherwise. I let her hold me for a long time. We cried together, and we comforted each other.

"Come with me," Aly said, taking my hand and leading me toward our bedroom.

"I'm not..." I started to say as she covered my lips with her finger.

"I just want to hold you closer. Those chairs hurt my ass. I don't know how your boney butt can handle them."

"Oh, okay. We can get cushions for the chairs," I said, absently.

"We'll talk about it another time."

With that, Aly lay back on the bed and pulled me close next to her. I have to admit it did feel good to be close. The past twenty-four hours had taken such a toll on me. I drifted to sleep within minutes. When I woke up several hours later, I was alone in bed. I got up and found Aly in our home office, reading a book.

"Hi," she said, looking up over the top of it.

"Hey," I said, still waking up. "I'm sorry I fell asleep."

"Don't be, that was the plan, well, I hoped you would feel comfortable enough to fall asleep."

"I love you, Aly, but some things need to change here if we are to continue."

"I know. Just let me know if I am smothering you. I can change."

"I don't want you to have to change. I just want us to respect one another's personal space and time. I'm sure there are things that you would like to do with your friends that you don't because you know that I wouldn't enjoy it," I explained.

"Yes, but you are my priority."

"You need to be your priority, not me."

"I'll try," she said, offering me a hopeful smile.

Chapter Sixteen

Things between Aly and I were going well. We had set some goals as a couple. One was that we would each be allowed to go out with our friends or by ourselves at least one night per week without the other one asking questions. This wasn't so much an issue with me as it was hard for her. She still had her clingy moments.

Grace and I went out at least once weekly just the two of us, and then sometimes with the three of us. I admit that I cherished the times it was just the two of us. It was just nice to be out without any pressure. Grace had seen the worst of my life. I didn't have to hide anything.

"How come you're still single?" I asked Grace one night while we were out playing pool.

"I haven't found anyone that I want to spend my life with," she replied nonchalantly.

"Are you trying?"

"Are you trying to get rid of me?"

"No! You have been my best friend since we were five. I just want to see you happy."

"I am happy. Plus, I've seen how messed up your life is or has been in the past. Why would I be eager to get myself into that?"

"Asshole," I retorted, bumping shoulders with her. "You get the next round."

"Fine, but you didn't deny my statement either,

so there," she said, sticking her tongue out at me.

"No, I didn't, but then again, you were part of that messed up dating life as well," I replied, sticking my tongue out.

Grace opened and closed her mouth several times as if she were going to reply, but then she flipped me off before turning and walking to the bar to refresh our drinks.

"Hello, Ms. Holt," said a deep male voice from behind me. I turned and saw a large man, easily six feet, six inches tall, weighing in at around three hundred pounds.

"W-who are you? What do you want?"

"I'm a special friend of your father's," he said. His voice was the one that I had heard in my nightmares. I felt a cold chill run down my back.

"What do you want?" I tried to puff out my chest and make myself seem bigger than I was. Let's be honest, five feet eight inches tall, and one hundred and twenty-five pounds. There was no making myself appear that big.

"Your parents have been looking for you, little girl."

"I am an adult. And I have no desire to see or speak to them. By all means, tell them that and to leave me alone."

"Well, we'll see what they think about that." The man smiled at me; his front teeth were rotted and black. "Have a nice evening, Ms. Holt." He turned and left.

I watched him walk away. How had he found me? What did this mean? Were Grace and Aly safe? Dammit. I had just gotten my life in some working order.

"You okay?" Grace asked, setting the drinks down

on the table I was standing next to.

"Huh? Oh, yeah. Sure," I said absently.

"Try again. You are paler than I think I have ever seen you and that is under bar lights. God, I bet you are almost translucent in the light."

"I'm fine, really," I said, unconvincingly. How could I be okay? How was I going to protect the two people I loved and cared most about? "Let's just play another game."

I should have stopped while I was ahead. I went to break, launched the ball off the table, and sent it bouncing down the stairs toward the dance floor. I would love to say that it was just on the break that I did that, but it wasn't. Grace kept trying to pry out of me what was going on, but I just couldn't bring myself to clue her in. Growing up, we had a system of clues that we would use so our parents wouldn't know what we were talking about. It came in handy when I had to miss school because my father had beaten me so badly I could barely move. It was a way for Grace to know I was going to be okay, but at that moment, I wasn't.

After we played that game of pool, Grace thought it would be safer for everyone in the bar if we stopped playing and just sat and relaxed. I got drunker that night than I think I have ever been in my life.

⚜ ⚜ ⚜ ⚜

I don't know when we left the bar, how I got home, how I made it to bed, or more importantly, I have no clue how I didn't end up hospitalized or worse from the amount of alcohol I consumed.

"Ugh," I groaned.

I felt the vestiges of sleep disappear. I wish that

would have been all I felt. Nope, I wasn't that lucky. I felt my stomach turn. I turned over to make a dash to the bathroom when a freight train slammed into my head, knocking me back flat on the bed. Not that I had moved far. Those whole two inches felt like a mile though.

"Yeah, I bet you're hurting," whispered Alyssa. I assume she was whispering, but to my head, she was screaming through a bullhorn into my ear.

I brought my hands up to my head. I had to feel what was left there, because I had never felt pain like I was feeling at that moment. Then the nausea hit again, and I started to gag.

"Oh no, you are *not* barfing in our bed," Aly said as she helped me roll onto my side and to the side of the bed where she had placed the garbage can. "Try to keep it in the can, please."

All I could do was grunt once before the nausea kicked back. I opened my mouth, and the toxic waste I had been smuggling in my stomach erupted. I must have blacked out or something, because the next thing I remembered was Aly wiping my mouth with one rag and pressing a cold damp rag to the back of my neck. I couldn't smell the toxic waste, so I guessed that meant that Aly had already had time to clean it up.

"Thanks," I croaked out.

"How did Grace let you get that drunk? I mean, you couldn't even walk when you left the bar. Do you remember the fun she and I had getting you inside and here in bed?"

"No, I don't really remember last night or yesterday for that matter," I rasped, my throat still raw from throwing up.

"How is your stomach feeling?" she asked as she

kissed the side of my head.

"Not well. I don't think I'm going to throw up a second time."

"Second time? Exactly how many times do you think you have thrown up?"

"Just once," I said, looking at her skeptically.

"Sweetie, you have thrown up seven times in the past two hours. Are you seriously telling me that you don't remember any of it?"

"Huh? I have? Two hours?"

"Yeah."

I could see the seriousness and concern in her eyes. I knew that she wasn't just messing with me. A knock on the door rattled my head, but Aly appeared to barely hear it. Aly went to answer the door and returned with Grace in tow.

"Hey," Grace said as she entered the bedroom.

"Hey," I said, nodding toward her and then instantly regretting moving. I felt my stomach flip, and I willed it not to expel any more waste.

"How is she doing?" Grace asked Aly.

"She is sick as hell. She said she doesn't remember yesterday and well, today either, apparently. She is still blacking out," Alyssa snapped.

"Why are you snapping at me?" Grace snapped back loudly.

"Shhh," I groaned.

"Sorry," Grace whispered.

"I'm snapping at you because you are the one that allowed her to get that drunk. What the hell were you thinking?"

"She's an adult, Aly. She is allowed to make her own decisions. I asked her to stop. I asked her to talk to me and tell me what the hell was bothering her. She, your loving fiancée, is the one that wouldn't tell me what was going on. All she would fucking do is drink."

"Will you two shut up? I am right here. It is my fault. I made the choice to drink," I said, hoping that they would stop arguing, or at least take it elsewhere. "I wanted to be numb. Me, nobody forced me. The blame starts and ends with me. I can't handle the two of you bitching at one another today. If I could get off the fucking bed, I would leave so that neither of you had to see or deal with me."

As the two women looked at one another, they both appeared stunned from my words. I felt another wave of nausea flying by, turned myself on my side, and leaned over the edge of the bed. I heard both women curse as Alyssa came around to the side of the bed to support me, while Grace scurried out of the room to re-wet the rags that Aly had been using to keep me cool and clean me up. I'm certain it was to get away from Aly as well.

"I don't know how it is that you have anything left in you," Aly said, wiping my mouth and then placing the other washcloth on the back of my neck.

"Luck?" I said softly.

"That was really gross, Kris," Grace said. She helped Aly get me adjusted so I didn't fall off the bed. They kept me close enough to the edge that if I did have another exorcist moment, I wouldn't have to move too far.

"That was nothing. You should have been here a couple of hours ago. That was gross. Are you planning on sticking around for a bit?"

"I was thinking about it," Grace said. "You look like you could use some help."

"I need a shower, and I was wondering if you

would babysit the boozehound."

"I don't need a babysitter," I groaned. The sharp pains in my stomach were causing me to lose some of my focus on their conversation.

"Yeah, no problem," Grace said, offering me a smirk.

After Aly had gone to take her shower, Grace had me as a captive audience. Under normal circumstances, that would have been okay, but today, under these circumstances, not so much. I thought about screaming for Aly to come back, but then, yelling would hurt, plus knowing Grace, she would manage to silence me.

"So, are you ready to tell me what had you drinking like an idiot frat boy last night? You realize that we aren't even close to being young enough to pull that shit off, right?"

"It was nothing. I just wanted to feel good, and then I wanted to be numb. I achieved what I set out to do."

"You were quite the hypocrite last night. You could have died. And yeah, I know that you probably gave yourself alcohol poisoning. And I am sure that it was much worse than I did that one time in college when you ripped me a new one. I should have taken your ass to the hospital to get your stomach pumped. I'm not certain that Aly and I shouldn't still take you to the hospital to be looked at."

"I'm fine, Grace. Really," I said as I tried to sit up and the room started to spin. "Whoa…"

"Fine, my ass. What did I miss? Come on, Kris, we've known each other for too long to keep secrets. You were fine before I went to get drinks. When I came back something was wrong."

"Just let it go, please. I love you for caring, Grace,

but please, for me, let it go."

"I can't. You could have died last night," she snapped.

"But I didn't," I replied. "I am right here."

"But you could have. I can't lose you…you mean too much to my life," Grace said, tears welling up in her eyes.

"I'm not going anywhere. You are stuck with me for life," I lied, sorta.

Well, it wasn't a complete lie, but I knew that I was going to have to think about how I was going to protect Grace and Aly. I had no idea how long it was going to be before that asshole told my parents where I was. I thought about leaving in order to keep them safe. I knew that my leaving would hurt Grace a lot. I don't know that she would ever be able to forgive me, and I really wouldn't blame her. I hated me for some of what I was thinking and what it was going to do to Grace and Alyssa. I need them safe and away from those monsters. I was going to have to leave them out of any decisions. I was going to have to protect them as best I could, no matter what the consequences were.

❧ ❧ ❧ ❧

It had been two days since my drinking binge to try to forget my run-in at the bar. Now, I had the daunting task of figuring out what to do. Do I run away? No, because they will use Grace and Aly to force me back. Do I send Grace and Aly away? Yeah, like that would work. I supposed I could tell them what was going on, but that would be involving them and putting them at greater risk. I knew that if Grace knew what was going on, she would never leave my side, and if my parents were to show their faces, she would probably get herself hurt. And that I couldn't live with.

"Kris? Can we talk?" asked Aly.

"What's up, beautiful?" I asked as I pulled her onto my lap. We were sitting on the couch in our home office.

I called it a home office, but really, it was our escape from reality room. True, there were two desks in the room, one for Aly and one for me. There was a small black, overstuffed leather sofa, and two different water fountain displays. Aly and I loved the sound of rain and running water. I had also wired the room with speakers so that we could turn on the fountains, turn out the lights, and listen to a thunderstorm in surround sound. Then there was the quaint little fireplace. I had some throw pillows near it so that we could sit in front of the fire on those cooler nights. Honestly, I loved this room. I think I spent more time in here than any other room in the house. Well, besides the bedroom.

"Grace said that something was bothering you the other night. She thinks it is why you drank so much." Aly took my hand in hers and gave me a reassuring smile. "I know you. You don't drink like that. Talk to me, what's going on?"

"Really, it's nothing." I could see that this answer wasn't going to work for her. "I don't know how to explain it. I saw someone that resembled someone from my past. It took me off guard and made me a little off balance."

"I see. So, why wouldn't you tell Grace?"

"Because if I tell her, she is going to over analyze it. She is going to become overprotective, and then she will get you worked up. It wasn't who I thought it was, so it just isn't important anymore."

"I see."

"Baby, I love you. I don't want to dwell on this anymore. Now, what do I gotta do to get a kiss?"

Aly smiled and brought our lips together. The kiss started slow and tentative, but as was common with us, it rapidly grew into heated and passionate. It wasn't long before we found ourselves making love. We had moved from the cold leather sofa to the floor pillows we had positioned in front of the fireplace. Our bodies moved as one. There was a hunger and need in our lovemaking, something that only she and I could satisfy within the other.

"I cannot believe that I get to make love to you like that for the rest of our lives," Aly said as we lay there sated.

"I love you," I said, placing a soft kiss on her lips. "I love you, too."

❧ ❧ ❧ ❧

Three weeks later, Aly and Grace had finally stopped badgering me about the drinking binge. It was a bright and sunny Saturday morning. Grace, Aly, and I had made a trip to the Farmer's Market. I don't recommend going with the pair of them. One at a time maybe, but I have never seen two women get so excited about fresh honey and vegetables. I would let them go together without me, but the last time I did that, they came home with enough fruits and veggies to keep a small army regular, and some artsy fartsy stuff that didn't match any decor in our house or Grace's house. They were dangerous together. Anyway, after we got back to the house, and they did whatever it was you do with flowers and veggies, I was going to swing into work to pick up some files that I had left. I was just about to get into my car when it happened.

"Hello, daughter," said the male voice from behind me. I felt an ice cold chill run down my spine. I wanted to run, I wanted to scream, but I couldn't. I was paralyzed with fear.

"I told you I found her," said the man from the bar.

"Yes, do you want a fucking cookie? Shut up and get her in the van," my father snapped.

I felt a sharp pain on the back of my head and then everything went dark. When I started to come around, the first thing I noticed besides the throbbing pain in my head was that my hands and ankles had been bound together. There was a gag in my mouth, but I was able to see what was going on around me. I felt as though I was living one of my many nightmares.

"Well, well, look who finally decided to wake up," my father said, looking down at me.

"Wha da fuh you wa wif me?" I said, around the gag.

My father took his dirty, grimy hand and pulled the gag out of my mouth. I felt my gag reflex kick in. His hands were gross, and he had put it in my mouth. Ew!

"What the fuck do you want with me?" I repeated.

"Oh, I have so many plans for you." The maniacal grin that crossed his face scared the shit out of me. I didn't have long to worry though. The grin disappeared as he backhanded me. I felt my head snap to left. The force of his swing made my neck burn. I've never had whiplash, I don't know what it feels like, but this is what I would imagine it felt like. I was scared to move my head. The burn in the muscles and tendons was so great, I was certain there was extensive damage. Or, maybe I was hoping so.

The room I was in had no windows, no light source other than the cliché naked bulb hanging from the ceiling above me. There was a twin cot and the walls were dingy, but bare. I had no way of knowing what day it was, how long I had been there. All I know is that every time my father came into the room, he beat me. He beat me until I passed out most times.

"Have you learned your lesson?" my mother asked.

"Please don't let him beat me anymore..." I pleaded. Yes, this was a sign of weakness, but I hurt and I was so sick of tasting my own blood, or seeing my own blood splattered around.

"You know that begging is not tolerated," said the man from the bar.

"Who are you?"

"What are you doing in here?" my father bellowed at my mother and the other man.

"What's it matter to you?" snapped the man.

I knew my father, and that was the wrong thing to say to him. I watched my father's face turn red before he swung at the man. His fist connected, and I heard the cracking of the man's jaw.

"Get him out of here!"

My mother scurried over and helped the man out of the room. When I heard the jaw crack, I had looked away. I didn't want to see the rage that my father had in his eyes. I knew that if I were to see that, it would stick with me for life.

"If I untie your hands, will you behave?"

"Yes, sir," I replied.

After he untied my hands, I sat where I was. I

knew that my father was mad, and that if I had done anything other than what he wanted, he would kill me. There was no doubt in my mind that he was willing and capable of it.

❧❧❧❧

Time passed. I don't know how much time. I had no real concept of day, night, week, or month. I was able to earn more freedom, but I was still watched very closely. I was locked in a room when it was nighttime or when nobody was home. I hadn't seen the mystery man since the day my father hit him. I hadn't heard him even mentioned. Maybe that played psychologically into why I followed my mother and father's rules so closely.

It was a long time before I was able to escape the clutches of my parents. One night they had both drank themselves into oblivion. I had been given more freedom and once they passed out, I slipped out the kitchen window. It was a tight fit, but I was thin enough that I made it work. I ran from the house. I don't know how far I ran; I just know that by the time I reached a town and police station, I was covered in cuts from branches and dirt from falling. I told my story about what happened. I told them about being kidnapped, beaten, about the private investigator, the blackmail, and everything. The police said that they had been investigating my parents and the private investigator for some time, but they never had any inside track. They asked me if I would be willing to assist.

"Ma'am, what we are asking is dangerous. I don't want you to be hurt more than you have been," said the sheriff.

"Please, call me Kris. Sir, I want these people locked up and the key thrown away. They have hurt me since I was a baby. I am willing to do whatever it takes."

"Kris, this is going to involve you going back there. Wearing a wire, and possibly enduring your pain and torture at their hands. I don't think that it is fair for us to ask you to do this."

"You aren't asking, Sheriff. I am volunteering. Just promise me that you will put them away and get me out as soon as you can."

He finally relented and agreed to do this. He called in additional police, FBI, something. I didn't care to know the specifics, I just wanted this over with and to get home to Aly and Grace. They got me back to the house. I had been gone for six hours. My parents luckily were still passed out. I got back into my room and the plan was set.

It took another three days before I was able to give the police the information that they needed and they were able to raid the house and get me out safely. They took me to the station, and I tried to call Aly, but her line had been disconnected. I called Grace next. He must have been deaf because his volume on the receiver was so loud that I could hear her end of the conversation as well.

"Hello?"

"Hello, is this Grace Barnes?"

"Yes, it is."

"Hello, ma'am. I am Sheriff Graham."

"How may I help you?"

"I'm sorry to bother you, ma'am, but do you know a Kristine Holt?"

"Y-yes? Is she okay? Please tell me she is okay."

"I'll let her tell you," he said, handing me the phone.

"Grace?"

"Oh my god, Kris? Is that you?"

"Yeah, it's me," I said, tears spilling down my face.

"Are you okay? Where are you? I have been so worried about you."

I explained where I was, and before I could get much further, Grace told me that she was on her way and would be here in two hours. I wanted to ask her about Aly, but she didn't give me time. She hung up quickly.

One of the deputies was my size, and she brought me something to change into. I showered and cleaned up as best I could. By the time I was done, I knew Grace would be there soon. I was sitting in the sheriff's office when she arrived. I saw her come in and talk to the duty officer. She then escorted her back to the sheriff. I couldn't hear what was said, but I could see Grace growing more and more anxious. The sheriff finally brought her to the office.

"Kris?" Grace asked.

I nodded, and she rushed the three steps forward and enveloped me into her arms. We both started to cry. I heard the door close and saw that we were alone.

"Thank you for coming," I dumbly said. I wasn't sure what to say. I was just so happy to see her and to have someone who cared about me holding me.

"Are you okay? You look so thin."

"I'll be okay. It is just going to take some time." I knew I looked like hell. I had been held hostage for over a year. I was nothing but skin and bones from the starvings that were given as punishment when I became too frail for them to continue to beat. "Grace, I tried to call Aly, but her number was disconnected."

"I-I don't…let's not talk about that now. When can I take you home?"

I didn't like it when Grace was evasive. "I believe we can leave whenever we're ready."

We left the office, and Sheriff Graham took down Grace's information, and she told him that she would be taking care of me. I knew it had been a long time, but had Aly forgotten about me? Did she lose hope? Then the most horrible thought popped into my head. What if Aly had moved on…what was I going to do?

Chapter Seventeen

The ride to Grace's house was quiet. I knew she was hiding something, and I was honestly afraid of what it was. Once we got to her house and were inside, Grace ordered food for us.

"Grace, why won't you tell me what is going on with Aly?"

"Aly was out of town, Kris. I reached her, and she should be here soon."

"What aren't you telling me?" I asked a bit sterner. It was just as I finished that question that I heard a car door close and saw Grace get up and move toward the door. Grace opened the door and in walked Aly.

"Oh my god, Kris," she cried as she raced over and hugged me close.

"Hi, baby," I said into her shoulder. I felt her stiffen when I called her baby. I pulled away from her and sat back down on the couch.

"Are you okay?" Aly asked. She sat down next to me and ran her hand along the side of my face.

"No, but I will be," I said, bluntly.

"Do you feel up to talking about what happened?" Grace asked. "I know you just got home."

"Um, some, I guess. I mean, what do you want to know?"

"Aly and I walked out of the house to find your car door open, and you were nowhere to be found—"

"Yeah, my dad and a scummy private investigator were out there."

"How did they know where we lived?"

"Well, the night of my drinking binge, while Grace was getting drinks, the private investigator came up to me, and we exchanged words."

"Why the fuck didn't you tell us?" Grace said, angrily.

"I didn't want you involved. I had already put you through enough. I just wanted to keep you both safe." I proceeded to tell them in very general terms what had gone on over the past year of my life. They both sat silent and with stunned looks on their face. Tears started streaming down their faces as I went on with the story. I wasn't giving them specific details. It was bad enough that I had to live with those memories. While I was telling the story, I noticed that Aly wasn't wearing her engagement ring. I guess after a year, I shouldn't have expected her to be wearing it still, but that didn't make it hurt any less. It wasn't until she started to speak that she realized that I was staring at her hand.

"Kris, how did you survive?" Aly asked.

"I held on to the memories of us, what we had planned for our future, and I knew someday I would get away from them. I'm really tired. I'm going to go to the guest room and get some sleep."

I didn't give either woman a chance to answer. I got up and walked out of the room. I could hear them whispering, but I was shutting down emotionally. I was just about asleep when I heard the door open. I could tell it was Grace. I wondered if Aly was still there. If she even still even cared, even a little.

I tossed and turned and barely slept that night.

When I finally decided to get up, I found Aly and Grace sitting in the living room.

"Good morning," I said, hugging myself. It was a safety mechanism I had used for years to help protect myself.

"Good morning," Grace and Aly said.

"Were you able to get some rest?" Grace asked, offering me a cup of coffee.

"Maybe a little, I mostly tossed and turned. I haven't rested soundly since before I was kidnapped."

"Do you want something to eat?"

"No, thanks, I just need to know where my life stands. I see you aren't wearing your engagement ring," I said, looking at Aly. "I know it was stupid of me to think or hope that maybe you would still love me."

"Kris, it isn't like that," Aly said, taking a deep breath. "We didn't have any idea what happened to you. The last we heard you were going to run to work. When you didn't return and we couldn't reach you, we went to go looking for you. Grace and I walked out the front door and there was your car with the driver's side door open, and you were nowhere to be found."

"Yeah, I lived that nightmare." I didn't mean for it to come out as harsh as it did, but right now, what I thought was my life was rapidly slipping away from me.

"I'm sorry. I didn't mean to trivialize what you went through. I do still love you—"

"But you aren't in love with me. You've moved on."

"You've been gone over a year..."

"Yeah, again, I lived that nightmare. How long did you wait? How long was it before you decided to give up on me?"

"Kris, that isn't fair," said Aly.

"What isn't fair? How long did you wait? I think I deserve to know that much."

"This isn't going to do anyone any good," said Grace, trying to get things back to a calm state.

"I wondered if coming back was a mistake. I don't want to be a burden to either of you. If you still have any of my things, I'll come and get them and find someplace else to be."

"The fuck you will," Grace said. "You are going to stay here with me. I just got you back."

"Life has moved on, Grace. Aly moved on, you have a life of your own. I'm just in the way and more damaged now than I have ever been."

"Kris, please, I do still care about you," Aly said, reaching toward my hand. I pulled it away just before she touched it.

"I don't want your pity. I was stupid to think that my life would be able to have some semblance of normalcy. I appreciate you coming to get me, Grace, I need…god, I wish they would have just killed me," I said as I stood up and started walking out of the room.

"Kris, wait," Aly said, jumping up and grabbing my upper arm tightly.

I froze. The way she grabbed my arm made me flashback to the past year and the way that my father had grabbed my arm before he beat me.

"I'm sorry," said Aly as she let go of my arm. I couldn't move; the fear had me paralyzed.

"Kris, look at me," I heard Grace say. I couldn't move, I could barely breathe.

"Grace? What do we do? What is going on with her?"

"What the hell do you think is going on with her?

She was kidnapped; she was traumatized. My god, are you stupid?" snapped Grace.

"Hey, don't snap at me."

"Aly, you have known her for long enough, this isn't new. You were there for the nightmares."

As Aly and Grace snapped at one another, I slowly moved backward until my back hit the wall. I felt trapped. I slid down the wall, pulled my knees to my chest, and started to shake. Life was so messed up. I was so messed up. I don't know how long I sat there, but eventually I noticed that I wasn't hearing Grace and Aly arguing. I raised my head and saw Grace kneeling in front of me, Aly standing behind her.

"Hi." Grace offered a smile. "Whatcha doin' on the floor?"

I couldn't respond. I wanted to, but it just wasn't happening.

"Kris, honey," I heard Aly say. My eyes snapped to her, and I felt myself glare.

Eventually Grace and Aly were able to get me back to the couch. I couldn't handle Aly being near me.

We worked out that, for now, I would stay with Grace. Aly was going to bring some of my stuff over.

"How long did you wait?" I asked again softly.

"I don't see what it matters," interjected Grace.

"Four months," said Aly. "It wasn't intentional or anything that I sought out."

"Wow, a whole four months." My words were bitter, but knowing that she only waited four months to move on, four short months of not knowing if I was alive or dead, I just couldn't believe how my life had gone so wrong.

Aly asked if I wanted to come to the house to pick out some things, but the last place I wanted to be was someplace where I would run into her girlfriend.

❧❧❧❧

"What's she like?" I asked Grace, a couple of weeks later.

"What's who like?"

"Aly's girlfriend, is she pretty?"

"Kris, don't do this to yourself. Don't torture yourself wondering about her. There is nobody like you. You are amazing, and Aly is a fool to let you go."

"Grace, that isn't true."

"You believe what you want, I'll believe the truth."

I had only seen Aly twice since I had been back. Grace had taken it upon herself to be there for me. She was there for the nightmares, the terrors, and the lapses in reality. I agreed to see a therapist, but only if Grace would come with me. I had trust issues when it came to others. Shocking, I know. Another shock was that I didn't tell the therapist and Grace all of what went through my head. I was afraid of what they would do…if they would have me committed.

We had seen the therapist a few times. One of the issues I was having on one particular day was dealing with the distance that Aly had put between us. I felt as though none of what we had was real. She cast me aside after four months and hadn't cared to check on me. Grace kept telling me not to dwell on it, but how could I not? I was going to spend my life with this woman, and she was completely blowing me off. Yes, she had a life, but dammit, I wanted her to care some.

That day's session was pretty standard. We discussed more of what I remembered from the dreams that I was having and then the struggle I was having with regards to Aly. I just couldn't bring myself to let go. Yes, I had only been back for a few weeks, but it still felt wrong.

"Kris, would it help if I had Aly come over and we talked with her?" Grace asked as we arrived back at her house.

"I doubt it. I get that she has a new life and that I don't matter. I get it in my mind, but my heart can't seem to let go yet."

"You do matter, Kris. She doesn't want to keep hurting you. That is why she stays away."

"Well, it doesn't help, but then again, seeing her and knowing that she feels nothing and felt okay to move on after such a short time doesn't help either. Maybe I just need to—"

"I swear if you don't stop blaming yourself I am going to kick your ass," Grace yelled. I was shocked because this was the first time anyone had lost their temper with me since I had been back. "You were not to blame in any of this. You didn't leave her by choice. You didn't opt to spend a year of your life in slavery to those assholes. Cut yourself a break here."

"Grace, we've been through a lot together. You've known that I was damaged for years now. Why you stick around, I don't understand. You saw my childhood, we dated—"

"And I fucked up and cheated…"

"I don't want to discuss that. I dated Aly. I was ready to spend the rest of my life with her. Granted, I didn't know it was going to be a matter of months—"

"That is not your fault."

"But holding on is. Do you want to truly know how I spend my nights in your guest room?"

"I'd like to," Grace said, honestly. "I wondered if you were telling us everything in therapy."

"I lay there daydreaming that I wasn't second best to people. I dream about being someone's number one. I cry myself to sleep because I'm lonely. I have nightmares that I sometimes wish would come true. I sometimes wish that they had killed me, and then I wouldn't hurt like this day in and day out."

Grace got up and walked away. I sat there. I wasn't honestly sure what to do. In the past, I would have followed Grace out of the room, although in the past, I wouldn't have had these types of thoughts either. I wouldn't have wished for something so final. The past year had taken its toll on me and now it was taking its toll on the people I cared about.

"You really don't get it, do you?" asked Grace as she re-entered the room, holding her cell phone.

"Don't get what?" I could see Grace struggling with something. She started to pace the room like a caged animal. "I don't understand."

"I…there are days I just want to slap the shit out of Aly."

"Why? What does Aly have to do with this?" I asked. I stood and walked over to where Grace was pacing and stood in her way. "Talk to me, Grace."

"You think that because Aly moved on that it was some flaw with you, something that you did wrong. Maybe it is just that Aly's a fucking moron. Has that thought ever crossed your mind?"

I shook my head. "It is my fault. What if I would have told you about the run in at the bar? What if I had screamed instead of letting them take me? What if I would have loved her more? What if—"

Grace cupping my face and kissing me cut me

off. The kiss reminded me of our first kiss so many years ago at her parent's house.

"You always wondered why I never dated seriously. It's because of you. *You* are the one that completes me. I didn't date because nobody measures up to you. Aly's an idiot not to jump at the opportunity to be with you."

Grace cupped my face and kissed me again. I felt her hands slide from cupping my face to wrap around my neck, pulling me closer. I wrapped my arms around her back. I heard a moan. I don't know if it was from Grace or myself, but either way, damn, it was hot.

"What the fuck is going on in here?"

Grace and I broke the kiss, and I turned and saw Aly standing in the doorway. She looked downright livid.

"Aly, what are you doing here?" I asked, trying to reel in my hormones.

"I asked what the fuck was going on in here."

"What do you mean?" I asked. I was still a little stunned from the kisses that Grace and I had shared.

"Why the hell were you kissing my fiancée, Grace?"

"Your what?" asked Grace.

"Since when am I still your fiancée? You moved on, remember?"

"Is that why you told me to come right over? So that I could walk in on that?" Aly said. The anger in her voice was rapidly rising.

"No, that, I had no idea that was going to happen. I invited you over because I was hoping you could help Kris."

"I don't think you need me to do that anymore. I think you helped yourself to her just fine."

Grace and Aly were standing face to face. "Stop!" I yelled, getting between the two women.

"Dammit, Aly, this isn't about you," Grace snapped. "Kris is the important one here."

"What did I walk into?" Aly demanded to know. "What the fuck is going on between you and my fiancée?"

"Grace, can we have a few minutes alone?" I asked. I knew it was going to be hard for her, but I needed to be able to confront Aly on stuff and I couldn't do that with the tension between the two of them. Grace nodded and left the room. Aly and I sat down on the couch. "Why do you keep referring to me as your fiancée? You have been dating and sleeping with someone since not long after I disappeared."

"Kris, I didn't know where you went. You just disappeared. I was devastated; you can ask Grace."

"If you were as devastated as you say, you wouldn't have moved on so quickly. Were you cheating on me or thinking about it? Did you even try to find me?"

"Of course I tried to find you. Grace went with me to the police. Did she tell you otherwise?"

"No, I never asked her. Grace isn't who I was engaged to marry. She wasn't whom I had pledged my life to. That was you. You were the one that I was ready to give myself to. Then you gave up on me. I noticed that you didn't answer the question about if you were thinking of cheating on me."

"No, I wasn't thinking of cheating on you. And I didn't give up on you, Kris. I still love you. I still care deeply about you."

"But it isn't enough. Why are you now declaring any feelings toward me? You have been distant since I got back."

"Kris, you were gone for a year. You cannot possibly expect that it wouldn't take some time to sink in that you were back."

"Is she prettier than me?" I knew I shouldn't ask, but I couldn't stop myself.

"Is who prettier than you?"

"Your girlfriend, you know, the woman who took my place in your heart?" It was a cheap blow, but I was hurt.

"Kris, it isn't like that," Aly said, taking my hand in hers.

"Then explain it to me. I thought we were ready to spend our life together. You got over me and moved on in less than four months."

"You were my world. Things were so good between us. I was so lost when you disappeared. Bailey and I got to know one another through work. She works in another department."

"Is she prettier? What is it that made you decide that *this* was the person that you were going to replace me with?"

"I didn't replace you, Kris. Stop saying that. There is no replacing you. God, Trisha still pines for you. I'm certain you are the reason that Grace hasn't gotten serious about anyone. You are impossible to get over. You know I don't do well on my own."

"It was four fucking months, Aly. Four months. Hell, you stalked me in college for longer than that."

"I know. I'm sorry. I don't know a good way to explain this. You keep asking if she is prettier than you. No, she looks almost identical to you."

Aly pulled out a picture of her and 'Bailey' for me to see. I agree there was a resemblance between her and me. That didn't really make things better.

"So, you replaced me with someone that looks like me."

"No, I filled a void that you left. I have been distant because I don't know what to do. I don't know how to help you. I don't know if I have the right to ask you to take me back. Hell, after what I walked into tonight, I don't even know what your relationship with Grace is."

"Well, I sure as hell don't have the answers. You have to do what your heart tells you. If it tells you to stay with Bailey, then do it. I'll sign over the house to you, and as soon as I figure things out, I'll get the rest of my stuff out and be out of your life."

"I don't want you out of my life. I still love you. I am willing to break up with Bailey—"

"You want me to tell you to break up with her? If you can't choose to do it on your own, then you don't want to do it. Something like what you are attempting to imply is a quick and easy decision. You just don't want to be alone. That is the real risk. You don't want to break it off for fear that I'll tell you no and you are left with nobody. I'm not going to do that. Roll the dice, flip the coin, write out the pros and cons, but do not ask anyone to make the decision for you."

Aly leaned forward quickly and kissed me. I can't lie and say that I didn't feel anything. I mean, I did still love this woman, but it was different than it was before I was kidnapped and it was different than my kiss with Grace was. If I were a lesser person, I would try to play them both, but I couldn't do that. Aly needed to make her choice, and I needed to figure out what I was going to do about the world-changing kisses that Grace and I shared.

Yes, I called them world-changing, because

kissing her was out of this world and not something to be just pushed aside. I was screwed, and depending on what they each chose, this love triangle could get rather complicated.

Aly and I said our good-byes. She kissed me again before she left. I wasn't certain, but I thought I heard Grace growl from the other room. I don't know if she was listening or not, but I don't care. We all had things to decide, and until decisions were made, life was going to be in this uncomfortable holding pattern.

Chapter Eighteen

Several days passed after Aly and I had talked. I hadn't seen or heard from her, but I wasn't surprised by that either. Aly was never thrilled with having to make tough decisions like this.

"Will you go out on a date with me tonight?" asked Grace, walking into the living room where I was sitting.

"Are you sure that is a good idea?"

"I think it is." Grace sat down next to me. "I know you are hoping for something from Aly, but I want to throw my hat in the ring again as well."

"Aly has to make her own decisions. And yes, I will go out on a date with you tonight," I agreed.

Grace told me to be ready by six, and then she bounced out of the room like a little kid. I couldn't help but smile as I watched her. It was nice to see Grace happy. I was still very torn between what to do about her and Aly. Yes, I knew I had to wait for Aly to make her decision, and I didn't want to hurt Grace by giving her false hope. But, damn…only waiting four months before moving on? That's a bit harsh. After a bit of dwelling in self-pity, I went to shower and get ready for my date.

I heard a soft knock on my door and, glancing at the clock, I saw it was six o'clock. I answered the door and saw Grace looking breathtakingly sexy and holding a small bouquet of flowers in a vase.

"These are beautiful," I said, taking the flowers out of her hand. She followed me into the room as I put the flowers on the dresser.

"You look incredible," Grace said. I could feel her eyes on my body.

I had chosen to wear my deep purple silk button up shirt. I didn't button it much more than to the valley between my breasts. I knew that I was tempting fate... well...Grace, but there was something exhilarating about it as well. To complement the shirt, I was wearing a pair of fitted black jeans.

"Thanks. You know how much I love you in that color," I said, playing with the collar of her royal blue shirt. Our eyes locked, and we got lost in one another.

"Shall we go?" said Grace, breaking the moment and offering me her arm.

"Lead the way."

Grace and I exited the house, and she drove us downtown. After we parked, we walked around. Grace took my hand in hers. It reminded me of when we were back in college. We would walk around campus holding hands. I didn't realize how much I had missed this. Aly didn't like PDAs. Once in a great while, she would hold my hand, but not often. Grace was always willing to do that. She didn't care who saw our love. If they accepted us as a couple or if they didn't, she couldn't care less. As long as we were together, that was all that mattered.

"So, beautiful, what are you in the mood for?" asked Grace. She placed her hands on my hips and pulled me close.

I could feel the warmth of her body against mine. I looked at her and smirked. "That, Ms. Barnes, is a very loaded question."

"It isn't as loaded as you think, at least not right now." Grace took my hand and brought it to her lips. "I know you have a lot to work though, and I know you are still working through your feelings for Alyssa. Just remember, I am here for you. There is no pressure."

"I appreciate that, I do."

"Good, now what do you want to eat? Anything specific making your mouth water?"

"Really?" I raised an eyebrow at Grace. It took a minute until she realized what she had said and what it could mean.

"Well, um…er…"

"Relax, Grace. Why don't we start with dinner and see where the rest of the night takes us?" I kissed Grace softly. Her lips were still amazingly soft, just like in college.

After stealing another longer kiss, Grace wrapped her arm around my waist, and we walked a little bit until the scent of the nearby Italian restaurant made my stomach growl. Grace smiled, and we went inside and had a nice dinner. We kept our talks to neutral subjects and touching was kept to a minimum, although we both explored the art of flirting as best we could.

"How about we get out of here, walk off a bit of that amazing dinner, and then I take you someplace better for dessert?"

"That sounds amazing to me. Can I make one request?"

"Anything," Grace said, offering me a sultry smile.

"Will you hold my hand while we walk? It is one thing I have missed from when we were together."

"Always."

We walked until we came to this little out of the way bakery. It hadn't been there when I was living here.

Even though it was out of the way, it appeared very popular. Grace and I placed our order at the counter, and Grace wrapped an arm around my waist as we headed to find a table to sit at and wait for our coffee and dessert.

"Grace?" We heard a woman's voice say as we were wandering around.

Grace and I turned to meet the voice and sitting three feet from us was Aly and her girlfriend. I thought I was going to throw up. Grace squeezed me tighter to her, and Aly paled.

"It's pretty full in here tonight, why don't you and your date join us?" Bailey offered.

I wasn't sure who was going to faint first, Aly or me. With Grace holding me so close, I felt like I was in the middle of a game of emotional chicken.

"Hon, I am sure that the last thing that Grace and her," Aly choked here, "date want to do is join us."

"Don't be silly, Aly. There isn't another table open."

"What do you want to do?" Grace whispered in my ear.

As awkward as this felt, her breath on my ear, the wine at dinner, and the flirting we had been doing all night caused me to struggle to put my hormones in check. Here was my ex-girlfriend, my ex-fiancée, and a totally clueless woman. This wasn't the time for the horny teenager to make an appearance. I glanced at Aly, and she gave me a forced smile.

"I'm not sure," I said quietly back to Grace.

"Please, sit," Aly said, painfully.

I nodded, and Grace and I sat down. I found myself seated between Grace and Aly. I'm certain that this wasn't ideal for either of them, but it was definitely going to make this a bit more interesting. Right after we sat down, our dessert and coffee arrived along with Aly and Bailey's.

I felt Grace's hand on mine under the table. I knew she was trying to be supportive, but I really didn't know how to react.

"I, um, guess I should do introductions." Aly let out a deep sigh. "Bailey Stephens, I'd like to introduce you to Kristine Holt. Kris, Bailey."

I watched Bailey's face. She seemed to recognize my name immediately and she was trying to place why. After a minute exactly, who I was became apparent to her. Her eyes widened, and she looked at the three of us.

"She's? When? How? Aly? Grace?" The woman stammered, her mind unable to process what it had just learned. "Somebody needs to tell me what the hell is going on. And it needs to happen soon."

Grace slid closer to me. I saw Aly's eyes narrow slightly. "Well, I got a call a few weeks ago…" started Grace as she told the story to Bailey. Aly offered in a few details here and there. Overall, Bailey and I sat there silent, dumbfounded.

"So, let me get this right. Kris, your thought-to-be-dead fiancée, has been back for a few weeks, and I am finding out in a restaurant by a fluke?" Bailey snapped, her eyes in an icy cold stare at Aly.

"Y-yes, dear," spoke Aly in a hushed tone. "I was going to tell you."

"When were you going to tell me? When you dumped me?"

"She isn't dumping you," I interjected. I knew it wasn't my place, but I felt as though I needed to say something.

"And exactly how do you know that she isn't dumping me?"

"Listen, she doesn't love me."

"Kris," Aly said in a pained whispered.

"You don't know that," Bailey said. "Has she said those words? I remember what she was like when you left."

"First off, I didn't leave, I was kidnapped. Secondly, Aly hasn't made an attempt in the past few weeks to work on us. She doesn't love me, so she isn't dumping you for me. We were together for years. We were engaged and she got involved with you four months after I went missing. Grace, can we go home? Please? I don't feel so well."

"Of course," Grace said. She stood and helped me up and wrapped an arm around my waist.

I forced a smile at both Aly and Bailey. I knew that Aly was in for a long night, but I just needed to get away from there. Confrontations weren't my thing before I was kidnapped; now, there were even less my thing. Grace and I walked quickly to her car, and then she drove us back to her place in silence.

❧❧❧❧

"Do you want to talk about it?" asked Grace as we arrived back at her house and sat down on the couch.

"I don't know what there is to say. I think I said it all to Bailey. Aly doesn't want me. Did she ever really love me? Why can't anyone just love me?"

"Sweetie." Grace wiped away the tears that had escaped and was making their way down my cheek. "I love you so much."

Grace brought our lips together softly. The kiss

was meant to be reassuring, but instead, it ignited something inside me that I didn't know was there. I took Grace's bottom lip between my teeth and played with it. I heard her let out a moan of pleasure that told me that we both needed this. I stood and extended my hand to Grace. She took it without words. We made our way to my bedroom.

"Are you sure?" Grace asked as we entered my room. I nodded, my words lost by the look of pure love and lust in her eyes.

Grace pushed me back against the door like she had done so many times before back in our dorm room. Her lips were on mine as she cupped my face in her hands. I pulled her body close before letting my hands roam. I cupped her ass in my hands and pulled her hips so that they rocked into my own. God, did she felt good.

"Oh, god, Grace," I moaned.

I don't know when I managed to do it, but I had unbuttoned the front of Grace's shirt and unhooked her bra. I brought my hands up to cup her breasts and felt her nipples hardening under my touch.

"Kris," whispered Grace as we broke our kiss, and she arched into my touch.

I walked us over to the edge of the bed. I slowly slipped Grace's shirt and bra off, and then I removed her pants and panties. She stood before me naked.

"God, Grace. You are the most beautiful woman on the planet," I said, before kissing her deeply.

Grace went to unbutton my shirt when I grabbed the front and pulled it open. We heard the buttons pinging around the room. Then her hands were pulling my bra and shirt off. Next, I felt my pants and panties being removed. I felt Grace's hand slip into the wetness that had pooled between my legs.

"Oh, baby," Grace groaned. I moved onto the bed, and she found her place above me, her hand returning to between my legs. "I love how turned on you get."

"Nobody has ever turned me on the way you do," I panted. What her fingers were doing to me was amazing.

I slipped my hand between her legs and felt how wet she was, and it just turned me on more. I wanted to tease her more, to prolong this, but I couldn't. As her hips rocked into me, I slid two fingers inside her. I watched her tilt her head back and her eyes roll back in ecstasy. It was only another moment before I felt her inside me.

We began to move like we did when we were dating before. We knew what the other wanted, what was going to please the other. The room filled with heavy breathing, grunts, and words of devotion.

"I love you, Grace," I panted as I neared my second orgasm.

"I love you, too," she responded as we both orgasmed together.

Grace collapsed on top of me. We were both trying to catch our breath. We lay together for a little bit longer before desire took over and we made love again. Finally, we were spent, and we drifted to sleep holding one another.

I slept better than I had in a really long time that night. I don't know if it was the exhaustion from the emotional roller coaster, the lovemaking, or just being in the safety of Grace's arms. Whatever it was, I was grateful.

I awoke to Grace's wandering hands touching me in ways that I hadn't been touched since the last time we slept together. No, it wasn't that Aly wasn't generous in bed. But it was just that they were very different. Aly was more about mutual gratification, where Grace would sacrifice her own pleasure to make sure that I was beyond fully satisfied.

I groaned as Grace placed a soft kiss on the tip of my nose and then kissed her way down my body. Feeling her just getting settled between my legs was enough to make me almost orgasm. The things that she did to me, I was in heaven. She teased and pleasured me until I could barely move. I pulled her up to me and kissed her. Tasting myself on her tongue gave me such a jolt that I flipped us over so I was on top.

"Inside, Kris," Grace begged. I allowed her the pleasure of her request. I used my hips to help me thrust into her with more force and to reach deeper inside her.

It was right after Grace called my name out that we heard her.

"*What the fuck!*" screamed Aly as she entered into my bedroom. I dropped my head to Grace's shoulder.

"What the hell, Aly," Grace said, pulling the covers up further, ensuring we were both covered.

"You couldn't wait to get her in bed, could you?" Aly accused Grace.

"What are you doing in my house?"

"I came to talk to Kris. I wanted to talk to her about last night with Bailey."

"Go start some coffee, and we'll be out in a few minutes," I said, my head still resting on Grace's shoulder.

"But..."

"Now, Aly," I said, more forceful.

Grace and I quickly showered together before getting dressed and heading out to meet Aly. When we reached the kitchen, I could smell the coffee. Aly was standing at the island with her hands on the countertop and a bottle of Tequila and a shot glass in front of her. She didn't look up as Grace and I made our coffee.

"Can I talk to Kris alone?" asked Aly. Her voice was hoarse and barely audible.

"That is up to Kris," said Grace, taking my hand and giving it a squeeze.

"As long as you swear not to yell." It was a typical request from me. Aly nodded.

"I'll be in my office."

Grace squeezed my hand again before leaving the room. Aly and I sat at the island in silence for what felt like an eternity. In reality, it was probably only a few minutes.

"H-how long have you been fucking Grace?" asked Aly bitterly.

"I have never 'fucked' either of you. If you are going to be crass, you can leave."

"I'm sorry. I am just in shock. The last thing I ever pictured was to find you in bed with Grace."

"Why would that be the last thing you ever pictured? You have stated several times that you have always known that Grace has been in love with me. You know we were out on a date last night—"

"Yeah, but can you blame me for wanting you to still be in love with me?"

"You don't get both of us. I'm sorry, but that isn't how it works."

"Kris, I do love you, and I am still in love with

you," Aly said as she took a drink of her coffee.

"Aly, you have a life with Bailey."

"It isn't what you are thinking. Yes, it seems like I moved on quickly, but that is far from the truth," Aly said. "Bailey looks a lot like you. She was a way for me to hold on to you. That may sound lame, but after you disappeared, it was the only thing that kept me sane. When I found out that you were alive and safe…I didn't know how to react. I wanted, want to take you in my arms and hold you, protect you, kiss you, and make love to you for hours. But I know how you feel about cheating, and you were right, I don't want to break it off with Bailey if there is no chance for us."

"Aly…" I didn't want to crush her world, but after last night with Grace, I don't think that I could be with anyone but Grace.

"I know. You and Grace have a heated, passionate past. I heard and saw enough when I got here to know that you and I never looked at each other like that, nor did I ever make you feel like that. Do you love her?"

"Yeah, I do."

"Would we have worked had you not been kidnapped? Or would I have eventually lost you to Grace?"

"I don't know, Aly. I know that I was fully committed to our life together. Thoughts and memories of you and Grace were what helped me stay sane while I was in that house."

"I keep wishing that I could have done things differently."

"We can't go back." I took Aly's hand in my own. "I really do hope that you find happiness. If it is with Bailey, great, if it isn't, I hope you find the woman of your dreams."

"You are her…" Aly said with a sad laugh.

"I must really be something. I still have Trisha, Grace, and you pining for me."

"You are. Grace is a very lucky woman."

"So am I."

Aly hugged me, and I felt her shoulders shake. I knew it meant she was crying. I held her while she mourned the official loss of our relationship. Once she composed herself, I escorted her to the door.

"Will I ever see you?" Aly asked. She reminded me of a helpless child with the innocence of her question.

"I'd like to think that this isn't the end of us as friends, but we'll have to see what the future holds."

"I love you, Kris. I am always here if you need anything. And if she hurts you again, I am not going to be nice about it."

"I love you too, Aly. I think Grace learned her lesson after the last time she hurt me."

We hugged one last time, and she left. I leaned against the door for a long time before I decided to go get Grace.

⁂

I knocked softly on the door to Grace's office but didn't receive a response. I opened the door and saw her standing at the window, lost in thought. Walking up behind her, I wrapped my arms around her waist and pulled our bodies together. I felt her lean into the embrace.

"I love you," I said, softly into her ear.

"Mmmmm, I love hearing you say that," Grace said.

"What were you thinking about?"

Grace turned in my arms and put her arms around my neck. "I was hoping that this is real and not a dream. That you are really here, in my arms."

I leaned forward and kissed her. "Nope, this is definitely not a dream."

"How'd it go with Aly? I expected to hear a lot more yelling and crying."

We moved to the living room and cuddled together on the couch. I told Grace about my conversation with Aly and that it was definitely over with Aly and me. I could feel Grace start to relax and then tense again. I could see the wheel turning in her mind. She was trying to work out what I meant, and if I was going to wait for Aly or if maybe, by some strange chance, she was going to have a chance. I knew Grace well enough.

"Baby, it is over with Aly, but I love you, and I'd like to explore the possibilities of where that could go. If you are interested, that is?"

"Yes, I am definitely interested," Grace said.

We spent the rest of the weekend lost in one another, reconnecting and reaffirming our connection. We decided that the following weekend, we would go to visit Grace's family and tell them everything. We hadn't told them that I was back or anything; I had to get through some of the horrors and deal with my inner demons. I know that seems rude and maybe a bit wrong, but I just couldn't handle them smothering me.

Chapter Nineteen

As the flight took off, I felt Grace take my hand in hers. I hadn't seen her family in at least two, maybe three years. Obviously, with my kidnapping, I lost a year, but before then, I hadn't seen them because, well, Aly and I were together and there had been no reason for me to go back with Grace to visit. I don't think that it really set in as to what we were doing until we landed. That was when the butterflies in my stomach became more aggressive.

"Are you okay?" Grace asked as we walked from the plane to the terminal.

"Sure," I said, unconvincingly.

"Talk to me, beautiful," said Grace as she pulled me over to a grouping of chairs.

"I haven't seen your family in years. With everything that went on between us, me being engaged to Aly, and then my going missing, and all that has happened since then. What if they think I'm too damaged? What if they don't want me to be in your life?"

"Kris, love, they have never once made a choice of who I was involved with. I love you; they love you. Yes, it is going to be a shock for them, but not in the bad way you are envisioning."

I wasn't sure how to respond. I just knew that I wasn't as confident that this was going to be a good thing. I loved Grace and her optimism, but I still couldn't help but worry. Some people come with baggage; I come with a U-Haul, and I don't mean the small ones.

"Do you remember how nervous you were the first time you came home with me in college?"

I had to admit, after Grace brought it up, this was a sort of deja-vu moment. I nodded.

"Well, they were so excited to see you then, and they are going to be just as excited now to see you."

"I also remember having a great nightmare while I was here that time as well."

"Yeah, but you also have to remember, that nightmare gave us our first kiss," Grace said, wiggling her eyebrows at me.

"You are such a goober," I said, before kissing her. Grace always knew how to help me calm down and feel better about things. "I love you."

"I love you, too. Let's go get the rental, and later if you promise not to scream as loud as you do at home, I'll help you relax even more."

"Mmmm, I'll do my best, but you just know how to make me feel so good…"

We kissed again and then went to get the rental car. As we got closer to her parents', I could feel the nerves creeping in again. The sound of the rain was doing little to calm my nerves. That was unusual because I loved to sit and listen to the rain.

"Do they know that you are bringing someone home with you?" I asked.

"Yeah, I told them that I had started seeing someone, that it was serious, and that I was bringing her home with me." Grace must have sensed that my fears were coming back. She pulled into the far end of the parking lot of the park just down the road from her parents' house.

Grace taking my hand in hers and then pulling me close comforted me. "Is Tyler going to be there?"

"Not tonight. He and Jenna had to go to some stupid thing with her family."

"I still can't believe that he married her."

"I can't either, but she has started to mellow out over the years."

"I'm sure that will change with my reappearance," I said, bowing my head.

Grace tilted my head up with one finger and kissed me. The kiss started out as a peck but grew into one of comfort and then desire. I looked around and saw nobody in sight. I was also grateful that the car Grace had rented had tinted windows. I leaned my seat back and pulled Grace over on top of me. I unbuttoned and unzipped her pants before thrusting my hand into her panties and felt the abundant wetness between her legs.

"Oh, god yes," moaned Grace as she unbuttoned and unzip my pants before slipping inside me.

"Yes," I said, slipping two fingers inside Grace.

We moved together, our hips rocking, hands thrusting in and out of the other, mouths pressed together, and the sounds of grunts and moans filled the car. I came first, Grace followed about a minute later. After a minute, I eased my hand out of her pants and brought my fingers up to my mouth. I knew that I was playing with fire, especially with her fingers still inside me, but I needed to taste her. I sensuously and torturously licked my fingers.

"Mmmm, Kris," Grace said as she kissed me, and then I felt her moving inside me again.

"Oh god, yes. Harder, baby," I said, thrusting my

hips into Grace rapidly. I could feel her grinding into my leg as well.

It wasn't long before we came together.

"I love you so much," Grace said, kissing the tip of my nose.

"I love you, too."

"You realize that we have to get going to my parents' house..."

"I know, but I needed that."

"Me too," said Grace, before moving back to the driver's seat and fixing her clothes. "Are you more relaxed now?"

"Yes and no. I'm definitely more relaxed and sated, but now I'm hoping that they can't tell that I just had sex with their daughter. Twice..."

"Well, if they notice, they sure as hell won't say anything."

"Well, I hope not. I may have to spend the weekend in the treehouse."

We laughed. Grace kissed me softly one last time before we headed the rest of the way to her parents' house. When we arrived, we found that Grace's parents weren't home. We were able to get our stuff inside, and we were cuddling in her room when we heard them come in.

"You ready?"

"If I said no, would it matter? Could I prolong the moment?"

"No, my love." Grace kissed me softly. "I'll go talk to them first. Why don't you take a moment and come out when you are ready?"

"Thanks."

Grace left the room, and I heard her talking with her parents. I heard them ask her where her new girlfriend was. Grace told them that she was shy and nervous about seeing them. She wasn't lying. I finally got up the guts to do this and walked out of the room. I could see Grace standing at the end of the hall. I couldn't see her parents, so I felt stronger when I walked up behind her, wrapped my arms around her waist, and kissed the side of her head.

"Hi, love," Grace said, in such a soft and loving tone that I just melted into her. Her parents turned and saw me standing there with my arms wrapped around their daughter's waist.

"K-Kris?" asked Erin, visibly shaken. I nodded my confirmation. "Oh god, honey." Erin stumbled over to us. She shoved Grace out of my arms, wrapped me tightly in hers, and held me close. I was having a hard time breathing, but I don't think that Mrs. Barnes would have cared.

"Mom, let her breathe," Grace finally interrupted. I'm wondering if she saw me turning into a smurf from the lack of oxygen.

No sooner was I out of Erin's arms than Sean had me in his arms. I had never seen Grace's father cry until that day.

"We have been so worried about you," he cried. "Are you okay?"

This question shocked me. Nobody ever started with it. I nodded into his chest. I was too choked up to speak. I felt Erin hugging me again as well. Here I went from being kidnapped and abused by my parents, to lovingly embraced by Grace's.

❧ ❧ ❧ ❧

Grace's parents agreed, though not entirely

willingly, to wait until the following day when Tyler and Jenna arrived for me to tell them what all had happened since I went missing. Instead, we talked about what had gone on from the Barnes family perspective. I loved how welcome and loved I felt in their house.

"Now, was that so bad?" asked Grace as we cuddled up together in her bed.

"I will admit I had imagined much worse. I have never felt as loved in my life as I do when I am with you and your family."

"That's good, because we happen to love you a whole lot. Are you sure that you want to tell everyone at once? I mean, we could have told my parents and have them pass on the info to Tyler and Jenna."

"It's okay. I think going through it once and being around to answer any questions right then and there is the best thing."

I was done talking. I pushed Grace onto her back and then rolled on top of her. I felt her legs wrap around me as I captured her lips in a hungry kiss. I could feel the heat coming from her body. The more we bumped and grinded together, the warmer and wetter Grace got. I felt her sliding my panties off, then taking my shirt off me. I did the same for her. Feeling her naked body below me fueled my desire to consume her. We took each other hard that night, a few times.

After a few short hours of sleep, Grace and I got up and ready for the day before heading out to the kitchen where we could hear her parents moving around.

"Are you ready?" Grace asked, putting her hands on my hips and pulling me closer.

I wrapped my arms around her neck and kissed her softly. "As long as I have you by my side, I am ready for anything."

We exchanged a couple of more kisses and 'I love you's' before exiting the room. As we entered the kitchen, I saw a look pass between Grace's parents, and then her dad blushed and left the room. I knew this couldn't be good.

"Did you girls sleep well?" Erin asked.

"Yes, ma'am," I answered softly.

"I woke up surprisingly refreshed," said Grace.

I saw a small smile on Erin's face before hearing her say, "I don't know how."

"Where'd Dad go?"

"He went to get some ear plugs and soundproofing material," said Erin. I wanted to die at that moment. I heard her laughing at the new shades of red I was turning.

"What'd I miss?" Grace asked, looking between her mother and me.

"It won't be an issue the rest of the visit," I said, mortified. Grace still had no idea.

"Kris? You are so red right now." Erin laughed.

"You are enjoying this way too much," I said, trying to glare at the older woman.

"Will someone tell me what is going on? Please?"

"Your parents heard us last night," I whispered in Grace's ear. Her eyes bulged. She looked at her mom, who nodded. Grace must have then replayed in her mind the conversation that had been going on. Now, I saw her turning several colors of red. Erin started to laugh harder.

"Oh god." Grace leaned into me, her head on my shoulder. "Seriously?"

"Yes, dear."

"Kris is right. It won't be an issue again."

"I am just happy that you two share such a strong and passionate love."

That was the last the subject was discussed. We made breakfast together, waffles, bacon, eggs, and pancakes. Sean did come back to join us, but he refused to make eye contact with any of us.

After breakfast, Grace and I cleaned up, and we were cuddled on the couch when Tyler and Jenna arrived. Grace and I stood up as we heard them enter the house. I heard Erin tell them that Grace and her 'girlfriend' were in the other room. I took my place behind Grace just as I had the night before with her parents.

"I love you," Grace whispered, leaning into my embrace.

"I love you, too." The closer that Tyler and Jenna got, the more nervous I got. I buried my face in Grace's hair.

"Hi, Grace," I heard Jenna say.

"Hey," Grace replied.

"What's up, Si...Oh my god, Squish?" squeaked Tyler as he ran over, shoved Grace out of the way, and hugged me. "It's really you, right?"

"Yeah, it's me." I squeezed onto him as tight as I could.

"When? How? Where have you been?" He asked, still not letting go of me.

"Why don't you let her go, and we can all sit down and hear the story?" Sean said. "We opted to wait until you were here so that Kris only had to go through this once."

"I don't get why she is such a big deal," Jenna said. "She probably did it just for attention."

Erin glared at her daughter-in-law and then

looked to me with sympathetic eyes. I smiled at her, letting her know that I appreciated that she was supportive of me. Everyone took seats. I was grateful that Grace and I were so close together that there was no way to tell where she began and I ended.

"You only tell us what you feel comfortable telling us. There is no pressure here," Sean said, giving me a reassuring smile.

I felt Grace thread her fingers in with mine before she kissed the side of my head, showing me her unwavering love and support.

"Theatrics," Jenna said, under her breath. This statement garnered a glare from her husband, his mother, his father and, had I not stopped her, there would have been words exchanged between her and Grace.

"I guess I should start with one night when Grace and I were out at the bar playing pool. She had gone to get drinks when this man came up…" I continued to tell them about that night, the drinking, why I drank so much, and then I moved to the day of the kidnapping. "I couldn't let anything happen to either Grace or Aly. This was my nightmare, not theirs." I told them, in limited detail, about my time being held captive. I told them about the threats used to keep me in line. I showed a few of the less embarrassing scars I had received from my time. I explained about my escape, and about the sting that I put together with the local law enforcement. This was something that Grace hadn't heard much about. There were sobs, gasps, and various other shocked noises. I heard some bored sighs from Jenna as well. When I explained about coming home and what had transpired over the past month, I could see anger in Sean's eyes, kindness, and love in

Erin's eyes. Tyler was harder to read, but I had known him long enough to see that below his calm exterior was a fire raging. Then there was the bored look on Jenna's face. That hadn't surprised me, in all honesty.

"I love you," Grace said, when I finally finished the story.

"I think I saw that same story on a television show," Jenna said, coldly.

"Jenna, I do not know what your issue is with Kris, but your attitude toward her is unacceptable and unforgivable within this household. Kris has been a member of this family for almost thirty years. This family has known you for barely five years. Kris has proven herself a caring member of this family, you I have questioned since the day my son brought you home."

"Mom, she's the one that outed Kris way back in our senior year of high school," Grace said. I wished she hadn't, but I wasn't going to say anything. This was a Barnes' family discussion.

"That was you?" asked Tyler.

"You act like it is a surprise. I have never made it a secret that I don't care for Kris," Jenna said, nonchalantly.

"Why?" Sean asked.

"Oh my god," I blurted out. I had just realized why Jenna had it out for me.

"Babe?" asked Grace.

The smile that crept across my face scared Jenna. I could see the fear in her eyes. I had finally, after all these years, figured out what the issue was. Now, the power was mine.

"Kris?" Erin asked.

I looked at Jenna; her eyes were pleading with

me. After all these years, I had the choice, tell what I knew or be the bigger person and let it go. The hell if I was going to let this woman get away with holding this any longer.

"Please," Jenna pleaded. She was seriously fearful.

"I can't believe I never realized this before. You did everything that you did to me in high school because I turned you down and then I turned your best friend, what's-her-name, down because I was already dating Trisha. You outed me because I wouldn't sleep with either of you."

"I'm sorry, what?" Grace said, sitting up straighter. The fury in her eyes could have scorched the sun.

"Seriously?" Tyler said.

Erin and Sean sat there stunned. Everyone knew I was telling the truth. The look of guilt on Jenna's face gave it away. I couldn't believe it had taken this long, but wow, I was so happy that I had.

"Fine, yes," snapped Jenna. "I was having a bit of an identity crisis so I thought that I would explore my options. How was I to know that little bitch would actually turn me down?"

"You thought that because you were popular that Kris would just bow and feel honored to screw you? Really? Did you know she was dating Trisha?" asked Grace.

"Who didn't know?" commented Jenna. "That was one of the school's worst kept secrets. I was highly amused when Trisha tossed your name out as the person Kris was sleeping with."

"Yeah, looking back, I wish it were true. The woman's got skills," Grace said, forgetting that her brother and parents were sitting there with us.

"Oh god," said Sean, bolting up and scurrying

out of the room.

"Grace, stop traumatizing your father with your sex life. Wasn't us hearing you both for five or six hours last night enough?" Erin protested. I knew that it was partly in jest to torture Jenna, but it was also to embarrass Grace and me. Erin was smiling as she left the room.

"Seriously? Six hours?" Tyler asked. I wasn't sure if he was jealous or just in awe of our stamina.

"We were tired after the flight," I said. "And yes, that is an accurate time, not just us messing with you."

Jenna was now very uncomfortable. And I was loving it. "And for the record, Jenna, I wouldn't have slept with you back then even if I wasn't involved with Trisha. I had self-respect. I wasn't going to let you use me to satisfy your sexual fantasies."

Grace pulled me close and kissed me with so much passion that she took my breath away.

"Gross, Squish, you put your tongue in my sister's mouth," teased Tyler.

"That isn't the only warm, moist part of your sister that I've put my tongue inside...today for that matter." Two could play that game. Plus, making him squirm was well worth the trouble I would be in later.

Chapter Twenty

We were sitting at a table near the dance floor of Leispiach, the local Irish lesbian bar. After all that had gone on today, we needed to get out of the house and burn some energy.

"I can't believe what you said to Tyler about your tongue," Grace said, leaning close to me. She was so close that I could feel her breath on my ear, and it made me shiver.

"What? It was true," I said proudly, waggling my eyebrows at my love.

"Mmmm, yes, it was," Grace said, leaning her body into mine and kissing me. "I love you."

"I love you, too. Now, dance with me." I pulled us up, and we moved onto the dance floor.

Now, I wasn't a good dancer; what I did really barely passed as being in the same distant family as dancing. So, we flailed around the dance floor for a long time before the DJ played a slow song. I wrapped Grace in my arms and held her close. This was what dancing was about, holding a gorgeous woman in your arms, feeling her body move with yours, kissing her deeply so that the entire club vanishes and there are just the two of you in the universe. We danced with our foreheads together kissing, lusting, making every moment of this closeness count.

"I need a drink," said Grace as we retook our seats at the table by the dance floor. "I'll be right back."

"I got it, my love."

I kissed her again. I loved kissing Grace. That was something that hadn't changed from when we were in college until now. I loved the feel of her lips on mine, the salty and sweet taste of her skin. After we broke apart, I made my way from through the crowd to the bar.

"Hey, beautiful, let me buy you a drink," said the woman next to me at the bar.

"Thank you, but I don't think that my girlfriend would appreciate that," I said, motioning toward Grace.

"You know that you are much too hot for that redhead."

"I appreciate the compliment, but—"

"Bitch, leave the hot chick alone," said the drunk woman, who now had her arm around me. "Can't you see that you are trying to play outside your league? As for you, hot stuff, what you say you and I find a place to get to know one another better?"

"I'll pass," I said. I turned to the bartender and ordered two White Russians. The bartender smiled at me and then quickly went about making our drinks. The drunken woman that was still hanging on me then squeezed my ass. That was the last straw.

"Mmmm, nice and firm."

"Keep your hands off me unless you want something broken," I hissed. I turned, recognizing the drunken woman. It was Trisha, my ex. I groaned and glared at her. She sat down on the barstool by her side. I paid the bartender and then made my way back over to Grace.

"What's wrong?" asked Grace as soon as I sat down.

"I got hit on by two women and—"

"Sexy, why'd you leave?"

"Trisha? What the hell?" snapped Grace.

"Hey, Grace! Have you seen this sexy goddess?" Trisha said, gesturing toward me.

"Yeah, and so have you. Are you too drunk to see that it's Kris?"

"No wa…holy shit! Kris…damn, baby, you are—"

"Finish the sentence, Trisha, and you won't speak the rest of the night," Grace said as she wrapped herself in my arms and kissed me.

"No way, you two are back together?"

"Yeah, we are," I said, smiling at the woman in my arms.

"Why don't the three of us go back to my place? We can talk and stuff."

"That is never going to happen, Trisha. You need to sober up," I said.

"Oh, no, I'm just getting started with the fun."

Grace and I looked at one another, and we knew that we needed to get some coffee into this woman and get her sobered up. We led Trisha out of the bar and down a couple buildings to a coffee bar and got her some coffee. It took about twenty minutes before we started to see a glimmer of the person that Trisha was.

"Ugh, where am I?"

"Welcome back to the land of the living," I said.

"Kris? Grace? Where the hell did you two come from?"

"Hey," Grace said.

"Kris? Where the hell have you been? What the hell? Do you know how worried everyone was about you?"

"Yes, I do know, and it is a really long story.

Short version is that I was kidnapped, I escaped, and now I'm trying to restart my life."

"Wow. Weren't you engaged?"

"Yeah, she…" I started, but I couldn't finish. I'm not sure why it hurt so badly at that moment. I was happy with Grace. I loved Grace.

"She didn't wait. It was her loss and my gain," Grace said, taking my hand in hers.

"How long have you two been back together?"

"Not long," said Grace. "So, what is up with the drinking?"

"Oh, I got dumped again. I'm starting to think that this is just karma's way of telling me that I never should have let you go," said Trisha, glancing up at me.

"I, for one, am glad you did." Grace moved closer, and I wrapped my arm around her.

"Ugh, I'm too sober for your mushy crap."

We talked with Trisha for a while, each of us finishing another cup of coffee. Then we escorted Trisha home before heading back to Grace's parents' house. On the drive home, traffic was rerouted, and we had to go past my childhood home. I wasn't prepared for the myriad of emotions and memories that hit me. It was right after we passed the house that I made Grace pull over because I thought I was going to get sick.

"Babe? What's going on?"

I could see the fear in Grace's eyes. I wanted to tell her that everything was or would be okay, but I wasn't sure that was the case. I just knew that seeing my childhood home scared the shit out of me. This time more than in the past because of what I had to live through for the past year.

"I just need a minute." I was doing my best to control the fear and panic that had welled up inside me. After a few minutes, the nausea started to pass, and I was able to take a deep breath. "Sorry."

"What happened?" said Grace, softly.

"I don't know. It felt like a panic attack."

"It doesn't surprise me, baby. You have been through a hell of a lot. Are you ready to go back home?"

"I think so. Promise me that you'll hold me tonight."

"Always," Grace said, kissing the side of my head.

We drove the two blocks to her parents' house and quickly made our way to her room. We changed and got into bed. Once we were settled, I took several deep breaths, trying to center myself before I opened up to Grace.

"When we drove by the past the house, it was like my childhood played through my head in fast forward. I saw moving in, meeting you, the various beatings I took. I mean, it was a split second, but I was just flooded with memories and emotions."

"Honestly, babe, that doesn't surprise me. I'm kinda shocked you didn't have that reaction more often around that place."

"I guess from being kidnapped it took a little more from me and that resolve is gone."

"Well, you are safe in my arms, so you can relax!"

Grace pulled me closer and held me the whole night. I fell asleep after she did. I was afraid to close my eyes. I was afraid that I would see the memories again. When I finally did drift to sleep, it was a dreamless sleep.

The rest of our time passed by without incident. I knew that I was noticeably quieter, but everyone respected me enough not to say anything. Trisha stopped by and apologized for her drunken breakdown.

Jenna was distant but nicer to Grace and me.

⁂

After the flight and short drive home, Grace and I found ourselves cuddled together on the living room sofa. It still surprised me with how comfortable and relaxed I was in her arms, or just having her close to me. We had spent so many years apart, and yet like this, everything felt as though it did when we were together before.

"How's the mind doing?" Grace asked.

"Huh?"

"You've been lost in your mind for a while, and I was wondering how things were going in there."

"I'm really sorry. I didn't mean to be ignoring you." I was embarrassed that I hadn't realized what was going on.

"You have nothing to be sorry about. We're here together, and you are in my arms where you belong. I'm glad you feel comfortable enough to relax and zone out. I just know your mind, and that isn't always a good thing."

"Yeah, it isn't. I was just thinking about how great and perfect it feels to be in your arms, after all that has gone on over the years. Thank you for loving me," I said, before kissing her softly.

"Mmmm, you never have to thank me for loving you. I am the one that should be thanking you for giving me another chance."

"What do you say we go forward from now on and what happened in the past stays in the past? We don't dwell on what happened."

"Deal," Grace said breathlessly. It was at that

moment I couldn't help but lean up and kiss her. "Oh god, Kris."

Hearing Grace moan my name was enough to put all the thoughts that had been going on inside my head to the back burner. I needed her. I needed to make love to her, to be connected in both body and spirit.

We moved to the bedroom and made love until we were too exhausted to move. I thought things were changing that night and that we were moving on to better things. Grace helped me find a job that was going to work around my therapy sessions and not cause added stress on me.

A few nights later, we were going over to Aly's for me to sign the papers giving her full ownership of the house and then for Grace and me to bring my stuff home. As we neared the house, panic filled my entire body. I didn't have any warning. I rolled the window down and threw up as we drove. Grace pulled over as quickly as she could. I continued to retch out the window.

"Kris? Love? What's going on?" Grace asked as she helplessly rested her hand on my back.

"I can't. I can't go there. Please don't make me go there," I cried hysterically. "Please don't let them get me." I was now frantically shaking in the seat next to Grace. Neither of us expected this little turn of events.

"Nobody is going to get you. You are safe. We don't have to go there. I will call Aly and have her come over when you are ready, and we can sign the papers then. I'll get a couple of the girls from work to come and help me get your stuff from the house this weekend." I could hear the desperation in Grace's words to calm me down. I knew she was afraid of something bad happening and me snapping. "Kris, look at me, my love."

I was hyperventilating and shaking so intensely that even turning my head to look her direction took some serious effort on my part.

"You are safe," said Grace slowly. "You are never going to have to deal with them again. Do you understand me?" I did this jerk, head bob, nod thing. "Good. I love you. We are going to go home. Can you try to calm down for me?" Again, the jerk, head bob, nod thing. "Do you want to hold my hand?"

I saw Grace slowly and cautiously extend her hand in my direction. I am pretty certain I broke the speed of light and sound reaching forward and grabbing on to her hand. I saw her wince in pain, but I couldn't ease up or let go. I hoped she understood that I wasn't doing it to hurt her. She smiled at me, and then while still holding my hand, she put the car in gear and turned us around and drove us back to her house. I let her help me inside and into the bathroom. She wanted me to have a shower to wash off all that had transpired. I was sitting on the toilet when she came back in.

"I called Aly and told her that tonight wasn't going to happen, and I invited her over tomorrow night to sign the papers."

"Thank you," I rasped. My throat was still raw from throwing up earlier.

"No need to thank me," Grace said, standing in front of me. I wrapped my arms around her waist and leaned my head against her stomach and the tears started to flow. I couldn't hold them, I couldn't stop them, and I couldn't control anything at this point. Grace just stood there and let me cry. She comforted me, but she never once tried to change positions or get me to move.

Once my breakdown was over, I numbly brushed my teeth and then the two of us took a shower together. It felt good to be close to her. I don't know what I did to deserve her, but I thank god I had her.

❧❧❧❧

The following day Grace and I called in sick. I was still pretty shaken up about what had happened and how I hadn't realized that returning to the place I was kidnapped from was going to do a number on my emotional system. I mean, what the hell was I thinking?

"Hey," Grace said as I entered the kitchen, where she was sitting at the island eating a bagel and reading the paper.

"Hey." I walked over and kissed her softly on the side of the head. "I'm really sorry about last night."

"You should be," Grace scoffed, jokingly. "I mean, freaking out the way you did was just so over the top."

I poked her in the ribs, and she jumped. I was even prouder of myself when I saw her bagel fall out of her grip and into her coffee. She glared at me and then started to fish the offending food item out of her coffee.

"What? You dunk donuts in your coffee."

"Cute, sweetie. Now that we've abused humor to avoid things, how are you feeling about last night?"

"Stupid as hell for not realizing that it was a bad idea. Embarrassed about how I reacted, and grateful as hell to have an amazing girlfriend like you who protected me and took care of me."

"None of us thought about the fact that we were taking you back to that place. I personally think your reaction was rather tame. I am pretty certain that I would have been screaming hysterically, and the entire neighborhood would have been out in their front yard gawking at the red-haired freak."

I smiled at her. I loved how she could make me feel better without even trying.

"You know, this would be a great time for you to say, 'honey, you aren't a freak' or something like that."

"Yeah, I would if it were true. But you, Grace Barnes, are a freak, and it is one of the amazing things I love about you." I wrapped my arms around her neck and pulled her forward until our lips touched. The kiss wasn't too needy, but it offered enough that I could tell we were and would always be okay on this.

"If I didn't love you, you would be in so much trouble."

"I know. And I love you too, freaky snot."

"I called your therapist to see if you could get in today. I know I should have asked you first, but I really thought that you might want to get a handle on this quickly. You know how your mind loves to twist events into nightmares."

"It is a good idea. Were you able to get me in?" Grace nodded and slid a piece of paper over to me with an address and three o'clock written on it. "What's this?"

"Today the therapist is working out of a different office. I wasn't going to assume that you wanted me to go with you, so I wrote the address down just in case."

"I think you are required to be there today. If not for my own sanity, for the fact that you will be able to recall a lot of what happened. When I have those episodes, I block most of it out."

"Then, gimme the paper back," said Grace, grabbing the paper away from me.

We went to see the therapist, and after going over the events of the previous night, we were given some exercises for me to practice to help with the panic attacks and to help me relax in general to hopefully stave off other attacks when my wonderful mind wandered. After the appointment with the therapist, Grace and I went to get groceries for dinner tonight with Aly.

"Hey, Kris," Grace called from the kitchen.

"What's up?" I asked, entering the room.

"Aly called, and she wants to bring Bailey. How do you feel about it? If you don't want her to come, she doesn't have to. I have no issues with that."

"It's okay, my love," I said, wrapping myself in her arms. "I don't have any issue with Bailey. Aly obviously felt the need to move on with her, and well, I do have you."

"Yeah, you do." Grace kissed me. I am certain that she meant for it to be a sweet kiss, but our hormones took over again and the kiss became much more.

Grace pushed me back against the island. I felt her hands slip under my shirt and find my breasts as she nipped and sucked on my neck. I moaned loudly and felt Grace smile as she made her way up to my lips.

"Do we…have…mmm…time for this?" I panted.

"Let me message Aly and we will."

Grace messaged Aly as we walked back to the bedroom. Once we entered, Grace tossed her phone onto the chair near the bay window. I pulled her onto the bed, and she rolled on top of me. The lustful look in her eyes made me shiver.

"Oh, baby," I groaned as we removed each other's clothes, and I felt her naked body slide against mine. At that moment, there was only us. The sounds of heavy breathing, moans of pleasure, and all the sounds you expect with passionate lovemaking filled the room.

"You realize that I'm not going to be able to keep my hands off you tonight," Grace said, sated and moving her hand across my stomach.

"Yeah, well, I am going to have a similar issue with you. Hopefully, Aly won't stay long."

"She's bringing Bailey…"

"It's okay. You may need to find a pair of big girl granny panties for me, but I can be a big girl for a little while. But if you leave me alone with her, I can't make any promises."

Grace kissed me softly. "I promise I will do everything in my power not to leave you alone with either of them."

"Thank you. When are they going to be here?"

I tried to control my hormones as her body leaned across mine as she looked at the clock. "Um, shit. Twenty minutes."

"We need to shower," I said, stating the obvious. "Alone or together?"

"Can you behave?"

"Most likely not."

"Well try, it is the only way we're both going to be ready."

I smirked. She knew there was no way in hell that I was going to behave. Hello, red hair, blue eyes, fair skin, naked, and wet. She was too tempting for me to resist.

We were just finishing getting dressed when the doorbell rang. I giggled and pulled Grace into my arms and gave her a chaste kiss. She quickly went and answered the door while I took a moment to compose myself.

I walked out to the living room and saw them all sitting down. "Hi."

"Hi," Bailey said in a short clipped tone.

"Hey. How are you?" said Aly. I saw her look at me and then at Grace. I glanced over in Grace's direction and smirked. I hadn't thought about the fact that we both still had wet hair. It was one of the drawbacks to having longer hair.

"I'm okay. Dealing."

"Can I get anyone anything to drink?" Grace asked, trying to ease the tension that had just crept into the room. "Beer?"

"Yes, please," both Aly and Bailey responded.

"I'll um, help you get it," I said, bolting for the kitchen.

Grace entered the kitchen right behind me. I turned to face her and was quickly enveloped in her arms. I clung to her as tight as I could without hurting her.

"Talk to me. What's going on, Kris?"

"I don't know. I just felt overcome with fear and sadness. I also think that Aly noticed our wet hair."

"Well, whose fault is it that our hair is still wet?"

"Yours," I said, before kissing her and then nibbling on her neck. "You were looking far too edible."

"I am not a dessert." I raised an eyebrow and just looked at her. "Seriusly? You want to go there?"

"Not while we have guests, but I will later. And, I will prove that you are dessert. A very yummy and tasty dessert." Grace let out a long groan, and I smiled innocently back at her.

We got the drinks and made our way back into the living room. An awkward silence overtook the room. I was trying not to sit too close to Grace, I didn't want to know how close Aly was sitting to Bailey, and I really wasn't sure what I wanted to know about Bailey. She was staring at me non-stop. I felt as though she was sizing me up.

"Can I have a minute alone with Kris?" Aly finally asked, breaking the silence. "Please?"

"That is up to Kris," Grace said, turning to me.

"I, um, okay." I looked at Grace and whispered, "Stay close, please."

Grace kissed the top of my head as she stood to leave the room.

"I don't know that I think that this is such a good idea," said Bailey quietly to Aly. She wasn't quite quiet enough for us not to hear her. "I know she says she is seeing Grace now, but who is to say that something isn't going to happen?"

"Trust me, please," Aly tried to reassure her girlfriend.

I was starting to wonder why she was with this woman. She obviously had trust issues. Did the woman not remember that she saw me out on a date with Grace the other night? Did she not notice the wet hair? Grace rolled her eyes and ushered Bailey out of the room.

"Okay, now it is just you and me. I'm sorry about her."

"What is her deal?"

"She knows that the reason that I started dating her was because she reminded me of you. Now that you're back, she is convinced that you are going to steal me away. That you and Grace are just pretending."

"Wow, I don't even have a clue what to say to

that." I was shocked. I was in love with Grace, not Aly. Well, not in a romantic way at least.

"What happened last night, Kris? Grace wouldn't give me details. I have been really worried about you." Aly sat down next to me and put her hand on my arm.

"I guess that I had a panic attack. Or at least that was what the therapist said today after Grace and I went to see her."

"I can't believe that you were able to get in right away to see her."

"Grace can be persuasive when she chooses to be."

"Will you tell me more about the panic attack?"

"I didn't think about the fact that I was going back to the place I was kidnapped from. I mean, I knew it, but I didn't really think how it was going to affect me. As we got closer, I felt my chest start to tighten, my head started to spin, I started to sweat, and it wasn't good."

"Wow, I guess none of us thought about how that was going to affect you. Are you okay? Really?"

"Yeah, Grace has been helping me." I explained the events of the previous night. The fear that I felt, the toll it took on my body and me. Aly patiently listened to what I had to say, and when I was done, I could see the sadness in her eyes.

"I can't imagine how you are so composed today," Aly said.

"Grace has been amazing. She—"

"Yeah, don't need you to say it. I saw the wet hair, and the looks you two have been sharing. I remember being in her position. The hornymoon phase. Are you happy? I mean, truly happy?"

"I am. The relationship with Grace is the same

intensity as before, but with the maturity that you gain with age."

"You make it sound like we're ancient." Aly laughed at the face I made.

"No, we aren't, but we are more mature."

"If I weren't with Bailey, would I stand a chance?"

"Honestly?" I asked, and she nodded. "No. I think with Grace is where my life is meant to be. I don't say that to be mean."

"I know, and I'm really happy for you. I'm jealous as hell that Grace has you, but if you are happy, I can learn to deal with it."

"Thanks. I do want you to be happy as well. If she doesn't make you happy, don't stay with her."

"She does, she just isn't you."

We stood, and I hugged Aly. Just as we parted, Grace and Bailey came back in the room. Grace made her way to my side and kissed me softly as she wrapped her arm around my waist.

We ordered pizza and talked about the past. When I saw it making Bailey uncomfortable, I changed the subject to try to get to know her more. I still seemed to irritate her a lot. I tried not to let it bother me, but that was easier said than done.

"I'll be back in a moment." I stood and hurried out of the room. I could feel the eyes watching me as I left, but I could only be expected to take so much.

I was stepping into the bedroom when I heard Grace call my name.

"What's going on?" she asked.

"I just needed to get away from the bullshit looks and stuff that Bailey was giving me." I sat down on the edge of the bed and buried my face in my hands. I felt Grace sit next to me. "I'm trying to be nice. I'm trying to like her, but she isn't making this easy."

"She feels threatened. Kris, Aly is still in love with you. I didn't realize it before, but tonight, yeah, I can tell."

"I know she is. She flat out asked me if she weren't with Bailey if she had a chance with me." I felt Grace tense up. I knew that her mind just went into overdrive. I took her hand in mine. "Relax, I told her no. I told her that I was with the person I was meant to be with."

I cupped Grace's face in my hands, leaned in, and kissed her. "I love you. You are who I was meant to be with."

"I love you, too."

There was a knock in the door before it opened a crack.

"Everyone still dressed?" asked Aly through the door.

"Unfortunately," Grace replied.

Aly entered the room, and I saw the concern in her eyes. "I got worried…"

"I just needed a moment."

"Bailey's giving her dirty looks and shit," Grace said.

"Yeah, I figured. As soon as you left the room, she asked when I was breaking up with her. I explained that I wasn't breaking up with her, that you had flat out told me that I wouldn't stand a chance with you."

"She had to at least be relieved by that," I said.

"No, she thinks I'm just lying and patronizing her."

"I'm, um, going to go talk to her. You two stay here."

I kissed Grace and then headed back to the living

room.

"What the hell is your problem?" I asked as soon as I got in the room.

"What do you mean?"

"You are a guest in this house, and you are giving me dirty looks. Aly has done nothing wrong, yet you think she is lying to you."

"Oh, come on, can't you see the way Aly looks at you? The longing and desire. I know the only reason she was interested in me was because I look like you. I'm not stupid. I'd seen your picture when we first started dating."

"But she is still with you. She knows that it is Grace that I've chosen for my future."

"Yeah, well, I still don't trust you."

"Don't trust me, I don't give a shit. Trust Aly, she deserves more respect from you."

"Listen, don't pretend to care about my relationship—"

"I don't," I interrupted. "I care about Aly. I have known her for a long time; I was engaged to her. She deserves to be treated better, and if you aren't going to do it, get the fuck out of her life."

As I finished this statement, I heard a gasp from behind me. I turned and saw Aly and Grace standing there, both of their mouths agape.

"So, what's going on out here?" asked Grace. The tension in the room was very thick.

"I think we should probably go. I think that is enough drama for one night," suggested Aly.

"Let me sign the papers, and then maybe Bailey will see that your ties to me are no more."

I saw Aly wince at this statement. I didn't say it to hurt her. I said it to put Bailey in her spot so that she would back off and give Aly a chance. I signed the papers, hugged Aly, and then moved to Grace's side. I felt her arm wrap around my waist. We said our good-byes, and then after Aly and Bailey left, we cleaned up and headed to the bedroom.

"You okay?" Grace asked.

"I'm here with you. I have what I truly need."

We went through our nighttime routine and then crawled into bed. Grace held me close in her arms as we drifted off to sleep.

Chapter Twenty-one

Two months had passed since I signed the house over to Aly and had fully started my life with Grace. My job was still going well. It felt good to be working again. The nightmares of the kidnapping and my time there were starting to subside. I attributed this to the fact that I was seeing my therapist two or three times a week. I got lucky in finding one that I could trust. Life was good.

I was in the kitchen preparing dinner one night when Grace got home. She came in with a huge smile on her face. Before I could say anything, she pulled me into a heated kiss. We aren't talking about the room getting a little warmer; we're talking steamy.

"Now, that is how you say hello," I said as the kiss ended. I was still holding her close in my embrace.

"Mmmm, yes it is."

"So, what has you in such a good mood?" I asked.

"You'll find out later," said Grace, before she bounced out of the room.

I laughed as I watched her leave. I smiled as I went back to my prep work and making dinner. I set the island and put a candle out for mood lighting. Once dinner was ready, I went in search of my girlfriend, who I hadn't seen since right after she got home. Usually she comes and sits at the island and keeps me company, but not tonight. I was really getting curious as to what she was up to.

I tried to open the bedroom door, but it was locked. I knocked on the door, heard her rustling around, and then she called back that she would be out in a minute. I went back into the kitchen and plated the food, poured us each a glass of wine. I had just finished pouring the wine when Grace came out in a pair of sweatpants and her favorite oversized shirt.

"Sorry, I was finishing getting things ready," she said with a smirk.

"I'm sure I should be scared, but I'm not."

Grace leaned over and kissed me. I felt her tongue skim across my lips. I opened my mouth as she slid her tongue into my mouth. I groaned at the incredible way it felt. I threaded my hand in her hair and pulled her tighter to me. We were both panting when the kiss ended.

"Mmmm, wow," I whispered.

"I agree. Thank you for making dinner."

"Hey, if that is what I get for making dinner, I may have to do it daily."

"I'm not going to complain. You know how much I hate cooking."

"Maybe we can negotiate something," I said, waggling my eyebrows.

We ate dinner and cuddled on the couch for a bit before Grace excused herself. I was left to sit there wondering what she was up to. Grace was never good at keeping a secret, so I didn't know how she was managing this one. About fifteen minutes later, Grace called for me to come back to the bedroom.

As I neared the bedroom, I heard soft music playing. I opened the door and the room was bathed in candlelight. Grace had placed about twelve to fifteen votives with tealight candles in them around the room.

There was a path of roses leading from the door to the bed. It was so beautiful that I wanted to cry, then I followed the path to the bed and my breath caught, my body temperature rose. There, kneeling in the middle of the bed, was Grace. That alone was an amazing sight, but tonight the bright blue satin chemise that she was wearing enhanced it. The color matched her bright blue eyes. Her stunning red hair was down, brushing just over her shoulders. I felt my mouth both go dry and some drool slip out of the corner and dribble down my face.

"Come here," Grace said, offering me a sultry smile.

"Y-you…I…damn," I managed to mumble out. My brain was focused on the breathtaking beauty in the middle of the bed.

By the time I reached the bed, Grace had made her way over to the edge. I leaned in and kissed her, my hands running along the sides of her body. I could feel the heat from her body coming through the thin material. Our mouths were moving together, tongues teasing the other; our breath was becoming ragged and dear god I was turned on. Grace didn't wear things like this. I think in all our time together she wore one twice. Granted they didn't last long on her body, but who can blame me?

I pulled back just enough to look her in the eyes. "You are the most beautiful, sexy, amazing woman in the world. I love you!"

"I love you, too. You are too overdressed to be allowed in the bed with me. And, mmmm, I really want you in bed with me."

I removed all but my bra and panties. I was going to remove them as well, but Grace stopped me.

"I'll take care of that. I need you in bed with me now."

I crawled into the middle of the bed, kneeling with her, our bodies pressed together. I felt her lips brush my shoulder and move in toward my neck. Then she was sucking on my pulse point at the base of my neck. She knew that spot drove me nuts.

"Oh god," I managed to say as she made her way up my neck.

I pulled her lips to mine. I needed to feel them. I heard her groan. My hands had made their way to her breasts. I could feel her nipples pressing against the fabric, begging for freedom.

Grace broke our kiss and moved along my jaw to my ear. I felt her tongue trace the outline of my ear, causing me to shiver.

"I have loved you for so long," Grace whispered into my ear. "I didn't know until that first night you kissed me." I let out a groan and pulled her body as close as I could to mine. "Marry me."

My hands stopped moving. I wasn't sure I had heard her right. Did she just ask me to marry her? Well, not really ask, but does she really want us to get married?

"Marry me. I want to spend the rest of my life making love to you," Grace said again. She then pulled back and looked at me.

"Y-you want me to marry you?"

"Yes. There is and has been nobody I have wanted to spend my life with other than you. Please, say yes."

I felt her eyes watching me intently. "Yes," I said.

I found myself being pushed backward onto the bed and her body on top of me. Her lips were on mine. I found the bottom of the chemise and reached under it. I let out a loud moan when I found out that she was wearing nothing under them. I slipped my hand between her legs. She was so wet. I couldn't have stopped had I wanted to. I slipped two fingers deep inside her.

"Oh, Kris. Yes," said Grace as her hips rocked in time with my thrusts. "Harder."

Grace arched back so that she was straddling me. I sat up, and I tried to pull the satin garment off, but I wasn't willing to stop with I was doing. Grace helped me pull it off, and I quickly started to tease her nipple with my mouth. I felt her unsnap my bra. In one motion, I flipped us so that she was below me. I quickly moved my hand out of her, tossed the bra aside, and then thrust back inside her. I used my hips to help me thrust deeper and harder. Grace pulled me into a heated kiss before she couldn't take it any longer and came and called out my name with a powerful shudder. I leaned forward and kissed her. I felt her hands push my panties out of the way and then her fingers were inside me. God, she knew how to make me feel things I don't think I was supposed to feel. I rode her into a rapid orgasm. I collapsed on the bed next to her.

"That...was..." I started to say between gasps.

"Fucking hot," said Grace, finishing the thought for me.

I nodded in agreement. After several minutes, as our breathing leveled out, Grace lay on her side and propped her head up on one hand, her other hand covering my still racing heart.

"I love you, Kris."

"I love you, too. Did we really get engaged?"

"Yep, you said yes. There is no backing out."

"I wouldn't want to do that anyway."

Grace turned to her nightstand, pulled out a ring, and slipped it on my finger. "There, now you are officially wearing my ring."

"You had this all planned out, huh?"

"Well, yeah. I had been planning on seducing you with the sexy clothes and romantic setting for a week. The proposal and stuff, well, that was a new development today. I was window shopping on lunch and the ring struck me as something you would like and wear, so I decided to get it and ask you tonight."

"What if I had said no?"

"I knew you wouldn't. We're meant to be together."

We took a short nap before spending the rest of the night worshiping each other.

❧❧❧❧

The following day, we managed to make our way out of bed, and we went to get Grace a ring. We had thought about doing matching rings, but the one she got me wasn't her style. I was just pleased that she was wearing one. Aly and I had never done that. I never got a ring while we were engaged. It was another way that this looked, felt, and was different.

"So, are you going to call and tell your parents?" I asked as we were walking down the street holding hands.

"Yeah, eventually. Right now, I want to enjoy us being the only ones that know. I want you to myself in that way for a bit. Does that make sense?"

"It does."

"Are you okay with that? If not, we can call them when we get home."

"Grace, I'm very okay with it. I think we do need to get home, though."

"Why? Are you okay? Is something wrong?"

"Something is wrong. You are wearing far more clothing than I want you to be. And since we are out in public, I cannot do the things that I want to you."

Grace smiled and took my hand as we raced home. We spent the rest of the weekend in an undressed state, mostly confined to the bed. It was perfect.

The following Monday was a rough day. I didn't want the weekend to end. We both went off to work. I was out on my lunch break when I ran into Aly. This was the first time I had seen her since the night she and Bailey had come over for dinner. It felt very awkward after everything that had gone on.

"Hi," said Aly, smiling as she walked up to me.

"Hi. How are you doing?" It felt forced, but I did still care about her.

"I'm okay. How are you?"

"I'm good," I said, before an awkward silence fell over us.

"I wanted to apologize about Bailey. She has some insecurities, and you coming back played on them."

"It's fine, Aly."

"Are things with you and Grace still going well?"

I don't know what the expression was that showed on my face, but I swear I saw Aly literally turn green with envy.

"Things with Grace and I are going very, very well." I smiled at her as I played with the ring on my finger. "Speaking of which, here she comes."

Aly turned and saw Grace walking up to us. She had a huge smile on her face and she winked at me. I admit my insides turned all mushy and my internal temperature rose. Grace kissed me, and I let our lips linger together a little longer than normal, but after the weekend we had, who wouldn't?

"Hello," Grace said.

I stepped behind her and wrapped my arms around her waist. I wasn't trying to rub our relationship in Aly's face, but I needed to feel Grace as close as I could.

"So, what is new with you two?" Aly asked.

I looked at Grace, and she looked at me and shrugged. It was a quick wordless conversation. We knew what the other was thinking. The three of us stepped over to a nearby bench and sat down.

"Well, Kris and I got engaged over the weekend." Grace blurted out this news. I don't think she meant to say it that way, but it came out and boy did it get cold in that area.

"I-I'm sorry, you what?" asked Aly, grabbing my left hand and staring at the ring.

"We got engaged," I stated, before kissing the side of Grace's head as she leaned into me.

"Do you really think that is a good idea? You haven't been back for that long, Kris. And, what the hell were you thinking, Grace? You are supposed to be helping her heal, not pushing her into things she's not ready for. Especially something like this," snapped Aly, her voice getting louder and louder.

"She isn't pushing me," I said, softly.

"Kris, I know that you don't think that she is pushing you, but sweetie, you are still getting a handle on everything. You haven't been back too long, and you went through so much."

"Don't you dare talk down to her," Grace snapped.

"I'm not. I am concerned for her. I still care a lot

about her, and I don't want to see you hurt her again. Kris, how do you know you can trust her? You have only been together a short while. You don't know who Grace is anymore. You were gone for a year, and before that, you and I were together."

"You aren't her keeper, dammit. She is an adult and fully capable of making her own decisions—"

"Not that you wouldn't try to influence them to go your way. You never got over her, did you? You have always been looking for the opportunity to steal her back. Even if it means taking advantage of what happened to her to get her to choose you."

"No, I never stopped loving her, and damn right I was looking for an opportunity to get her back. But I would never take advantage of her or the ordeal that she went through. You seem to be forgetting that Kris is an adult. She is capable of making her own decisions."

"Both of you stop acting like I'm not sitting right fucking here," I said, standing up and causing Grace, who was still leaning up against me, to almost fall off the bench. I started pacing back and forth, pressing my hands to my head. The pressure inside my head was growing rapidly.

"Kris?" said Aly.

"Baby?" Grace said.

"Grace is right. I am able to make my own fucking decisions. But I am not a pawn or trophy for either of you. Nobody wins me."

I saw Aly start to get up, and I put my hand out to stop her. Grace sat there. I could tell that it was taking everything she had to not get up and take me in her arms. I appreciated her effort. I knew it couldn't be easy for her. It was never easy for her to sit back and watch me grapple with my inner turmoil.

"Aly, Grace hasn't done anything wrong. I could have told her no when we first kissed, but I love her. Yes, you and I were engaged, but that ended a long time ago. You ended that when you decided to date someone else. You made that choice. Not Grace, not me, you."

"Yes, I did, and I regret that and I regret losing you. But seriously, Kris, think about what you are doing. Grace cheated on you in the past. Do you remember how horrible that felt? I don't want to see you get hurt like that again. You were so devastated."

"And you dating Bailey like four months after she disappeared wasn't cheating?" Grace interjected.

"Hey, we didn't know if she was alive or dead."

"So you moved on?"

"*Hey*!" I yelled. "Enough, both of you." We were causing a bit of a scene, but I didn't care at this point.

"Sorry," whispered Grace. Aly just glared.

I walked over and stood in front of Grace. She looked up into my eyes. I gave her a slight nod, and she wrapped her arms around me and buried her head in my stomach. I put my hands on the back of her head, letting her know that I was okay.

"You are out of line, Aly. Yes, Grace did something stupid in the past. I am not going to hold it against her for the rest of our lives. She has stated that it won't happen again, and I believe her. I can't live life holding on to the past." I pulled away from Grace and took a couple of steps toward Aly.

"Interesting choice of words there," Aly said, bitterly. "I guess that means that you can't hold on to me and don't need me in your life."

"That isn't what I said. I am simply not going to hold the past over Grace. I love her, Aly. I would like for you to be happy for us," I said, softly.

"I can't be right now. I'm sorry."

I watched as Aly hurriedly walked away from us. I had hoped that she would be happy for us, but she wasn't. She was far from happy, and I had no clue how to fix it.

"Just give her some time," said Grace as she took my hand.

"I didn't mean to hurt her." I felt the tears creeping toward the surface.

"I know you didn't."

Grace wrapped her arms around me and held me. I knew I had to get back to work soon, but I didn't want to leave her embrace.

The rest of the week passed quickly. I hadn't heard from Aly. I had tried to call her a couple of times, but she didn't answer. This weekend we were going to tell Grace's family about our engagement.

❧ ❧ ❧ ❧

I was pacing the airport terminal while we waited for Grace's parents to arrive. We had hoped that Tyler would be joining us, but he and Jenna had other plans. I wasn't totally upset that Jenna wasn't going to be there. Things never did get resolved after what happened the last time we were back.

"Hey," Grace said, wrapping her arms around my waist and pulling me to her on one of my many passes. "What's going on? Why are you so nervous?"

"Aren't you nervous about telling your parents that we're engaged?"

"No, and I don't see why you are either. Care to enlighten me?"

"Let's see, my past from age five until two weeks ago."

"Kris, they know all that stuff, and they still love you. Try again," she said as I nuzzled my head into her neck.

"I just…I don't know what it means to be a part of a family. I love you, and I don't want to disappoint you or anyone else."

"That could never happen." Grace kissed me softly. We heard over the PA that her parents' flight had landed. We moved to the gate to greet them.

On the drive back to the house, Grace's parents filled us in on their flight and the amusing things that happened. Once we got to the house and got them settled, we all made our way to the living room. Erin and Sean were seated on the couch, Grace was standing in front of me, and we had our fingers entwined together as she leaned into my embrace.

"So, are you going to tell us whatever this news is?" asked Sean.

"You guys are moving in together," said Erin.

"Um, we've been living together since Kris got back, Mom." Grace chuckled. "No, um, how do I put this…"

"Just spit it out, kid," said Sean in an exasperated tone.

"Kris and I are getting married," Grace said, raising our hands and showing them the rings.

"Don't mess with me. Are you serious?" asked Erin.

I felt fear well up inside me. I was certain that this was the moment that they were going to tell Grace that they thought it was a bad idea, that I wasn't good enough or welcome in their family. Grace must have felt me tense because she brought our entwined hands up and kissed the ring she had put on my finger.

"I asked Kris to marry me a week ago today."

Her mother let out this squeal/yell, I really don't know what it was, but it was loud and I'm certain that I heard two of the neighborhood dogs bellow out as well. Within seconds, we found ourselves wrapped into a group hug with Grace's parents. I felt bad for Grace since she was in front of me, and she caught the brunt of the squeeze.

"I want all the details," Erin said, once we finally separated from the hug. I felt myself blush, remembering how and when Grace had proposed.

"The official story we are telling people is that Kris made us a nice romantic dinner, we cuddled for a bit, and then I knelt in front of her and asked her to marry me."

"What do you mean the official story? Is it not the real story?" asked Sean.

"Those details are better left between Kris and me."

I knew I had to be as red as Grace's hair or a few shades darker. It took a minute, and then Grace's parents caught on and joined in the blush.

Saturday, we spent the time catching up. Sean and I talked about sports and remodeling ideas for the house, while Grace and her mother discussed wedding ideas and gardening.

Chapter Twenty-two

As I looked around the room, it felt cold, sterile, isolated. The walls were a light blah beige, and the floor reminded me of the flooring from school. One-foot by one-foot squares of linoleum. There was a semi-large window overlooking the roof of another part of the building. The roof was covered with rocks. The horizon outside felt familiar, but I wasn't sure what to make of it. It was nighttime and there wasn't a lot to see. There were lights, but nothing defining, nothing with a 'you are here' arrow. As I watched the lights, I started to hear a rhythmic beeping.

Beep…beep…beep…beep.

I turned looked around the room. That was when I saw a bed. My eyes followed along the edge of the bed from the foot to the head of the bed. I could make out the outline of a body in the bed from a distance, but I wasn't able to see whom it was. I followed some wire leads and was able to identify the beeping. The wire leads were leading from the body lying in the bed to a heart-monitoring machine. I watched the line going across the screen and that the spikes coincided with the beeps. Another monitor beeped and then a faint motor noise started. I felt a pressure forming on my right arm. It kept getting tighter and tighter. I looked at the body and saw a blood pressure cuff on the arm. When the pressure subsided, I slowly walked over to the bed and looked down at the person in the bed.

"Oh, god," I gasped. It was me lying there. "How was this possible? Was this real? Was this a dream? Oh, please let this be a dream."

I stared at the body. It looked so weak and frail. I looked so weak and frail. "How long had I been like this?" I heard a noise and turned to see the door opening.

"Hey, Kris," Grace said, entering with a bouquet of flowers. "How are you doing today?"

I watched as she set the flowers in the empty vase on the tray table by the window. Grace looked tired. I watched as she moved the lone chair in the room next to the bed and took the hand of the woman in the bed. I felt my left hand warm slightly.

"What the hell is going on?" I said to myself as I looked between my warming hand and the body in the bed.

"The nurse said you had a good day today. I'm glad you have had a few more of those lately. Although, I'm still not happy about that episode you had when you went into cardiac arrest and started to seize, that wasn't good. You scared the shit out of me. I can still close my eyes and see it. Please, don't do that to me again."

"How long have I been like this? I wonder what she is talking about. Why did I go into cardiac arrest? Why did I have a seizure? Wait, what the hell am I saying? This isn't real. I have to be dreaming. This cannot be real."

"I miss you, Kris. God, I wish you would wake up. I have so much that I want to talk to you about. Well, I talk to you this way, but I would rather you be able to answer me. I have some big decisions to make in my life. I need you...Please, wake up."

I felt the wetness from her tears on my hand, running down my arm.

"What decisions did she have to make? What happened to me?" I heard the beeping increase in frequency as the panic started to rise within me.

"*No!*" I awoke, gasping for air, my heart thundering in my chest.

"Kris? Baby?" Grace asked, sitting up next to me.

I continued gasping for air. Grace wrapped her arms around me and held me close. It took a few minutes, but I was finally able to regulate my breathing.

"Are you okay?" asked Grace, whispering softly in my ear.

"Yeah, I think so." I leaned into her embrace. I told her about the dream, about how it made me feel.

"That is really fucked up," Grace said.

"Thank you for stating the obvious, dear," I said. Sometimes, she was such a goof.

"Well, it is. What is it with your mind that it won't let you have a break from this stuff?"

"I don't know, but I fear someday it will be too much for you to handle."

"Never. I love you. You are stuck with me."

Grace kissed the side of my head, we got comfortable again, and she held me until I fell asleep.

We went out for brunch with Grace's parents before we took them to the airport. I was sad to see them go, but overall it was a really good weekend.

❧ ❧ ❧ ❧

Three weeks had passed since our encounter with Aly. Something still bothered me. Deep down, I knew that Aly was hurt, but she had moved on. She had made that choice; nobody forced her.

As I was walking downtown, I let out an audible

groan when I saw Bailey walking with a purpose in my direction.

"You and I need to talk," she said.

"I don't really think that there is anything that you and I have to talk about," I said.

"I do." Bailey grabbed my arm and directed me toward an out of the way bench.

"Take your hands off me." I could feel the anxiety and fear well up inside me. I tried not to let it show. I didn't want this woman to know that she could easily have that level of power over me.

"Sorry," said Bailey. She let go of my arm, and we sat down at opposite ends of the small bench.

"What do you and I possibly have to discuss?"

"I don't know what the hell you and Grace did, but Aly has barely been able to function lately, and when she does, she is angry, hurtful, and downright mean."

"We didn't do anything," I said.

"Well, someone did something, and she said it was because of the two of you. So, tell me, what the hell did you do to my girlfriend?" The anger in Bailey's tone was causing her voice to become louder. I really didn't want another scene.

"Listen, talk to your girlfriend about it. She won't talk to me so why in the hell should I talk to you?"

"You owe me that much. You are destroying my life and my relationship. Unlike you, I love Aly."

"You don't know me, and you have no idea my feelings toward Aly. As for owing you anything, no, not even close. I don't owe you a damn thing."

"You have devastated my girlfriend."

"No, I didn't. I don't control how your girlfriend acts, how she feels, or any of that shit. So, you can just stop blaming me for her attitude."

I stood up, and Bailey stood as well and grabbed hold of my upper arm. She squeezed it very tightly, causing me to wince.

"Listen, bitch," she started.

"Bailey, take your hands off her," said a voice from behind me. I recognized it as Aly's.

"Baby, what are you doing out here?" asked Bailey, letting go of my arm and moving to hug Aly.

"Kris? Are you okay?" Aly asked, moving up to my side and putting a gentle hand on my shoulder. Her tone was calm and soothing. I knew she could see me barely treading water under the surface. "Kris?"

"I'm, I'm fine," I managed to get out in a raspy tone that told any and everybody that I was far from being fine.

"Aly, why are you out here?" asked Bailey again.

"I needed to get away and, well, this is where my life changed quite drastically a few weeks ago."

Bailey turned and glared at me. "Aly, tell your girlfriend what is going on with you so that she'll leave me the fuck alone. Right now, she is blaming me for it all," I said.

"Well, in part, it does have to do with you." Aly turned from me to Bailey before continuing. "The reason my mood has been so hit and miss lately is because Kris and Grace informed me that they are getting married."

"You knew they were dating. Why is this a shocker?"

"Dating yes, but marriage is a whole different level when it comes to relationships. When you get engaged and are ready to marry someone, your relationship completely changes."

I turned and saw Aly was now looking at me, love still apparent in her eyes. She used to have this love and look when we got engaged, when she was ready to spend her life with me. I avoided looking at Bailey. I could feel the angry vibes she was sending in my direction.

"Aly, why haven't you returned any of my calls or text messages?" I asked, meeting her eyes.

"I needed time to process, to mourn."

"She didn't die, Aly," Bailey scoffed.

"No, but the Kris I was with and going to marry did. The woman that I knew like that was now gone. That needed to be dealt with."

"And has it been?" I asked.

"I don't know. I thought it had been until I saw the look in your eyes when Bailey had your arm."

"Of course, poor, poor, pitiful Kris. What about the shit I've had to deal with for the past three weeks? Do you even care that you have hurt me?"

"Yes, I care about that," Aly said. "I do love you, Bailey—"

"But I'm not Kris."

"I'm nothing important. I have to go. Grace is going to be worried if I'm late getting home."

"We aren't done here," Bailey called behind me.

As I walked away, I heard her and Aly exchanging heated words. I didn't want to come between them, but I really didn't like Bailey.

⁂

When I arrived home, I could see that Grace was stressed and appeared to have been pacing. I wasn't that late, so I didn't think I was the cause. Okay, I hoped I wasn't the cause.

"Are you okay?" asked Grace. She hurried to me and wrapped me in her arms.

"Why?" I asked.

"Aly called. She told me what happened. Are you okay?"

"There was a mild panic attack when Bailey grabbed my arm, but yeah, I'm okay." I leaned in to kiss her, but she pulled back.

"Bailey did what?"

"She grabbed my arm."

"Uh huh, and she has a death wish? Who the hell does she think she is putting her hands on you? Does Aly know this?" I nodded. "What the hell!"

"Baby, relax," I said, wrapping my arms around her waist in order to hold her body close to mine.

"But—" Grace started to say, until I kissed her neck softly. "You don't play fair."

"Nobody said I did. I love you."

"I love you, too. But I am not going to forget what Bailey did. And why the hell didn't Aly tell me about it?"

I took Grace's hand and led her over to the sofa. I had a feeling this was going to take a bit to pass.

"She probably didn't tell you because she thought that she had the issue covered. She got Bailey to let go of my arm, and then she made sure I was okay. Please, let's not dwell on this."

"All right, so tell me about this little meeting you had with them."

I explained to Grace what had happened since I left the office. She was still angry with Bailey, but she promised me that she would let it go. While Grace made dinner, I went and got changed before setting up her laptop in the living room.

"So, wanna start planning our wedding?" I asked Grace. I was hoping this would add to her distraction and help her forget about earlier.

"Hmmm, watch TV or plan our future?"

"Fine, I suppose I can go plan it by myself," I teased. I started to get up, and Grace pulled me onto her lap and kissed me with so much passion I almost forgot what I was going to go and do.

"Where do you think you're going?" she said into my lips.

I moved and straddled her lap, and I felt her hands rubbing my thighs. "Well, I was going to go plan our wedding." As her hands moved toward my inner thighs, my hips jumped on their own.

"Well, let's get to planning, and then we can celebrate," Grace said, seductively.

"I love that idea."

"Mmmm, I love you."

We kissed for several minutes before I slid off Grace's lap, and she pulled the laptop over and brought up her calendar. We looked over various dates before finally agreeing on one. It was the anniversary of our first-ever kiss. Yes, I realize that it was because of a nightmare, but had I not had that nightmare, my life would be so very different. That was going to give us ten months to plan and arrange our wedding.

"So, we have a date. Do you want to look at venues?" asked Grace as I cuddled closer.

"Did you have some place in mind?"

"Well, I was thinking that maybe we could go to Treehouse Point in Issaquah, Washington."

Grace pulled up the website and right there on the front page of their site was the most romantic looking venue. The fact that it was a treehouse only added to what made it so perfect. Our childhood was spent in the treehouse in her parents' backyard. Grace opened the pictures, and we looked at the different styles of treehouses, standard ones, and ones you accessed via a bridge.

"That is perfect," I said leaning over and kissing Grace. "Where did you find or hear of this place?"

"I may have been thinking about our wedding recently." I saw a sly grin cross her face.

"Did you already reserve it?"

"No, because we hadn't picked a date. I just wanted to find some place that was going to be special and remind us both of our history together."

"You realize that we have no romantic history with treehouses, right?" I teased.

"Yes, but in looking back, I do think I had a crush on you growing up."

I took the laptop from her hands and set it back on the coffee table before pulling Grace up and leading her to the bedroom without a word. I pressed our bodies close before whispering in her ear, "I agree, I believe that we have been attracted to one another for a very long time." I felt her shudder, which caused me to smile.

Grace pushed me onto my back on the bed before covering my body with her own. Her lips hungrily met mine. I felt her hands under my shirt and unfastening the front-clasp bra I was wearing. Then her hands were on my breasts, my nipples going instantly hard. I arched into her touch.

"Oh, Grace," I moaned.

Grace moved my shirt up and lowered her mouth to tease my protruding nipples. I could feel her sucking on one while rolling the other with her fingers before switching sides.

"Kris, touch me."

My hands slid under her shirt. I let out a loud moan when I felt her naked breasts cupped in my hands. I needed to feel our bodies pressed together, skin to skin. We removed our shirts and then came together. I felt just how hard her nipples were as they rubbed against my own. I flipped us over so that Grace was beneath me. I leaned down and sensually kissed her neck. As I did, I felt her legs wrap around my waist, pulling our lower halves together. As I ground my hips into her, I could feel the wetness seeping through her underwear and shorts. I knew she was as wet as I was. I could smell the arousal. Mmmm, she was making me dizzy with desire.

"Make me scream," Grace said. I didn't need to be told twice.

I kissed a trail from her mouth, to her ear, down her neck, to the valley between her breasts. I could feel her heart racing as I moved lower, slowly removing her shorts and panties until she was completely naked. I kissed her mound before dipping my tongue lower and tasting her. I teased her swollen clit before taking it in my mouth. I felt her raise her hips to gain more friction. I couldn't help myself; I sucked harder on her center before plunging inside her. I could feel her hips rocking with me. I felt her hand on the back of my head, holding me tight against her.

"Mmmm, Grace," I groaned at the amazing woman allowing me to make love to her.

I continued thrusting and sucking. I could hear her breath catching. I could feel her inner walls spasm. I knew she was close. I increased the speed and force of what I was doing to her. Her panting and moans grew louder and louder with each thrust. Finally, Grace couldn't take it anymore, and she let the orgasm wash over her. I continued what I had been doing until she arched up and came again. I felt her tug at my hair, and I allowed her to pull me up to her mouth. I kissed her passionately.

Grace came one more time before flipping me over and ripping the clothing on my lower body off me. She then firmly attached herself to my center and thrust inside me. I knew I was so close. Tasting her and hearing her always made me so hot. The fact that we were planning our future before making love amplified tonight.

I came several times before Grace moved to lie next to me and pull me into her arms. We lay together, feeling every twitch and every breath. It wasn't long before she rolled on top of me, and we made love again, and again. We made love until we were too exhausted to move.

I love you's were the last words exchanged before we drifted to sleep.

It was several hours later when I faintly heard Grace saying my name, but I couldn't open my eyes. I was trying, but it wouldn't happen.

Beep...Beep...

"Kris, baby. Baby, wake up, please," Grace kept repeating as the damn beeping continued.

Beep...Beep...Beep...Beep...

Chapter Twenty-three

G-Grace?" I struggled to say. My voice was hoarse and raspy. I felt as though a truck or maybe two had run me over.

"Kris?" Grace said, sounding surprised. "Oh, god, am I hearing things again?"

"Grace?" I said again, moving my hand this time.

"Kris? Move your hand again," Grace said, and I complied. "Aly, get the nurse. She's waking up."

I heard a door open and close. I had just opened my eyes and made eye contact with Grace when within seconds there was a flurry of action surrounding me. I felt Grace pulled from my side. I tried to find her, but I heard her being ushered out of the room.

"Ms. Holt, I am Dr. Gomez. Do you know where you are?"

It took me a few moments to ground myself before I looked around the room and saw several machines. "The hospital?"

"Yes, do you know how you got here?"

"No."

"Do you know your full name?"

"Kristine Kay Holt."

"Do you know what year it is?"

"Why are you asking me these questions?" I felt the panic starting to build within me.

"We are trying to assess what you know about what has gone on."

"I-I want to see Grace," I said, fear taking over. I heard the heart rate monitor start to beep faster. "Where's Grace? Please?"

Dr. Gomez put his hand on my hand and gave it a reassuring squeeze. "Okay, this has to be pretty disorienting for you. Why don't you talk with Grace, and we'll be back in a little while to talk? Us getting you all worked up isn't going to do anyone any good."

I saw everyone leave; I was alone for a couple of minutes and then Grace entered. She hurried over to the edge of the bed and took my hand in hers.

"Hi," she said.

"What the hell is going on?" I asked, panic evident in my voice.

"You are in the hospital—"

"I gathered that. Grace, how did I get here? Why are they asking me all those odd questions?"

"What questions?"

"Like what my name is. Do I know where I am? Do I know what year it is?"

"Kris, what is the last thing that you remember?"

"I remember you and me, a very romantic night after we finished picking our wedding venue..."

Grace looked at me, shock and confusion accenting her face. In all honesty, it scared the shit out of me.

"Kris, I don't know how to tell you this, but you've been in a coma for five years."

"What? No. How? I don't understand." I could feel the tears welling up in my eyes. The damn heart monitor and its beeping were going to drive me bat-shit crazy if they didn't shut it up.

"Kris, we were in high school. It was our senior year. I don't know the specifics, but I found you barely alive in the treehouse in my parents' backyard."

"No, Grace, I remember that. When you found me, I hurt. You wanted to take me to the hospital, but I said no. You stayed with me that night. You went to get blankets for us to sleep in the treehouse, and Tyler came back with you. I had some bruised ribs and a black eye, but that was it. We graduated high school and left for college two days later."

"No, Kris, we didn't," Grace said. I tried to pull my hand away from her, but she only held on tighter.

"Why are you lying to me?"

"I'm not."

"Grace, please. I don't understand," I said, a tear rolling down my face.

"Kris, I found you unconscious in my treehouse. Tyler, Dad, and I called an ambulance. You've been here ever since."

"If I have been here, then why do I remember graduating? Going to college? Getting a place after? I remember being kidnapped, and then escaping."

"That didn't happen. Yes, I went to college, but I did it nearby so that I could come and see you as often as possible."

"I...I am so confused." I put my head in my hands and started to cry. "I don't understand why I have all of these memories, and you're telling me that they aren't real."

"Hey, we'll figure it out," Grace said, wrapping me in a hug. God, it felt good to be in her arms. I leaned into her embrace. "Are you ready to let the doctor in again?"

"I-I don't know. Will you stay?"

"Of course. I'll be right back. I'm always going to be here for you."

I watched Grace leave the room. I didn't know what to think or believe. Had I really been here for five years? Was everything I knew a dream? How was that possible? What was going to happen with the rest of my life? What life?

The doctors came in, and Grace perched herself at the end of the bed. They tried to get her to leave, but I told them that I needed her to stay. They took blood, did several physical tests. I had a lot of muscle atrophy, but not as much as I would have, had Grace not helped me with exercises while I was in the coma. Knowing that she did that for me made my heart swell. Dream or no dream, I loved this woman.

"I'll be back tomorrow to discuss your future," Dr. Gomez said.

Everyone cleared out of the room except Grace. She was still perched at the end of the bed. I hated how distant everything felt. I wanted her to hold me, to kiss me and tell me that everything was going to be okay. I couldn't help it. I felt the tears well up in my eyes and then pour down my face.

"Hey, what's wrong?" asked Grace softly as she took my hand in hers again.

"I...It doesn't matter."

"Kris, of course it matters. What's wrong?"

"What isn't wrong? I just found out that what I thought was my life, wasn't. I think I need some time to process things. It is a lot to take in."

"Do you want me to leave?"

"I don't know why you would stay," I said. It was a harsher statement than I planned, but I still had a fuzzy brain, and I needed time to understand what my life was now.

"Kris, you are my best friend. I would stay for

you. I'm here for you."

"I just need to let things sink in. Maybe you can come by tomorrow? I mean, I'm sure you have a life and everything. Who would want to hang out in a hospital with someone in my situation?"

"I'll be here first thing in the morning."

"Thanks," I said.

"I'm glad you finally woke up. I've missed you a lot."

Grace kissed the side of my head before leaving the room. Once she was gone, I let the tears flow. I turned on the television and well, yep, it was five years later. They weren't lying about that. What about the memories? What about my life? Grace and I were supposed to be getting married soon. It couldn't all be fake.

❧❧❧❧

It wasn't long after Grace left that I drifted off to sleep. You would think after sleeping for five years I wouldn't be so tired, but everything that went on emotionally and physically wore me out. When I woke the next morning, Grace was sitting at the side of the bed.

"Hey," she said, her eyes sparkling in the sunlight.

"Hey." I reached out and took Grace's hand in mine. Out of habit, I entwined our fingers together. When I saw the look that Grace was giving me, I quickly let go of her fingers and diverted my eyes from her.

"You don't have to pull away from me."

"Yeah, I think it is best if I do."

"Why don't you tell me about the memories?"

"Why?"

"I want to understand. I want to know the other life, the other you."

"Why?" This seemed to be my new favorite word. "They aren't real…nothing I know at this point is real."

"I know that, but maybe it will help if you talk about it. We used to share our dreams when we were kids. Please? I want to know what you experienced. Start at the first thing you remember."

"I remember our freshman year in college. I played the field a lot, enjoyed, if you will, the college scene. You got mad at me, and we even stopped speaking. I figured you hated me so I started to avoid you. I went out of my way not to see you, to make it easier for us. Towards the end of our sophomore year, we started to talk again. You save me from the nightmares. It was after one of those nightmares that we had our first kiss. Not long after that, we started dating and you moved in with me. I remember that you had a horribly smelly roommate. I teased you that it was more the reason that you wanted to move in with me. You always denied it though."

"I don't know how you know about my college roommate, but you and I never went to college together. We never dated."

"I get that you are telling me that my life, all of these memories are fake. To me, though, they are very, very real."

"I'm sorry, Kris. I'm not going to lie to you. None of what you have said so far happened. I'm not saying this to be mean, I just don't want you to get hurt more."

"Yes, because what could possibly hurt more than being told your life is a lie and all that you know is made up. Please just leave," I said, coldly.

"Kris…please."

"You ask me to tell you about what I remember of my life, our life, and then you just rudely say that it never happened. To me, it did. Get the fuck out of my room," I snapped. "I don't know why you are even bothering with me."

Grace wrote her number down on a piece of paper that was on the tray in front of me. I wanted to throw it in her face, but there were too many wires attached to me, and I didn't want to pull one and have to listen to another damn machine beep.

"Call me. I'm not letting this be the end of us."

"Why even bother with me?" I mumbled as I watched her leave the room.

I sat there alone with only the beeping of the heart monitor machine to keep me company. Well, that and my thoughts. How could everything in my head be a dream? It happened. I know it did. Grace isn't telling me something. I picked up the empty water pitcher in front of me and hurled it across the room. The plastic shattered.

"Miss? Are you okay?" asked the orderly or nurse as she entered the room.

"I'm not sure. I don't think it matters to anyone either way," I said, defeated.

"Would you like some company? Maybe someone to talk to?"

"I don't want to impose or be a burden. I apparently have been doing that from this bed for years now."

"Let me go sign out, and I'll come back," she said, smiling at me.

I watched her leave. I thought to myself how fitting it was that the one person who truly seemed to care was a complete stranger. If Grace was telling the truth, I was a high school dropout, I'd been in a coma for five years, and I was alone because we never fell in love. What do I do now? I was wallowing in self-pity when the door opened again.

"Hi, again."

"I really don't want to be a burden. If you have some place else to be, really, I understand."

"I want to be here. My name is Mya."

Mya was pretty. She had black hair, green eyes, and an athletic build. She looked to be my height or a little taller, but her face just showed kindness, and that I needed right now.

"Hi, I'm Kris, unless that is a lie as well," I said. I watched Mya move the chair closer to the bed and sit down near me.

"I'm sorry, I don't understand."

"I'm sorry. I'm throwing myself a pity party. I was informed yesterday that I was in a coma for the past five years. Today I found out that all of these memories I have aren't real."

"I'm sorry. I know how frightening and disorienting that can be. I had a similar thing happen to me. That is why I volunteer in this department."

"So, you are here out of pity?" I said, bitterly.

"Not at all, I am here because I want to be. I've seen you here for the past three years. Which is also how long I have been volunteering. In case you were wondering."

"I'm sorry. I don't mean to take this out on you."

"It takes time to process. I was in a car accident and had some severe head trauma. I spent two years in a coma. My fiancée decided she didn't want to wait for me, so she moved on. My brother was the only person that still took the time to come and visit me. Hell, my parents didn't even take the time to come see me after a while."

"Did you have false memories when you woke up?"

"No, but I did feel lost and alone. Do you want to talk about your memories?"

"I don't know that I see the point. According to Grace, none of them happened. Even though they feel as real, maybe even more realistic, than what I am experiencing now."

"Is Grace one of the two women I've seen hanging around here?"

"Probably, Grace has red hair, amazingly blue eyes."

"Yep, she is here a lot. I don't know if that helps or not, but I do recall seeing her here almost daily."

"Yeah, she felt some guilt or some obligation to show up."

"Kris, if you don't mind me saying, people don't hang around hospitals out of guilt and/or obligation for as long as she did without the person they are visiting meaning something very important to them."

"I don't know what to believe anymore. Grace says I have been here for five years, and that she and I never had a relationship, that I never graduated high school, and that I never went to college. It is all very overwhelming. To me, it all happened."

"I can imagine that it is very overwhelming, and frightening. May I offer a suggestion?"

"Sure." Knowing that Mya had been in a coma and knew some of what I was going through made it easier for me to trust her.

"Talk to her. Find out from Grace what has been going on for the past five years. Maybe if you talk about what you remember, she can help you work through things. It is what I had to do," said Mya. "Maybe it was a dream. Maybe it was your subconscious taking in what was going on around you?"

"I don't know. I don't know if I am ready to face this yet."

"Well, for what it is worth, I'll be around, and I am always here to listen if you want someone impartial to talk to."

"Thank you. And, I'm sorry I was such a bitch when you first stopped in. I do appreciate you talking with me."

Mya reached up and squeezed my hand. It was reassuring and welcomed. If what Grace said was true, then I'm alone, I have no future. Why didn't they turn the machines off? What was the point to keeping me alive? To me, at this moment, it felt like just self-cowardice on their part.

"I'll leave you to your thoughts. And if you don't mind, I'd like to stop back tomorrow."

"I'd like that," I said, offering her a brief smile.

❧ ❧ ❧ ❧

Dr. Gomez came in shortly after Mya left. I told him that Grace had told me that I had been in a coma for the past five years. He said that they would like to do some more blood work and take some brain and body scans, just as a precaution. I agreed and then he headed out, stating that they would be in to get me in a while.

I was lost in my thoughts when I heard a knock at my door. I looked up to see Grace peek her head in.

"Grace? I thought you left," I said, surprised to

see her standing there.

"I couldn't leave you or leave things like they had ended. I told my girlfriend to go home."

When she said the word 'girlfriend', I thought I was going to throw up. In my mind, we were in love. She was my girlfriend, my fiancée. In all reality, she was my everything.

"I see. Can I ask one question to start with?"

"Of course, you can ask me anything," Grace said. She sat down in the chair that Mya had left next to the bed.

"Why did you keep me alive for so long? Why not just pull the plug? Let me die," I asked. The horrified and hurt look that crossed Grace's face about killed me.

"Why did we keep you alive for so long? Why didn't we just pull the plug? Seriously?" asked Grace. I think that she was stalling. "Kris, you were my best friend—"

"Were being the operative word here," I interrupted. "Why didn't my parents just pull the plug?"

"That isn't fair, Kris. When I found you in that treehouse, I thought for certain you were dead. Yes, your parents wanted us to pull the plug almost immediately. My folks got an attorney and went to court to get an injunction to stop your parents from killing you. Not that they hadn't already tried. We didn't pull the plug because you were my best friend. You are part of my fucking family. We had been through so much since we met when we were five. I wasn't ready to lose you. My life needed you. Hell, it still needs you."

"Why though? You have a life; you've had a life for years without me in it."

"You don't get it, do you? You are still very much

a part of my life. I come here almost daily."

"That I don't get either. Is it out of guilt or obligation? Because, I am awake now. You are free to live your life."

"You are a part of my life. I don't come here out of obligation or guilt. I come here because every day I hoped that you would wake up, that I would finally get you back."

"And now I did, and you got more than you bargained for. What does your girlfriend think about you coming here so often? Or, even being here now that I'm awake?"

"Aly understands. She knows all about you and me."

"Aly? You're dating Aly?"

"Yeah, we've been together for like three and a half years."

"What the hell is going on?" I said to myself but made the mistake of using my outside voice.

"What do you mean?"

"I, ugh, in my 'bizarro' world, I dated an Aly. Well, I was engaged to her at one point."

"At one point? What did your Aly look like?" Grace asked, curiously.

"She had light brown hair, auburn eyes. She was five-foot-seven, athletic build."

"Wow, that's what Aly looks like."

"Was she a complete bitch when you first met her?"

"Yeah," said Grace.

I could tell that Grace was getting creeped out by what I was saying. I have to admit, so was I. What I really wanted to know was how I knew this stuff.

"Ma'am, visiting hours are over," said the nurse,

entering to take my vitals.

"But," started Grace.

"It's okay. You have a life to get back to. I'm not going anywhere just yet. I'll be here if you want to come and see me tomorrow or whenever you get time."

"I'll be back tomorrow." As Grace hugged me, I heard her sniffle. "I'm so glad you are awake."

I didn't sleep well that night. I don't know if it was because I had already had five years of sleep, or if it was because my life or the life I knew was a lie. Every time I closed my eyes, I saw my reality. I didn't know how to stop seeing it. My life with Grace, the future we had planned. The hot and steamy night we had before I woke up to this hell.

❧❧❧❧

I had finally given up hope of getting some sleep on my own and asked the nurse for something to help me sleep. When I woke up the next morning, I was very disorientated. I felt like I had the other day coming out of the coma. Then reality hit me like a two by four. I was more alone than I ever thought I could be. The love of my life wasn't mine. She was the love of someone else's life. I had no clue about my family, what I was going to do when I got out of here, nothing. The only thing that I knew for certain was that my name was Kristine Holt, and I was in the hospital.

Dr. Gomez came in and said that over the next few days I would be having the tests and scans he wanted to be done. He stated that depending on how they turned out, I should be able to go home within a week. That thought scared the shit out of me. I didn't know where home was. Maybe it was a cardboard box near a park or something.

After Dr. Gomez left, I heard a knock at the door, and a woman poked her head in.

"Do you have a moment?" she asked. I nodded and she came in. "I'm Dr. Bauman. I am a counselor. I was told that you were having some issues since waking up, and I wondered if I may be able to help."

"I don't know. I feel like I am beyond help. I feel like the world would have been better off if I were to have died five years ago instead of living in that coma."

"I know it's frustrating, but would you feel up to telling me what is going on?"

I nodded and I told her about what Grace had told me as opposed to what my mind remembered. She told me that she had a theory on things like this. She said she believes that while you are in a coma you can still hear those around you. She suggested that what I was 'dreaming' was what was going on around me. I dreamed about school because either Grace was talking to me, or she was talking to someone in the room. She thought it was the reason that I knew what Aly looked like. She said that the hard part for me was going to be identifying the real and the fake memories. She gave me her card and said that if I wanted to talk more to call her, and she would stop by. I thanked her for the help. She had given me something to think about rather than to dwell on what my life had become.

I was staring out the window when Mya came in.

"Hi, Kris," she said, softly.

"Hi," I said, grateful that it was her and not Grace.

"How are you doing today?"

"I'm about the same. I'm still very lost and confused. I did talk to Grace briefly last night. The nurse came in and told her she had to leave because of visiting hours."

"What did you talk about?"

I told her about my conversation with Grace, about knowing what Aly looked like. I told her about my conversation with the counselor and her theories. Mya seemed to agree with the counselor that my mind took what I was hearing and turned it into my own reality. I then told Mya about my fears about leaving the hospital, about being alone. She said that she understood my fears and feelings. Mya explained that when she left, she had no place to go either. She told me about a place called Caring House that takes in people while they are getting themselves re-established.

"I'll get you the number. That is where I went when I left the hospital. I refused to be a bother on my family."

"Thank you, Mya. You don't know me, and you are being so very kind. I am very grateful."

"I know how scary it is to be in your place. I just want to help in some way to ease some fears."

There was a knock on the door, and Grace poked her head in.

"Oh, sorry, I'll come back," said Grace.

"Please, stay. I have to get back to my rounds. Would you like me to stop by before I leave today?"

"Yes, please. I'd like that," I said.

"Great, I will see you later."

"Hi, I'm Grace." I could hear jealousy and anger in Grace's voice.

"Hi, I'm Mya. I'm a volunteer here. I hope you have a great visit."

Mya smiled back at me and waved as she left. Grace took the spot that Mya had vacated.

"How are you today?" she asked me.

"I'm still very confused, but now I'm scared as well. I've just got a festival of emotions going on here."

"I understand the confusion. Why are you scared? Did something happen? Did the doctor get some test results back?"

"No, they haven't told me about any test results. When Dr. Gomez told me that I would probably be leaving within a week, I realized I don't know where I'm going to go. What happened to my parents? What am I supposed to do with my life? I lost five years, and everything I knew before no longer exists. My dream world is just that, a dream world. I have no one and nothing here in this world. I'm all alone."

"Kris, you aren't alone. You have me, Tyler, my parents. As for what you are to do, we'll figure it out, together."

"You have a life Grace, a real girlfriend. I don't understand why you are wasting your time with me. Hell, after what I told you yesterday, I am surprised that you are here even."

"You are my best friend. I am not going to lose you any more than I already have. Yeah, I'm confused about what you told me last night, but that doesn't change my wanting to be here to help and support you."

"What happened to my parents?" I asked, unsure if I wanted to know the truth or not.

"They are in jail right now. It took us a while, but we were finally able to prove that they were the ones that did this to you. Once we proved that, the police and courts took over. They won't be getting out any time soon. They will never hurt you again."

"Wow, I, wow," I said, shocked at the news.

"Kris, can you tell me more about what was your

reality?"

"I don't come out looking good in several parts."

"I don't care. I want to know and hopefully understand what it was like for you."

I spent the next three hours explaining to Grace what my world had been for the last five plus years. She was quiet throughout most of it. I got a couple of raised eyebrows, but she let me speak. When I finished, I expected her to run out the door and never look back or for her to tell me that she was going to request a psych evaluation while I was here as well. Then I told her about the counselor stopping in and her theory.

"That's amazing. I can't believe all that you went through in your mind. And for the record, my parents wouldn't have had an issue with us getting together."

"You can't say that for certain. In my world, they adored me until I started sleeping with you. Then it changed things, and they saw me becoming my parents."

"But you aren't them. You are nothing like that. They know that."

"They knew that in dreamland as well, but that didn't stop them from trying to sway you from me. I get that it was to protect you, but it didn't make it hurt any less."

"I called my parents and Tyler. They want to come see you when you are ready for visitors."

"I'd like that, eventually. I need to have a better grip on reality before I can see anyone. Grace, I feel you should know that I almost told you to leave earlier today."

"Why would you do that?"

"I'm so embarrassed and ashamed at what I thought was reality."

"You can't help it," Grace said, taking my hand in hers.

"You can't keep doing that," I said, cautiously pulling my hand back. I saw a hurt and confused look crossed Grace's face. "Grace, in what was my reality, you and I were engaged. We were hopelessly in love. Dream or not, that is where my feelings for you are. I need time to accept that you are not and will never be mine."

"Shit, I'm sorry, Kris. I didn't think about that. Can I do anything to help?"

"I'd say be less attractive and desirable, but that isn't possible." I blushed at the boldness of my statement.

"I'll do my best," Grace said, looking at her watch. "I have to go to work. I'd like to come see you again, but I don't want to make things harder or more painful for you."

"How about I call you when I think that I am able to handle seeing you again?"

"Okay. Can I give you a hug? Please?"

I opened my arms, and she hugged me. It felt like my world was complete. After Grace left, I broke down and started to cry. I loved her with all my heart, and it wasn't real, she wasn't mine. It hurt so much; I wanted to die. I wished I had died instead of waking up.

Mya found me laying in the fetal position, still crying. As I explained what had happened, she held my hand, she let me cry on her shoulder, she did what she said she would; she helped and supported me.

"I know how hard it is and how much it hurts, but it will get better," Mya said, once I started to calm down.

"Part of me doesn't want it to get better. I want

Grace. I want what I had before I woke up."

"I know, but that isn't going to happen. You need to get your mind to start accepting it, and then it can help your heart accept it."

"How long did it take you?"

"It took over six months to get my mind in order, and then another five or six months for my heart to let go."

I let out a groan. Another year of pining after and hurting for Grace.

Chapter Twenty-four

Two days passed before I called Grace. I could hear the relief in her voice when we talked. I told her that I would love to see her and her family. I did ask if she would be offended if I weren't ready to meet Alyssa yet. She said she understood and that it would just be the four of them. Mya had been in several times per day to make sure I was surviving. When I told her that Grace and her family were coming to visit, she was happy but cautious. She knew that this was going to be very hard for me. In my reality, these people had been there for me until I started to date Grace, then my relationship with her family crumbled. Yes, we did make it better, but I still remembered them stating that I wasn't good enough for Grace. Mya reminded me to try to keep the worlds separate. Mya also made me promise to call her afterward and if I needed her.

"Knock, knock," said Grace, poking her head in the door.

"Come on in," I said. My stomach fluttered when she smiled at me. This was going to be harder than I thought.

"All of us, or do you want to take it slow?"

"You can all come in." I really just wanted her, but I knew that it wasn't in my best interests.

In walked the family that I had spent most of my life wanting to become a part of. I wasn't sure if I was elated or irate to see them. I felt my stomach clench when I first saw them. I kept reminding myself that things were different, but it was very hard to control my emotions.

"Oh, Kris," cried Erin, hugging me tightly. "I've missed you so much."

"Kris, sweetheart," said Sean, hugging me. "I am so happy you are awake and a part of our lives again."

"Hey, Squish," said Tyler. We both smiled at the nickname.

"Hi," I said, wiping a tear out of my eye.

"How did your tests go?" asked Grace. I could tell she was fighting the urge to reach for my hand. I appreciated her effort.

"So far, I am in perfect health. I guess my years of hard dream living didn't hinder my physical health," I joked, or tried to joke about it. I was hoping that, by joking, it would ease the pain. I was wrong.

I talked with Grace and her family for a couple of hours before the emotional toll exhausted me completely. Grace's parents offered for me to come and live with them when I got out. I told them that I appreciated the offer, but in light of my mental state and my perception of reality, I needed to think about it. They understood and said that they wanted me to know that I wasn't alone, and they would be there for me. I hugged Erin, Sean, and Tyler again, and they left, leaving Grace and I alone. Not a position that I was entirely comfortable with.

"Promise me that you will think about their offer. I know that you have reservations, but I don't like the idea of you going to that Caring Home place. If I thought you would consider it, I'd say come stay with Aly and me, but I think that is too much too soon."

"It is definitely too much too soon. I'm glad you

are happy, but I still want to be the one to make you happy," I admitted. "To build a future with you."

"I know it is selfish on my part, but may I hug you?"

"Sure," I said, hesitantly. I was agreeing purely for selfish reasons as well. I wanted the woman I was head over heels in love with in my arms. Yes, I knew that would make it hurt more, but after seeing her family, I hoped that it would help me deal with some of those emotions as well.

After Grace left, I called Mya. We talked for about a half hour, and then I told her I was going to try to sleep. My dreams were about the good times with the Barnes family when I was a kid.

※ ※ ※ ※

It was the day before I was scheduled to be released. Mya was wheeling me around the floor since my muscles were still weak and not able to carry me long distances. Hell, they barely carried me short distances.

"What am I going to do tomorrow when you aren't here to talk to?" Mya asked.

"Well, you'll have more free time to spend with the other patients," I joked.

"Yeah, but they aren't as much fun as you."

"We'll keep in touch and do stuff outside of here. That is if you want to."

"I'd love that."

"Hey, Mya, Kris," said Grace as she stepped off the elevator.

"Hello," said Mya.

"Hey," I said. Grace was wearing a pair of jean

shorts, a black fitted T-shirt, and a black baseball hat. I fought not to drool on her.

"Grace, would you mind pushing Kris back to her room? I just realized the time. I have a physical therapy appointment to get to."

"No problem," Grace said, smiling. I had noticed that Grace seemed more annoyed whenever she saw me spending time with Mya.

"Stop by later?"

"Of course. Thanks again, Grace," Mya said, heading toward the elevators.

Grace pushed me back to my room. She then helped me get into bed.

"You and Mya seem to be getting along pretty well." Grace was anything but subtle when she was jealous.

"She's been a lot of help, and a good shoulder to lean on."

"I'm glad that you have her for that, but…well… nothing. It's not important."

"Grace, she is just a friend. I've still got a long way to go before I'm ready to date anyone."

"I know, and I'm sorry. I don't know why I said that."

"Why do you get so upset when she's around?" I asked bluntly.

"I don't know. I guess it is because you are able to let her help you, and you can't let me. I want to be the one there for you."

"I want you to be the one too, but until I get over the feelings dream me has for you, it isn't easy for me to let my guard down." As I said this, the explicit sexy dream that I had the previous night about Grace flashed through my head.

Grace was sitting on the edge of my bed. I could feel her so close. I sat up, pulled her close, and I kissed her. We aren't talking a peck either. We are talking full-blown tongue action and mental explosions of pleasure. It felt better than kissing her ever had before, or at least in my dream world. I heard Grace moan into the kiss, which just turned me on more and made me pull her even closer. I felt her lean more into the kiss. Her hand threaded into my hair as she held our mouths together.

"Mmmm, Kris," Grace said, breathlessly when I ended the kiss as quickly as it had begun.

"I'm sorry. What the fuck is wrong with me? I'm such an idiot," I said, berating myself for my actions. I couldn't meet her gaze, but I could feel Grace's eyes on me.

"Kris, I am flattered, and you are a damn good kisser, but you know that I love Aly."

"I know, I'm sorry. Momentary loss of control and sanity?" I hoped that she would let it go at that. I didn't want to have to point out that she kissed me back.

Grace nodded and then said that she had to go, but she would call me later. After she left, I called Mya and told her what happened. She came up and tried to help me make sense of it. We agreed that it was the emotions of my going to the Caring House instead of to Grace's parents' house, and the loss of my seeing Grace whenever I wanted. That night I dreamed about that kiss and how amazing kissing Grace made me feel. How amazing it would feel to make love to her.

Morning arrived, and Dr. Gomez told me that I would be discharged around noon. Mya had arranged to be there to take me to the Caring House. I had effectively avoided any further contact with Grace. I don't think I could have handled it.

Tyler had gotten me a cell phone, and I sent him, his parents, and Grace a text message that I was being released, and I would keep in touch.

"Ready?" said Mya as she came into my room with a wheelchair.

"Yeah, I think I am."

As Mya wheeled me out, I saw Grace standing outside the building. She was off to the side watching us. I don't know why, but she looked so lost. She took steps toward us then went back to the side of her car. I couldn't help or fix her. I had to start to focus on me and transitioning from being haunted by darkness to being haunted by lies.

About the Author

BL Clark lives in Southern Wisconsin. As a child, BL dreamed of becoming an author, she is now living her dream. In her free time, you can find BL working on various story ideas, or playing with some form of technology.

You can follow BL Clark at:
Twitter: bl_clarks
Facebook: blclark.author
Website: blc.bkclark.net

Check out BL's other book.

To Love Again - ISBN - 978-1-939062-99-4

Jade Donovan felt like she had everything in life, a great marriage, a beautiful daughter, and then fate intervened. Now she needs to learn how to move forward, not only for herself, but her four-year-old daughter. Jade's best friend Kristel hopes to help her get back on track by attending a grief counseling group run by Rachel Cassidy, a widow herself. With time, Jade is able to take the steps forward to heal and finds herself falling for Rachel. Not everybody is happy with the path that Jade has started on. Will Jade be able to overcome the loss of her wife and the other obstacles life has in store for her, to be able To Love Again?

Other books by Sapphire Books Publishing.

Zero Ward - ISBN - 978-1-943353-19-4

Danny Felts grew up in the heart of the Midwest on a dairy farm, expected to follow in her mother's footsteps and marry a farmer and become a mother. Danny had other ideas. As World War II heats up, she makes a decision that will change her life forever as she becomes a lie, serving with the Seabees in the Navy as Daniel Felts.

Kate Adams is about to graduate high school in her prestigious and elite San Diego neighborhood when she's dragged to the USO for a dance with friends and servicemen. There, she meets the person that will catch her eye and her heart, only for jealousy and vengeance to tear her apart.

Are Danny and Kate strong enough to win the battle within and fight for their love?

Touched by Starlight - ISBN - 978-1-943353-23-1

Kiernan O'Shay, one of the most powerful and richest people in the solar system, dreams of building a light-speed spaceship. She can achieve this goal if she owns all of Stellardyne, a space freighter manufacturing company founded by her late grandmother. To accomplish this, she must meet stipulations in her grandmother's will that require her to marry and have an heir by her fortieth birthday. Time is running out. Kiernan has a reputation as a ruthless business tycoon letting nothing and no one stand in the way of getting what she wants. And she wants the beautiful and intelligent Ariel Thorsen as her wife and the mother of her child.

Ariel Thorsen is content with her family life and her profession as a college physics professor. She meets Kiernan O'Shay at a dinner celebrating her mother's promotion to a junior executive in Stellardyne. Ariel is impressed by Kiernan's interest in physics and spaceships. She also finds Kiernan attractive. One week after the dinner, Kiernan offers monetary wealth to Ariel if she enters into a marriage agreement and bears Kiernan an heir. Ariel is appalled by the offer. She's not for sale, believing love should bind two people together—not the promise of wealth.

But when Kiernan accuses Ariel's mother of corporate

espionage, Ariel feels she has no choice but to accept Kiernan's marriage proposal on the condition that no charges are brought against her mother.

Can love grow when trust isn't in the equation?

Previously published as The Dreamer, Her Angel, and the Stars.

Best Lesbian Erotica - ISBN - 978-1-943353-11-8

Lusty and Fun

Better set aside some "me time" once you have your hands on this award-winning collection of hot, sheet-twisting erotic stories that will leave you squirming.

With group sex, first times, exhibitionism, domination, and toys, this 2015 Golden Crown Literary Society Award Winner (Erotica) has something for every lover of lesbian erotica. These stories burn with details so vivid you'll swear you can see, hear, smell, taste, and feel the women loving women within.

Best Lesbian Erotica - It's the next best thing to being there.

This book was originally published as Best Lesbian Erotica 2014.